The
RESURRECTION
of
MARY MABEL McTAVISH

The
RESURRECTION
of
MARY MABEL McTAVISH

The RESURRECTION of MARY MABEL McTAVISH

ALLAN STRATTON

DUNDURN
TORONTO

Editor: Shannon Whibbs
Design: Jennifer Scott
Printer: Webcom

Library and Archives Canada Cataloguing in Publication

Stratton, Allan, author
    The resurrection of Mary Mabel McTavish / Allan Stratton.

Issued in print and electronic formats.
ISBN 978-1-4597-0849-5 (pbk.).-- ISBN 978-1-4597-0850-1 (pdf).-- ISBN 978-1-4597-0851-8 (epub)

I. Title.

PS8587.T723R47 2014   C813'.54   C2013-906070-7   C2013-906071-5

1 2 3 4 5   18 17 16 15 14

  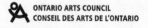

We acknowledge the support of the Canada Council for the Arts and the Ontario Arts Council for our publishing program. We also acknowledge the financial support of the Government of Canada through the Canada Book Fund and Livres Canada Books, and the Government of Ontario through the Ontario Book Publishing Tax Credit and the Ontario Media Development Corporation.

Care has been taken to trace the ownership of copyright material used in this book. The author and the publisher welcome any information enabling them to rectify any references or credits in subsequent editions.

J. Kirk Howard, President

The publisher is not responsible for websites or their content unless they are owned by the publisher.

Printed and bound in Canada.

Visit us at
Dundurn.com | @dundurnpress | Facebook.com/dundurnpress | Pinterest.com/dundurnpress

Dundurn
3 Church Street, Suite 500
Toronto, Ontario, Canada
M5E 1M2

Gazelle Book Services Limited
White Cross Mills
High Town, Lancaster, England
LA1 4XS

Dundurn
2250 Military Road
Tonawanda, NY
U.S.A. 14150

For Daniel Legault, my lightning bolt for
twenty-five years and counting

CONTENTS

I

The MIRACLE

The VISION

Mary Mabel's decision to kill herself wasn't taken lightly. She'd considered it off and on ever since she was ten. That's when she and her papa, Brewster McTavish, had arrived on the doorstep of the Bentwhistle Academy for Young Ladies, a Gothic flurry of turrets, parapets, corbelled chimneys, gargoyles, dormers and widow's walks, more apt for the housing of bats than the delinquent daughters of the idle rich.

The Academy sat on a four-acre field in the west end of London, Ontario, a colonial outpost in the Dominion of Canada. Unlike the real London, London, Ontario, was a reconstituted barracks town of retired farmers, accountants, and insurance salesmen, who fancied the place a city. At eighty thousand souls, it was certainly large enough and moneyed enough, with its army of stone churches, steel bridges, and broad tree-lined streets of ample yards, each with a solid brick home sporting a Union Jack. It had its own fairgrounds, too, and a hockey rink, men's club, and a train station — even its own east-end underbelly of unpaved, potholed roads and clapboard houses. What it lacked was imagination; Londoners were a practical, thrifty lot who said their prayers, and saw the Devil's work in anything that threatened the predictable.

Construction of the Bentwhistle Academy had begun in 1910 under the supervision of the town's greatest financier and leading citizen, Horatio Algernon Bentwhistle V. Horatio had conceived the Academy not only as a monument to his family's name, but as a hobby for his only child, Miss Horatia Alice, who'd become increasingly difficult since her return from school. Now, twenty-odd years later, Headmistress Miss Bentwhistle had halted improvements to the Academy in the wake of the Great Depression and her father's untimely death. This had left the moat half-dug, its clay basin filled with leaves and stagnant runoff. School brochures conjured "a magical lagoon, ideal for the contemplation of Lord Tennyson, Longfellow, and Sir Walter Scott"; a breeding ground for mosquitoes was more like it.

Mary Mabel had had a bad feeling about the Academy from the moment she and her papa were shown their quarters, a basement dungeon below the Great Hall comprised of two windowless, low-ceilinged rooms with cement floors, an icebox, and a stove. Her papa had been hired to do odd jobs for room and board, as he'd done for the past five years in towns throughout Wisconsin, Indiana, Illinois, and Michigan. She was to work in the laundry and kitchen, in exchange for which she could attend classes with the young ladies.

Her schoolmates were a nightmare, especially Clara Brimley, ringleader of the ruling clique. They'd taunt her for being poor ("What's your real name? Penny Less?"), for having lost her mama ("Where did you lose her? In a whorehouse?"), and, above all, for being plain ("Here comes Miss Potato Head"). At night, Mary Mabel would stare into the small mirror in her bathroom, praying for her mama to appear to tell her she wasn't as ugly as all the girls said.

It's true I have big eyes and a mop of curls, she thought, *but my "auntie" in Indiana said my mole is a beauty mark, and my features are something I'll grow into, whatever that means.*

Mary Mabel refused to let anyone see she was unhappy. When the young ladies taunted her about her mama, her papa, or her looks, she didn't cry like they wanted. Instead, she spat in their soup and blew her nose on the inside of their pillow cases.

"Devil child." That's what Miss Bentwhistle called her the time she pitched a ladle of vegetable slop at Clara. The headmistress was of the opinion that a week spent scrubbing the Academy's toilets with an old hairbrush and lye powder would settle her down.

"Serves you right." Clara smirked. "You're a nobody's brat. I trust you've learned your lesson."

"Take care," Mary Mabel replied, "or I'll stuff your face in the toilet bowl where it belongs."

Clara snitched. Mary Mabel got a second week, and her papa warned her that if she caused any more mischief, Miss Bentwhistle would send them packing. "Well," Mary Mabel said, "if that's a promise, I'd better get cracking." He chased her down the hall and round the boiler, cursing her lip till an overhead pipe laid him out cold.

Mary Mabel would've gotten into greater trouble, if it hadn't been for play-acting. She started with puppets. One night, she drew a face on a finger and stuck it through the toe of a dead sock. Production standards soon improved, thanks to decorated thimble-heads costumed with a wardrobe of worn hankies. Alone in her room, she'd entertain herself with epics, switching characters with the flick of a thumb. It reminded her of when she was eight, living with "Auntie" Irene, a mortician's wife who directed theatricals for the Milwaukee Little Theater Guild.

At fourteen, fancying herself a grown-up, she set the puppets aside and acted the tales herself, performing the roles of Jo March, Little Nell, Dora, and, one memorable night, smothering herself on the sofa as Othello and Desdemona both. Inspiration came from her library. She collected it in the middle of the night. Families fleeing the bailiff would take off after dark with whatever would fit in a borrowed wagon; leftovers were strewn everywhere. Mary Mabel would sneak out to front lawns and pick books like fishermen pick worms, then stack them in her closet on jerry-built shelves of boards and cement blocks that wobbled up to the ceiling.

These books were her best friends, her only friends, if truth be known. To enter their worlds was to encounter possibilities wondrous and magical, certainly more so than any she could picture in the here and now. Her papa disapproved. "Get your head out of the clouds," the beanpole lectured. "Life only gets worse. Accept your lot, or you'll end your days weeping over your ironing board."

His words went in one ear and out the other, though he was right about life getting worse. As she approached the age of seventeen, Mary Mabel thought about suicide daily. Not in the wild, hysterical way some of the girls did over boys or examinations, but with a calm, quiet resolve. She no longer wondered whether to do it, but rather when and how.

Rat poison was her first idea. It was easy to come by, as the Academy had a large supply to keep down fall infestations. Still, she shuddered at the fate of the mice and squirrels that died in the walls and smelled for weeks. Next, she thought of hanging herself from the clock tower, like a character out of Victor Hugo; but, however romantic, she hated the idea of letting the world look up her skirts. Leaping in front of a train like her heroine Anna Karenina, or shooting herself with a pistol like Hedda Gabler, were also out of the question; she was determined to die in one piece.

Mary Mabel weighed and discarded options until the week following her birthday. That night, out of the blue, she woke up to find her mama in glowing white robes, floating at the foot of the bed. She'd prayed for a visitation for as long as she could remember, but her mama had never come, and she'd almost given up hope. Her mama's arrival now meant the visitation must be about something important: her entry into womanhood, perhaps?

"Meet me tomorrow at noon on Riverside Bridge," her mama said, "and we'll be together forever."

Mary Mabel reached out to hold her, but the moment she did, her mama disappeared. *What a peculiar dream*, Mary Mabel thought. Yet the meaning was clear, and for the first time in ages she felt at peace. She knew when to die. And where. And how. The plan made such sense. Sunday was her one day of the week without chores; she wouldn't be missed for hours. Riverside Bridge was perfect, too, out of the way, private and beautiful. And the height of it and the rocks beneath — it was a death that couldn't be botched.

She got up. On the way to brush her teeth, she almost tripped over her papa, snoring on the floor of what passed for their living room, legs splayed out, back upright against the couch. Brewster tended to slide off when he passed out. As usual, his bottle was secure beside him, upright if empty. Mary Mabel stood for a moment and watched him twitch. He'd be upset when they gave him the news. Not because of her death, but because he feared scandal. She imagined his lament: "What will Miss Bentwhistle say?"

On that score, she knew he could rest easy. The headmistress was as skilled at deception as the Artful Dodger. She'd advertise the leap as a tragic accident. Privately, she might even rejoice, seeing as the funeral would provide her sympathy and attention. She'd see to it the service was a social event on the Middlesex County calendar, held at St. James with the Reverend Rector Brice Harvey Mandible presiding, and herself in charge of the eulogy, a moving oration correct in all particulars.

Mary Mabel pictured Miss B., a monument brave in grief, declaiming from the pulpit: "Our Miss McTavish was a motherless child whom we cherished as our own. Despite her circumstances, her hard work in the laundry and kitchen earned her a desk at the Academy alongside our young ladies. Here she flourished, winning academic honours in English Language and Literature as well as the Bentwhistle Prize for penmanship. A flower nipped in the bud, God has taken her to His bosom to blossom by His heart." After the interment, Miss B. would arrange a memorial assembly in the Academy chapel at which her young ladies, decked out in black lace and crinolines, would be obliged to offer up prayers. Mary Mabel planned to give them all a good haunting.

Her reverie was interrupted by her papa, mumbling an order in his sleep. *With me gone, he'll be up to his ears in dirty under-wear in no time, damning my memory for the bother*, she thought, and surprised herself with a laugh.

There was still an hour to sunrise. Mary Mabel had half a mind to go to the bridge then and there, while her determination was awake and the world asleep, but she held back. The vision had been specific as to the time, and, as she knew from her books, "the constellations have purposes we mortals must attend."

Besides, the truer reason, she hadn't finished *A Tale of Two Cities* and was desperate to know how things turned out for Sidney Carton. He was a drunk, but a noble one. Mary Mabel couldn't imagine her papa risking his neck for anyone. Would she love him any better if he got his head chopped off? What a pity she wouldn't have the chance to find out.

She took her Dickens to the rocker, opened it to the page marked with the feather retrieved from one of Miss Bentwhistle's Sunday hats, and began to read, eyes darting as fast as Madame Defarge's knitting needles. She whittled down the pages till ten o'clock, when her papa woke himself with a loud fart, the explo-sion starting him bolt upright. "What time is it?" he blinked.

"Ten," she said. "Would you care for some porridge and toast?"

Brewster grunted, padded unsteadily to the john, peed, and poured his weekly bath. Following the Sunday morning ser-vice at St. James, he had a standing engagement to clear Miss

Bentwhistle's drainpipes. She had, as she put it, "sensitive nasal capillaries, owing to good breeding and refined genes," and he took care to keep her nose in joint.

By the time he was spruced up, Mary Mabel had his food on the table. Her papa at feed made eating an adventure in nausea. She shot him a look. Sidney Carton was about to die, and all he could do was belch. She consoled herself that this was the last time he'd disturb her reading.

Porridge guzzled, Brewster wiped his toast around the bowl, mashed it into a ball, popped it in his mouth, chewed twice, and gulped. Then he pushed back his chair and gave his tummy a pat. "What mischief will you be at while I'm out?" he asked, as he went for his toolbox and plunger.

"I'm going to jump off a bridge."

"Mind you don't make a mess." Brewster snorted and lurched out the door.

The heroines in her books would have cried out, "Farewell, Papa, I love you." Not Mary Mabel. She returned, dry-eyed, to Mr. Carton's redemption. At last, the final page, the final paragraph, the final sentence, the final word. It was then that she cried, rocked for a bit, and thought that like brave Mr. Carton it was a far far better thing she was about to do than she had done, and a far far better rest to which she was about to go than she had known. A curious peace descended.

With great calm, she returned the book to its friends on the shelves, closed the closet door, and went to the teacup on the apple crate beside her bed. The cup wasn't much to look at — late Victorian, green, with gold trim about the rim and handle — but it was the only thing of her mama's she'd managed to grab the night she and her papa had fled Cedar Bend.

Mary Mabel held it tight, closed her eyes, and saw the large woman with big, warm breasts who sang to her and read her stories. She remembered how she cuddled next to her mama for afternoon naps. And about the three days that her mama lay very still at the end of the parlour, the house full of grownups, while she ran around getting lost in a sea of black skirts and saying to anyone who'd listen, "My mama's in that box," without quite knowing what that meant, except that when she said it, it made the grownups cry.

She remembered other visitors, too: her mama's sewing circle that brought baskets of food; and the strange women who tucked her papa into bed when he was lonely.

One night, a man with big red ears barged in when her papa was out. He came from the lodge and smelled of raw meat. The man turned the place upside down yelling for someone called Marge to come out and face the music. When he realized the little girl was alone, he said, "When your pa gets back, tell him Slick Skinner dropped by, and he'll be round again to gut him clean."

Mary Mabel passed on the news. In a heartbeat, she and her papa were on the run with no more than they'd tossed in a pair of bags.

"Who's Marge?" she asked.

"A mistake," he wheezed, dripping sweat so bad the suitcase handles slipped his grip.

They hopped a freight at Peak's Gully and hit the Sault border by dawn, fleeing into the States, west to Wisconsin. "Know why Skinner's got elephant ears?" her papa asked. "He never forgets. As long as you live, you see them ears, you head for the hills."

From that night on, the pair wandered as gypsies through a wilderness of small towns. Sometimes Brewster got odd jobs, and when he did, they'd stay, and when they'd stay, Mary Mabel would meet a new "aunt." It seemed that aunts were like dandelions: a common nuisance found everywhere, and you couldn't get rid of them.

They, however, could get rid of *you*. Inevitably, they'd complain of her papa's late nights abroad, the upshot being that they'd be out on the street by daybreak. To hear him tell it, it was always her fault — she'd got on their nerves with her games of pretend — that's what he'd grumble as they'd hitch a ride to the next town and the next aunt. It was like that from north Wisconsin around Lake Michigan, and back into Canada at Detroit — like that all the way to London, Ontario, where they happened upon the Bentwhistle Academy for Young Ladies, and its headmistress, the illustrious Miss Horatia Alice Bentwhistle, B.A., a.k.a. her Auntie Horatia.

Mary Mabel checked the clock on the wall. It was time for her to put away the past and end the future. She gave her mama's teacup a little rub and replaced it on the apple crate.

There were a few loose ends. She figured she owed her papa a clean start, so she did the dishes, wiped the ring from his tub, sewed the small tear on the underarm of his plaid shirt, and put a fresh bottle and a tumbler on the table. Finally, she took pen and paper and sat down to compose her note. She wished her last words could be as beautiful as Mr. Carton's, but he went to a Paris guillotine to save the husband of the woman he loved, so how could he not be eloquent?

She got to the point: "Dear Papa, Forgive me. Please don't blame yourself or worry. I've gone to a better place. Your loving daughter, Mary Mabel. Postscript. For supper, you'll find a plate of macaroni and cheese leftovers in the icebox."

It was all done but the crying; that, she'd leave to others. She propped the note up against the bottle. Then, before procrastination could cool her heels, Mary Mabel took a deep breath, rose smartly, and set off to be with her mama.

The WICHITA KID

Three days before, Grace Rutherford had stood on her front verandah across town and peered down her long nose at the little rascal tethered to the railing. "Timothy Beeford," she'd said, tapping the right toe of her black hobnailed boot, "do you honestly expect me to believe that after a morning's church service and Sunday school at First Presbyterian, you'll be of a mind to attend an evening gospel revival?"

"Yes, ma'am," her nephew replied, with all the innocence his ten-year-old eyes could muster. "Billy and me, we'll be with Billy's mom and dad. I aim to get saved."

Aunt Grace was having none of it. Since arriving on her doorstep, Timmy had been the very devil. Neighbours shook their heads and muttered, "There goes that Wichita kid." Well at least they didn't call him "that Rutherford kid." She and her husband Albert had had the good sense to steer clear of children; they hadn't wanted any, and the good Lord had answered their prayers. That is until they'd received that late-night telephone call from Kansas.

It was Albert's sister Belle on the line — Belle, who'd been sent as a youth delegate to the International Assembly of Presbyterians in Wichita eleven years before, and made hay with the first farmer she set eyes on. Aunt Grace shuddered to think of the missionary funds squandered on her sister-in-law's disgrace; it had been hard for the Rutherfords to live it down. Now here was Belle, calling from her neighbour's farm at three in the morning, if you please, begging her and Albert to take in her mistake.

"It's about Ralph," Albert whispered, his hand over the mouthpiece. "It's serious this time."

Grace crossed her arms. It was always serious with Belle. She knew about Belle's begging letters, the ones Albert hid in the shoebox under his side of the bed. If the Beeford farm wasn't being eaten by locusts, it was dying of drought, or suffering dust storms so ferocious they buried livestock whole. Could Albert send a little money? Just a little? For seed? To fix the tractor? To replace the henhouse carried off in the last twister? "Please, Albert, I beg of you. Ralph and I will be eternally in your debt." Wasn't that the God's own truth.

Albert always gave in. "Times are tough," he'd say. Well, except for the likes of Rockefeller, life hadn't been a cakewalk for anyone since the Crash, now had it? Besides, what was the point of buying seed, or repairs, or a henhouse, when Ralph Beeford couldn't pay his mortgage? Sure enough, three months ago Ralph and Belle had lost the farm, and all the savings that Albert had shovelled their way had gone up the flue with it. Now, as the prodigals sat waiting for the bailiff to evict them, scarce a day went by without Belle scribbling even more letters; letters which, after much prayer, Grace had been led to intercept and misplace in her wood stove. With Belle so hard up, Grace wanted to know how she could afford so many stamps. And now this telephone call.

"It's serious," Albert repeated. "Ralph's taken to reading the Book of Revelation. Tonight he brought the shotgun in from the barn. Belle's with Timmy at their neighbours. There's enough in the cookie jar to send Timmy here before Ralph does something we'll all regret."

Grace tightened the belt of her housecoat: How could he lay that guilt on her shoulders?

"The Lord never gives us more than we can bear," Albert said.

Grace had her doubts.

Her suspicions were confirmed the morning she and Albert met Timmy at the station. Despite the long journey, he'd bounced from the train the image of mischief incarnate: dirty hands, smudged face, and clothes fit for the oil drum.

Grace recognized him from the Brownie snapshot Belle had sent the previous Christmas. "So you're Timmy," she said. "I'm your aunt Grace and this is Uncle Albert. Let's save the hugs till we get you washed up, shall we?"

A scrub with a lather of soap and a rough facecloth had revealed dimples the size of dimes, like the dents of baby fingers plunged in pastry dough, and a mass of freckles — a spill of cinnamon on rice pudding. Aunt Grace sniffed. Oh yes, this was a face that spelled trouble; the acorn doesn't drop very far from the tree.

"Don't judge a book by its cover," Albert said.

From what Grace could make out, the cover was the least of their tribulations. Bullfrogs, cowpies, firecrackers, and stink bombs fascinated the Wichita kid, especially in combination and indoors, as did bodily functions and any hair-raising experiment involving fire and combustibles. When she and Albert demanded that Timmy explain why he had done this or that, he had two cheerful all-purpose replies: "Because" and "To see what would happen."

Why did God create little boys? Aunt Grace wondered. Give a girl a doll and she'd sit happily under the dining room table all afternoon and play house. Give Timmy a doll and within two shakes its limbs were clogging up the toilet.

Aunt Grace tried to curb Timmy's instincts. When she caught him playing cops and robbers she confiscated the toy gun he'd swiped from Kresge's. Without batting an eye, he replaced it with a stick. When she forbade him playing with sticks, he used his finger, cocking his thumb like a regular gangster.

Aunt Grace blamed it on the picture shows. Naturally, she refused Timmy permission to attend, but with or without her say-so she was sure he snuck into the Capital on Saturday afternoons with his little pal Billy Wertz. It frightened her to speculate on the sights he saw therein. If it wasn't James Cagney shooting up the town, it was Boris Karloff robbing graves or Bella Lugosi sucking blood. What kind of example did that set the nation's youth? Certainly not the kind found in the Good Book. At least when God ripped Jezebel into a thousand parts the better to be, consumed by wild boars, He provided young people with a cautionary tale of sound moral instruction.

Things came to a head the day Timmy blew up the tool shed in a chemistry experiment gone bad. He spent the next two weeks tied to the verandah by a rope. If the Rutherfords thought this punishment would curtail the mortification he caused them, they were mistaken. Passersby watched as the Wichita kid stood at the lip of the top step and practised long-distance spitting, self-induced belching, and the host of other skills with which little boys endear themselves.

Small wonder that Aunt Grace was suspicious of his desire to attend the upcoming revival. She knew all about the Tent of the Holy Redemption Tour. Run by a pair of American evangelicals, it breezed through town each fall before heading south to over-winter in the Florida panhandle. Folks praised the preaching of Brother Percy Brubacher and the charm of his partner, Brother Floyd Cruickshank, but the good reverends weren't what drew the crowds, not in a month of Sundays.

Aunt Grace sucked her teeth. "Timothy Beeford, don't tell tales. You've no intention of finding Jesus. What you really want is to get inside that tent. That tent with its history of horrors."

"All right, okay," Timmy confessed. "So can I? Please? I'll be good for a whole week. I promise."

．．．．

Timmy'd heard about the tent the previous Saturday after seeing *The Mummy* with Billy Wertz. They arrived back at Billy's to find an impromptu party in full swing. Mr. Wertz and a few of his friends, big hairy men like himself, were hunkered in a circle out back, while their wives were indoors exchanging cookie recipes. The way the men snickered, Timmy figured they were drunk.

Billy set him straight. "Us Pentecostals don't drink. We just have apple cider."

A whoop from the men. Cries of "kaboom, kaboom."

"What're they talking about?" Timmy asked.

"The revival tour. It's coming next week."

Timmy looked puzzled.

"You know, the tour, the tent?"

Timmy still looked puzzled.

Billy rolled his eyes. "Daddy," he called out, "tell Timmy about the Tent of the Holy Redemption!"

The men blinked, then let out a collective guffaw. "Go on, Tom. Tell the kid. Make a man of him."

Mr. Wertz cocked his head at Timmy. "If I tell, promise you won't let on to your Aunt Grace?"

Timmy could hardly breathe: If this was a grownups' secret, it must be important. "Cross my heart and hope to die." He plunked himself cross-legged at the foot of the oracle.

"All right then." Mr. Wertz took a glug of apple cider and leaned forward. "Next week, a couple of preachers are coming to town with the Tent of the Holy Redemption. But before the reverends got their hands on it, it wasn't a revival tent, see? It was a den of iniquity. Belonged to the Bennetts, rich folks from Pittsburgh, made their money in coal."

"Robber barons," interrupted the man on Mr. Wertz's right. Timmy pictured a family in Zorro masks sitting on shiny black thrones.

"Robber barons is right," Mr. Wertz said. "Now these Bennetts, these robber barons, they had themselves an estate near Hornets Ridge, a village 'bout a slingshot east of Mount Pawtuckaway, off in the Merrimack Valley of New Hampshire. And they'd get their richy-rich pals to come up by sleeper train to join 'em on pleasure trips. By day, they'd hunt. By night, they'd party in the tent. Stuff themselves sick on game, French pastries, and booze. Oh, yes! And dance to jazz bands bused in from New York!"

"Never mind about that," the man said. "Get to the good part."

"I'm getting there, I'm getting there," said Mr. Wertz. He had another glug of cider. "Now the Bennetts had this son by the name of Junior. The worst of a bad lot. He had slick hair, silk ascots, and wiggled his eyebrows at every gal in the county."

A chorus of hoots: "A walking erection!"

"Doubled the town birthrate!"

"Wore out the back-seat springs on his daddy's Hudsons!"

"At least he was good for something!" said a man to the left.

"Who's telling the story?" Mr. Wertz demanded.

"You, Tom, you," the men cackled.

"Right, so anyways, this Junior, he finally bites off more than he can chew. Starts making time with Nellie Burns, wife of the sheriff's deputy, Reggie. Reggie gets wind of the hanky-panky. Late one night, he grabs his shotgun and heads to the Bennett tent. There he finds his wife and Junior naked as jay birds 'cept for their party hats. What happened next wasn't pretty."

The men fell silent. Timmy's eyeballs were out of their sockets.

"'The wages of sin is death,'" the man on the left observed.

"Amen," said Mr. Wertz. "That's Brother Percy's very text. Adultery happened in that tent, lad. A double murder-suicide to boot. To this very day, you can see the holes where the lovebirds had their skulls blasted through to Kingdom Come. And if you look real hard, you can even see some brains."

• • • •

Timmy nagged his Aunt Grace for days. He nagged his Uncle Albert too. "I gotta see inside the tent. I just gotta." The couple discussed their nephew's request into the wee hours. Aunt Grace was inclined to say no. As a Presbyterian, she found the idea of tent evangelists embarrassing. "Too much singing, clapping, and general mayhem, not to mention those tambourines."

But as Uncle Albert pointed out, the Wertzes were pretty respectable for Pentecostals. "Maybe our Timmy could learn something from a God-fearing sermon on the wages of sin."

Aunt Grace counted to ten; Albert gave in to everyone, except her. She wrung a concession. "We'll give you our blessing," she told the boy, "providing Mrs. Wertz promises you'll be home for tuck-in by nine o'clock."

Billy and his mother arrived at five to collect Timmy for the twenty-block walk to the fairgrounds; Mr. Wertz had gone ahead to help raise the tent. Before the revival, they planned to meet up with other families from Bethel Gospel Hall for a potluck picnic; then, after the testifying, to have Timmy home by nine as promised. Uncle Albert and Aunt Grace were waiting with Timmy on the verandah, Uncle Albert clutching the family Bible, Aunt Grace cradling a container of her special potato salad.

"Sorry we're late," Mrs. Wertz hollered from the street.

Aunt Grace smiled primly. Pentecostals could carry on like pig-callers in a barnyard, but Presbyterians knew better than to make a ruckus. "Why, Betty," she said when Mrs. Wertz was within speaking distance, "aren't you looking festive." This was in recognition of Mrs. Wertz's pleated navy dress and string of imitation pearls. For herself, Aunt Grace wore only black on the Sabbath — as Christ had died for her sins, it was the least she could do — but she understood that in fashion, as in most other things, Pentecostals had their own notion of the appropriate. Ah well, who was she to judge? God would let Pentecostals know what was what in the fullness of time, and in any case it wasn't as if she had to invite Betty Wertz inside.

Mrs. Wertz showed off the frock with a spin. "Thanks muchly. It's nearly new from my sister Bess, out Ingersoll way. Lucky for me, she's been enjoying her suppers of late. Heavens, I wish I could put on some flesh, but there you are."

"And here *you* are," said Aunt Grace, presenting Mrs. Wertz with her special potato salad before the conversation could descend to body talk.

"You shouldn't have," Mrs. Wertz replied, packing it next to the bologna sandwiches and celery sticks in her picnic basket.

"No trouble," Aunt Grace allowed. "I make it with olives and pimentos, you know. With a speck of pepper for zest." Aware of a wriggling at her side, she glanced at Timmy, and faced an unspeakable horror. "Timothy! Get your hands out of your pants!"

"But my nuts itch."

"Timothy!"

"Well, they do!"

Aunt Grace gave him two quick spanks. "That's for scratching. And that's for sass." She pivoted back to Mrs. Wertz, red as a beet. "If Timothy gets himself into any mischief, give him a good smack. It's the one thing he understands." Timmy made a face. Aunt Grace grabbed him by the ear. "If we hear of any hijinks, there'll be more where this came from." With that she gave Timmy a third and final spank that sent the lad scooting down the verandah steps.

"I'm sure he'll be just fine," Mrs. Wertz said, as the boys

ran laughing in circles to the street, the picnic basket swinging between them.

The Tent of the Holy Redemption was a forty-by-sixty-foot blue-and-white monster. Timmy fell silent the moment it came into view. As he approached, all he could think was: "Once upon a time, a man was *naked* in that tent. With a *woman*. And now they're dead. And in Hell. Both of them. Together. I wonder if they're still naked?"

"Hi there." It was Mr. Wertz, fresh from securing the last support. He gave Mrs. Wertz a sweaty bear hug and she didn't even mind. Timmy bet they did things that would make his Uncle Albert and Aunt Grace drop dead of a heart attack.

Mr. Wertz turned to the youngsters. "What would you kids say to a tour?" The boys were in heaven.

Their first port of call was the portable generator and trailer-truck at the rear. The truck was bright enough for a carnival caravan, covered in colourful curlicues, squiggles, and capital letters. "She's quite the beast, eh?" Mr. Wertz enthused. "Everything you see — tent, poles, generator, the whole shebang — folds up and fits inside."

"Are those the eyes of God?" Timmy asked, pointing at the trailer wall. Circling the command PREPARE TO MEET THY GOD were a dozen gigantic bloodshot eyes, more scary, all-seeing, and all-knowing than even the eyes of his Aunt Grace, who claimed to have an extra set in the back of her head.

"Sure thing," said Mr. Wertz. He gave them a knowing wink: "So what do you want to see next?"

"Blood, blood!" Timmy squealed.

Mr. Wertz tousled the little ghoul's hair and threw him in the air. "You got it." He trooped his charges up front, lifted the tent flap, and hustled them into the sanctuary of horrors. Ahead stretched a wide centre aisle, flanked by twenty rows of benches and chairs, which led to a platform with a pulpit on its left and a piano on its right. Above the stage, shards of light entered where brains had once been blasted out.

Timmy was beside himself. He imagined naked people running back and forth, dodging bullets like mechanical ducks in a penny arcade. Bang! Bang! AAAH!!! Bang! Bang! AAAH!!!

What he loved most were the gore stains radiating from each hole. Ten years of rain and sun had failed to wash, weather, or bleach them away, as if God had decreed the tent's taints would never fade, but remain an eternal warning to sinners. (Brother Floyd prized this effect, which made worthwhile his periodic efforts with slaughterhouse guts and a paintbrush.)

Outside, Mrs. Wertz and the women were calling the menfolk to supper. Timmy made a beeline for the food lineup, appetite whetted no end. What a spread! The fairground tables bowed under a weight of roast and boiled meats, fresh vegetables, salads, sandwiches, and pies of every description.

Timmy was a prize piglet, even gobbling a scoop of his aunt's potato salad, except for the olive bits. These he stored in his pants pockets, where he hoped they'd dry into ammunition for his peashooter.

"You're like a little oinker fattening up for slaughter," Mr. Wertz said, laughing. How he'd regret those words, wish to gobble them back as surely as Timmy did butter tarts. For if the Wichita kid was as stuffed as a mounted deer head, within two hours he'd be as dead.

GOD'S JUDGMENT

Eyewitness reports of the tragedy were as varied as the Gospels. Nonbelievers, outside the tent, focused on the explosion of the generator, and the sight of the eyes of God, ripped from the side of the trailer, whirling in a metallic ring of fire into the heavens. Believers within recounted visitations by the beasts of Revelation, and of electrical wires transformed to the snake of Eden spitting fire as they whipped and darted in demonic pursuit of sinners.

Most famous within this apocalyptic tradition was the account of Mr. Bud Smith, featured in the *Stratford Beacon Herald*. Mr. Smith declared that the Pit of Hell had opened up to the right of his lawn chair, releasing a Satanic legion of armed skeletons that he'd single-handedly dispatched with the aid of his cane. The *Herald* declined to report that old age had been bringing the grizzled ancient similar visions on a more or less weekly basis.

Most widely circulated, however, was the version of Mrs. Betty Wertz, written for *King Features Syndicate* by then cub reporter K.O. Doyle.

```
I SAW TIMMY BEEFORD DIE
by Mrs. Betty Wertz
As told to Mr. K.O. Doyle


It was a terrible night, the night
Timmy Beeford died. Died, dead, in
the Tent of the Holy Redemption!
    Under the big top, the air was
so hot you could bake muffins. And so
high you'd swear the Bennett brains
were fresh from yesterday.
    Worst of all, the service was late.
According to Brother Floyd Cruick-
```

shank, his partner Brother Percy Brubacher had been detained by the Lord. "That's all very well," said I to my Tom, "but it means we're left suffocating in an abattoir."

Brother Floyd could see the flock was restless. He urged a singalong. So me, Tom, and the rest of the Bethel gospel choir took to the stage with our song sheets.

No sooner had we launched into "Power in the Blood," than a snap storm hit. Thunder and lightning to beat the band, building to the third chorus, when out of nowhere Brother Percy staggered up the aisle, soaking wet, hollering in tongues.

We have the like at church each Sunday, hands heavenward, palms up, but never before the invocation. The sounds lit the crowd like a brusher, tongue-speaking blazing through the tent. It was as if we'd been beset by demons.

I wonder if folks went strange on account of the heat or something in the mayonnaise. Whatever it was, it was madness, and above it all the squeals of a child. "Apple cider! Apple cider!"

I looked over to the boys. Timmy Beeford was standing on the front-row pew, pointing at Brother Percy with one hand, while he made the crazy sign with the other.

Right then and there, I should have marched off that stage and given those kids what-for. Instead I froze. And in the seconds that followed, I lost the chance to act forever. For I wasn't the only one to hear wee Timmy.

Brother Percy's eyes bulged and his index finger flew forward. "THOU SHALT NOT TAKE THE NAME OF THE LORD THY GOD IN VAIN. EXODUS 20, VERSE 7."

The congregation snapped to attention. A moment of silence, except for the storm. Timmy woke to the rage before him. Too late.

"WOE TO BLASPHEMERS, FOR THEY SHALL BE STRUCK DEAD, AND GREAT SHALL BE THE TERROR THEREOF!"

No doubt Brother Percy only meant to give the lad a scare. But no sooner did those words fly from his mouth than lightning hit the metal cross on top of the tent.

A roar like Armageddon. The pole split in two, cords severed, wires fried, bulbs exploded, glass sprayed, as the bolt shot down the line outside and hit the generator. An explosion. In the pitch black, the creak of bars bending! The tent was caving! Bedlam! Everywhere, a mob of screaming worshipers scrambling to escape!

I feared the boys would be crushed underfoot. A raging bear, I tore through the dark to find my cubs. Found them. Grabbed them. Carried them to safety.

But something was wrong. Timmy was a lump, as pale as the moon.

"He got tangled in wire," Billy wailed. "It sparked something crazy. Mommy — Mommy — he's dead!"

As God is my witness, so he was.

RESURRECTION

Mary Mabel could swear on a stack of Bibles about what happened when she arrived at Riverside Bridge. She'd climbed on top of the railing, peered down, and felt a chill at the sight of the river rocks. Her mama's voice had rung in her head like church bells: "Let go. Let go." She'd closed her eyes, stretched out her arms, and then ... and then? She hadn't a clue. The next thing she recalled was twirling barefoot, like a dervish, before a radiant young man bathed in light.

At the sight of the angel, she'd dropped to her knees in wonder. "Am I in heaven?" she asked. "Are you God's messenger, Gabriel?"

"No, ma'am," he replied, "I'm George Dunlop. Ambulance driver from London General."

Mary Mabel shielded her eyes from the sun, and saw that her angel had chin stubble, pimples, and a grass stain on his left knee from scrambling down the embankment. They were standing on the rocks by the river's edge. The driver looked embarrassed. "The Petersons spotted you," he said. "They called for help. Are you all right?"

"I don't know. Am I?"

He said she ought to come with him, which seemed a good idea. Though otherwise unharmed, her dance on the sharp stones had cut her feet.

Thing were slow at the hospital, typical of a Sunday. The town was taking the Lord's Day to rest, what with Saturday night hangovers and church. Aside from a couple of orderlies and a janitor, Dr. Hammond was alone with his trusty sidekick, Nurse Judd. Dr.

Hammond had been a drill sergeant on home duty during the Great War, and used his army whistle to boss the wards. He had a reputation as a crusty sonovabitch who saw the sick as a nuisance, and forestalled discussion by making their diagnoses as incomprehensible as possible. His motto, "What they don't know won't hurt them," was a comforting thought, though patently untrue judging by his contribution to the local cemetery.

As Nurse Judd wrapped her feet in gauze, Mary Mabel imagined herself an Egyptian princess being prepared for burial, her grieving Pharaoh father leading the court in lamentations so profound that the river Nile o'erflowed its banks with tears. Meanwhile, Dr. Hammond was calling the Academy. He told the porter to inform Mr. McTavish of his daughter's whereabouts. Then he returned, took out his notepad, and began asking Mary Mabel questions so silly she thought he was teasing.

"Do you know where you are?"

"Westminster Abbey."

"What is the date?"

"1812."

"Is George Dunlop the Archangel Gabriel?"

"Of course not, he hasn't a trumpet."

Dr. Hammond paused. "Are you a humorist, Miss McTavish?"

"No, sir."

There followed a heavy silence animated by medical jotting. Mary Mabel glanced from Dr. Hammond to Nurse Judd. It was clear they thought she was crazy. She decided not to mention her conversations with her mama. "May I go now?"

"No. You're to spend the night under observation, subject to your father's approval."

"Oh, he won't approve," she assured them. "I'm to be at work come five in the morning. Even if I was dead, Papa wouldn't let me off my chores."

Dr. Hammond furrowed his brow, muttered "melancholia," and scrawled furiously in his notepad. At the mention of melancholia, Mary Mabel giggled, which made Dr. Hammond scribble even more. But the truth was, since her escapade at Riverside Bridge, Mary Mabel had been suffused with a joy so warm that nothing could extinguish it — not even the realization she was alive.

Nurse Judd escorted her to a sickbed to await Brewster's arrival. "He'll be along shortly," she said. Mary Mabel knew otherwise. By the time the ambulance driver had found her, her papa would've read her suicide note and hit the bottle, terrified of impending scandal. The porter knocking would have sent him scuttling under the bed. It would be supper before he got word that she was alive, good news that would occasion a fresh bottle by way of celebration.

There were thirteen other beds in the ward, a long rectangular room divided by yellowing muslin privacy screens. Mary Mabel wasn't sure how many souls she had for company, but counted at least eight: five coughers, two snorers, and a woman across the room with hiccups. Together with the hum of the ceiling fan, the rattle of the dinner trays, the squeak of the medicine carts on cracked linoleum, and the periodic buzz from the fly strips, they made napping difficult. By dusk it was more so, a snap storm beating a tarantella on the window panes.

Still, Mary Mabel daydreamed happily till eight, when she was overcome by an acrid waft of body odour, booze, and raw onions. Her papa had arrived, a buzzard in from the wet. She listened to Nurse Judd give directions to her bed, then closed her eyes tight shut as she heard the approaching squish of his soaked boots, the screen rolled back, and the sound of him slumping heavily onto the chair to her right. He sat in silence, save for the drip off his rain slick.

She opened her eyes. He was peering at her with the intent gaze of a stuffed bird. She pictured him on a mantel. "Shall we go?"

A heavy groan. "I love you."

"I know."

He groaned again. "No you don't. I love you. Very much. Very, very much." A shudder. "Do you love *me?*"

"Of course, Papa. So, shall we go?"

"We can't. We have to wait. The doctor's with a patient. You're the picture of your mama. I love you, Mary Mabel. I love you very, very much."

Lord, Mary Mabel thought, *how many times will he tell me he loves me before Dr. Hammond comes and rescues me?* Spending the night at the hospital was beginning to look attractive.

Brewster horked a wad of phlegm and spat it in his hand-kerchief. More laundry. "I haven't said a word to your Auntie Horatia," he confided.

"I don't have an Auntie Horatia."

"Suit yourself. I've kept this from her all the same. It would drive her wild. And after all she's done for you. "

"Please, Papa." She indicated the world beyond the screen. "You're shaming me."

"No more than you shame me, with that cow face of yours." He rose from his chair. "Hey, you folks with your ears in our business, my slut of a daughter ran off to kill herself!"

The woman across the room stopped hiccuping. Mary Mabel hid her face in her pillow.

Brewster fell back into his chair. "I'm sorry," he wept. "I'm a bad father." He wanted her to contradict him, but she wouldn't. "I'm a bad father," he snivelled again.

"So you say. Now be quiet. I'm alive. There won't be a scandal. Lucky you."

"How could you think I'd care about scandal if my little girl was dead?"

Mary Mabel laughed. Her papa looked so startled that she forgave him despite herself. She got up and kissed him on the forehead. He let out a wail. And that's when the mayhem struck.

Down the hall, the emergency doors burst open and a flood of Pentecostals washed into the waiting room. A clatter of chairs and trays. Cries of "Doctor!" "Devils!" "Save us!"

Mary Mabel ran to the door of the ward and looked down the corridor. It was a war zone. Home duty had not prepared Dr. Hammond for a horde of Holy Rollers. He let rip with a toot on his whistle. "Smarten up. Get in line. Take a number."

No one paid heed, least of all a frantic couple who'd clawed their way to the front with a lad as limp as a rag doll. "Doctor, please help," the woman cried.

"Shush," Dr. Hammond roared. "Can't you see I've a riot to take care of?"

"But this boy may be dead!"

"Then take him to an undertaker."

Her companion clutched the doctor by the throat. "Examine him now!"

Dr. Hammond peered at the youngster. The child's face was a light blue, the lips purple. His jacket was burned through, the exposed skin raw. Orderlies kept the crowd back as Dr. Hammond ripped open his shirt, and listened through a stethoscope. "There's no heartbeat," he said. "How long has he been like this?"

"Twenty minutes."

"Then you're right. This child is dead." Dr. Hammond scratched his initials on a death certificate handed him by Nurse

Judd. The woman howled, but the doctor had no time for consolation. "I didn't kill him. If you want a second opinion, go down the road to St. Mike's."

That was too much for the man. "Sorry, Jesus," he exploded, "but I got business to attend to!" With that, he decked Dr. Hammond, leapt on top and pummelled away.

Mary Mabel felt her mama's presence. "Go to the boy," her mama said. The room disappeared. All Mary Mabel could see was the child. As if in a dream, she floated beside him. She knelt, smoothed his hair, and clasped his hands within her own. There was a whirring, a dark fluttering. Heat flooded her body, coursed down her arms, and out through her fingers.

It was then that the boy gave a cough. And a second. His chest began to move as he inhaled. His cheeks flushed. His eyelids twitched. Opened.

"Ow," he said. "I hurt."

Mary Mabel glowed. With her mama inside her, she'd raised the dead.

II

ENTER MISS BENTWHISTLE

MISS BENTWHISTLE GIRDS HER LOINS

Miss Horatia Alice Bentwhistle, founder and headmistress of the Bentwhistle Academy for Young Ladies, president of the Middlesex county chapter of the Imperial Order of the Daughters of the Empire, and guiding light of the St. James Ladies' Auxiliary, clutched her covers to her ears and prayed for the private telephone on her bedside table to stop ringing.

What time was it? She squinted at the grandfather clock to her left, in the hope that its hands might swim into focus. Oh, never mind. Whatever the hour, it was too damn early. Yesterday, her handyman, Mr. McTavish, had inspected her pipes. As usual, he'd been very thorough with his plunger, clearing the full range of her ductwork. The drainpipe in her basement was a particular revelation, in memory of which she'd toasted herself with champagne till the middle of the night. Now her entire body throbbed; she ached for rest.

The telephone fell silent. Thank you, Jesus. It rang again. Christ Almighty.

Miss Bentwhistle eased herself up, placing a brace of goose-down pillows between her back and headboard. She lifted the receiver gingerly to her ear. "Miss Horatia Alice Bentwhistle. I trust this is an emergency?"

"It's more than an emergency," declared the Reverend Brice Harvey Mandible, rector of St. James. "It's a scandal." According to the rector, the *London Free Press* had reported that an American tyke was electrocuted the previous night at the Tent of the Holy Redemption.

"A tragedy, surely," Miss Bentwhistle allowed. "But a scandal, why?"

"They say he was resurrected."

"Resurrected?"

"Resurrected!" The rector's stout tenor pitched two octaves north. "Miracles are well and good in their proper place. But their proper place is in the Bible. They don't belong now. And they don't belong in London, Ontario. And even if they *do*, they most certainly *don't* at a Pentecostal freak show."

Miss Bentwhistle's bum hurt. She rolled to her side. "Harvey, dear, what time is it?"

"Miss Bentwhistle, I don't think you appreciate the seriousness of the situation. If this miracle is believed, what temptations lie in store for followers of the true Cross? Who may be led into prophecy? Or tongue-speaking? Good Lord, tent evangelists are next to pagan! Rumours of this so-called 'resurrection' must be discredited! Squashed!"

"I see. And you have called upon me to set the record straight?"

"Well naturally I've called you. Who else would I call? After all, you —"

Miss Bentwhistle placed the receiver on her bedside table and sucked a lozenge. She had no need to listen to the rector of St. James prattle on about her importance to the community. As he had pointed out, who else could be called on a matter of such importance? She was, after all, the last of the Bentwhistles, a family of United Empire Loyalist stock that traced its lineage to a barony in the north of England — in commemoration of which the Academy dining hall boasted a Bentwhistle Coat of Arms and Family Tree as certified by the Heralds' College of Westminster, inscribed on parchment in gilt with the royal seal, thank you very much — and that had established and maintained the social parameters of local society since the end of the eighteenth century.

Without question, Miss Horatia Alice Bentwhistle knew that she was the one to be called. The voice on the end of the line appeared to have petered out. Miss Bentwhistle retrieved the receiver. "Never fear, Harvey," the dowager sighed grandly. "I shall address the situation as is my duty. I am, after all, a Bentwhistle."

"Yes, and the girl's employer."

The lozenge stuck in Miss Bentwhistle's throat. "Beg pardon?" she choked.

"The miracle worker. It's Mary Mabel McTavish. She's yours!"

Miss Bentwhistle reached for the smelling salts.

Ten minutes later, she stood naked before her bedroom mirror, considering the weight of responsibility under which she laboured as she girded her loins for the confrontation at hand.

She had already rung the porter, instructing him to summon Mary Mabel and her father to the office. They'd be there this very moment, sweating. Let them sweat. An hour more and she'd descend to tell that brat, in no uncertain terms, that in the laying-on of hands she had exhibited inappropriate behaviour, and in so doing had threatened the hard-earned reputation for sobriety and moral rectitude of the Bentwhistle Academy, indeed of the Bentwhistle family itself. Let the trumpet sound. There would be hell to pay, with Miss Horatia Alice Bentwhistle, B.A., the instrument of God's will.

Hmm. There seemed to be more of her today than there was yesterday, an observation Miss Bentwhistle had been making with frightening regularity. "I look like a teapot!" she exclaimed, surveying her Rubenesque charms.

She hoisted her corset: "Deny and contain!" The motto of her late father, Horatio Algernon Bentwhistle V. If he had overcome scandal, Miss Bentwhistle determined, so could she. Wrestling with laces and clasps, she drew strength from the great man's battle with the clutch of elderly widows who'd sought his ruin.

East-enders, Miss Bentwhistle sniffed. *What right had they to do business with a Bentwhistle in the first place?*

The vixens had asked her father to put their money in government bonds. More wisely, he'd invested the funds in stocks, depositing profits equal to bond interest in their accounts while pocketing the balance in his own. These transactions went unnoticed during the run-up to the Great Crash; but when the market collapsed, taking the widows' money with it, they'd had the effrontery to charge him with fraud.

Lesser mortals might have crumbled. But not the Bentwhistle *paterfamilias!* "Deny and contain!" Horatio had bellowed and headed to the court house. He claimed — and who could doubt it? — that the widows had insisted he speculate wildly. "They were thrill seekers; desperadoes, the lot of them." And why had he withheld profits in excess of interest? "It was for their good that I sequestered the dividends. Otherwise those insatiable grannies would have run hog-wild, squandering the treasure of their declining years on trifles."

Oh, how the little people howled for his blood. But as their betters well knew: wealth is the backbone of virtue; the wealthy, models of probity. Judge Benjamin T. Vanderdander, a fellow Tory and one-time school chum, found for the defence: "In the absence of written instructions, the charges are without merit or foundation."

Horatio promptly sued the widows for libel. Unable to afford a competent lawyer, they were found guilty and sent to the slammer.

Miss Bentwhistle indulged a smile remembering her father's boozy victory party, following which he'd died "happily in his sleep," as the *Free Press* put it, when the car he was driving crashed into a telephone pole. His venerable remains, eulogized by the premier and local dignitaries, were trundled to the family mausoleum in a horse-drawn carriage led by the Royal

London Regimental Pipe Band whose members, in addition to comforting the bereaved with "Amazing Grace" on the bagpipes, intercepted pensioners throwing rotten eggs concealed beneath their hankies. The poor can be so spiteful.

Winched into her corset, Miss Bentwhistle waddled to the vanity table to complete her transformation to Dowager Empress. The only problem was sitting down, next to which breathing was a positive snap. She consoled herself that a wince of discomfort from corsets or gas can pass for displeasure and may actually be of assistance when dealing with the help.

A heavy application of alabaster pancake to fill the crevasses, followed by a blush of rouge, a streak of mascara, a tease of lipstick, a dusting of lavender powder, and Miss Bentwhistle had made her face. It was a monument to authority, precisely the sort of countenance to squash a bug like Mary Mabel McTavish. There remained but the hair, a Brillo pad of light brown curls that suggested a chubby Harpo Marx. It vexed the headmistress to see new strands of grey around the temples. While too numerous to pluck, these could still be concealed with an artful application of shoe polish administered by means of a deft wrist and her favourite old toothbrush.

But before the Merlin of makeup could work her magic, she was overcome. Eyebrows twitched, jowls shook, and tears poured down her cheeks, smudging, eroding, and generally playing havoc with her carefully constructed mask. Quite naturally, the waterworks flowed from the remembrance of her father. Not of his death, mind, but of the terrible secret she'd discovered in its wake. A secret that this Mary Mabel scandal threatened to expose:

Miss Horatia Alice Bentwhistle was bankrupt.

The Crash — more smelling salts — had destroyed not only the widows' mites, but the Bentwhistle family fortune, as well. Horatio had concealed the ruin ("Deny and contain!"), the power of his reputation sufficient to mesmerize creditors. But with his death, Miss Bentwhistle had found herself alone, faced with a mountain of debt against which she had but her name and her Academy. Both were in immediate jeopardy.

Privileges conferred by her name would disappear if she were known to be insolvent. Therefore, the Bentwhistle Academy had to be milked to pay down debt. At the same time, the Academy's pedigree, the Bentwhistle name, had to be maintained, lest wealthy clients send their heirs to more reputable havens. Maintaining her name, in turn, meant maintaining a facade of wealth, which in turn meant increasing the flow of the very red ink she was desperate to staunch.

The poor have no understanding of true financial need, Miss Bentwhistle thought, weeping. *They require tens and twenties, while I require thousands. Life is so unfair.*

To forestall talk, she dropped references to foreign accounts, and hosted a dizzying array of occasions. She also embarked on a recruitment drive to enroll more students to generate more funds to pay for more parties to polish a name designed to attract more students to generate more funds and so forth. It was a vicious circle, all the more desperate as Hard Times had wiped out much of her potential clientele. Like Scarlett O'Hara, Miss Bentwhistle resolved to think about that tomorrow.

London was too small a pond in which to fish for additional students, so Miss Bentwhistle poached in the exclusive waterways of Toronto. It was a daring long shot. The nation's navel had an ample supply of private schools, capable of conferring social status without the financial drain obliged by boarding.

Despite this drawback, Miss Bentwhistle pressed ahead. She knew from personal experience that the rich were habitually bored, and that bored rich adolescents had even more opportunity to get into trouble than their downtrodden counterparts.

Consequently, she used her Toronto contacts to ferret out the names of well-heeled families with delinquent daughters. To these, she sent an illustrated brochure touting the Academy's high moral tone and academic standards, as well as its commitment to Christian redemption and reasonable rates.

Toronto's troubled bloodlines took the bait. At the very least, ensconced a good three hours drive from the city, their adolescents would no longer embarrass the family by rolling in drunk at 4:00 a.m., *sans* panties, to throw up on the shrubbery. Here was a chance to ditch their headaches while keeping their heads held high.

The Academy prospered financially. Its academic standards, however, sustained significant collateral damage. This could have been stickhandled without tears if only Miss Bentwhistle's teachers had been as clever with their mark books as she was with her bank books. Unhappily, they were a linear lot who failed to grasp that while standards are all well and good, it's the appearance of standards that counts.

Miss Budgie, the long-suffering English teacher, was the first to be summoned to her office. A nervous sort given to rashes, she blamed her doomed love life on Miss Bentwhistle's edict that single female staff could only socialize with the opposite sex on Sunday afternoons, chaperoned. This had something to do with "setting an example," though what sort of example Miss Bentwhistle refused to say. ("If it's something I have to explain, it's something you wouldn't understand.")

The moment Miss Budgie entered the office, the headmistress pounced. "The average English mark has dropped twenty percent this term. Our parents don't pay good money to get these results."

"Miss Bentwhistle, the students didn't do their work."

"Don't make excuses. You were hired to inspire. If you'd done your job, the young ladies would have done theirs."

"Not this lot. They're juvenile delinquents."

"Are you questioning the admission standards at the Bent-whistle Academy? Our young ladies come from the best Toronto homes. Homes where names such as Budgie are unknown."

"Nonetheless, they don't want to be here."

"And do *you* want to be here?"

Miss Budgie gasped.

"These marks will be raised by this afternoon."

Parents were thrilled to see improvements in their children's test scores. "It's a miracle," they raved to friends with similarly troubled teens; enrollment rose as quickly as the marks on incomplete assignments. Nor did provincial examinations threaten Miss Bentwhistle's shell game; teachers collared cheaters at their peril.

Thus, four years after her father's death, the Academy appeared to flourish and Miss Bentwhistle to reign supreme, monarch of all she surveyed. "I am the Virgin Queen," she joked with staff. Too frightened to bell the cat, they stroked in public and mocked in private, a sad packet of neutered mice.

Miss Bentwhistle didn't care. She had no need for friends, as she commanded the company of an extensive stock of wine bottles. Ostensibly on hand for parent events, crate after crate found its way to her boudoir. They proved good friends, providing sympathy during late-night tipples, and courage on those occasions when she called upon the services of her odd-jobs man, Brewster McTavish.

Brewster McTavish. A man with the sort of essence encountered in the novels of that wicked Mr. Lawrence. Thin as a pipe cleaner and covered in boils, his face was set in a permanent leer that Miss Bentwhistle liked to pretend was facial paralysis brought on by a childhood bout of diphtheria. When he'd arrived on her doorstep, Mary Mabel in tow, she'd been looking for someone to cut her grass. McTavish swore he was aces at yard work, and would swab the floors, bully the boiler, and deal with infestations of rodents — all for room, board, and pocket money. Delighted at the bargain, the headmistress snapped him up.

He was soon her darling, not for his janitorial services, but because of his grasp of theatrical lighting, a hobby he'd picked up from a Milwaukee matron devoted to little theatre. To Miss Bentwhistle's elation, Mr. McTavish introduced coloured gels to the auditorium's incandescent lamps. In the past, she'd suffered through assemblies under the ruthless glare of white light. Now she was radiant, her charms enhanced thanks to the glow of a soft pink front and an amber behind.

Oh, Mr. McTavish! Oh, oh, oh! Was ever a man such as this? A hard worker devoted to his child! An artist devoted to her interests! A common man worthy of her compassion!

Soon she was looking for reasons to call Mr. McTavish to her office and to see him after hours about one project or another. She professed to be astonished at the number of things that needed to be screwed in and out, and at the surprising array of nooks and crannies needing his manly attention. How she'd managed to live without him was quite beyond her.

Londoners noticed a change in the headmistress, but refused to contemplate the obvious. The image of Mr. McTavish and Miss Bentwhistle engaged in animal husbandry was simply too grotesque. Moreover, Miss Bentwhistle wisely included Mary Mabel in their outings. "How our Horatia dotes upon that little gumdrop," remarked Mrs. Herbert C. Wallace, secretary-treasurer of the St. James Ladies Auxiliary Bridge Club. "She's an example to us all."

One Sunday, inspired by the Reverend Mandible's homily on charity, Miss Bentwhistle visited the McTavishes bearing an orange. "This orange is especially for you, my dear," she beamed at the girl, breasts swelling with the special joy that comes from giving. "From now on, you may be pleased to call me your 'Auntie' Horatia." Mary Mabel looked up sweetly. "Thank you very much," she said, "but I have more aunties than I can remember. If it's okay, I'd like for you to just be a grownup." Miss Bentwhistle chewed her dentures. Determined to teach the child some manners, she set her to work in the laundry and kitchen.

Meanwhile, female teachers were not so delighted with the new janitor. The third schoolmarm to lodge a complaint was that well-known rabble-rouser Miss Budgie, she with the fetish for "standards."

"I don't know quite how to put this," Miss Budgie began, "but whenever I pass Mr. McTavish he starts to play with his fly. And he leers at me."

Miss Bentwhistle was understandably appalled. "How dare you attack a poor victim of diphtheria!"

"Miss Bentwhistle, he stares at my breasts!"

"And what do *you* do to provoke him?"

"Nothing! And I'm not the only one to complain. Miss Lundy has spoken to you already. Miss Brown too. He pressed them up against the broom closet and invited them down to the boiler room to see his toolbox."

"That is their point of view," Miss Bentwhistle acknowledged with a thin smile. "Mr. McTavish has quite another."

"Are you saying our word can't be trusted?"

"I'm saying that Miss Lundy is a hypochondriac, and Miss Brown a known hysteric. Everyone has an agenda, Miss Budgie. Everyone. I, however, am the headmistress. It is my duty to rise above agendas."

For once, Miss Budgie was not to be cowed. "I have witnesses!"

"What need have I for 'witnesses'? Are you suggesting I'm afraid to deal with Mr. McTavish."

"No. Just that you haven't."

"Tell me, my dear," Miss Bentwhistle asked, as sweet as jam tarts, "are you in any position to make waves?"

Miss Budgie trembled. "Are you threatening me?"

"No. I believe I'm asking a question."

Miss Budgie hesitated. "I'm not trying to make waves. It's just that Mr. McTavish ... well ... he makes it hard for me to do my work."

"Well *you* make it hard for me to do *my* work. I have a school to run, Miss Budgie. I haven't time for tattletales. If you are unable to do your job without vilifying your colleagues, I shall find someone who can. I expect a letter of apology on my desk by this afternoon."

Miss Bentwhistle's decision to betray her staff for Mr. McTavish was not the result of romantic infatuation. Rather, the charges implied that she had employed a lecher, a lapse in judgment that threw into question her moral discernment. In light of this, the headmistress saw the accusations for what they were — an attack against her person.

There was also every chance that the little backstabbers were delusional. Mr. McTavish's essence was undeniable, and it would not in the least surprise her if Miss Budgie and her conspirators had picked up the scent and were indulging themselves in lurid sexual fantasies. Was she to sacrifice Mr. McTavish to satisfy a coven of sexually obsessed deviants?

In any case, even if the Academy janitor *had* been indiscreet, what of it? Men are well-known to be slaves to their dangly bits, especially men of common breeding. As members of the fairer sex, it was up to his detractors to comport themselves so as to discourage propositions. Why, if anyone was to blame, it was they! The trollops must be punished! And they were — Miss Budgie was humiliated in front of her students for allegedly stealing chalk from the office supply cabinet.

Still, Miss Bentwhistle fretted about the charges. At last, she confided them to her handyman. He denied them outright, allowing that at most he may have given his accusers a well-intentioned smile, which they no doubt misunderstood on account of his facial paralysis. Miss Bentwhistle stroked his sweet, beleaguered brow. Poor Mr. McTavish. How she would comfort him tonight.

It occurred to her that, having saved his skin, she had him in her debt.

A remembrance of this debt was at the forefront of Miss Bentwhistle's mind as she completed the reconstruction of her face. At this morning's confrontation, she'd call upon Mr. McTavish to force his daughter to recant the miracle. Miss Bentwhistle knew that nothing short of a denial would keep this scandal from her door.

After all, what kind of headmistress employs a publicity hound who claims to raise the dead? How could she discipline her students if she couldn't control her staff? Toss in a Pentecostal freak show and Miss Bentwhistle's head reeled with nightmares of a convoy of limousines emptying the Academy of its young ladies. Then what? The Academy collapsed, her debts unpaid, and her family name disgraced, it would be a mere hop, skip, and a jump to the poorhouse.

It was the vision of that grim future that had caused Miss Bentwhistle's explosion of tears. She'd seen herself shacked up in the hobo jungle at the outskirts of town, a sad old derelict with nary a penny to wash her drawers. Imagined herself shuffling up for a ladle of broth at the St. James soup kitchen, cowering before Mrs. Herbert C. Wallace, Reverend Mandible, and the rest.

Well, it wasn't going to happen. As God was her witness, by the time she'd finished with the McTavishes, Mary Mabel would be on her knees. She'd issue a public proclamation that the Beeford boy was never dead, but merely stunned; she'd seen him move and helped him to his feet. She was a young woman wronged by fabrications of the press, an innocent whose life within the halls of the Bentwhistle Academy had taught her to place integrity, honour, and dignity before all else.

There was, of course, the awkward detail of the death certificate, but that was small potatoes. Dr. Hammond wouldn't admit to signing death certificates for the living; it would scare away his clientele. Besides, it wasn't in London's interest to have its hospital seen as a happy-go-lucky loony bin shipping healthy out-of-towners to the morgue; that would be bad for tourism. In the end, the death certificate was just a piece of paper waiting to be misplaced by an underpaid clerk.

She made her way to the wardrobe. Selecting a frock was easy; she'd been wearing black since her father's death. The decision, a sly cost-cutting measure, had proven good for business, a constant allusion to the Horatio Algernon Bentwhistle Memorial Fund. "Funerals provide such a dignified excuse to pass the hat," she observed.

All that was left was to steady her nerves. Miss Bentwhistle took two tablespoons of laudanum, a homebrew she concocted from the lifetime supply of opium she'd found in her father's effects. (He'd acquired it during his tenure as chairman of the Middlesex County Hospital Association. When the drug was outlawed, he'd generously overseen its disposal from the county's repositories.)

Miss Bentwhistle washed the laudanum down with a glug of brandy, the smell of alcohol contained by a peppermint drop, and glanced at her watch. Nine o'clock. Battle stations. She stood in front of the mirror and repeated the mantra "I am a Bentwhistle, I am a Bentwhistle, I am a Bentwhistle." With that, the regal barge navigated to the door and floated forth to rendezvous with destiny.

IN *the* LION'S DEN

The instant Timmy Beeford resuscitated, the assembled Pentecostals erupted with whoops of joy, cartwheels, and grand huzzahs for Jesus.

"We'd best be off," Mary Mabel whispered to Brewster. She grabbed him by the arm, and made for the door.

"Wait!" Mrs. Wertz called after. "We have to celebrate!"

"I'd love to," Mary Mabel sang over her shoulder, "but I have to be up at four."

In bed, Mary Mabel couldn't sleep for the silly grin on her face. Her mama'd had a reason to send her to the bridge: it was to get her to the hospital to save that boy. She gave thanks and promised to follow her mama's guidance forever.

Soon it was time to rise and shine. By five the stove was stoked, the tables set. By six, milk, porridge, and scrambled eggs were on the serving trays. By seven, she'd ladled breakfast to the Academy's young delinquents. And by eight, she was up to her elbows in dirty dishes, when the porter arrived. "You're to report to Miss B. immediately."

"She'll have to wait or there'll be no clean plates for lunch."

"Don't worry about that. Miss Budgie's been assigned the wash-up before her morning class."

Mary Mabel couldn't figure what could be so important. It hadn't occurred to her that her miracle might have altered her relations with the world. Not that there hadn't been warnings. On the way home, her papa had gaped like a goldfish, and Miss B.'s young ladies had lined up for breakfast as slack-jawed as a row of pithed frogs. Still, it wasn't until she hit the office that she realized the enormity of things.

Two police officers were hauling off a scruffy man in a trench coat. The secretary, Miss Dolly Pigeon, a wizened rat terrier with small breasts and big hips, was beside herself. "You're the cause of this!" she yipped at the girl. "I hope you're satisfied!"

"Are you her?" the man demanded as he was dragged out. "Are you Mary Mabel McTavish?"

"Who's he? How did he know my name?"

"He's from the *Free Press*. There's more at the gates."

Before Mary Mabel could think, her papa barrelled through the door. "Look at the trouble you've got us into!"

"Shut your traps," Miss Pigeon ordered. "To the Bench!"

The Bench was a church pew retrieved from St. James. Hard and unforgiving, it was the Academy's version of the stocks. The pair waited an eternity before the headmistress sailed in, a copy of the morning's paper tucked beneath her arm. "How are we this morning, Miss Pigeon?"

"As might be expected."

"Quite so." Miss Bentwhistle swept into her private study and closed the door. A pause, and then she pulled the servants' cord, tinkling the little brass bell that announced she was ready to receive appointments.

Miss Bentwhistle's inner sanctum was hushed and dark, the heavy velvet curtains secured to ward off light. *Oh-oh*, Mary Mabel thought, *she's having a migraine.*

"Shut the door," came a low purr from the far end of the room. Her papa obeyed.

"Come closer," the headmistress growled. "I'm not about to bite."

Her papa gave a nervous chuckle and pushed her forward. "The both of you."

Brewster gulped and stepped onto the dusty Persian carpet, almost tripping on the head of the Bengal tiger rug splayed across it. Miss Bentwhistle claimed her great-grandfather, Horatio III, had bagged the beast on safari. In truth, he'd stalked it down in a dusty Toronto curiosity shop. Either way, it was a skinned warning to any who'd dare to cross a Bentwhistle.

Now in range, their eyes accustomed to the muslin light, Mary Mabel and her papa saw a vision gave them pause — Miss Bentwhistle in the highest of high dudgeon, a grand inquisitor to make the angels quake, as imperious a judge as the combined host of Bentwhistles past who glowered through the gloom from the baroque frames that lined her lair. Mary Mabel felt faint, the air heavy with powders, pomades, and lavender potpourris. She glanced at her papa. He looked set to vomit.

An awkward pause. The Iron Maiden cocked an eyebrow. "Well, Miss McTavish, you've been quite the busy bee."

"The girl is sorry," Brewster said. He stuck an elbow in his daughter's ribs. "Apologize to your Auntie Horatia."

"Don't interrupt," their captor snapped. She fixed Mary Mabel in her sights. "It is barely nine o'clock in the morning, and we find ourselves besieged by the Middlesex County press. Muckrakers from the *Gleaner*, *Bugle*, and *Beacon*, not to mention our London rag, have decamped at the Academy's front gates. We've been obliged to call in constables, Miss McTavish. Constables. It's a positive scandal."

"But what's it got to do with me?"

She flung the *Free Press* on her desk and tapped her right index finger three times on the banner headline: LONDON GIRL RESURRECTS DEAD BOY.

"Oh my."

"Oh my?" Miss Bentwhistle's breasts elevated to the heavens. "All you can say is *'Oh my'*? A young lady knows better than to draw attention to herself, but you, you flibbertigibbet, you made a scene! And on a Sunday! In so doing, you sullied the Academy's hard-earned reputation for propriety!"

"I didn't mean to."

"Of course not. You're just a sweet, little Florence Nightingale. Although even *she* was never ascribed the powers of our Lord Jesus."

"I didn't say a word to the press."

"Why bother when three hundred witnesses, Holy Rollers, God spare us, are happy to babble away on your behalf. Well, you just march outside and tell the press their story is absurd."

"But it happened. I can't deny it."

"Listen to me," the headmistress said, "and listen hard. I am telling you: there was no miracle. That boy was never dead."

"He *was*. Dr. Hammond signed the death certificate."

"A piece of paper can easily be ripped up."

"I don't care. The boy was dead. A power surged down my arms, out of my fingers, and he came back to life."

"You make it sound like jump-starting a car." Miss Bentwhistle circled her prey. "Some might say the lad was simply unconscious. That the affair was a stunt. Adolescent theatrics."

"They'd be wrong."

"It's those books of hers," Brewster blurted. "They've turned her wits."

Miss. Bentwhistle bristled. "When it comes to scandal, insanity is a complication not a defence." She cast her eye on Mary Mabel. "Though you have shamed the Academy, my pet, I am willing to compromise. You may think what you like in private, provided you say what I want in public."

"What sort of compromise is that?"

Smoke might have shot from the dowager's ears. She stormed to the window — migraine be damned — and threw back the curtains. "Do you see those clouds? They take such pretty forms. I imagine I see the shapes of people. Little homeless people scudding across the sky. Why look — an odd-jobs man and his lumpen daughter. Do you see them, my pet? It's a picture clear as day. Or perhaps not, for look, even as we speak the wind is blowing them apart. Take care, precious, *my* visions have a habit of coming true."

Mary Mabel threw back her shoulders. "Do what you like. I won't deny the reason I'm alive."

"Indeed, little martyr?" Miss Bentwhistle laughed dryly. "And are you prepared to sacrifice your father for your arrogance?"

"How dare you threaten Papa!"

"Damn right." Brewster leapt to attention. "If the girl insists on being wilful, do what you must. But why punish me?"

"Heavens, what do you take me for?" Miss Bentwhistle gasped. "I'd hardly put a young thing on the streets alone."

Miss Pigeon flew into the room. "Toronto's on the line! A man from the *Globe*!" The *Globe* was the paper of record for Academy parents.

Miss Bentwhistle spun on her heel. "No more delay. Recant. Now."

"No."

The headmistress whirled back to her secretary. "Inform the *Globe* that we no longer have McTavishes on staff. Furthermore, should they intend to feature us in their account, provide them with the name of our solicitor."

Miss Pigeon scuttled off.

"You have one hour to pack and be gone," Miss Bentwhistle said, with a glance at her watch.

"For God's sake," McTavish pleaded, "don't cast your darling Brewster to the wind!"

"'My darling'?" Miss Bentwhistle's hand fluttered to her throat. "Imagination must run in your family! How dare you think I'd stoop to the likes of you?"

"Stooping's the least of it," Brewster rose to his feet, no longer the supplicant. "If I'm kicked out, I'll leave with lips flapping. Your 'special interests' will turn this county on its ear."

"Lunacy!"

"Don't play the innocent. You're no more virgin than I am. Why, you take to acrobatics that'd make the Devil blush."

"Depraved ravings!"

"Not half so depraved as your delight in feather dusters!"

Miss Bentwhistle's eyes twitched. "Mr. McTavish, your rant is nothing short of slander. Nor is slander the least of your sins. You've been denounced by the Misses Budgie, Lundy, and Brown. Their accusations are documented in my filing cabinet. Gross indecency. Attempted rape. Why, I myself had cause to fend you off."

"That's a lie!"

"Oh? And who do you suppose will be believed: a McTavish or a Bentwhistle? We know the local magistrate, my dear. Be careful how you tread. Any loose talk and you will find yourself locked in the Kingston Pen with a bounty on your bottom! Now — get out of my school, my town, my county!"

"Mercy for Papa," Mary Mabel begged.

Miss Bentwhistle curled her lip. "That, my dear, would take a miracle. And you're fresh out."

Back in their quarters, Brewster went on a tear. "Trouble, that's all you've ever been. Well, now you've ruined us. Happy? You only had to say it never happened."

"I don't have much, Papa. I couldn't give her that."

"But you could give away our home? I'm too old to start over. There's younger men can do the things I do, and better."

"Don't worry. We'll find something else."

"There's no more 'we.' It's time to be rid of you." He snatched some coins from his money tin and threw them at her. "There. Don't say I left you nothing."

Mary Mabel wilted onto the cot.

"Ah, here come the tears. I'm to feel guilty, am I? Well, you can boo-hoo till doomsday. You brought this on yourself, you and your games of pretend." He brushed a tear with his sleeve. "It's for the best, us parting. You've hated me your whole life. I don't mind. Just have the guts to say it. Say that you hate me, so I can leave in peace!"

She couldn't. He went to smack the hurt off her face. Instead, he grabbed her mama's teacup and smashed it against the wall.

"Now, curse me," he wept. "Curse me to hell!" He grabbed his knapsack and ran out the door.

She listened as he blubbered down the corridor, and up the steps to outside. Heard the heavy door slam. She stayed very still for a time, as if, if she stayed still long enough, it would all go away. At last, she crawled across the floor, collected the shards of her mama's cup, and shrank into a ball in the corner. It was time to pack and go. Go? Where?

"Mama," she called out, "what am I to do? I need you. Help me. Please."

But there was only silence.

III

HUNTERS *and* HUNTED

A NIGHT of TERROR

The next thing Mary Mabel knew, the porter had arrived to collect her. "You're to be stowed in the trunk of the Packard and spirited past the newshounds at the gates." The indignity was a relief. She was too upset to think, much less be swarmed by reporters. She tossed a few clothes in her bag, along with *The Collected Works of William Shakespeare*, said goodbye to the rest of her books, and left home forever.

The porter dropped her across town, at Highway 2, on the outskirts of London's east end. "Hike your skirt, you'll hitch a ride no problem." He handed her five dollars.

"Thanks," she said. Together with the spare change her papa had thrown at her, she'd have food for a couple of days.

The porter drove off. Mary Mabel planted her suitcase at the side of the road and stuck out her thumb. The fourth car stopped.

"Where to?" the man asked as she got in.

"Wherever you're going."

"Aren't you the sly fox." He put his arm around her shoulder. She slapped his face, hopped out, and raced back into town as fast as her legs would carry her.

The rest of the day she wandered the east end, incognito. Parishioners from St. James didn't go near these dead-end streets, and her picture hadn't appeared in the papers. Not that her mug on the front page would have changed anything; she went unrecognized by a pair of Pentecostals who'd been at the hospital. Out on a missionary patrol, they spotted her sitting on a bench, and ran over with their Bibles, eager to testify how they'd witnessed the Beeford resurrection with their very own eyes, and how Miss McTavish was one of their own.

"Well, I'm she, and I'm not one of anybody's," Mary Mabel said, "though if you could spare me a room for the night I'd be obliged."

"You're not Miss McTavish!" the elder huffed. "You're a two-bit whore! A pox-ridden clap-breeder! How dare you pretend to be who you aren't?" The pair turned on their heels and took off in search of likelier candidates for salvation.

At dusk, Mary Mabel found herself at the entrance to the Western Fairgrounds. The revival tent stood silhouetted against the sky, the centre collapsed, tears in the canvas brilliant with sunset. "So this was where Timmy Beeford was electrocuted," she marvelled. She gaped at the shell, what was left of the gener-ator, and the hulk of the trailer-truck. It was a wonder that only the boy had died.

Night fell. Shadows slipped under the tent flaps and into the trailer. Was it safe to fall asleep among strange and lonely men? She decided not to chance it. Luckily, the truck's cab was empty. She crawled in, locked the doors, and fell asleep, a full moon shining through the windshield, God's night light to the forsaken.

Next morning, she was up before the rounds of the London Parks Department. She freshened up in the Fairgrounds' wash-room, managing a sponge bath in one of the stalls with a pair of socks she wet in the sink. For food, she settled for a late afternoon bowl of pork and beans which, with a slice of buttered bread, rice pudding, and a Maxwell House, could be had for sixty cents at Minnie's Good Eats across the road.

By sundown, she was back in her cab, curled up for bed, proud of herself for surviving her first full day on the streets. "It's not so bad," she thought. "At least it could be worse."

• • • •

Mary Mabel was right. It *could* be worse. And it soon *was*.

She woke up in the middle of the night with the feeling she was being watched. Rolling over, she saw a man standing outside the passenger door, his nose squashed flat against the window. Her Peeping Tom was a vision from the crypt. His eyes gleamed wild from deep sockets, sunk in a head papered in gauze like Boris Karloff's Mummy. Ears, unnaturally large, sprouted from the bandages, along with clumps of matted hair. Seeing her awake, the monster began to jabber. Saliva drooled from his mouth, a mouth with jaws that appeared to be wired shut with clothes hangers.

Dear God, she thought, *it's a lunatic escaped from the town asylum!*

The creature began to claw at the window. Long, bony fingers rattled the door, fiddled the handle. Mary Mabel scrambled to the driver's side and pressed the horn with all her might, praying the nearby tramps would save her. No such luck. They fled in all directions.

The lock popped up. The door swung open. The madman grabbed her by the calf. She flipped over, yanked up her free leg, and landed a boot to his chin. He reeled back, howling. She turned to escape out the driver's side. A second stranger blocked the exit. He shone a flashlight in her eyes. She hoisted her bag from the cab's floor and held it like a shield.

Flashlight chuckled. "We've got us a live one."

"Godda beesh!" swore the madman.

Mary Mabel looked from one to the other. "Back off or I scream!"

"As if anyone would care. What's your name?"

"None of your beeswax!" She cast a nervous eye at the maniac. To her relief, he'd shifted his attention to the glove compartment, rifling through a grab-all of maps, receipts, pencils, old toothbrushes, and crumpled sandwich bags.

"I admire your spunk," Flashlight continued, "but you're in a heap of trouble. Break and enter. Tell us your name or we turn you in."

"Clara Brimley," she answered warily.

"Liar. Not to worry, I've other ways to find out." He emptied her bag and searched it, opening the cover of her *Collected Works*. He read the inscription: "'From the Library of Miss Mary Mabel McTavish..'" His jaw dropped. "You're Mary Mabel McTavish?"

"What's it to you?"

Flashlight whooped like he'd hit the bingo jackpot. "Criminey, crackers, and tangerines!"

His monster pal joined in: "Ass an ee sha ruhseef!"

"You can say that again," Flashlight said. "Miss McTavish, God has answered our prayers." He saw her confusion. "My apologies. The name's Floyd Cruickshank. And this here's my partner, Brother Percy Brubacher."

LIFE *in the* VINEYARD

B rother Percy Brubacher would live to regret finding Mary Mabel in the Holy Redemption trailer-truck, would live to curse her name and all her works, fulminating from soapbox pulpits on Los Angeles street corners to the cell of the prison where he would be held on charges of kidnapping and murder. Yet at the time, finding Mary Mabel made Percy feel as close to Heaven as he was ever likely to get.

Now forty, he'd been undergoing a spiritual crisis. The promise of his first years evangelizing had turned to dust and he'd found himself in a pitched battle with the Forces of Darkness. "Help me, Jesus!" he'd scream in the middle of the night; but the Lord was not to be found in those lonely small-town hotel rooms with their peeling flowered wallpaper, mouse droppings, and tick-infested sheets.

Percy would leap out of bed in a frenzy and ferret from his suitcase the little black books in which he'd written up the history of his ministry, a literary labour undertaken as an assist to future biographers. He'd seek inspiration from page one, volume one, "The Day I Got the Call," a recounting of the morning he'd stood, age five, in the alley behind his family's bakery in Hornets Ridge, and served a communion of day-old Chelsea buns to a congregation of squirrels and chipmunks. As the rodents munched, tiny claws pressed together as if in prayer, the clouds had parted and a halo of sun had shone down around him, the sign of God's anointing.

Percy's mother encouraged his call, taking him to local meetings of the Women's Christian Temperance Union. He was an immediate sensation in his little blue blazer, grey flannel shorts, and bow tie, leaping to his feet as the Spirit moved, to preach away on the evils of drink. His father, a backsliding Baptist with a taste for bathtub gin, was none too pleased at his son's denunciations. But as Percy reported, "The old devil said little, being generally passed out."

While Percy's religious vocation was attractive to rural women of a certain age, it caused trouble with the village boys, especially at recess, after he'd trumpeted their sins in front of the teacher. Percy didn't mind. He wore his shiners proudly. "The badge of the Lord," he called them. "'For so persecuted they the prophets who came before me.'"

He took comfort from a postcard he'd received from famed baseball player-turned-evangelist Billy Sunday. Sunday had been touched by the letter from the little boy from New Hampshire, who'd written for advice on how to handle an alcoholic father. His reply became Percy's salvation, recognition from the next best thing to God Himself that he mattered in the world beyond Hornets Ridge. He waved the postcard under everyone's nose, made it the frequent subject of school Show and Tells, and created a small shrine to it next to the Bible by his bed. At night, he'd kneel, clasp it in prayer, and, running his finger gently over the postage stamp, listen to the still voice of the Lord.

"*Yea, God spake unto me through Reverend Billy's postcard,*" — (volume one, page 126) — "*revealing a Great Plan, a Divine Destiny for His humble servant. In cause of my deep and abiding faith, He promised that the day would come when I would be summoned to preach His Gospel throughout the land, and would be known, now and for all eternity, as the greatest of His prophets in the New World.*"

Like all prophets, Percy endured a time of testing. In his early twenties, he wandered off for a prayer retreat atop Mount Pawtuckaway. From its peak, he saw the fiery furnace of Shadrach, Meeshach, and Abednego brought unto Hornets Ridge. His father, in a drunken stupor, had pitched a tank of kerosene into the bakery oven; his family died instantly in the explosion.

Percy anguished. *"Why had I been saved, while my mother and siblings had perished? The Lord spake unto me in my agony. He had need to temper my faith, He said, the better for it to withstand the temptations of Hell."*

Percy retreated to a shack outside the village. Here he prayed without cease, readying himself for the promised day when God would summon him to mission. A few elderly women who remembered him from the W.C.T.U. left plates of food and spare coins outside his door, but this was the extent of his following. Even village clergy kept their distance; they resented being called to account by a hermit half their age. Children, emboldened by their parents' mockery, threw stones as he passed. He paid them no mind, his eyes alight with glory. Let them call him "Beggar Loon" and "Scarecrow"; he'd have the last laugh.

Sure enough, when he hit thirty, God smiled on His poor servant. Reggie Burns, praise Jesus, went and blew the heads off himself, wife Nellie, and Pittsburgh playboy Junior Bennett — and Percy Brubacher got his break.

Within four days of the murders, the Bennetts put their estate on the market, and sold its contents at auction. In "Sinner On My Doorstep" — little black book, volume three, pages 21 to 50 — Percy recalled the curious visit he'd received that evening from Floyd Cruickshank, a former classmate who minded the till at the general store where Percy bought soap, macaroni, and tacks. Floyd, ever the would-be dandy in his secondhand worsted windbreaker and matching plus-fours, rocked on the heels of his Oxfords and asked, "Could I have a word?"

Percy was wary. Since their school days, the most Floyd had ever said to him was, "That'll be sixty-five cents." But the Lord put a flea in Percy's ear, so Perce said, "Fine."

After a little this-and-that about the weather, Floyd got down to business. He'd been at the auction. "All day, folks ponied up to buy the Bennett's effects. They claimed they wanted a piece of history. Bull. What they really wanted — you could see it in their eyes — was a piece of secondhand sin. They wanted to hang their hats on the rack where Nellie hung her cloth coat, or put their lips on Missy Bennett's bone china, or — pardon my French — have a bounce in the sheets of a murdered adulterer."

Percy nodded grimly. He imagined Satan's flames licking the pillowcases.

"At the end of the day," Floyd continued, "everything sold but the tent. No surprise. It'd take a pretty big backyard. Even repaired, the stains'd put a damper on get-togethers. Which is why I got it free for the hauling."

Percy's heart raced. "You got the tent?"

"Amen." And now Floyd got serious. "Perce, we've known each other since we were kids. I'm ashamed to say I did you wrong."

Percy could hardly breathe. He was suddenly back in the playground, swearing down God's vengeance, as Floyd cleaned his clock. Again and again and again.

"I'm here to say I'm sorry," Floyd said.

Percy's eyes welled. "You're sorry?"

"Yes. I'm sorry. Very sorry. Forgive me?"

The next thing Percy knew, he was hugging Floyd and sobbing on his shoulder. Floyd eased him onto the porch step and handed him a handkerchief.

"I'm no do-gooder," Floyd said quietly, as Percy blew his nose. "I'm just a sinner who wants to get the hell out of Hornets Ridge. That bloody tent's my main chance. All afternoon, I've thought, if folks find thrills in tea towels, what'll they find in the tent of horrors itself? Only thing is — I can't just sell tickets. Respectable folks'll need an excuse to go inside."

"Maybe a sermon?" Percy blurted. He shook his fist over his head. "That tent is the Lord's living proof, The Wages of Sin Is Death."

"My thought exactly," Floyd enthused. "A God-fearing barn burner on that theme'll pack 'em in. But heck, Perce, I'm no speaker. I can barely sell toothpicks, much less God."

"So the Lord has sent you unto me!"

"More or less." Floyd stuck a finger in his collar. "I remember school, Perce. You gave me nightmares for weeks. No kidding. You were one scary bugger. So here's what I'm driving at. You're a preacher without a pulpit. I have a pulpit without a preacher. Whadeja say?"

"I say the Lord has worked a wonder in your heart, Brother Floyd!" Percy wrung out the handkerchief and gave his eyes another wipe. "Yea, it be murder, suicide, adultery, and drink have brung this tent unto us, but through our ministry shall innocent souls be snatched from the Pit. Oh Brother Floyd, I say unto you, all things work together for good for those who love the Lord. Let us pray."

By midnight, Brother Percy was packed; he had but his Bible, his postcard, a few old clothes; a second pair of shoes, the soles patched together with squares of birch bark, bicycle tires, and tacks; a toothbrush and a comb; and his emerging set of little black books. Unable to sleep, he lit his kerosene lamp, and wandered to the cemetery to spend his last night in Hornets Ridge beside his mother's grave. As he later wrote:

> *I knelt beside the wooden cross that marked dear Mother's resting place and traced the grooves of her name with my finger. "I won't be able to come by so often, Mother," I said, "for God has laid a mission on me. But you already know that,*

smiling down from Heaven. You're the only one who believed in me, who never made fun, besides blessèd Billy Sunday. As he wrote in my postcard, 'From a little acorn will grow a mighty oak.' It's true. For I'm growing, feet planted in the Word of God, arms branched open in the Light of the World. Before I'm through, I'll be as famous as Brother Billy. More famous, even. They won't laugh at me then. They'll bend their knees and pray before me. I'll make you proud, Mother. I'll be crowned with glory and have money enough to buy you the biggest stone in the whole darn cemetery. Better than a stone: you'll have the statue of an angel. For that's what you are, it's what you deserve, and it's what you'll have, so help me God."

For a time, God's Promise looked to be fulfilled. As recorded in Percy's little black books, those were the glory days, a time of redemption with Satan on the run. The Bennett murders packed the tent that whole first summer; and come frost, Floyd had finagled invitations from the Deep South, where righteous brethren from the hills of Arkansas to the Florida orange groves were keen on hellfire sermons featuring Yankee sinners bobbing in brimstone.

The collections had been equally good: love-offering envelopes sufficiently stuffed to keep up payments on the truck, and on that marble angel for his mother, which he'd got at a discount on account of the left wing being chipped in transit, though not so's you'd notice, praise the Lord. There was even enough to shell out for beds in private hotels; these inspired more uplifting prayers than those delivered from lumpy mattresses in the basements of local deacons. Nor did the evangelists stint on such accommodation. As Floyd pointed out, "Jesus may have preached to whores, but stay in some flophouse, you think there won't be talk?"

The evangelists also agreed that the Almighty wanted His employees to look their best. "Rags and sandals are fine for Bible times, but holes in the socks make a lousy advertisement for the Kingdom of God." So Percy got himself outfitted with two navy, off-the-rack suits from Tip Top Tailors, three starched white shirts, one pair of suspenders, and a snazzy charcoal-grey fedora.

Percy kept a careful tally of all such expenditures on the flesh in his little black books. Here, too, he recorded tallies of the tent's nightly take, as well as the count of those who hit the sawdust trail, parading up the aisle to fill out decision cards for the Lord. Some of these converts made a habit of getting saved. If Percy knew, he didn't let on. He was proud of his numbers, and prayed they'd be celebrated like those of his hero, Brother Billy, whose salvation stats had been touted in box scores on the front pages of dailies from L.A. to Washington, Albuquerque to New York.

Percy's triumphs, however, went unheralded. Local reporters covering the arrival of the tent simply wrote a rehash of the murders. "Those degenerate fornicators get more ink than I do," Percy groused. To add insult to injury, no one appeared to know how to spell "Brubacher," an indignity that invariably set Percy to work on some variation of the following letter-to-the-editor.

> *Dear Buttonbrook Gleaner,*
>
> *Buttonbrook should count itself good and lucky to have had the internationally renowned revivalist Brother Percy Brubacher preaching out at the bandstand last Saturday night. He has chased the Devil out of Arkansas, Rhode Island,*

and points between. So it is a crying shame that your editor is so ignorant as to spell his name with a "k." This is an embarrassment to your paper, a black day for Buttonbrook, and an insult to the Reverend Brother Brubacher, who is more famous than the lot of you put together.

Yours sincerely,
Mr. Herb Potts

As time rolled on, attendance at the tent began to thin. The Bennett killings were stale, jostled out of the spotlight by Al Capone, the Lindbergh baby, and above all else the fallout of the Great Crash. It's hard to raise a sweat over the death of some playboy when big city skies are raining bankers.

The Depression did more than upstage their act. While a few churches continued to play host, most cut off invitations lest dwindling tithes be siphoned to the competition: charity begins at home. Consequently, Brothers Percy and Floyd had to underwrite production costs, while fending off accusations that they were stealing bread from the mouths of local widows and orphans. It was a strain, especially as the offering envelopes they were accused of filching were increasingly stuffed with newspaper.

Costs up, revenues down, the evangelists scaled back. They lodged at modest bed and breakfasts, which had the attraction of landladies prepared to darn socks, or raise pant hems to disguise frayed cuffs. There was a price for this needlework: widows with a clutch of dead lace at their throats and habitations appointed with dusty bouquets of dried flowers. Such would insist on favouring them with recitals at the parlour piano. "Do you ever dream of domestic bliss?"

The Widow Duffy was a terror in this regard. Her attentions to Brother Percy caused the poor man much consternation, especially at night when she prowled the corridors, ultimately surprising him in the biffy. "Get thee behind me Satan," he cried, scrambling to cover his privates. The Widow Duffy claimed herself an innocent sleepwalker, but Percy was no fool. "She meant to have her way with me," he whispered to Brother Floyd. "We must quit this den by daybreak: 'Flee from temptation, nor let the shadow of it come nigh!'"

While Percy knew the Bible, he scarcely knew himself. Sex was no temptation to him whatsoever. An enthusiastic virgin, he held the entire process to be as distasteful as it was messy, a dirty chore necessary to propagate worshippers. Fortunately, being a preacher, he'd been given a more dignified means to populate the Kingdom, and a damn sight more sanitary to boot.

Floyd, on the other hand, laboured under no such misapprehensions. Frankly, the Widow Duffy's nocturnal ramblings had aroused more than his curiosity. "Brother Percy," he admonished, "we have a Christian duty to remain. If that dame sleepwalks unattended, she may fall down the stairs and break her neck."

"Don't think to pull the wool over my eyes," Percy scolded. "You've a mind to spill your seed in that harlot! How shall you answer up to Jesus at the end time?"

"Nag, nag, nag. If I wanted a wife I'd have married one."

"Repent or burn!"

"Go suck an egg."

Percy stormed off, spending the rest of the night at the local fleabag. He didn't sleep. Then again, neither did Floyd. Yet whereas Percy spent the morning's drive to the next town muttering into his Bible, Floyd was frisky as a pup, pedal to the metal, whistling rags. They stopped for gas. Brother Percy closed the Good Book and held it to his breast. He cast a baleful gaze in the direction of his colleague.

Silence.

"What?" Floyd demanded.

God's prophet flared his nostrils. "Apostate!"

Brothers Percy and Floyd never again shared accommodation. Percy confined himself to respectable S.R.O.s with sharp-eyed proprietors who snooped the halls to nix shenanigans amongst unmarried guests. Famous for shared baths with rust-stained sinks, the smell of mothballs, and the sound of lonely geriatrics weeping at all hours behind closed doors, these hotels were a perfect match for the evangelist. Once management realized he was alone, they paid no heed to his arguments with the dresser mirror.

Floyd, truth to tell, had always kept his pump primed. He'd simply held off till Percy'd fallen asleep, figuring it was better to sneak off like a kid out for a smoke than to set himself up for sermonizing in the truck. He'd had nightmares of being strapped to the wheel with Percy haranguing him from North Bay to Memphis. But discovery of Floyd's appetites had put a cork in Brother Percy's pipes; his censure registered instead by heavy sighs. This was a mite creepy on all-night drives, but a definite improvement over the yapping to which Floyd had hitherto been subjected.

As Percy's private life grew progressively solitary, his nature became more bilious. "Billy Sunday wasn't stuck in hicksvilles with a whoremonger! He was beloved! Adored! It isn't fair!" His theology followed his mind into nightmare, his God transformed from disciplinarian to psychopath.

"The Lord thy God is a bloody god," he'd rage across the stage, "His plan of redemption, a slaughterhouse dripping with the blood of the Lamb, our Lord and Saviour Jesus Christ! Who's off to the lake of fire? You know yourselves, you hellborn, hog-jowled, whiskey-soaked assassins of righteousness!

You cigarette-smoking, fudge-eating lechers in spats and green vests! You hags of uncleanness dolled up in fool hats for card parties, serving spiced meats on hand-painted china with nasty music on your pianos while your spawn run the streets like a rummage sale in a secondhand store, gadding about in the company of jackrabbits whose characters would make a black mark on a piece of tar paper! Well, you're off to judgment, my friends. You, too, Granny, your white hairs won't save you from a swim in the Devil's chamber pot! You're off to a judgment fierce as that of those damnable rum-soaked Bennetts, suffocating in the rank, fetid sweat of their fornication, drowning in the juices of their abomination! A judgment fierce as Sodom and Gomorrah, when the Lord God made Mount Vesuvius puke a hemorrhage of lava!"

Congregations were disconcerted. In theory, they accepted that they were all sinners, but in practice it was generally understood that the preacher's wrath was to be directed at sinners *outside* the tent. By the end, only Pentecostals had the stomach to attend. They could count on the Holy Spirit descending, transporting them with the gift of tongues, God's proof-positive that they'd been saved by the blood of the Lamb and were bound for glory with Percy and the angels.

Floyd had known that life in the Lord's vineyard was not for the upwardly mobile, but after expenses he barely had the scratch to pay for his French ticklers. He decided to pull the plug. He waited till they hit London, Ontario. Here Percy would be as happy as he'd be liable to get, haranguing one of the last crowds to consider him a somebody.

••••

And so, the afternoon of that fateful revival, Brother Floyd moseyed his partner into the van of the trailer truck. "I've been doing some thinking."

"Praise the Lord. The first step to repentance."

Floyd bit his tongue. "The ministry's had it," he continued. "It's time to call it quits."

Percy staggered backwards. "*Quits*? Where would the world be today if Jesus had called it quits?"

"Our receipts don't amount to a pinch of heifer dust," Floyd persevered. "We're a corpse begging to be buried."

"And what if we are? Lazarus came back."

"For heaven's sake, Perce, you're misery on a stick, you scare the kids."

"God didn't put us on this earth to be happy. We were put here to serve."

"There's other ways to serve."

"Not for me! This ministry's my calling. It's where I belong. It's my home."

"It's not your home, it's a tent. Repeat after me: 'This is a tent. A tent of horrors kept fresh with slaughterhouse guts and a paintbrush.'"

"Nooo!"

Floyd wasn't good with tears, but he wasn't about to let a wave of compassion sink his resolve. "Perce," he stared in embarrassment over the poor man's left shoulder, "I've been doing some calculations. There's a way we can close up shop and go our separate ways with a little something to tide us over."

Percy sniffled. The absence of other vocalizing encouraged Floyd to believe that reason had a prayer.

"We got ourselves seven thousand square feet of tent near as I can reckon. At four six-inch squares per square foot, that's twenty-eight thousand squares. I propose we do one final farewell tour. Each night we'll sell Redemption squares, to be cut from the tent and delivered at tour's end: two bits a piece, or a buck for one with blood on it."

Percy gaped like a gopher on a spit. "YOU'RE NOTHING BUT A GODDAMN STOOL UP THE DEVIL'S ANUS!" He hurled a folding chair at his partner and flew from the fairgrounds, tears of rage, horror, and helplessness flooding down his cheeks. "Dear God," he beseeched, falling at the foot of a mighty oak, "steep me in Your wrath! Do such a Work through me tonight that it will tear the firmament!"

The next thing Percy knew, he was on stage screaming at Timmy Beeford, lightning shearing the main pole, ripping the wires, popping the light bulbs, exploding the generator — and his mother's childhood caution ringing in his ears: "Percy, my pumpkin, be careful what you pray for. God may be listening."

K.O. DOYLE and CO.

Bright and early the following morning, Brother Floyd had surveyed the damage to ministry assets. It was calamitous. The generator and trailer were write-offs, ditto the lights and supports. As for the canvas, the cost of repair would be prohibitive.

"Hot diggity!" Floyd crowed. This would lay to rest any hopes his partner might have harboured for their ministry's resurrection. Good thing he'd kept up the insurance payments. Brother Percy'd urged him to drop the policy and put their fate in God's hands. "Trust in the Lord and He will provide." However when dealing with God, Floyd had preferred to keep one hand on his wallet.

His caution vindicated, he savoured the wreckage, then skipped to a telephone where he placed a call to their underwriter. He was promised that an adjuster would be up from Toronto on next morning's train. If God were as helpful as the United Dominion Insurance Company, Heaven would have a lot more takers.

Visions of Easy Street filling his head, Floyd made his way to London General Hospital to visit his partner. In the past evening's upheaval, the poor man had broken his jaw. With the wires and swelling, he was in no condition to answer back. What better time to rub in the good news?

Floyd cataloged the carnage with glee. "The Almighty's will is writ large," he concluded. "He wants us shut down pronto."

Percy was beside himself, his attempts at interjection digging metal into bone, tissue, and nerve ends. "Aaaa! Aaaa!" he howled in pain.

"Why, Perce, is that the glorious sound of rejoicing?"

"Aaaa! Aaaa!"

"Aaaa! Aaaa! Aaaa-men!" Floyd winked to the heavens. "Thank you, Jesus."

Brother Percy grabbed the Gideon Bible on his nightstand. He was about to pitch it at his partner's head, but Floyd cocked a fist. Percy cowered.

"Blessèd are the meek," Floyd reminded with a grin.

Floyd stopped grinning with the arrival of the adjuster, Mr. Fischer. In the view of the United Dominion Insurance Company, the destruction of ministry property fell under the clause dealing with Acts of God. ("A subject about which you're no doubt familiar.") Floyd blanched. Dreams of a lucrative settlement were up in smoke, but so were plans to market tent squares. Without a final tour, how could they pitch the merchandise? And without the tent, truck, and generator, how could they have a tour?

Complicating matters, work on Percy's jaw had taken a bite from their reserves. Released from hospital that afternoon, the evangelist stooped to a dingy room in the cheapest digs he could find, the C.P.R. Hotel, a.k.a. The Ceeps. Floyd likewise swallowed his pride, and had management squeeze in a cot at the foot of his partner's bed.

After supper, while Percy prayed to the Almighty for deliverance, Floyd toddled downstairs to the hotel tavern to worship at the altar of Jack Daniels.

The kid at the end of the bar was one cocky bantam. Vest open, tie loose, slick hair parted in the middle, he left off talking to the bartender, and plunked himself down at Floyd's table. "K.O. Doyle," he stuck out his paw. "I hear you're Floyd Cruickshank, brains behind the preacher man."

"What's it to you?"

"I'm looking for a Mary Mabel McTavish. You know her?"

"What if I do?"

"I'd like to jog your memory," Doyle said. He was with *King Features Syndicate*, a Hearst operation, up from Buffalo for a peeka-boo. "A tousle-haired all-American tyke, right out of a Norman Rockwell, dies and gets brought back to life. The story's a four-star wank-yer-crank, 'specially if the dame's got stems."

"News travels fast."

"I got sources."

Doyle's source, courtesy of *King Features*, was the telegraph operator in Wichita, Kansas, who took the cable Uncle Albert sent his sister.

TIMMY HAD A DUST UP WITH MOTHER
NATURE. THE FREE PRESS SAYS HE DIED
AND GOT HISSELF RESURRECTED. HORSE
FEATHERS. GRACE SENDS HER REGARDS.
SHE IS HAVING A SPELL. ALBERT.

A call from *King Features* to the *Free Press* confirmed the article. The paper offered to sell its copy, but the skeptical syndicate opted to send up a staffer for an independent fact check. After all, "Canadian news" was a contradiction in terms.

Doyle had hit town that morning. Like travelling salesmen and other ne'er-do-wells, he'd checked into The Ceeps because it was cheap, next to the station, and came with a bar. After dropping off his bag — a change of underwear and a toothbrush — he went in search of the gal of the hour. According to the *Free Press*, Miss McTavish worked at the local private school. Doyle traipsed over, only to be confronted by the headmistress. "That damn Gorgon tore a strip off me," he sputtered to Floyd. "Her butt's so puckered, I'll bet when she farts, she hits high C."

From there to the hospital. Doctor Hammond refused comment, but his broken nose told a tale, as did the shaken demeanour of a certain Nurse Judd.

Doyle had better luck at Bethel Gospel Hall. The pastor was a hayseed with breath that would strip linoleum, but he was four-square behind the miracle; he also tipped Doyle to Tom and Betty Wertz. The couple made shy, but Doyle got past the front door when he said he was a lawyer come to offer his services cheap, on account of he'd heard the good doctor planned to charge Tom with assault.

Last port of call: Timmy Beeford's. Aunt Grace had the house sealed up tighter than a nun's panties. But she'd overlooked Timmy's upstairs bedroom window. Doyle lured the little nipper onto the verandah roof and got what he wanted with a couple of lemon sours.

With enough for a column, Doyle skedaddled back to the hotel bar, phoned in what he had to *King Features*, and tucked into supper: a pickled egg washed down with a pail of suds.

"You Canucks brew it strong," Doyle told Floyd. "Then again, you gotta be pissed to live here." He excused himself for a leak.

"I couldn't help but overhear."

Floyd looked up into the florid face of the drunk from the far corner. A big guy with a lumpy nose, the drunk slapped Floyd on the back. "Scoop Jones from *Scripps-Howard*. I got a quart of Four Roses in my room. Ditch the kid, come up for a nightcap. Give Scoop the scoop, get double for your trouble."

"Sorry, pal, I gotta hit the hay," said Floyd, rising unsteadily from his chair.

"A rain check then. Scoop Jones. Room 202."

As Floyd lurched to the elevator by the front desk, he heard the clerk say to the new arrival in the rumpled fedora, "Scratch

Micallef, *Associated Press*? I must say, we've been getting a lot of newsmen lately. The bar is that way."

Wobbling down the hall to his room, Floyd felt a spot of envy. Some young missy'd grabbed the spotlight he and Perce had dreamed of. She'd be rich. Damn. There was nothing so cruel as the good fortune of others.

However, Floyd was a visionary, not long for regret. By the time he fumbled his key into the lock, he'd had a flash. By the time the door swung open, it was a full-blown inspiration. And by the time he switched on the overhead light, he saw his career resurrected in glory. He was going to hitch a ride on Mary Mabel's star, be her manager, be a millionaire.

"Perce," he cried, "get your ass in gear. If you want to save that damn ministry of yours, get on your knees and pray for God to bring us Miss McTavish. Tell Him to make it snappy. Given the shit He's flushed our way, it's the least He can do."

Percy tumbled out of his sheets. If this could save his pulpit, he'd get cracking like eggs at a diner.

A few hours later, Percy prayed out and Floyd passed out, Herschel MacIntosh of the London Parks Department came pounding on their door, fresh from chasing lovers out of the fairground. "There's bums in your tent. Any trouble, there'll be hell to pay."

The evangelists got to the site in no time. In the cab of their truck, they found a tramp in a dress. Percy was outraged when Floyd took up flirting. *No way is that whoremonger going to fornicate at the foot of my bed with some hoboess*, he fumed, as he checked the glove compartment for theft. That's when he heard Floyd say the magic words: "You're Mary Mabel McTavish?"

Mary Mabel McTavish! Lo, the Lord had delivered her unto them, just as Percy'd prayed! The reverend's eyes filled with tears. He had a direct line to the Almighty after all.

The CALL

No sooner had Mary Mabel been introduced to the evangelists than they were interrupted by visitors. "It's the Three Stooges," Floyd whispered. "Don't give them your name, or there'll be trouble." She decided to trust his advice: better the devil you know than the devil you don't.

"If it isn't the gentlemen of the press," the evangelist called out. "What brings you boys out on a 3:00 a.m. constitutional? The Londonderry air? Or are you after some London derrière?"

"I'd ask the same of you," the youngest snorted. "Who's the doll?"

Floyd grabbed her by the elbow. "Why, Mr. Doyle, this is a vagrant we caught on a tip."

Mary Mabel took her cue. Imagining herself the ruined heroine of *The Fallen Shopgirl*, she went knock-kneed. "Is you me Daddy?" she asked, clinging drunkenly to his lapels.

"High on turpentine," Floyd confided.

Clucking tongues and shaking heads. How exciting! Mary Mabel decided to go all out. "I've been a bad girl, Daddy," she pouted. "Take me home and spank me!"

"I'm not your Daddy, child."

"We can purr-tend," she hiccuped, and threw her left arm open to the newsmen. "Which one-ov-you wants to be my Daddy?" She batted her eyes.

They took a step backwards, half-interested, half-afraid.

"No takers?" she sobbed prettily. "Then I'm all alone in the big bad world, and me with a bun in the oven." She shook her fist at the moon. "Curse you Billy Bounder!"

Floyd stepped hard on her instep. "Shut your trap. Your

Daddy's in the county jail! And that's where you'll be headed too, soon as we raid the tent!"

At word of a raid, the newsmen perked up. Floyd turned to his partner. "Lead the way, while I guard our potted Petunia. En route, you can regale the lads with your conversion stats."

That was all the encouragement Brother Brubacher needed. Despite his wired jaw, he puffed his chest and led the scribblers away with a spirited, if incomprehensible, account of his ministry.

"Let's make tracks," Floyd whispered to Mary Mabel. Lickety-split, they did.

"How did I do?" she asked, once clear of the park.

Floyd laughed. "Lord love us, you peddle more ham than a meat market."

"Thanks, but you shouldn't have stopped me before I'd made my speech about Billy Bounder. He's the cad who ruined Agnes Boyle in *The Fallen Shopgirl*, chapter six." Before Mary Mabel knew it, all the words that had been bottled up in her head since leaving the Academy came flooding out. She told him every-thing: about her books, her puppets, her papa, Miss Bentwhistle, and Academy theatrics. She even told him about being in "Auntie" Irene's *Midsummer Night's Dream* for the Milwaukee Little Theater Guild. "I was the fairy Peasblossom," she babbled. "Bits of my wings kept falling off, but the grownups said I was very good just the same. I love play-acting. It sure beats scrub-bing toilets for Miss B. Oh, I'm talking your ear off. You'll be thinking I *am* high on turpentine. Where are we going?"

"To the Thompson twins, to find you a bed."

"The Thompson twins?" Mary Mabel was over the moon. To meet the Twins was too delicious. She'd heard their tale when she was little, on a drive with Miss Bentwhistle and her papa. The Twins, one-time classmates of Miss B., were the spinster daughters of Mr. Ezekiel Thompson, a local pooh-bah whose cane had had a mind of its own. Despite much abuse, the Twins had devoted their lives to his care. "On his ninetieth birthday, the doctor pronounced him good for ninety more," Miss Bentwhistle had confided. "Imagine the shock when that very night he got booked for the boneyard after tumbling down three sets of stairs and hitting his head with a shovel."

Financial hardship followed. Despite lives of service, Misses Millie and Tillie were left nothing but the family home, their father having bequeathed the rest of his estate to St. James, since "The Lord God can put it to better use than a couple of old maids." Now living in poverty, they made ends meet by running a bed and breakfast that served visitors produce cultivated in their front garden.

Floyd confided that because of their circumstances, the Twins suffered chronic sleep apnea. "You mustn't worry if you hear strange noises in the middle of the night," he said. "I'm frequently called upon to perform resuscitation." He told Mary Mabel to crouch among the tomato plants while he knocked, on the excuse that he'd forgotten to discharge his bill when he'd left the past morning, and wanted to make amends before making introductions. As it turned out, the Twins were more than forgiving, until they saw Mary Mabel emerge from hiding.

Floyd assured them that everything was above board: the girl had been abandoned by her father; he, a Good Samaritan, was looking for a home in which she could take refuge; as for the moment, he'd appreciate the use of their sitting room for a pastoral consultation.

And so, with the Twins in the adjoining dining room chaperoning over a game of two-handed euchre, Floyd and Mary Mabel had tea. He inquired after Timmy Beeford's resurrection, grilling her at length. "I trust you won't take offense, but how much pretend would there be in all this?"

"I'm no angel," she replied, "but every word I've said is true. Standing up for that truth has cost me my home and family. You can believe me or not, I don't care two pins. Now, if you're through with the insults, I'd like the Misses Thompson to show me to my room."

"Hold on," he said. "I'm certain of two things. First, you believe what you're saying. Second, you have a calling."

Mary Mabel let out a hoot. "I have nothing, much less a calling."

"As God is my witness," Floyd persisted, "I want you to be a partner in a new travelling revival show. I'll produce, Brother Percy will sermonize, and you'll be the star attraction."

The thought thrilled her. Nonetheless, she'd read about producers. "I can look in a mirror. I know what looks back. I'm nothing special, so don't try to seduce me with my vanity."

"God doesn't care about the wrapping paper. It's the gift inside that counts. Yours is the gift of miracle. I want to help you bring that gift to the world."

"I was blessed with one miracle. I may never have another."

"I'm not asking for any. All you need to do is step on a platform and tell your truth. You've no need to be scared."

"I'm not," she lied.

"Yes you are. You're afraid to fail, to be laughed at. It's a fear born of sin! The sin of pride. Take courage! Pure hearts prevail! As for the jitters, your turn for the press proved you have nerves of steel. A life on the boards is yours if you'll have it. Your food and lodging'll be taken care of, and there'll be money for as many books as you can read."

Mary Mabel bit her lip.

"Picture Miss Bentwhistle's face when you're famous," Floyd tempted. "Picture Clara Brimley and the other Academy brats as well. Your papa, too — he'll come crawling, you mark my word, begging for you to take him back."

Mary Mabel barely realized she'd stopped breathing.

"We live in a wasteland, Miss McTavish. Despair roams the land. Folks want a miracle to change their lives. You're living proof that anything is possible. Join with me. Through our ministry we'll offer hope. Dreams. The chance of a new start. Whadeja say? Will you give it a shot?"

Mary Mabel prayed very hard. Her mama filled her head: "Say yes," she whispered.

"Yes," Mary Mabel gulped.

Floyd slapped his knee. "I'll write up a contract to legalize our venture."

"That's very kind."

"One little thing." He hesitated. "When you talk about your resurrection, don't mention your mama. Feel free to keep her in your heart, but give the glory to God."

"Why?"

"We don't want folks thinking you're crazy. Don't get me wrong. I believe you. But it's a cruel world."

"He's right," her mama told her. "Besides, it's the truth. I'm your guardian angel. And who sends guardian angels if not God?" She had a point.

"Have your papers ready for me in the morning." And with that, Mary Mabel shook his hand and joined the circus.

IV

The HEARST PRESS

The CHIEF

William Randolph Hearst lay very still, staring up at the velvet canopy over his oak baldachin bed in the Gothic Suite of his castle at San Simeon. It was the middle of the night. His forehead glistened. Heart pounded. Was he awake? Was this a dream?

Someone else was in the room. Millicent? No, his wife was in Manhattan, stowed away among the antiques in his three-floor apartment at the Clarendon. Marion? He slid his hand under the covers to her side of the bed. Empty. Of course — Marion was on a shoot with his Cosmopolitan Pictures in Burbank, wouldn't be back till tomorrow. So who was in the room?

He heard breathing. "Who's there?" Was that a whisper in the air? He brushed his ear. A glimmer of moonlight slipped through the half-closed curtains casting a shadow by the Persian vase. Was it the stranger? Hearst sat bolt upright and yanked the chain on the lamp next to the headboard. The shadow vanished in the light. He peeked under the bed. Nothing. He was alone. The only eyes staring at him were the eyes from the photographs of his deceased parents, Senator George and Phoebe Apperson Hearst, and of the fourteenth-century Madonna by Segna sitting on his chest of drawers.

He'd keep the light on. There'd be no getting back to sleep. If he was awake. If this wasn't another of his damnable dreams.

He checked his watch. Four in the morning. Best to work. To keep busy. That was the way to keep those dreams at bay. To keep that shadow out of sight. With the size and grandeur of his estate's other fifty-six bedrooms, he knew folks wondered why his own was a measly eighteen by twenty feet. He never told them, but the truth was that the bigger the room, the more nooks and crannies there were for shadows and bogeymen to hide in.

Hearst wrapped his thick terry-cloth dressing gown over his toasty, cream flannel pajamas, slipped his feet into his lined lambskin slippers, and called his secretary from the desk phone.

Joe Willicombe answered on the third ring.

"Can't sleep. Off to the study. About the papers —"

"Still laid out, W.R. Would you like me to join you?"

"No, I'm fine. Restless, that's all." God bless Willicombe. "Sorry to wake you."

"Any time."

Hearst hung up. He'd reward Willicombe for his patience. Maybe get him an inlaid sandalwood box to display his favourite shells. He lumbered his solid frame across the hall to his pink marble bathroom, splashed his face with cold water, watched the water empty down the gold-plated drain pipe, patted his face dry with a towel monogrammed in gold thread, and padded his way to the study, taking care to turn on each of the tall, delicate *torchères* along the passage, each refitted as floor lamps with shades created from the pages of Gregorian chant books.

He wished Marion was home. He could sleep then. She made him feel young, not like an old trout set to wash up on some riverbank. Dear Marion. What did she see in him? Not the money. She'd made her own dime with Ziegfield and the silent flickers. Hearst wished her career was doing better, but the joy of her company was one advantage of the recent slowdown. Louis B. Mayer, that fat toad, said her stutter didn't work in talkies. What did he know? Jack Warner had been only too happy to have him move Cosmopolitan Pictures onto the Warner lot — Marion's twenty-room dressing room, servants, and daschunds along with it. She'd be the nation's top star yet, no two ways about it. He — Hearst — would see to it. All she needed was the right property. The right part.

At the entrance to his study, Hearst paused to catch his breath, enjoying the burnt oranges, rusts, and reds of the antique Spanish ceiling; the intricate grillwork of the Florentine bookcases filled with rare treasures spined in silver, ceramic, and ivory; and of the Camille Solon arches with their murals of Biblical and mythological tales. He removed his slippers. These wouldn't be needed on the warm Bakhtiari carpets.

It was time to begin his ritual. Laid out across the study's carpets were the latest editions of the hundreds of newspapers in his publishing empire. He'd already been over them with Willicombe. He'd go over them again, turning their pages with dexterously boney toes, scanning the headlines, the placement of the photographs, searching for that special detail to make his day complete.

He remembered the excitement of the old days. His reporters had doubled as amateur dicks, dishing up sleaze for a public keen on private dirt. His favourite stories? That trip with Sarah Bernhardt to the opium den in Chinatown. Or the one about the masseur of a Turkish steam bath found bobbing headless in the Hudson. Or the lollipop who broke marriages when she leapt naked from a pie at the Pooh Bah Club.

Above all, he relished his dispatches on the sinking of the *Maine*. Sure, his stories should've been filed under fiction. But they started a real-life war with Spain that had left America the sole power in the hemisphere and propelled Teddy Roosevelt up San Juan Hill to the White House. Starting wars and electing presidents: if that didn't prove the power of the press, what did?

But where were the stories now? Where was the power they gave him? Since the Crash it was nothing but grim Depression, enlivened by dance marathons and the funnies. Papers were turning into billboards, just another space to place an ad. What was the point of that? No wonder he felt old.

A chill ran down his spine. Someone else was in the room. "Willicombe?"

Silence.

"Who's there?"

A high, girlish laugh like his own, came from the mustard wingback at the far end of the mahogany conference table. The wingback faced the wall, its occupant hidden from view. "You own the world, but I own you."

Hearst swallowed hard. "Who are you?"

The wingback rotated. Seated before him was a young man who looked exactly as he had looked over fifty years ago: a young man with a lean face, hair slicked and parted in the middle, a lush mustache waxed at the tips.

"I'm dreaming," Hearst said. "This is a dream."

The young man smiled. "What's real and what's not? Sometimes things can be real and not real at the same time. Sometimes things that aren't real can *make* things real. 'Remember the *Maine!*'"

"I'm going to wake up now."

"Are you? Maybe you've fallen asleep and you're never waking up again."

Hearst pinched his hands. He slapped his cheeks. "I'm waking up. I'm waking up!"

"You own the world, but I own you." The young man smiled, and suddenly he had no eyes, no skin, no hair. He wasn't like young Hearst at all. He was a gaping death skull.

Hearst screamed. The next thing he knew, he was alone in his study, sprawled on the floor where he'd fallen asleep reading yesterday's *Journal-American*. The phone was ringing in the alcove by the wingback. Hearst stopped screaming. He lay on his warm Bakhtiari carpets unable to move, gasping for breath. The phone continued to ring.

Someone was running up the stairs, now, too hurried to wait for the elevator. "W.R., are you all right?" It was Willicombe.

"I'm fine," Hearst called out. He scrambled to his feet, made it to the phone, adjusted his robe, and slouched in the wingback as Willicombe hit the study. "What's the matter, Willicombe? You look like you've seen a ghost."

"I heard screaming."

"Oh?" Hearst laughed. "And here I thought it was the telephone." He motioned Willicombe to a chair, and picked up the receiver. "The Chief here. What's up?"

The call was from one of his syndicates, *King Features*. Hearst listened as the senior editor told him about a young staffer, name of Doyle, who'd just confirmed a whopper. Apparently some Canuck gal had resurrected the dead.

"What?"

"Exactly what I said. Some tyke from Kansas. Tell it to Toto, I says. But Doyle, he swears he talked to the kid, a preacher, and others. They'll swear to the deed on a stack of bibles."

Hearst's heart skipped a beat.

"So what do I do?" asked the editor. "Run it? Bury it?"

Hearst gripped the phone. His voice spiralled into the stratosphere. "Front-page banner. You hear me? Every day. All week. And more! Get me more! I want more!"

ON *the* CASE

K.O. Doyle rolled back to The Ceeps at sunup, mighty sore at falling for Floyd's midnight con. A trip to the London lockup had confirmed that the evangelist hadn't hauled the doll anywhere near the joint. He flopped on his bed for some shut-eye, but within minutes the desk clerk was at his door with a cable from his editor.

> THE CHIEF IS HOT TO TROT. HAS SENT
> METROTONE CREW. ARRIVAL TWO
> THIRTY. GET THE KID. GET THE GIRL.
> GET GOING.

Christ on a pogo stick! Hearst's Metrotone crew cranked out newsreels for Bijous coast to coast! It could be his big break! Doyle scribbled a toothbrush across teeth and tongue, splashed his pits with aftershave, flew to the downstairs greasy spoon, inhaled a Maxwell House, fished ice cubes from his water glass and pressed them against his temples as he ran to the curbside cab.

Aunt Grace set aside a batch of muffin batter to answer the front door. Who could be calling at 7:00 a.m.? If it wasn't that scrawny little weasel with the lemon sours. What could he be up to? By the smell of him, no good.

Doyle apologized for the hour; it couldn't be helped. Perhaps she'd heard of Mr. William Randolph Hearst? He was Hearst's representative come to make arrangements for a newsreel on

Timmy's resurrection. If it'd be convenient perhaps, he could shoot a scene of the family in the front parlour at three?

The doughty Presbyterian tilted her chin. As a matter of fact, it would *not* be convenient. Her Timmy was convalescing, her husband was indisposed with sciatica, and she was baking muffins, following which she'd be visiting shut-ins. In any event, neither she nor hers would ever consent to parade themselves for the newsreels. Movie houses were nothing but dark, dingy holes of temptation leading the unemployed to indolence, youth to ruin, and lovebirds to hell in a handbasket. So, no, it would not be convenient to be filmed in her front parlour this afternoon, or on any other, come to think of it, and she would thank Mr. Doyle to remove himself from her property forthwith and henceforward.

Doyle allowed as he'd respect her wishes and instruct the crew to steer clear. He'd go down the road apiece and talk about Timmy in front of that old tarpaper shack with the oil bin on the front porch.

"Not the Dickie place!" Aunt Grace gasped.

Was that the name of it? With the front yard covered in rusty car parts, and the broken windows by soiled bedsheets?

"Jack Dickie is a good-for-nothing Methodist gone bad. Don't you dare shoot your story there! Folks'll be getting the idea it's *our* place."

They might, he shrugged. Might fancy as well that she and her hubby were the sort to live within — gin-soaked rubes no better than they ought to be — or wonder what sinister goings-on had led them to keep wee Timmy under wraps. Was the lad an American captive in some foreign hicksville hellhole?

Aunt Grace pursed her lips. Under the circumstances, perhaps an interview in her front parlour *could* be arranged. So, if he'd excuse her, she'd best be getting the place in order — by which she meant scrubbing the floors, dusting the knick-knacks, waxing the woodwork, wiping the walls, airing the closets, cleaning the stove, tending the icebox, doing a wash, and beating the rugs till they screamed for mercy; for if cleanliness was next to godliness, Aunt Grace was bound and determined the world would see that she lived in the lap of the Lord.

Doyle still had to ferret out Mary Mabel. Here, he had a break. On returning to The Ceeps, he was handed a letter by the desk clerk, the ink barely dry on the envelope.

> Greetings and salutations in the Lord,
>   Pray forgive our reticence on the matter of Sister Mary Mabel. She has been on a spiritual retreat. At sunrise prayers, I put in a word on your behalf. She has agreed to meet you at 9 a.m. at the Twins B&B, 495 Wharncliffe Road.
>   Yours in Christ,
>   Brother Floyd Cruickshank
> P.S. As for that lassie in the park, after pastoral counselling she has welcomed Jesus into her heart, abjured the Devil, and is presently on a bus to the country, there to repair her soul in the care of her belovèd granny. To God be the glory.

Floyd had deposited similar invitations for Scoop Jones and Scratch Micallef. To Perce, however, nothing. In fact, before scampering back to the Twins, he hadn't even popped upstairs to tell his partner where he'd been nor what he was up to.

If this was rude, it was also business. Floyd's first thought had been to incorporate Mary Mabel into the existing act, her hope a balance to Percy's hellfire. Yet the more he chewed on the idea, the tougher it became to swallow. The Great Unwashed, out to see a fetching curiosity, would have no time for the ravings of some distempered preacher.

At the same time, he couldn't cut Perce loose. The reverend had an imagination and a mouth. Floyd shuddered at the whole-cloth tales he'd spin from the yarn of a middle-aged man and a teenage girl traipsing about the land unchaperoned "with a suitcase full of rubbers!" It would be a cross Floyd couldn't bridge, a scandal repelling the public, with denials fanning the flames.

The showman was stymied, but short-term, one thing was clear: the less Perce knew, the less he'd have to bugger up.

Doyle skimmed Floyd's invitation and pocketed it, along with those left for Scratch and Scoop. "I'll deliver them personally," he told the desk clerk, a dollar bill putting paid to silence awkward questions. "By the way, I've traced that miracle girl, Miss McTavish. She's holed up at the Salvation Army in Toronto." He tapped his nose and headed off to the Twins, secure in the knowledge his rivals would shortly be bribing themselves into a wild goose chase to the provincial capital one hundred miles away.

TRANSFIGURATION

Following her late-night conversation with Floyd, Mary Mabel had been treated to a hot bath spiced with a tincture of rosemary, then given a nightdress and taken by Miss Tillie up the narrow circular staircase to the sewing room at the back east corner of the third floor. It was a cramped, airless affair, filled to the brim with old hat boxes, ends of quaint fabric, and baskets of appliqués, thread, scissors, and yarn, variously stacked and draped over a junk shop of disused furniture as awkward as it was antique.

"You'd not get a moment's rest below," her hostess explained, as she moved piles of dusty dress patterns from the fainting couch to the sewing table by the window. "Me and my sister, we snore something terrible."

Miss Tillie paused to catch her breath, looking through the turret window at the moon. "This used to be my favourite room," she said. "Father kept us hopping, but given his game leg, he couldn't navigate the servants' stairs. So here's where we'd come to escape. It was such a blessèd retreat, till he took to banging the ceiling below with his cane. Ah well, may he rest in better peace than he ever allowed us."

She grabbed the bedclothes, fresh from the linen cupboard, and shook them out with a good deal more force than necessary. "Thank your lucky stars your father's disappeared," she observed through the dust cloud. A pause, and she began to make up the couch. "You know, I always wanted a daughter. One of my 'Things to Do' that will never get done. Don't let life slip away on you." She fluffed the pillow, gave it a quick pat, and headed to the door.

"Thank you," Mary Mabel called after, crawling under the sheets.

Miss Tillie turned. There was a tear in her eye. "Let me tuck you in." She pulled the covers up under the young woman's chin, stroked her hair and kissed her gently on the forehead. "Good night, sleep tight, don't let the bedbugs bite."

Mary Mabel hadn't been tucked in since Cedar Bend. It felt good. Like being six with a brown sugar sandwich. Before Miss Tillie'd left the room, she was fast asleep.

She dreamed she was sailing on a cloud harnessed by ribbons to a crow. "Where are you taking me?" she asked.

The crow turned. It was Miss Bentwhistle, rowing a black boat. Or was it a black coffin? "This'll teach you to give sass to your auntie," the headmistress cackled, snipped the ribbons, and flew off. A gust of wind. The cloud blew apart. Mary Mabel fell and fell and woke up gasping for air.

The room was alive with dust, a rich haze of gold glittering with morning sun. What time was it? Where was she? The last few days skittered through her head. They hardly felt real. She had a sudden terror.

"It's all right," came a voice from the foot of the fainting couch.

Mary Mabel's forehead tingled. "Mama?" She sat up. The sun shone in her face. She had to squint, but her heart saw perfectly. Her mama was standing before her, a beautiful angel swathed in white robes surrounded by a shimmering light. "Mama!"

A sharp rap at the door. "Breakfast's on the table," chirped a twin. "No time to dawdle. We're expecting company."

Mary Mabel glanced at the door. "I'll be right down." Beaming, she turned back to her mama, aching for a hug. But the room was empty. At the foot of the couch, where her mama had been standing, was a dressmaker's dummy draped in a flowing white sheet. Surely it hadn't been there before.

Am I crazy? she thought. *No! I was awake, I know what I saw, I know what I heard. I talked to Mama. And if she's come to me this often, I know she'll come again.*

Ten minutes later, she was downstairs, eating a boiled egg and toast as Floyd crowed about his morning exertions. "At nine o'clock, the top American syndicates'll be at the door!"

Mary Mabel sputtered crumbs. "Those men from the fairgrounds?"

"You got it."

"But they'll recognize me."

"Not a chance. People see what they want to see. Besides, last night you were in shadow: seedier than a rotten tomato. Your bath's already done wonders. By the time Millie and Tillie get through with you, you'll be unrecognizable."

"Ready or not, here we come," the Twins chimed. In a spritz, the breakfast table transformed to a beauty salon, her hosts brandishing scissors, combs, makeup, and brushes with evangelical fervor.

"Yank her hair in a bun," Floyd coached from the sidelines. "Chop out the matts. Pluck the eyebrows. And how about rouge? Lipstick? Eyeliner? Don't be shy with the blush. And as for that birthmark, trowel on the base."

After the paints and powders, the costume. The Twins had laid out a nurse's uniform, their souvenir of the last poor soul hired to help their father, back in the days when the bugger was spry enough to give chase. "An appropriate get-up, given your bent for healing," Miss Tillie remarked. "Upon my word, twenty years' storage has even improved it, for look, it's turned the most delicate yellow."

"And the cap, Tillie! The cap!" Miss Millie enthused, adjusting the headpiece just so. "It's the crowning touch, set off by those lashes and sparkling eyes! The menfolk won't know where to look!"

"You're fit for a heavenly choir!" Floyd agreed. "Now collect yourself in the powder room, while we collect ourselves on the porch. We'll call you for your entrance."

A GAME of POKER

Doyle arrived to find Floyd on the verandah rocker, a twin on either side. They made an arresting trio. The Misses Millie and Tillie had effected their own reconstruction and were in fine fettle, slender and bright as a pair of hollyhocks, a vision in ruffled peach taffeta, white feathered hats, and floral parasols. Floyd, by contrast, was grey as cement, the drab garden gnome between them.

So where's he stashed the girl? Doyle wondered, as he stepped gingerly over the pumpkin and zucchini vines that snaked across the crumbling stone walkway. *Squirrelled away, I'll bet, until I pay the handler's fee.*

Floyd struggled to his feet. "Mr. Doyle, you're in good time,"

"The early bird catches the worm."

"May I introduce the Thompson Twins."

Doyle tipped his hat. The Twins arched their backs and nodded smartly.

"Brother Floyd tells us you're a reporter up from the States, Mr. Doyle," Miss Millie chirped. "On behalf of my sister, may I say what a privilege it is for the Twins Bed & Breakfast to entertain an important visitor such as yourself."

"Our late father loved Americans," Miss Tillie leapt in, handing him a freshly dusted business card, rescued from behind the radiator in the vestibule. "He once took a trip to Cape Cod, and we have cousins in Des Moines."

"Oh yes, rest assured, we keep out the welcome mat for our American guests. Make sure to mention that in your article."

"Your readers will also want to know we offer meals."

"And for the price of a smile we treat our visitors to homemade apple cider and a slice of our very own rhubarb pie."

"A tour of the town on horse and buggy can also be arranged."

"And remind your readers that there's no snow in summer."

"And in winter we're well supplied with hot water bottles."

Floyd realized he wasn't the only entrepreneur on the porch. Since they'd heard that American press would be dropping by, the Twins had been impossible. In ten years, their only publicity had been the handful of flyers they'd left at the tourist information booth on Highway 2.

"Millie, if they write us up, think of the visitors!"

"We can air out the third floor!"

"Put cots in the study!"

"Hang the Stars and Stripes!"

"Hire a maid!"

Visions of greenbacks had driven them nutty as fruitcake. This accounted for their peach taffeta outfits, resurrected from matching attic hope chests. It accounted as well for the heavy, oversized three-piece suit in which Floyd sweltered. When he'd emerged from his tub, the pair had informed him they'd bundled his clothes into the old wood stove in the kitchen, replacing them with articles from their late father's bedroom. "This is far more respectable. Papa only wore it to funerals, and even if it's a mite ancient, good taste never goes out of style."

(In truth, Floyd's clothes hadn't been burned at all: they were hiding out under the sisters' big brass bed, along with odd socks and underpants pilfered over the years from the suitcases of various gentlemen guests. These made the most delightful mementos, something to snuggle next to late at night, or wear about the house with the drapes drawn. Who knew sin could be so thrilling?)

The sisters were now a runaway train, their conversation rapidly running away along tracks headed far from Floyd's destination. Clickety-clack, they barrelled through Family History.

Clickety-clack, through Tales from the B&B. And then — *toot toot* — "Let's take a tour!" as they set upon Doyle, grabbing an elbow each and making a beeline for the front door.

Floyd slammed on the brakes. "Ladies, ladies! We've business to attend to."

Miss Millie bit her tongue. "Come Tillie, we mustn't disturb the menfolk. But before you repair to the States, Mr. Doyle, you must have a taste of our pie. There's a piece with your name on it." And with that, she and her sister linked arms and swept indoors.

The men prepared for their game of poker. Doyle hadn't been dealt much. He needed access to Mary Mabel, but he hated to fold to a fee dictated by Floyd. Careful not to tip his hand, he feigned indifference, ambled to the edge of the porch, stretched, slouched on the railing, and casually surveyed the yard.

Floyd sidled over. "So pleased you could drop by."

Doyle fixed his gaze on a haphazard patch of corn by the birdbath. "Un-hunh," he yawned, inhaling the garden air, along with the faint smell of mothballs from Floyd's long-storaged suit. "I was expecting to see Miss McTavish."

"She's at her devotions. There's so much to pray for, what with our upcoming pilgrimage to the Holy Land."

Doyle turned from the corn in the yard to the corn on the porch. "You're going abroad?"

"We aim to take Sister's healing touch to the lepers of Jericho."

Doyle tried not to choke. "When are you embarking?"

"As soon as God provides the wherewithal." Floyd batted his eyes, as beatific as a stained-glass window. "The costs are fantastic. Passage, trunks, travel clothes, toiletries. And once landed, food, lodging, and the rent of a herd of camels to carry our cargo of Bibles."

"In short, I'm to cough up for the interview?"

"Should the Holy Spirit so move you."

"How much?"

"'Blessèd are those who give, for they shall receive.' Your colleagues from *Scripps-Howard* and *Associated Press* are expected shortly. I'm sure they'll want to give plenty."

Doyle fingered the ace up his sleeve: "Scratch and Scoop have split for Toronto. I'm the only game in town and I'm afraid my wallet's as thin as my patience."

Floyd faltered. Doyle might be bluffing, but he couldn't afford to find out. "Not to worry," he patted the reporter's arm. "Sister will co-operate, whatever the contribution. In fact, I'll give you a deal. An interview on the house. Why should a few lepers stand in the way of our friendship?"

Doyle checked his nails. He saw the sweat on Floyd's neck. "I'm afraid I've wasted your morning." A cocky salute and he headed down the walkway. "Good luck in the Holy Land," he hollered over his shoulder. "Give my regards to Jesus."

He was halfway to the gate before Floyd caught up. "I don't think you heard. You can have Sister for free."

"Who cares? There's a reason I'm the only one here. I'm being patsied to write a story leaky as a sieve."

"No. On my honour as a gentleman."

"Like I said."

"But Mr. Hearst wants the story. You told me."

"That was last night." Doyle's eyes danced. He hadn't had so much fun since he'd snapped the mayor of Tulsa getting spanked at Diamond Lil's. Time to drop his bombshell. "The Metrotone boys hit town this afternoon. I'm in charge."

"Newsreels!" Floyd exclaimed.

"There's two stories I can tell," Doyle continued. "One's about wee Timmy Beeford, never dead, but very injured, thanks to you. We'll shoot him at the train station in a wheelchair pushed by his sainted aunt and uncle, heading back to Kansas and life in

a new home paid for by the Hearst chain of family newspapers."
He paused. "Or I can tell the tale of a Miracle Maid sent by God
to heal the sick. Praise the Lord and jiggle the cash box."

Floyd took a deep breath. "How much do you want?"

"Ten percent of next year's take."

"Ten?" Floyd staggered. "Five!"

"Suck a turd," Doyle sneered, and hopped the fence.

"All right! Ten!" Floyd called after.

"Fifteen! That's ten, plus five for the insult. Wire the money
every six months to a numbered account. Strictly on the Q.T.
Understood?"

Floyd nodded.

"I'll be back with the crew at three."

"Okey-doke."

They shook hands.

"You're a smart man," Doyle said. "Stay smart, my stories'll
make you rich. Screw me, I'll nail your nuts to a tree."

LIGHTS, CAMERA, ACTION

At three on the dot, Doyle and his crew squealed up to the curb in a pair of rented jalopies. The boys, fresh from a Grand Trunk bar car, were ripe as roadkill. Hauling equipment over shoulders and under arms, they trampled through the garden, dripping sweat, waving off flies, and cursing a blue streak.

The Twins, waiting on the verandah with Floyd, pretended not to notice. "Back for that piece of rhubarb pie?" Miss Millie flirted. She gave her parasol a provocative spin.

"As a matter of fact, I'm back for a piece of that Mary Mabel McTavish," replied Doyle.

The crew laughed.

"I must have gone deaf," Miss Tillie bristled. "Did you say something funny?"

The boys stared sheepishly at their shoes.

"Sister's in the west-wing conservatory," Floyd intervened.

Mary Mabel, who'd been watching through a tear in the parlour curtains, scampered down the hall and hid behind a jungle of potted palms, the better to make an entrance. Not a moment too soon. She'd barely had time to pinch her cheeks than Doyle was at the portal.

"Holy Hannah!" he blurted.

Indeed, the Twins' conservatory would knock anyone's socks off. An airy room with pretensions to match, it had windows and French doors on three sides; a grand piano, legs modestly clothed in lace pantalets; a large wicker birdcage, vacant since Polly Parrot fell afoul of their father's cane; and a clutch of extravagant wing chairs. The chairs were arranged in conversation nooks separated by a robust array of ferns that burst from iron pots and ceramic urns sporting Japanese motifs as imagined by Victorian decorators. Like the rest of the house, the conservatory had seen better days — several panes in a panel of small bevelled windows had been replaced with sawed boards wedged tight by strips of folded cardboard — but it was nonetheless impressive, a Dowager Duchess so grand no one would dare to remark on the runs in her stockings.

"This'll make one helluva backdrop!" Doyle whistled. "So where's the skirt?"

Mary Mabel let forth a ripple of laughter and emerged from the greenery, imagining herself Florence Nightingale bringing good cheer to the Crimea. "No need to be coarse, Mr. Doyle," she teased. She strode across the room with a confidence surprising even to herself, and shook him by the hand. Doyle was struck dumb.

Mary Mable tried not to giggle. Floyd had warned her that he was a bad apple, but up close, he appeared no more fearsome than a lamb. To be sure, his cowlick defied brilliantine, and his collar could do with a scrub, but wicked? Hardly. Without suspenders his pants would fall down.

She saw him gawk at her bosom. "Have I spilled something?"

"Not at all," Doyle sputtered. "Let me introduce my colleagues."

Mary Mabel nodded to each in turn, astonished to find that Miss Millie had been right. None of them could look her in the eye, each as awkward as the boys bused in to squire Miss Bentwhistle's debutantes at Academy formals. Might they actually consider her attractive? The idea made her palms sweat. She hoped no one noticed, especially Doyle, whom she was finding more alluring by the minute.

Luckily, observing Miss Bentwhistle's young ladies had taught Mary Mabel the perils of infatuation: the most one can expect from young men are lies and bad poetry. She imagined herself the iron matron in one of her Rebecca Ramsay nurse novels. "I understand I'm to answer a few questions, Mr. Doyle," she said. "Let's get to it, shall we?"

"You bet." He cleared his throat, cracked his knuckles, and ordered the crew to secure their camera to a dolly at the entrance to the conservatory and to create a makeshift stage by the palms.

"Right away, Mr. DeMille," the crew chief clicked his heels.

Doyle motioned her to a pair of wing chairs near the baby grand. "I'd like to have a private word," he said, with a sharp look at Floyd, hunched on the adjacent piano bench perusing sheet music with the ever solicitous twins.

"I've a duty to protect Sister's interests," Floyd objected.

"Come now, I can protect myself," Mary Mabel said. Scowling, Floyd relocated to the birdcage at the far side of the room.

Doyle glanced at the Twins. "Don't worry about us," Miss Millie sang. "The kitchen beckons!" She took her sister's arm and away they sailed.

"Alone at last." Doyle smiled.

Mary Mabel blushed. "I'm supposed to be afraid of you."

"Is that a fact?"

"They say you're a ruthless so-and-so. Still, I don't believe everything I hear." She'd intended to be charming, but he wasn't amused.

"Your preacher pal's been telling me a story about you resurrecting some kid," he said. "No disrespect, but I've a nose for liars."

"I'll thank you to speak well of Mr. Cruickshank. He rescued me from the streets."

"No doubt. But he's still a preacher. A snake-oil salesmen touting God as the ultimate elixir."

Mary Mabel paused. "You're trying to get me angry, aren't you? You think if I'm mad enough, I'll say something I shouldn't, and you'll have a better story."

"I just want the truth. See, I don't take to supernatural hocus-pocus. Only fools believe in things they can't see. Are you a fool?"

"No," she said. "And neither are you. You believe in Mr. Hearst, but I'll bet you've never seen him."

"I don't need to see him. He's given me a job."

"Well I've been given a job, too."

"So I see. A mission from God."

"I never said that."

"If not a mission from God, then whom? Let's talk straight. This 'heaven-sent' miracle stands to make you a bundle."

She wanted to say that she'd starve before breaking faith with her mama — but if Doyle mocked God, what would he say about *her*? "I don't mean to hurt your feelings," she answered calmly, "but if you only believe what you see with your eyes, you're blind to life."

"Is that a fact?"

"Yes. You can see pain and suffering — who can't? — but you'll never see the magic of hope. The mystery of grace. Given the horrors of this world, the real miracle isn't that I raised a boy from the dead. It's that people like you can get out of bed in the morning."

"You think I'm in need of pity?"

"Most folks are. Human beings suffer so much, they're afraid to dream."

"I've no need for dreams."

"But you're not a human being. You're a reporter."

"True enough," he laughed. "And I have eyes." He shook a playful fist at the ceiling. "'Curse you Billy Bounder!' Sorry, Sister, the gig's up."

Mary Mabel choked. "About last night ..."

"Relax. The Chief wants a story. I'm game. Just wanted you to know I'm not one of your suckers."

"We're ready," called the crew chief.

Doyle swept his arm toward the stage, an improvised dais of milk crates, masked by coleus and angel wings. "It's magic time. The camera will dolly up. I'll ask a few questions. You'll answer."

She wanted to cry. Who did he think he was? Why should she care what he thought anyway? The fact that she did hurt most of all.

"Quiet on the set," Doyle barked. "Roll 'em. And — action!"

The camera wheeled forward.

"What is your name?"

She stared straight at the lens. "My name is Mary Mabel McTavish."

"Did you raise the dead?"

She felt the sting in the voice. No sound now but the camera's whir. She was alone, naked, pinned like a bug. An emptiness opened in the pit of her stomach and grew till it threatened to swallow her whole. Nowhere to run, to hide, save by fleeing the room in tears. What — run and betray her mama?

She took a deep breath — and as she did, she saw stars, felt tingles. A river of warmth coursed up from the tip of her toes to the top of her head, flooding her with power. She was aglow. A Joan of Arc. Did she raise the dead? Her eyes blazed. "Yes!"

REUNIONS

After the inquisition, Doyle insisted that Mary Mabel accompany him around town for additional footage. "We need a reunion with the miracle kid."

Floyd accepted on her behalf.

Fine, Mary Mabel thought, *but I'll make his life miserable.* She planned to do it by smiling. It was a trick Clara Brimley used at the Academy when she wanted to drive Miss Budgie crazy. Miss Budgie was Mary Mabel's favourite teacher, the one who'd stayed after school and listened to her problems and lent her books. Clara didn't care how nice Miss Budgie was. She chattered away and made faces right in front of her. And no matter what Miss Budgie said, she'd reply, in the sweetest voice, "Dear me," or, "I'm sorry," or, "I'm afraid I don't know."

Conversations had gone like this:

Miss Budgie: Miss Brimley, this is the tenth time I've asked you to be quiet!

Clara: Dear me.

Miss Budgie: You're the most difficult student I've ever had.

Clara: I'm sorry.

Miss Budgie: How am I supposed to teach with you carrying on?

Clara: I'm afraid I don't know.

Miss Budgie tore her hair out, while Clara batted her eyes. There was nothing to do. If she'd sent Clara to the office for saying, "Dear me, I'm sorry, I'm afraid I don't know," she'd have looked like a hysteric. Which is exactly what she'd become.

With Clara in mind, Mary Mabel sat beside Doyle in the lead jalopy, hands clasped primly on her knees. He asked her about the local landmarks, what she thought of the weather, and who were her favourite movie stars. "Dear me," she simpered, "I'm sorry, I'm afraid I don't know." But to her dismay, Doyle didn't get hysterical. He laughed!

Fortunately, she was able to ignore him once they hit the Rutherfords'. Timmy didn't recognize her. Hardly surprising, he'd been off in a another world. What *was* surprising was that she didn't recognize *him*. Memory had conjured a child more delicate than the boisterous tyke now picking his nose.

A couple of shots in the spotless front parlour, and Doyle had them headed to other locations. Aunt Grace insisted on coming along to supervise. Throughout the shoot, she hid in the back seat, gnawing her bran muffins. Doyle was pleased for her company; she'd brought along Timmy's leash. If the kid hadn't been tied to the nearest tree, who knows what he'd have gotten up to.

"So you're from Kansas," Doyle said, as they drove to the cemetery.

"Wichita," Timmy nodded.

"I'm an American, too."

"Are you going to take me home?"

"Not today."

Timmy frowned, then brightened. "My daddy has a gun. We shoot gophers. Daddy says if people come from the bank we're going to shoot them, too."

"Your father said no such thing!" Aunt Grace exclaimed.

"Did too. My job is to get them to stand in front of the kitchen window. Daddy says I'm a decoy. When I grow up I'm going to be a soldier."

"Sounds like fun," Doyle teased. "Only one problem. Soldiers have girlfriends."

Timmy made a face.

"It's true. Soldiers have so many girlfriends, they can't turn around without bumping into them. Isn't that right Aunt Grace? Your little Wichita is going to be such a heartbreaker, he'll be emptying out the convents."

Timmy'd had enough of girlfriend-talk. "Guess what?" he piped up. "There's brain-guts on the God tent! Real brain-guts. No kidding. Outside of people's heads. All stinky and everything."

Come four o'clock, Herr Director had what he needed. He snapped his fingers, declared the shoot wrapped, and bundled Mary Mabel back to the Twins. "Adios, Sister," he said. "Me and the boys, we're headin' back Stateside. You'll be coast to coast, top of the week." He wiggled his ears and roared off.

"He's sweet on you," Miss Tillie whispered as the dust settled.

"He's sweet on himself," Mary Mabel replied.

As for Floyd, he looked like a corpse with a second wind. He slipped off his jacket and vest, loosened his tie and collar, stretched, and collapsed onto the old Muskoka chair on the porch. His wet shirt slapped the wood. "We're on our way," he beamed, as the Twins mopped his brow with a pair of tea towels.

The way he said it, to be "on our way" was to be in glory. However Mary Mabel had been on her way with her papa enough times to know that hope usually ends in despair. And if "on our way" meant constantly being insulted by the likes of Mr. Doyle, she'd rather have stayed put. At that very moment, she wanted nothing more than to remain in that yard, a garden so still the only sound was a blue jay ruffling its tail feathers in the birdbath. To be here, now, forever, amid brown-eyed susans, cosmos, and chrysanthemums — that would be happiness enough.

It's a strange thing, happiness, Mary Mabel thought. *It sneaks in when you least expect it, filling you up like a helium balloon, flying you high above clouds of doubt; but the tiniest thing, and you're back in a swamp of worry.* That's where she was now. After soaring in unaccountable bliss, a troubling question floated through her head and out of her mouth: "Why didn't Brother Percy get interviewed?"

"We didn't want to scare anyone," said Floyd, picking at a paint chip on the armrest.

"I'd quite forgotten about that poor man," Miss Tillie tutted, "and him all alone in his sick bed. We ought to invite him for supper."

"Nonsense," said Floyd. "Brother Percy hates bother."

"We're having pot roast. It'd be no bother at all."

"It would be for him. Nothing but chewing, chewing, and more chewing."

Miss Tillie's eyes filled.

"Mr. Cruickshank," Mary Mabel asked, "is there a reason you want to keep us apart?"

"Curiosity killed the cat," he muttered darkly, and went indoors.

In her heart of hearts, Mary Mabel knew the reason. From their first encounter in the trailer-cab, she was certain Brother Percy was deranged. Her opinion was confirmed at supper. The household had just sat down when there was a caterwauling at the front door.

"God spare us," cried the Twins, clutching their silverware to their bosoms.

Floyd investigated with the carving knife and tongs. Lo and behold, they weren't beset by thieves and murderers, but by God's own prophet, squealing like a pig, having sprained his ankle on the doorknob.

"For the love of Christ," Floyd swore, and slipped outside.

From her post in the parlour, Mary Mabel had a front-row seat to the reunion. Brother Percy flapped his arms so much she thought he'd take flight. With all the wires in his mouth, she didn't know exactly what he said, but the gist was clear. He'd nabbed Doyle, heading from The Ceeps for the train home, and heard about the newsreel and their new lodgings. What kind of fast one were they trying to pull?

"There's no 'fast one,' Perce. The Yankees ambushed us with their movie cameras. Don't worry. We sung your praises to the rafters."

A loud grunt. If Floyd had made him out to be so fine, why hadn't Mr. Doyle so much as snapped his photograph?

"Have you checked the mirror lately?"

Brother Percy wept. He'd lost his chance to be in the pictures. His first and only chance. He was a nobody; he'd always be a nobody.

"Buck up," Floyd said. "You'll be in newsreels galore, once your head's shrunk. Why, we're about to embark on the mother of all revivals with the Hearst press in our pocket. You're going to be famous, Perce! Famous!" Spinning such dreams of tomorrow, he danced his partner down the block and out of sight.

Shortly after, they returned carting Brother Percy's suitcase. Mary Mabel and the Twins watched as he hobbled up the path, next to lame owing to his altercation with the door.

"Should we offer him one of father's canes?" asked Miss Tillie.

"Has life taught you nothing?" Miss Millie gasped. "If they have to crawl, you have a better chance to escape."

Brother Percy tiptoed into the vestibule as if sin was lurking in the pantry. The Twins shook his hand, brought him to the table, and announced that after supper, they'd fix him up with a cot in the laundry room.

"If you wake up feeling peckish," said Miss Tillie, "you can treat yourself to the pickled preserves next door in the root cellar."

Percy was asked to say grace. From what they could make out, he began with the Lord's Prayer, repeating the plea to be delivered from evil; proceeded to the Twenty-third Psalm, stressing how the Lord had prepared a table for him in the presence of his enemies; and concluded with a rousing admonition against the sin of gluttony.

The Twins praised his oratory and passed the platters. Brother Percy was forlorn. Owing to his wired jaw, he could only suck food through a straw.

"Poor thing," Miss Tillie clucked, and scooted to the kitchen to fetch him "something special," which turned out to be a thin purée of turnip and cauliflower. "It was a favourite of father's, after he lost his teeth," she said.

"Very nutritious," her sister agreed. "And good for the bowels."

Of that there was no question. Within minutes, Brother Percy became quite musical. His concert provided the excuse to leave the table. Floyd went to get some fresh air, while the Twins cleared the dishes. Mary Mabel was about to help, when Brother Percy fixed her with a hard look. "Ah af ma eye ah oo," he whispered.

"Well, take your eye off me or I'll give it a poke," she shot back.

He fled the room with a shriek.

METROTONE PRESENTS

Mary Mabel's newsreel debut was a triumph, a feast of images and testimonials intercut by Metrotone editors to maximum effect. Goosing the pictures was K.O. Doyle's commentary, a script of unapologetic hagiography, all the more effective when Metrotone brass overdubbed his pesky tenor with the uncredited baritone of Ronald Coleman — and underscored the lot with Beethoven's Fourth.

Timmy Beeford proved an audience favourite, cute as a button in his Sunday suit, waving up at the camera with one hand while scratching his bum with the other. Gasps were heard when the camera pulled back to reveal him standing in a freshly dug grave; and a woman in Iowa fainted when he popped into a coffin, a prop recruited from the Blackstone Funeral Parlour in exchange for a shot of its homey facade.

Tom and Betty Wertz likewise held appeal. Wholesome as freshly churned butter, they held hands as they testified to the miracle, their tale as guileless as a baby's smile. These were no hucksters. These were Canadians for heaven's sake, as down-to-earth as Tom's plaid shirt.

Lest Doubting Thomases remain, there followed the stern image of Aunt Grace and Uncle Albert, she holding a pan of bran muffins, he clutching the family Bible. Even the grumpiest curmudgeon had to admit that these rock-ribbed Presbyterians with the pinched cheeks and tight jaws lacked the imagination to entertain a con.

Still none of the cast, neither child nor adult, came close to eclipsing the star of the show, the miracle worker herself, Sister Mary Mabel McTavish. Eyes electric, skin delicate, features strong, the camera loved her. From the opening close-up, that pale lustrous face, set against the rich backdrop of conservatory vegetation, appeared nothing less than an icon of purity and strength. And when the scene shifted to Aunt Grace's front parlour, and Timmy flew into her arms, snuggling close for a teary embrace — a composition Doyle stole from *The Kid* — there wasn't a dry eye from Baltimore to Pasadena.

Emotions also ran high in the private screening room at San Simeon. Marion was weeping into a highball on the leather sofa under a pile of dachshunds, while the Chief gave an order to his secretary. "Willicombe, get *King Features* on the horn. That kid Doyle's a comer. Give him a raise, and ship him back to Canada. This story has legs."

V

MANUFACTURING DREAMS

AT *the* ROXY

"**D**on't count your chickens before they hatch," Doyle puffed as he jogged down the street to the Roxy.

It was hard not to. Last night, he'd seen the crowds who'd come to laugh at the Marx Brothers, weep buckets for Mary Mabel. It was a response replicated across the country, the girl's connection to the audience confirmed by the call he'd received that afternoon from his editor at *King Features*. On instructions from the Chief, he was to head back to Canada tomorrow — to the girl's hometown, Cedar Bend — there to scare up locals "who-knew-her-when."

Doyle grinned. In no time she'd be on tour. With the press syndicates hyping the tale in a race for readers, how could she fail? It didn't matter if folks believed her; her status as sideshow curiosity would pack 'em in either way. Doyle pictured sold-out auditoriums, jacked-up ticket prices, and sacks bulging with freewill offerings. "Fifteen percent, fifteen percent," he panted, legs trotting an ever-quickening pace as he calculated his cut of Holy Redemption revenues.

Doyle needed the money. His mother wasn't well. Most nights she sat by the window with her pipe, swaddled in an old housecoat, feet propped on a metal folding chair to relieve the water-pressure bruising puffed legs and ankles. He pretended he didn't know about her nighttime accidents, but there was no getting around last week when he'd found her in the kitchen, flopping around on the linoleum. "Leave me alone!" she'd wept. "I'm not some beached fish!"

Doyle was terrified. For now, Mr. Bradley from downstairs could check in, but he wasn't up for round-the-clock care. And a paid nurse was impossible. That left a county home. Out of the question. Doyle had done exposés for Hearst. They were squalid holes staffed with brutes who beat their clients and stole the tuck money from their pockets.

That the future should loom so bleak was especially cruel for a spirit as fiercely independent as his mother, Mrs. Bonnie "Ma" Rinker. The eldest of twelve children, she'd been a new bride, barely twenty, when her husband and parents died in the great Allentown train derailment. The state came calling with plans to place her brothers and sisters in foster homes, but the orphaned widow refused. "I'm all the mother and father they need," she announced. To support the family, she'd rented their hundred acres to neighbouring farmers for meat and produce, and earned pin money by taking in sewing and selling eggs from a handful of scrawny chickens out back.

Life was tough, but Ma was tougher. So tough that, once grown, the kids were determined to get as far away from her as they could. All except for the baby, Estelle, who only escaped at night, and then no further than the arms of old man Drummond, two farms down. By fifteen, she was pregnant. "If that old pervert comes near you again," Ma raged, "I'll cut off his balls with the pinking shears." Three months later, she delivered the baby. Estelle never saw him. Her water'd burst on the buggy ride to town and she'd died of complications.

It was expected that Ma would put the child up for adoption. Instead, she took him to St. Andrew's to be christened. Father Rafferty declined. "I won't profane the holy sacrament of baptism by conferring it on a bastard." To which Ma snapped, "There's only one bastard in this room, and I'm looking at him!" She never darkened a church door again.

To protect the boy from gossip, Ma sold the farm and moved to Buffalo, where she presented herself as a widow with child.

"Mrs. Bonnie Rinker," she'd say, flashing her wedding ring. "This is my son, Lester."

Lester Rinker. Neither name stuck. "Lester" was for sissies and got the lad into any number of scraps until his knockouts earned him the nickname K.O. (As an adult, Doyle loved the double initials; they gave him literary credentials.) The name "Rinker" disappeared when former neighbours arrived in town. One night police showed up on the doorstep. Ma's young delinquent had been caught breaking into the county archives. "The rumours are true!" he sobbed. "I never had a dad."

From then on, he went by the maiden name of both his mothers — Doyle. "I'm a bastard, sure as spit. Well, I'm gonna make them know I'm proud of it. So proud, they'll never be able to make me ashamed again. Truth — only and always!"

Ma wept with pride and worry. Young men with that sort of attitude either go far or die young. Usually both.

Doyle's passion for truth, that innocent faith in moral absolutes so charming in the young and appalling in the old, led him to a career in newspapers. But truth is a slippery beast, its pursuit neither for the faint nor pure of heart. The faint recoil from sniffing out dirty laundry. As for the pure, deceit is the surest path to candour. Doyle soon discovered that a reporter's "honest day's work" involved no end of corruption.

This conundrum plagued him till he received the counsel of an elder scribe. The sot was revered by Doyle for his ability to hit the spittoon at the far side of his desk while blindfolded. "Villainy in the cause of virtue is no vice," the rheumy veteran hacked, "and as truth is the greatest virtue of them all, there is no sin too vile to employ in its service. After all, what's a little skulduggery when set beside the greater good — the public's right to know?" With that, the great man reared back and horked another lunger into the pot.

If pressed, Doyle would admit that the public's right to know might best be defined as the public's right to be titillated. Nonetheless, tales of love nests, cockfights, and speakeasies draw readers; and without readers there can be no free press; and without a free press there can be no democracy. In the words of his mentor: "Peddling sleaze helps save the world from tyranny."

The Roxy manager was a buddy, Larry Bundy, a crocodile of a man with glassy eyes, leathery skin, and a wall of yellow teeth. He'd saved a spot for Doyle in the back row, a good thing too as the joint was packed and humming. Folks were passing stories about the Miracle Maid, things they'd read in the paper, or heard on the radio, at the barbershop, the corner store, or over their neighbours' verandahs.

Doyle slipped into his seat as the houselights dimmed, and a fanfare of trumpets announced the Metrotone newsreel. The audience responded on cue with gasps, tears, and awe. After the show, Doyle slouched in his seat and listened to the crowd mingling giddily up the aisle. How could that girl's improbable story transform grown adults into a pack of trained seals? Doyle shook his head in wonder: people said they didn't believe what they read in the papers, but the power of the press to shape opinion spoke otherwise. To that, add the power of talkies, dreamlands in the dark luring spectators as a flame does moths.

Doyle suspected that a good night's sleep would bring more than a few to their senses. What of it? Controversy is publicity money can't buy.

He closed his eyes. Fifteen percent. Fifteen percent.

"Want to come up to the booth for a nip?"

Startled, Doyle looked up at Larry Bundy. They were alone. The audience had long since cleared out, and the young woman from the candy counter had finished her cleanup. "A nightcap? Sure." He'd promised his mother he wouldn't go to the bar, not that he wouldn't have a drink.

Bundy ushered Doyle into the lighting booth. It was his private sanctuary, a cramped room full of stacks of yellowed newspapers and the smell of cigarette butts, apple cores, and old bologna sandwiches. Aside from the projector and the beat-up card table where Bundy counted receipts and amused himself with crosswords and solitaire, everything was caked with a crust of dirt and stink.

"Have a seat," he offered, pulling mugs and a bottle of cheap Scotch from a filing cabinet. There was something fuzzy growing in the bottom of the cups. Bundy gave them a wipe with his shirttail, poured a couple of stiff shots, and plunked them on the table. Then his ritual. He started the projector, sound off. Most nights he drank here alone, the flickering stars keeping him company till dawn.

Bundy eased himself onto an upended Coca-Cola crate. He knocked back his first drink, poured a second, and began to talk. At first he rambled about weather, baseball, the pain-in-the-ass of chipping dried chewing gum from under the theatre seats. By his fourth drink, however, he'd found the courage to spit out what he'd meant to say all week.

"What's life for, K.O.? Any ideas?" He waved at the room. "There's gotta be more to it than this. Last week I was thinking of taking the splicer and slitting my wrists, or wrapping reels of film round my neck and hanging myself from the booth. Then I see this gal of yours, this Miss McTavish, and I think ..." A light glimmered in those glassy eyes. "Her miracle's a sign, isn't it? A sign, no matter how tough life gets, there's someone, something, looking out for us. We can't be here for no reason, we can't just be spinning alone in a cold, black void. Can we?"

Doyle was humbled. He'd assumed the girl's success was owed to puffsters like himself. Yet looking at Bundy's hangdog face, he had a flash of boozy insight. Every con needs a willing pigeon, and life turns souls into dumb clucks primed for plucking.

"Tell me the truth, K.O.," Bundy gripped his mug. "She did it, didn't she?"

Doyle hadn't the heart to say no. He put his hand on his friend's arm. Bundy was confused, but Doyle's touch told him everything was okay.

Everything but the smell of burning celluloid.

"Yikes!" The film was jammed, the frame melting. As Bundy staggered to turn off the lamp, Doyle looked from the booth to the auditorium. There, frozen on the screen, was Mary Mabel's face, twenty feet tall, a wall of beauty and grace, suddenly bubbling, blotching, crinkling, and — vanished.

Freed, the newsreel leapt from its sprockets, and merrily unspooled across the floor. A drunken stab at the projector's off switch sent the beast into fast-forward. The film whizzed a mad jitterbug through the air, snaking under the chairs and over the table, dancing in and out of the waste basket, around stacked newspapers and debris. By the time Bundy regained control, he was up to his knees in a thicket of tiny pictures of Mary Mabel.

Doyle sensed the party was over. "Thanks for the Scotch."

"Any time," Bundy muttered, defeated by the hours of untangling ahead.

"Say, do you think you could spare me a snippet?"

Bundy threw up his arms. "Why not?"

"Much obliged." Doyle clipped a souvenir and skipped off, a bit of Mary Mabel in his pocket.

By the time he got home, Ma had tucked herself in, and was pretending to sleep. Doyle tiptoed to his room, sat on the edge of his bed, and held the film clip to the lamp light. A moment of time, trapped between his fingers: a young woman, a blank slate on whom the public fixed its dreams. There was magic in that image. He knew it. He felt it. And, like the clip itself, he could see right through it.

CEDAR BEND

Cedar Bend was founded in the early nineteenth century by the Bentham Boys, Thomas and Egerton, a couple of quarrelsome squirrels unfit for civilization. They'd heard land was cheap up north, so that's where they'd headed, families in tow. When winter hit, they set up camp by a bend in Wolf River. Game was plentiful. The Boys stayed put. Over time, they were joined by a clutter of misfits.

Agriculture was out of the question, given the thin, rocky soil, but there were plenty of trees. The pioneers built a sawmill on the river bank. Barges floated the wood to ports downstream, till a rail link was established in 1892. The trains shipped lumber out, and tourists in. Specifically, rich Americans keen to shoot Canadian wildlife. Hunting lodges sprouted like mushrooms, the population exploded, folks said before no time it'd top a thousand. Then came the Crash. The price of timber tanked, the mill shut down, the tourists stopped coming. The town began to die.

Not fast enough, thought Doyle, as he checked into Slick's Lodge.

He'd come by bus on the milk run. All night the beast had bumped along perilous gravel roads before conking out ten miles from town. Doyle had hitched the rest of the way in a rusted-out Model T pulled by bones in the shape of horses. He asked about a place to stay. "That's a toughie," said the driver. "Main Street Hotel's boarded up five years. Same with the huntin' lodges. 'Cept for Slick Skinner's. A mile outa town, but I s'pose it'll do in a pinch."

Slick's Lodge was a collection of one-room cabins dotted around an imposing log house in need of a new roof and shutters. The reception desk was the kitchen table. Doyle signed the guest book under the watchful eye of Marge Skinner, a large woman with a black eye and bruised cheek. A second woman, sporting a fierce, hairy chin and orthopedic shoes, sat in a rocker by the window knitting socks.

"Stayin' long?"

"Day or two."

"Whatcha here for?"

"Holiday."

Marge showed him to his cabin. The floor was sprinkled with mouse droppings; a dusty June bug lay belly-up on the window-sill; the sheets smelled of mildew. Doyle asked the whereabouts of the washroom. Marge pointed to a nearby outhouse. "It's a two-holer. There's a latch if you're shy."

A peek inside convinced Doyle he'd be using the bushes.

Marge headed back to the house. "I'll get you some news-paper."

Doyle noticed the bearded lady eyeing them suspiciously from the window.

An hour later, armed with a camera, the young reporter stood at the outskirts to the village. He'd decided to go disguised as a tourist. Folks in small towns resented reporters; men who were paid to snoop on their neighbours. After all, *they* did it for free. A bridge lay ahead. Next to the bridge, a weathered sign:

WELCOME TO CEDAR BEND

SHINGLE CAPITAL OF THE WORLD

The population figure underneath had recently been painted over, replaced with the historic advisory:

BIRTHPLACE OF MARY MABEL MCTAVISH

At least, that's what the sign *should* have read. A shotgun blast had blown the name McTavish to smithereens.

Doyle crossed the bridge and took a sharp right, following the road as it hugged the shoreline. It had been paved once.
Now it had potholes deep enough to drown kittens. A hundred
yards away, the sawmill rose from the water's edge. Dilapidated
boards mocked a once-bright future. Across the road a cross-
hatch of laneways sported houses no bigger than pillboxes. Most
were tumbledown, weeds growing in the shingle walls, eaves like
planter boxes. Others stood poor but proud, kale and squash
growing in neat front yards.

A large public park separated the shantytown from the rest
of the settlement. It featured a bandstand, rusty playground
equipment, a nonfunctional drinking fountain, and a statue of
the Bentham Boys in heroic pose, which doubled as a war memorial. It also served as the grounds of the Cedar Bend Meeting
Hall, home to the village council and the volunteer fire brigade.
Churches followed, each built of river rock, and nestling a small
cemetery by its side. Beyond these, a school, a library, the county
courthouse, and a row of two-storey shops. The stone and stucco
homes of the Cedar Bend elite provided the tour's grand finale.

Doyle decided to start his fact-finding mission at the dry-
goods store. A little bell tinkled when he opened the door.
"Hello?" He wandered the thinly stocked aisles of dresses, hammers, rubber bands, and rifles, but there was no sign of the
proprietor. The dentist's was empty, as well. So was the grocery
store, the funeral home, and the gas station/souvenir shop.

His luck changed at Mr. Woo's Canadian and Chinese Food
Restaurant and Laundry. Mr. Woo was all smiles and chit-chat.
In the course of getting Doyle a glass of water, he confided that
his father'd been blown up working on the Cedar Bend railroad,
his family'd stayed in town because they had no place else to go,
and today's special was won ton soup and a hamburger.

"Sounds good."

Mr. Woo was happy to talk about Mary Mabel. She was the daughter of that devil who'd thrown an open bucket of paint through his front window. The police told him not to press charges; the man's wife had just died. "I sorry," said Mr. Woo, "but what that have to do about my window?" It wasn't the only time his window was broken. Whenever people had bad luck, they attacked his property. They got away with it, too. "Cedar Bend, it full of devils."

Doyle edged the conversation back to Mary Mabel. "Her daddy, he like devil ladies," Mr. Woo announced. "She alone by self. No mama. No friend. Talk to air. Talk to air, all time. I feel sorry. Give almond cookie." Mr. Woo tapped his head. "She crazy girlie."

Doyle agreed. He snapped Mr. Woo's picture, and left a big tip.

Outside, a flash of inspiration. The red-and-white-striped barber's pole across the street. He zipped over. Peering through the window, he saw half a dozen men on wooden chairs having a jaw. He opened the door. The men turned. Stared.

"What can I do you for?" the barber asked.

"Shave and a haircut."

"Cash?"

Doyle noticed the clump of turnips beside the aftershave, the bundle of pressed shirts over the coat rack, and the live chicken in the wire cage by the wastebasket. This was a town accustomed to barter. "Cash."

The barber had a new best friend. In no time, he had Doyle in his swivel chair, wrapped in a paper collar and knee-length bib. "A little extra off the sides?"

"Sure."

The barber began to snip, periodically stepping back to assess his handiwork. With a twitch of horror, Doyle realized the man was near blind. Meanwhile, the others sat solemnly, arms folded, brows furrowed, studying the progress of the haircut like witnesses at an autopsy.

"So," the barber said at last, "how's things at Slick's?"

"Who told you I was at Slick's?"

"Little bird."

The man opposite scratched himself. "You met the Chaperone?"

"Who?"

"The one with the beard. Slick's sister. Stays over when he's away."

"Don't let her catch you making eyes at Marge," advised the gent in the red suspenders. "When Slick gets the wrong idea, fellas go missing."

"Don't listen to him," said the barber. "They wander off, is all."

"Search parties never find them," Suspenders muttered darkly.

"Big deal. Bush goes on forever."

"Well, not to worry," Doyle ventured, "I've only got eyes for the scenery." The man with the overbite laughed. The room relaxed. "I understand this is the birthplace of Mary Mabel McTavish."

The barber reclined Doyle's chair. "She's a local gal, all right." He covered the young man's face and neck with a damp cloth heated on the radiator.

"Any relatives in town?"

"Her ma," said the man beside the chicken. "She's buried at Wesley Free Methodist."

From under the towel, the reporter tried to guess whether the following silence was respect for the dead or the haircut. Before he could figure it out, the barber hoisted his chair upright and whipped off the cloth. The men's eyes lit up, as if Doyle's head were a dove conjured by a magician from under a silk scarf. But hold the applause. The tonsorial artist was already brushing pillows of shaving cream over the young man's hairless cheeks, around his ears, and the back of his neck. He flashed a straight razor. Leaned back so he could see where to stroke.

"I don't need a shave."

"On the house!" Before Doyle could run, the barber grabbed his head with one hand and swooped the blade down his cheek with the other. "About our Mary Mabel," he said without missing a beat, "she was remarkable right from the start. Once upon a time she found a missin' kid through the power of prayer."

Doyle had read that story in the competition. It smelled of Floyd. He waited till the razor was past his throat. "You're pulling my leg."

"Heck no. It's public knowledge. Don't you read the papers?"

Overbite leaned forward. "Between you, me, and the fence post, the kid was the baby of a friend of my cousin. Mary Mabel found him in an icebox."

"Actually," said the man by the chicken, "it was a girl she found, niece of my neighbour, down a well, over Beaver Creek way."

"You're both right," said the barber. "From what I hear-tell, she found lots of folks." He swooped the razor down Doyle's other cheek, narrowly missing his ear.

Doyle gripped the armrest. "You boys must know lots of stuff. Stuff the papers haven't printed."

"Nope. That's about it. She and her pa left years ago. A fella forgets."

"Too bad. Miracle stories would sure scare up the tourists."

"You think?"

"No two ways about it. You'd have bus tours in no time."

Hmm. "Now that I think about it," said the barber, with a sly nod, "I seem to recall, just shy of five, she may have resurrected one of Bert's sick puppies."

"That she did," said the man with the Adam's apple. "Juggs. Best damn hunting dog I ever had."

A chorus of, "That's a fact."

"Then there was the time this robin laid its eggs in the palm of her hands."

A chorus of, "So it did."

"'Nother time, she faced down a grizzly bear set to eat Fred's granny at the Sunday school picnic."

A chorus of "God bless her."

"You'd swear to that on a stack of Bibles?" asked Doyle.

"Stack 'em high."

Hokum or not, these were scoops from "official town sources." Doyle grinned, as the men spun yarns woollier than his mother's mittens, and turned their minds to potential tourist sites.

"You know, we could turn the library into a museum. Build a Mary Mabel shrine out front."

"And Bert, the minute Juggs kicks the bucket for good, make sure to get him stuffed. He can be Exhibit A."

"Plus, we oughta make a list of all them holy wells. Put up plaques."

Lord, there was so much to dream ... to dare ... to do ...

Doyle checked the back of his haircut in the barber's mirror. Another Cedar Bend miracle: it wasn't half bad. The barber slapped on an aftershave-*cum*-hangover-cure, dusted his neck with talc, whisked off the bib, and bowed. The reporter flipped him two bits. The show was over. It was time to go.

The men gave him a standing ovation. "Thanks for your suggestion as to how to kick-start this shitebox. Make sure to talk us up back home." They let him snap their picture in front of the striped pole out front. Local colour for Hearst's rotogravure.

One final question. "How come stores are open but the owners are out?"

"'Cause we're here," said Suspenders.

"That's right," said Overbite. "Can't be two places at once."

"What if you get customers?"

The men snorted. "Folks know where to find us."

Heading back to Slick's, Doyle paused at the entrance to Wesley Free Methodist cemetery. A crow perched atop the heavy wrought-iron gate. Doyle rolled his eyes; he had no patience for gothic effects. Camera at the ready, he went scouting for a marker.

There was one other visitor on the grounds: an old man crawling around a tombstone, clipping bits of dead grass with a pair of scissors. Doyle approached.

"Excuse me. I'm looking for the grave of a Mrs. McTavish, mother of Mary Mabel."

"Ruthie McTavish, eh?" The old man kept clipping. "What's your interest?"

"I'm a shirt-tail cousin. On the McTavish side."

"A McTavish, eh?" A flicker of amusement. "And you're staying at Slick's?"

Doyle sighed. "There seem to be a lot of 'little birds' in town."

"Yep." *Clip, clip, clip.*

"About Ruthie ..." He toed the ground.

"What about her?"

"Can you help me?"

Clip, clip. "Course I can." *Clip, clip.* "Question is: will I." *Clip, clip, clip.*

"Please?"

"That's more like it." The old man rose gingerly, brushed the dirt off his knees. "Jimmy McRay," he said, giving Doyle the once-over.

"K.O. McTavish."

They shook hands. Jimmy signalled for Doyle to follow and

headed toward the back of the cemetery. He stopped by a trough of weeds in a patch of nothing. "That's what you're lookin' for. The resting place of Ruthie Kincaid McTavish. Best friend my daughter Iris ever had."

Doyle was confused. There was no memorial; not even a wooden cross.

"Grave collapsed a while back," Jimmy volunteered. "Pineboard coffin. Brewster never sprung for a proper marker. Painted a scrap piece of flagstone. Earth swallowed the tail end of it last winter. Me and Iris are gonna do something."

A moment's silence. Doyle snapped a picture. "Do you have a photo of Ruthie?"

"Why?"

"Souvenir. Like I said, I'm family."

"The hell. You're no McTavish."

"Family friend, then."

"You ain't that, neither."

"I can pay."

It took some looking, but the snapshot was finally located in one of the many boxes of photograph books under McRay's bed. He'd been quite the shutterbug in the old days. In fact, a village event wouldn't be complete without Jimmy making a nuisance of himself with his trusty Brownie box.

The snapshot in Doyle's hand was taken at one of the annual Cedar Bend Mill picnics. Iris, Ruthie, and the infant Mary Mabel were sitting on a blanket eating watermelon. Jimmy had clearly surprised them. Iris had her hand up, and her head turned away to make him go away. That's why the picture had ended up in one of his "spoilsport boxes" and not in one of the books on display by the mantel in the parlour.

The snap cost Doyle a princely five bucks, but he got the story for free.

"It wasn't a year and a half after this picture, poor Ruthie was dead. Middle of February. She woke up before dawn with a blizzard howling through the house. Back door was open. Mary Mabel was gone. Ruthie ran into that whiteout screaming her little one's name. They found her next day, one leg poking out of a drift in the park. She was clutching the teeter-totter, froze solid. There should've been a closed casket."

"Where was Mary Mabel?"

"Wrapped in a blanket, protected by the woodpile, corner of the house."

"What was she doing there?"

"That's what everyone wanted to know, yelling and shaking her, when she wasn't being hugged. She sobbed about hearing a scratching at her window, how she couldn't see nothing for the blizzard and frost, how she went to give whoever it was a blanket, and ended up at the woodpile."

"I don't understand."

"Nothing to understand. She was all mixed up. Folks figured the scratching was tree branches. Little Mary Mabel had quite the imagination. And a fever. And she knew she'd done wrong, didn't wanna catch heck, you know kids."

"How did she take her mother's death?"

"Had no notion what was up. Barely two, eh? When she realized Ruthie was in the coffin at the end of the parlour, she ran up and knocked, like it was all a game of hide-and-seek. She was cross when Ruthie wouldn't come out. She went round pulling on people's dresses and pant legs saying, 'My mama's in that box.' We put her to bed, only she didn't stay put. She dragged her little stool in from the kitchen, wanted to climb into the coffin to have her afternoon nap beside Ruthie like she always did. Oh, the tears when we pulled her away. She called for her daddy. Course, Brewster was in no condition to help, passed out by the stove."

A discreet pause. "And later? How was she once things sunk in?"

Jimmy's back tightened. "You're from the newspapers," he said softly.

Doyle shuffled.

"No point lying. The whole town knows it."

Doyle hung his head. "I'm sorry."

"Never mind. Just be good to Ruthie's memory. It's not right, she should disappear like she never existed."

Doyle nodded.

Jimmy patted his knee, and walked him to the door. "I expect you'll be wanting to see the McTavish homestead. What's left of it, anyway. Bear right at the corner, third house in, the one with the tree growing through it."

"Thanks for the tip."

Jimmy gripped his hand. "You asked about Mary Mabel, once things sunk in. Poor kid was a mess. Take care of that picture."

The McTavish place was a drunk on a bender: the picket fence, a row of broken teeth; the yard, an upchuck of fallen shingles and shattered glass; the house itself, passed out against the trunk of a neighbouring maple. As advertised, a branch grew in through the kitchen window, and out through a section of collapsed roof. Nor was this the only breach. Front and back doors were missing, casements were cracked, and several cedar planks had been pried from the rear wall. Nature had accepted the invitation. Years of dead leaves and evergreen needles had blown indoors. Kept damp by rain and snow, they'd decayed into a mulch that rotted floorboards and fed an indoor shade garden.

Doyle stood at the threshold. Ahead lay the open parlour. Several shotgun blasts had ripped large holes in the far wall, revealing a kitchen. Vandals had also had fun with a hunting knife; the words DIE MCTAVISH were carved in the crumbling plaster above the wainscotting, and the couch had been disemboweled. Every other stick of furniture in the room had been looted. It was the same story in the two bedrooms opening to the right; nothing but DIE MCTAVISH on the walls, and hacked bedding. Even the straw stuffing from the mattresses had been stripped, plundered by birds and squirrels to line nests.

He proceeded to the door of the kitchen, delicately testing each floorboard en route. The wood stove was gone, but he could tell where it had stood by the pipe hanging down from the ceiling. He could tell where the cupboards and counter had been, too, by the unpainted rectangles on the wall. The bolts that had secured them littered the floor, along with the odd cracked pot, bent fork, and a heap of smashed green china. Only a small saucer survived.

Doyle closed his eyes. For a moment, he imagined the house alive: Ruth McTavish at the end of the parlour in her plain pine coffin; a crowd of mourners eating sandwiches; and a little girl running through their legs, bewildered by her mother's silence, and by the silence of her old man, back from Mr. Woo's, lying stinko by the stove. Home sweet home.

Suddenly, he became aware that the little girl in his mind's eye was staring at him. He turned away, disconcerted, pictured himself circulating among the mourners. Yet wherever he went, she followed. "Stop it," he said. "You're part of a daydream. You can't see me."

"I can see lots of things," she replied. "Would you like to see my mama? She's in that box."

Doyle's eyes popped open. He *was* being watched — and not by a figment of his imagination. Someone was behind him.

"Hello? … If this is your squat, I'm sorry. I should have knocked."
The watcher remained very still. Doyle considered his situation.
He raised his hands in surrender. "I didn't mean any harm," his
voice shook. "So if it's okay with you, I'll be on my way."

A furtive movement. Whoever was there had edged closer.
Silence.

The young man began to sweat. If he was murdered, he'd
never be found. His body could be stuffed through the floorboards or dumped down the hole of the backyard outhouse.
"Please. I look after a sick mother."

A guttural chatter.

Doyle determined to die bravely. He swallowed hard, and
turned to face his doom. A woodchuck peered at him from a tear
in the side of the couch. "Aaaaa!" Doyle screamed. The woodchuck fled. He blushed.

There was a chill in the air: late fall, early dusk. Doyle was
about to make tracks, when he cast a glance at the heap of china
on the kitchen floor. That saucer would make a nice souvenir.

Back at his cabin, Doyle scribbled notes till the cowbell summoned
him to the log house for supper. Marge was nowhere to be seen.

"Mrs. Skinner's taken poorly," said the Chaperone. A heavy
iron key hung around her neck. She tossed her head toward the
kitchen table. Doyle took a seat as she hobbled to the pot on the
wood stove and dished up a hearty bowl of rabbit stew seasoned
with buckshot. "Help yourself to seconds," she said, plunking it
down in front of him, along with a thick slice of bread and a jug
of water. Before he could say thanks, she was out the back door.

Doyle eyed the stew. He scraped it back into the pot. Through
the window, he saw the Chaperone enter the outhouse. He had
two minutes to snoop undisturbed.

The young reporter always got excited when he searched through other people's things. It wasn't so much from the act of running his mitts through underpants, or reading private correspondence — although these pleasures were not to be denied — as from the thrill of being someplace where he wasn't supposed to be. Happily, his occupation made voyeurism a professional responsibility.

This particular master bedroom was unique. Its walls were covered with heads. Wolves, deer, bobcats, bears, muskrats, squirrels, porcupines, chipmunks, skunks, rabbits, foxes, lynx, and snapping turtles stared at him blankly, their skulls hung on spikes. Clearly, Skinner was a do-it-yourself taxidermist. The beasts' eyes were dime-store marbles, while their flesh had been left to desiccate on the bone. This left a few looking emaciated. Others had cheeks stuffed with socks, bits of wool poking through rotted snouts. Sometimes Slick had gone overboard; the bear over the bed seemed to have a bad case of mumps. All the same, there was no denying the hunter's artistic flair. Fangs were bared, lips propped in place by finishing nails stuck between teeth like toothpicks. Most startling was the fox near the chest of drawers; the shrivelled remains of a hen were fixed in its jaws by a drool of white paste. Then there was the collection of sparrows nesting in a brassiere cup, and the porcupine sporting a pipe.

Doyle turned his attention to the Skinners' personal effects. A peek under the bed revealed little. A few slippers, a ball of tangled fishing line, and a pair of snowshoes. The dresser was also a disappointment. Marge's drawers were filled with girdles, other unmentionables, and a bag of homemade potpourri, while Slick's were a cornucopia of soiled long johns, shell casings, playing cards of naked ladies, and half-empty packets of chewing tobacco.

Of interest, however, was the photograph album on the Skinners' night table. Each page featured a different man in hunting gear. Former guests, Doyle presumed. Some were on their knees in prayer, as if seeking the Lord's assistance for the hunt. Others appeared to be dead drunk, splayed out against tree stumps, their eyes as glassy as the stuffed wildlife. Still others were apparently shy, their photos shot while they ran away from the camera with their arms in the air.

Suddenly, Doyle found himself staring at his own name. It was on a scrap of newspaper ripped from the *Cedar Bend Herald*; a wire-service version of the first story he'd written about Mary Mabel. The article bookmarked the only blank page in the picture book. At the bottom of that page, in a childlike scrawl, were the words: B. MCT. THE ONE THAT GOT AWAY.

Doyle put the album back on the night table. Instinct told him to return to the kitchen, but there was still the bedroom closet to inspect. He turned the knob. The door was locked. Damn.

From inside the closet, a woman's voice: "Go away."

"Mrs. Skinner?"

"No. Santy Claus. Who do you think?"

"Are you all right?"

"Of course I'm not all right."

"I'll get you out."

"You'll get yourself killed is what you'll get. Now leave me alone, you little shit-for-brains. If I want your help, I'll ask for it."

A cough. Doyle turned to find himself staring down the wrong end of a rifle.

"How's your 'vacation'?" asked the Chaperone.

"F-fine," Doyle stammered. "That's quite the gun."

"Yep. Makes mighty big holes."

"I'll bet. I, uh, I was just admiring your brother's trophies."

"Is that a fact?"

From the closet: "Gerty, get this slicker out of my bedroom."

"Sorry to have disturbed you, Mrs. Skinner," Doyle apologized. "I, uh, I was looking for your husband."

"Well he ain't here. You blind as well as stupid?"

"He's huntin," said the Chaperone. "But he'll be back."

"When?"

"Maybe a month, maybe a minute." She cocked the rifle and aimed it at his groin. "If I was you, I wouldn't stick around to find out."

Doyle took the hint.

VI

LEAVE-TAKINGS

TRUTH *versus* TRUTH

Seeing herself on the silver screen gave Mary Mabel palpitations. The Twins said she mustn't feel self-conscious, that the mole above her lip hardly showed at all.

"Nonsense," she wept. "Everything shows. My face is so big the entire town could crawl up my nose."

"So what?" Floyd consoled. "A little plainness makes a person look sincere."

Mary Mabel could have smacked him. Most embarrassing to her was having to stand outside the theatre each night in her nurse's outfit. She tried to refuse. "People will stare!"

"That's the idea," Floyd said. "Just imagine you're an actress. The uniform is your costume."

Brother Percy yammered that he "wannad a cos-doom doo." To shut him up, the Twins provided him with a top hat and tails from their father's wardrobe.

So there they stood under the marquee, Mary Mabel and the reverend, while the manager walked up and down the sidewalk wearing a sandwich board reading WELCOME SISTER MARY MABEL, STAR OF METROTONE PRESENTS, and hollering greetings into a megaphone while Brother Percy waved.

The first night, Miss Budgie came to the show with a couple of other teachers. "I'm so glad to see you're doing well," she said. "You've no idea how I've missed you in English." Mary Mabel gave her a hug. Miss Budgie's eyes went misty and she hurried away. Some classmates showed up, too. They stood across the street in small packs whispering and giggling. Except for Clara Brimley. She made a point of walking past the lineups as if they weren't even there.

Then there was the contingent from St. James who arrived to pass judgment on the fuss. Mrs. Herbert C. Wallace presented herself. "I suppose you're proud of yourself," she sniffed before sweeping to the ticket wicket. Mary Mabel was delighted she couldn't get in. The show was sold out.

No wonder. In the days leading up to the opening, she'd attracted a lot of attention. Doyle's articles for Hearst had been carried by the *Free Press*. So had the stories by Scratch Micallef for *Associated Press* and Scoop Jones for *Scripps-Howard*. The latter two, having swallowed Doyle's bait, had made a ruckus at the Sally in Toronto. They'd terrorized the place, prowling the halls, squeezing bottoms, and offering to trade bootleg for scuttlebutt. The cops were called, and they spent a night in the clink. This too made news: if American press syndicates were snooping after Miss McTavish, she must be important. Consequently, when the Misters Micallef and Jones sailed up to the Twins, they trailed an armada of local scribblers.

Floyd had spotted the advancing posse from the window. He told Mary Mabel to go to the conservatory; he'd field questions from the porch, then send the reporters down with their cameras to snap her at prayer. Brother Percy insisted that he was going to be in the pictures, too. "Then put on a fresh shirt," Floyd barked. "And pop a mint while you're at it."

"I'm not too keen on having my picture taken," Mary Mabel said. "I've come down with a cold and my eyes are watering."

"There's nothing like runny eyes to make a gal look spiritual," Floyd winked. "Folks like their saints a little sickly. Heck, you ever seen a picture of Jesus in the pink?"

Luckily, neither Mr. Jones nor Mr. Micallef recognized her from the fairgrounds. Perhaps they'd been distracted by their recent misadventures. Or perhaps they didn't have time to play detective. In any case, they and the others passed through quicker than Brother Percy's turnip soup.

Their coverage was extensive and positive, featuring word of the planned American tour, and inviting interested parties to contact the ministry in care of the Twins. Despite the good press, Brother Brubacher was upset. He'd been cropped out of all but one photograph. Its caption read: SISTER MARY MABEL PRAYS FOR CIRCUS FREAK PERCY RUTABAGA. He tore up the articles, burst into tongues, and passed out.

"We better strap him to his cot till he's sensible," said Miss Millie. "Either that or take turns guarding him with the shovel."

Floyd agreed. He dragged his partner's body downstairs to the laundry room, then stepped outside. Mary Mabel followed. She found him sitting on a stump at the back of the garden, picking his teeth with a blade of grass.

"What exactly did you tell the press about Brother Percy?" she demanded.

"Not much."

"Then why did they write that he was a circus freak?"

"Dunno. They oughta be ashamed of themselves," he grinned.

"I suppose you had nothing to do with those stories about my childhood, either. Like about how I found a missing toddler through the power of prayer!"

"Those were good stories."

"You lied!"

"No I didn't. I just made the truth more interesting."

She gave him a hard look "I appreciate everything you've done for me, Mr. Cruickshank, but I can't bear falsehoods."

He smiled. "You know as well as I do that things can be true and not true at the same time."

"Don't try to pull the wool over my eyes."

"I'm not. The characters in those books and plays you read — you talk about them like they're real. You laugh and cry over patterns of ink on paper."

"Fine," she said. "Call me crazy."

"No. It's not crazy to believe in stories. Each Christmas, millions of common-sense people put up Nativity scenes. Ask them if they believe about the star and the three kings and the shepherds, and they'll say, sure, why not? Well for Pete's sake, if a star was hovering over a stable, the planet would incinerate. And there'd be more folks gawking than a handful of farmers and wise men."

"That's sacrilege!"

"It's the truth. It's also the truth that babies are special. They remind us of how perfect we used to be, and of how far we've fallen. Even though we've messed up, they offer hope that humankind has a fresh chance to get it right. That's the point of the story. If the Gospel writers figured they needed to toss in a few whoppers to get people's attention, who's to blame them?"

"Those fantasies you told the press weren't about Christmas. They were about my life."

"Your *story*! Nobody gets to choose their life, but everybody gets to choose their story. What's yours? Are you just another kid with a troubled past, or an innocent touched by grace? Spit it out — what's your truth? Hope or despair? If it's despair, buzz off — people can slit their wrists without your help. If it's hope — well that's a truth worth selling. So get off your high horse. If fudging facts was good enough for Jesus, it oughta be good enough for you."

Mary Mabel wavered. "If things aren't the way we say, men like Mr. Doyle will find out. And *then* what?"

"Reporters don't care about facts. They care about selling papers."

"Still, if they ask about your stories, what'll I tell them?"

"Put your hand on your heart and say, 'In the words of the Good Book, miracles only take love, and love is easy to give.'"

"The Bible doesn't say that."

"Who's going to check?"

Suddenly Mary Mabel remembered her mama shelling peas, her asking what made them grow, and her mama talking about the miracle of life. "Miracles just take a bit of love," her mama'd said, "and we've all got lots to give."

She looked Floyd in the eye. "Those words aren't in the Bible. But I *can* say they're something my late mother told me."

"Your late mother?" He paused. "How touching. Did she really say that?"

"Yes," Mary Mabel said. "I think so."

With the press abuzz, booking the tour was a snap. Floyd negotiated the venues and the ministry's percentage of the gate. He drove a hard bargain. "Each penny we collect goes to good works," he explained to organizers. "We owe it to God to get the best deal possible."

The hoopla climaxed with the premiere of Doyle's newsreel. The morning after, Mary Mabel was reading in the back garden when Miss Tillie came running from the kitchen. "We've got a special visitor," she panted. "Make sure your nails are clean."

Mary Mabel hurried to the drawing room. Brothers Percy and Floyd were already in attendance, the guest of honour to their left. It was none other than Miss Bentwhistle. Nesting on the sofa, bedecked in black taffeta and a black feathered hat, she looked like a well-fed vulture. The fox stole draped around her shoulders might have been lunch. She craned her neck toward the young woman. "Come," she cawed, "give your Auntie Horatia a hug."

Mary Mabel froze. Miss Tillie led her over. The buzzard clutched her in her talons, swooped her down, and gave her a peck on both cheeks. "May I congratulate you, my sweet. The world is your oyster. We at the Academy have taken note, and we are very proud. You are, *sans doubt*, our most illustrious *alumna*. In recognition of your accomplishments, we intend to feature you in our upcoming enrollment campaign, and to erect a plaque in your honour at our front gate."

Squeals of delight from the Twins. A grunt from Brother Percy.

"The unveiling will take place Monday next, at 2:00 p.m.," she preened, "a reception to follow in the Great Hall. We trust you shall be able to attend."

"I'd rather eat glass."

The room blinked. Floyd fell about with apologies: the recent excitement had gone to Mary Mabel's head, she wasn't herself.

"I'm myself and nobody else," Mary Mabel contradicted. "That two-faced witch put me and Papa on the street."

Miss Bentwhistle pursed her lips. "What an odd construction of events. We set you free to explore a limitless future. It would have been a crime to hold you back."

"Because of you, Papa left me!"

"Your father's disappeared? So that explains the petulance." She patted Mary Mabel's knee. "Not to fret. Word of your success will bring him home."

"How? Papa doesn't read. He hasn't got a radio. For all I know, he's riding the rails, sleeping in barns."

"I wouldn't want that getting out. There are those who might question your filial devotion."

"Miss Bentwhistle," Floyd interjected with a firm look in Mary Mabel's direction. "We're grateful for your efforts. Community endorsements will benefit our work for the needy."

Mary Mabel knew he was right. It was also true that she'd enjoy seeing Clara Brimley and the rest of her tormentors forced to sit through an assembly in her honour. "I apologize," she said. "I'll be thrilled to attend."

"Good girl." Miss Bentwhistle beamed. "Life's too short for pettiness and regret." A grand inhale and she rose like a hot air balloon, billowed across the room, and hovered at the threshold. "Till Monday next, my dears. Never fear. We shall be the highlight of the Middlesex County social calendar."

The ACADEMY RECEPTION

Floyd planned for the tour to hit the road following Miss Bentwhistle's ceremony. He'd lined up a dizzying itinerary to keep Mary Mabel in public view. "You're hot," he told her, "But today's papers line tomorrow's bird cages." His ultimate dream was to play New York. First, though, they'd have to do regional tryouts. This meant touring the American Midwest. "When we hit the Big Apple, we gotta be slick as spit. Flop there and forever after we'll be stuck winding our way through the loopier loops of the Bible belt."

The first event was in Flint, Michigan, sponsored by the Chamber of Commerce. It had rented the auditorium at Ulysses S. Grant Memorial High School, seating capacity seven hundred. Floyd thought that was perfect. As well as keeping down costs and expectations, a high school auditorium was both large enough to bring in a decent gate and small enough to guarantee a full house. "Folks want what they can't have. If our first shows sell out, ticket sales'll skyrocket. At top dollar, too."

Box office wasn't his only consideration. He announced that no matter how popular the tour got, he'd always advertise fifty free seats for the poor to demonstrate Christian charity. Mary Mabel asked why they couldn't just open the doors and pass a plate. He rolled his eyes. "That's how we ended up at the Twins."

Charity would also figure in the ministry's choice of hosts. Floyd selected groups who planned to put their proceeds toward good causes. "This'll build a loyal fan base. For instance, the Flint Chamber's plowing its profits into a bucket brigade to clean abandoned storefronts. When folks see the improvements, they'll think of us fondly."

"Terrific," Mary Mabel said. "And what's our share of the profits to be used for?"

"The greater of glory of God."

"Could you be more specific?"

"In the fullness of time."

In the fullness of time, the greater glory of God turned out to be a secondhand Oldsmobile. Floyd made the surprise purchase with the advance money. He drove it back from Frank's Auto Repair the morning of the leave-taking. The honking brought the household outside.

"Wouldn't it be cheaper to travel by bus?" Mary Mabel asked.

"God's work can't be tied to bus schedules."

The Twins admired the chrome. "Very snazzy. Does this mean you're able to pay your bill?"

"Not quite."

"But you've bought a car."

"It's not a car. It's an investment. Don't fret. You're first in line, next round of advances, as God is my witness." The Twins looked doubtful. "Ladies, nothing hurts more than an absence of trust."

Meanwhile, Brother Percy fulminated from the verandah. It wasn't the automobile that had him hopping. It was the new paint job. The Olds was a blinding white emblazoned in bright red capital letters. The driver's side read: GOD LOVES YOU!!! This drove Brother Percy up the wall. To paraphrase the good reverend: "It's a damned lie. God only loves you if you declare Jesus Christ to be your personal Lord and Saviour. Otherwise it's off to the lava lake."

If Percy was upset by the words "God Loves You," it was a blessing that he failed to do a walk-around. On the car's passenger side the lettering screamed: THE MIRACLE MAID TOUR!!! And on the trunk: SISTER MARY MABEL!!!

Mary Mabel was so embarrassed, she wanted to sprout wings and fly away. No such luck, so she ran to her room, crawled under the covers, and held her breath, hoping to pass out.

Within minutes, Miss Tillie was tapping at her door. "May I come in?" She took the silence as an invitation. "You scurried off in such a hurry. Are you okay?" The young woman looked such a sight that Miss Tillie swept over and touched her forehead to check for a temperature. "What's the matter, dear?"

"Nothing. I just want to die."

Miss Tillie sat on the edge of the bed and cradled her. "There, there. It's all right."

Mary Mabel knew otherwise. Life was going so well, but the world felt topsy-turvy. All monsters under the bed. She wanted her mama. The recent visitations had been a blessing, but their glow was fading into memory.

"I miss her," Mary Mabel blurted. "I'm afraid to forget what she looked like. I try to picture her every day, so she won't disappear. Sometimes I can't. And even when I can, I'm not sure I'm remembering right. She's vanishing. Why can't I hold on to her face? How can I be so awful? She loved me."

Miss Tillie didn't ask whom she meant. She didn't ask anything, just held her. And Mary Mabel held her back. "I'm going to miss you very much. Promise me you'll stay beside me this afternoon at the Academy."

Miss Tillie hugged her tighter still. "I wish I could. But Millie and I won't be there. We'd spoil the occasion."

"Never."

Miss Tillie cupped Mary Mabel's head in her hands and stared deep into her eyes. "Folks in this town, they think they know everything there is to know about other folks. My sister and I … our father … well … it's difficult."

"I don't care about the rumours."

"Others do."

"Miss Bentwhistle's no saint."

"It's not just Miss Bentwhistle." Miss Tillie kissed her hair. "Don't fret. We'll be there in spirit. Now you stay under these covers and I'll bring you some tea and cookies."

"I'm not hungry."

"It doesn't matter. Tea and cookies make the world a better place." Miss Tillie paused at the door. "You know, Mary Mabel, somewhere up there your mama's looking down at you. And she's very proud. I know it in my heart."

Miss Bentwhistle's function was death on wheels. Local dignitaries, staff, and students, decked out in their Sunday best, sat on rows of folding chairs on the front lawn before a podium draped in Union Jacks. Mary Mabel was stuck centre stage, surrounded by the worthiest of the worthies. The mayor, the local member of Parliament, and the Reverend Brice Harvey Mandible, all gave speeches congratulating her and commending the headmistress under whom she'd flourished.

Miss Bentwhistle provided the keynote address. "Miss McTavish came to us a motherless child whom we took to our bosom." Et cetera. This led to an announcement: the creation of a Mary Mabel McTavish Scholarship to be awarded annually "to a young lady of diminished circumstance." Donations toward the award would be gratefully accepted, and publicized in the *London Free Press*. *Oohs*, *ahhs*, and much clapping. Miss Bentwhistle acknowledged the applause and turned to the Academy marching band. As they struck up "The Maple Leaf Forever," she unveiled the plaque of honour. It was actually more of a billboard.

THE BENTWHISTLE ACADEMY, EST. 1910
ALMA MATER TO MISS MARY MABEL MCTAVISH
"WHERE LITTLE MIRACLES BEGIN"

Mary Mabel was summoned to the lectern to deliver her thank-you speech. It had been prepared by the headmistress and was as flowery as an Easter bonnet. The words caked in Mary Mabel's mouth. She cleared her throat and took a sip of water. It didn't help. Searching the crowd for a friendly face, she spotted Miss Budgie, her eyelashes fluttering like butterflies. Mary Mabel put aside her text. "Above all, I would like to thank my English instructor, Miss Budgie. Her love of learning, dedication to fairness, and generosity of time, have meant more to me than she will ever know."

Miss Budgie fainted.

Mary Mabel leapt from the stage and ran to her side. Miss Budgie rose to a round of applause from the gentlemen. In the background, Clara Brimley could be heard joking about her "fabled healing touch." Mary Mabel didn't care. Miss Budgie was all right, and she'd escaped the speech.

The reception that followed was mercifully brief. The stuffed and the starched shook her hand, while munching on petit fours. Then, none too soon, it was time for the show to hit the road.

Mary Mabel never saw London, Ontario, again. Would that she could say the same of Miss Bentwhistle.

MISS BUDGIE FLIES *the* COOP

One week later, Miss Budgie sat alone on the floor of her classroom at the Bentwhistle Academy for Young Ladies. The desks were pushed against the walls, and she was surrounded by cardboard boxes. Boxes hauled out of the bank of filing cabinets at the back of the room, pulled off the long rows of shelves under the front blackboard, dragged from beneath the work table by the windows to her right, and from the supply closet to her left where they had been piled helter-skelter in a dizzying tower of such height and weight that they threatened the life and limb of anyone foolish enough to open the door.

She gazed vacantly at these stacks of boxes, and at the shadows of these stacks of boxes — ghastly spectres that quivered to the ceiling, thrown up by the smoky light of the coal-oil lamp beside her. Tears dripped onto the pile of foolscap sheets on her lap. What in the world was she going to do?

Miss Budgie had never wanted to become a teacher. Like most everything else in her life, it had just happened. Even her birth had been an accident, a ten-year gap separating her from the youngest of her four brothers. As for her parents' deaths, nothing had prepared her for those, either. Indeed, nothing had prepared her for anything.

She'd grown up expecting to stay on the family farm near Tillsonburg, helping her mother until she caught the eye of some young man at a box social. They'd marry and she'd raise a family of her own. Daughters would be nice, she'd thought, although she knew she ought to have at least one son to make her husband happy.

It was not to be. When she was just shy of twenty, her mother took sick with pneumonia and was gone within the week. Her father followed, of a heart attack, six months later. The family farm and all its belongings went to her eldest brother, John. His shrew of a wife made it plain that the kitchen wasn't big enough for the both of them. Nor was there room with her other brothers. Murray lodged in a disreputable boarding house, while Robert and Henry worked at a cheese factory in Ingersoll, where they shared a room over the local menswear store.

The advertisement in the *Globe* seemed the answer to her prayers. The Bentwhistle Academy for Young Ladies, est. 1910, was seeking a person of Christian character to teach English Language and Literature, Home Economics, and Religious Studies. Miss Budgie had always cursed her high school certificate. She'd attended Tillsonburg Secondary as a means to expand her pool of potential husbands beyond the dire prospects along Concession 4, but her proficiency at academics had scared them all away. "Success brings nothing but failure," she'd wept. Now, however, her education offered her the chance to redeem her life.

The interview had gone well. Miss Bentwhistle was impressed by her references, her Sunday school teaching experience, and the second prize taken by her deep dish boysenberry pie at the previous year's bake sale in St. Thomas. She offered Miss Budgie the position on the spot: "You shall receive room and board, a small gratuity, and the prestige afforded by association with the Academy." Miss Budgie accepted, convinced that her teaching days would be few. London was of a size to offer abundant matrimonial possibilities.

There were only three men on the Academy staff and each was problematic. The geography teacher was dull as dust, the

Latin teacher dry as chalk, and the music teacher, Mr. Felix Fontaine, was a confirmed bachelor of impeccable taste, manicured nails, and a passion for Mozart.

Happily, Miss Budgie secured herself a place with the Wesley Methodist choir. Most of her male pew-mates were married or lived with their mothers, but Miss Budgie soon had the attentions of two tenors and a baritone. The tenors liked to talk, especially about themselves, and the baritone liked to listen. They had many a happy tête-à-tête over biscuits and tea in the Academy drawing room, but these ended abruptly when Miss Bentwhistle allowed that Miss Budgie should not mistake her school for a brothel. Henceforward, she would be free to entertain gentlemen callers only of a Sunday afternoon under the beady eye of head secretary Miss Dolly Pigeon.

The gentlemen callers disappeared.

And then, before she knew it, Miss Budgie turned thirty.

She consoled herself that at least she had a job. Or to be more exact, a vocation. For over the years, Miss Budgie had become an outstanding teacher, devoted to her subjects and her students. She owed her love of education to Mr. Fontaine. They had become fast friends, who liked to giggle and gossip over a game of crokinole in the Academy library. He taught her about music and art and literature. He made the classics come alive.

The day he left town, Miss Budgie was devastated. Miss Bentwhistle had gone looking for something in the long-abandoned coach house. What she found was never made entirely clear, but Miss Budgie understood that it involved Mr. Fontaine, the groundskeeper, and a garden hose.

Things were never the same. The new groundskeeper was an oily rake, an odd-jobs man by the name of Brewster McTavish. His advances were as frequent as they were unwelcome. Miss Budgie had always longed to be pursued by a man. Now she was and it terrified her. Attempts to secure the protection of the headmistress were in vain. Marking papers in her classroom after hours was a particular danger. She'd lock the door, but McTavish had a key to every room in the school. One night, things threatened to get out of hand. She barely managed to scare him off by blasting away on the bugle she kept in the lower left drawer of her desk. The instrument had belonged to Mr. Fontaine, who'd been a bugler in the Great War. It had been overlooked in the haste of his untimely departure, and she'd slipped it out of his room to keep as a memento.

Mr. McTavish had not been her only distraction. Standards at the Academy had taken a precipitous drop. High marks were not something which the young ladies were required to earn, but which their teachers were obliged to award. The school's decline reached its nadir with the arrival of Miss Clara Brimley, spawn of prominent Toronto lawyer Mr. Howard K. Brimley, Q.C. She and her set, a circle of privilege whose families contributed handsomely to Academy endowments and fundraisers, forged a tight-knit cabal that faculty challenged at its peril.

Miss Budgie fell afoul of the clique over an essay Miss Brimley scribbled on comic irony in Shakespeare's *Twelve Nites* (*sic*). The paper was a thicket of spelling and grammatical errors submitted on crumpled foolscap smeared with ink scrawls. Miss Budgie circled and identified each embarrassment, made crisp notes regarding structure, form, and presentation, and confidently assigned it an *F*.

Clara was not amused. "If you don't improve your attitude," she said, "I'm going to speak to my father."

"Be my guest," Miss Budgie replied. Next day, the headmistress obliged her to raise the grade to a *B*, in front of a smug Miss Brimley.

"Does this satisfy you?" Miss Bentwhistle inquired of the complainant.

"I'd like her to apologize," Clara simpered. "Also, to pay for my long-distance telephone call to father." And it was so.

In the days that followed, Miss Budgie struggled to keep her grip. She asked Clara to stay after school. The girl sat at her desk and stared at the ceiling as Miss Budgie tried to explain the importance of responsibility and respect. Clara yawned and rose. "I have to go now," she said. "I'm expected at the soda shop."

"Sit down!" Miss Budgie ordered.

Clara smiled. She opened her mouth and screamed, "Ow! Ow! Stop it, Miss Budgie! Help!"

Miss Budgie fled the room.

With Miss Brimley in command, students no longer bothered to pass each other notes. They simply wandered the aisles and struck up conversations. It was Miss Budgie's fault. If she had motivated her students, there wouldn't be a problem. Or so Miss Bentwhistle had said before Mary Mabel McTavish claimed to raise the dead.

Ah, Mary Mabel, Miss Budgie's one bright light. It had been difficult to forget that she was the daughter of Brewster McTavish, but the girl had been such a keen pupil that even that could be forgiven. Mary Mabel was the one student who hung on her every word. The one student who came to her outside of school hours to talk about books. The one student with the brass to stand up to Clara Brimley.

"That resurrection tale!" Miss Bentwhistle had thundered, moments after the girl's expulsion. "You're to blame for her imagination! You and your creative writing assignments! You encouraged her!"

"I understood motivation was my job," Miss Budgie peeped.

"Insolent toad! You've motivated her onto the street. You'll join her, too, if you don't shape up!"

Of course, the headmistress changed her tune once association with Mary Mabel became desirable. Miss Budgie remembered the ceremony in the young woman's honour. What a joy to know that happiness remained a possibility for a deserving few. And what a heavenly shock to hear herself praised from the podium.

Yet despite Mary Mabel's kind words, Miss Bentwhistle had sent her neither a card of commendation nor a toffee. Instead, after the function she'd upbraided her on the front lawn before a gaggle of young ladies. "Your collapse was a sorry spectacle. It embarrassed the assembly, set a poor example for our pupils, and ruined the festivities.

Miss Budgie shrank as she watched her students titter and scurry off to gossip in the dormitories.

She didn't remember much after that, of the days leading to tonight, with her on the classroom floor dripping tears, covered in foolscap, surrounded by boxes. She had flashes only: of the air alive with paper airplanes, of thumb tacks slipped onto the seat of her chair, and of turning away to stare out the window. Memories of staying late to tidy up, of wiping lewd drawings from her students' desks, of fretting how to hide the swear word carved on the door frame, and of covering it up with a doily.

She also seemed to recollect that sometime — when? — she had been hit in the head with a flying piece of chalk, and had stood there like nothing had happened.... Nothing *had* happened ... *had* it? And recalled the scene this morning, when her entire first-period class had staged a mock faint, all forty of them swooning to the floor *en masse* amidst a fit of giggles. She had an idea of herself weeping and of Clara Brimley batting her eyes and smirking, "Want a hankie?" Somehow she had ended up pressed against the blackboard, while Clara conducted her classmates in a chant of, "Boo-hoo, boo-hoo," as they skipped out the door. There had followed the inevitable interview with Miss Bentwhistle. Why were her pupils roaming the corridors? What was the matter with her? And, by the way, where were the preliminary reports for the upcoming parent-teacher interviews?

Miss Budgie remembered apologizing: she had been sure the period was over, there must be a problem with the classroom clock; as for herself, she was perfectly fine, and the reports would be on Miss Bentwhistle's desk first thing in the morning.

However the truth was that there *were* no reports. Since her students refused to do homework, Miss Budgie filled their class time with essays, tests, and work sheets. These had been collected every day since the beginning of the term. Unfortunately, none of them had been marked.

It wasn't that Miss Budgie hadn't *wanted* to mark them. It was that she *couldn't*. No sooner would she pick up her red pen than she'd find herself heaving into the toilet. Her students' work was deplorable, incomplete, and covered in doodles. If she graded it honestly, the brats would have her humiliated. On the other hand, if she inflated the scores, she would humiliate herself. So she'd done neither. She'd simply bundled the assignments into cardboard boxes, resolving to do them tomorrow. Soon, so many tomorrows had turned into yesterdays that she didn't know where to begin. Paralyzed with terror, she had attempted to hide the boxes on curtained shelves, in filing cabinets, and behind the closet door, in the desperate hope that somehow they'd disappear. Only they hadn't. They'd grown into the monstrous stacks whose giant shadows now filled the walls.

It was 2:00 a.m. Miss Budgie had yet to mark anything. She couldn't manage to hold her pen, nor could she read. Words swam off the sheets in front of her. They floated in front of her face. What did they mean? Why wouldn't they stay on the page?

And how could she mark by lamp light? To impress parents, Miss Bentwhistle permitted her young ladies to use electricity at all hours, while, to cut costs, her teachers had been reduced to oil lamps!

In mid-sniffle, a smile flickered across Miss Budgie's face. Why hadn't she thought of this before? It was the answer to her problems. She began to hum. She wasn't sure if it was something she remembered or something she was making up. Either way, it was a cheerful tune and put her in a very good mood as she danced about, emptying her boxes into a paper mountain at the centre of the room.

"Goodbye," she laughed at the assignments.

And lit a bonfire.

Miss Bentwhistle was in her nightie, tucking into her fourth nightcap when the alarm was sounded. She'd felt rather toasty, but had put it down to the alcohol.

"Good heavens," she mused, hearing the tumult in the hall, "are there boys from the university on a panty raid?" She opened the door. Her rooms were immediately engulfed in smoke, but that wasn't what caught her attention. It was the sight of her secretary as sooty as a chimney sweep.

"Fire! Fire!"

Miss Bentwhistle blinked. Why, so there was.

"The school is lost!" Miss Pigeon cried. "We must save the girls!"

"To hell with the girls!" Miss Bentwhistle bellowed. She covered her mouth with a pair of old knickers, shoved Miss Pigeon aside, and barrelled down the corridor to the Academy Dining Hall. Inside were a pair of documents as precious to her as life itself.

MISS BENTWHISTLE RECUPERATES

Miss Bentwhistle dabbed her lips with the best linen napkin of the Reverend Rector and Mrs. Brice Harvey Mandible. She had just completed an especially fine mid-morning breakfast of coddled eggs, sausage, cured ham, and crumpets with plum jam, washed down with a little tea and honey — a breakfast that had been delivered to her bed, here in the master room of the St. James manse, by Mrs. Mandible herself. The Mandibles had taken her in following the fire. They had given her full use of their home, including their very own bedroom.

Sun poured through the casements and drenched the room, spilling over the twin easels sporting the Bentwhistle Coat of Arms and the Bentwhistle Family Tree. Thank heavens she'd rescued them from the Academy dining hall during the conflagration. The parchments, curiously, had been improved by the ordeal. The ornate gilt calligraphy and decorative seals of the Heralds' College of Westminster still glittered, while the recent soot and singeing intimated ancient family lore and *gravitas*. God was smiling on her master plan.

The headmistress had a little stretch, and settled back against the bank of fluffed pillows propped against the oak headboard. Another teaspoon of laudanum and the world would be tickety-boo.

It had been a challenging few weeks.

Miss Bentwhistle's tribulations had begun the night following the reception for Mary Mabel. She was prowling the corridors when she was overcome by a death stench coming from behind the door to the laundry room. Rat poison had been put down the previous week, but this smell signalled more than a dead rodent. Surely an army of raccoons lay putrefying under the tubs. Miss Bentwhistle entered the room and traced the stink to a clothes hamper. Using the end of a nearby mop, she lifted a crumpled sheet. Underneath was a beast all right, but of the two-legged variety. A big palooka in hunting gear. He was burrowed in a mound of undergarments, garters hanging from big red ears.

Miss Bentwhistle was so outraged, she forgot to scream. "What are you doing in my laundry room?"

"Nothin'. I was out for a stroll. Must of taken a wrong turn somewheres and got lost."

"I see." Miss Bentwhistle noticed his shotgun. "Sorry to have disturbed." She calmly dropped the sheet back on his head, fled to the hall, and locked the door.

What to do now? A call to the police was out of the question; word that armed brutes prowled her corridors would empty the school. On the other hand, the intruder couldn't be set free. Nor could he be kept as a house pet. If only she could have stuffed his mouth with a mop, trussed him in sheets, and cemented him behind some pipes.

There was no more time to think. Inside the laundry room, her gentleman caller had removed the pins from the door hinges. A mighty heave and the portal ripped from its moorings. The beast stood before her in a cloud of plaster dust. He had a shotgun under his arm; a skinning knife hung from his belt. "No more hide-and-seek, woman. Where's Brewster McTavish?"

"Ah! So you're here for Mr. McTavish?"

The woodsman was confused. Normally people didn't ask questions. They spilled the beans and screamed for mercy. "Yeah," he said warily. "We're old pals."

"I might have guessed. Sorry to say, your friend's left town for parts unknown. I suggest you do likewise."

The hunter fingered his trigger. "Where's his young'un, Mary Mabel?"

"Do you live in a cave?" At a glance, perhaps he did. "Miss McTavish is off saving souls, my dear. Her itinerary is posted in the *Free Press*."

"You'd best be telling the truth," the hunter said, "or I'll be back to shoot your girlies." With that, he blasted out the nearest window, hopped through and disappeared.

If Miss Bentwhistle had been upset to have her school invaded, she was outraged to have it burned to the ground.

Trust Miss Budgie. The little snip had been the only fatality, count your blessings. Still, her funeral was a trial. All those hankies to clean. Finding something nice to say had been no picnic, either. Miss Bentwhistle made a dozen false starts on the eulogy. "Miss Budgie was a teacher who fired up her students." Perhaps not. "Miss Budgie was a special favourite of the janitorial staff." Hmm. "Miss Budgie was well-known for the liveliness of her classes." Yes, well. She settled on the theme: "Gone, but Not Forgotten."

The St. James Board of Session had sent flowers and arranged for Miss Bentwhistle to stay at the rectory. Over the generations, her family's tithes had contributed mightily to the church's good fortune, and the session thought its act of charity would be a useful down payment on favours yet to come. The Mandibles were upset at being evicted from their matrimonial bed, but who paid the bills?

London had opened its heart, as well. Churches immediately offered to rent their Sunday school classrooms to the Academy, while community-minded citizens eagerly invited the young ladies into their homes in exchange for the school's boarding fees. "Vultures," Miss Bentwhistle fumed privately. Publicly she expressed gratitude. She and her students would move in forthwith, though naturally she couldn't discuss money matters while mourning her dear friend, Miss Budgie.

Unhappily, association with Miss Budgie became increasingly awkward. At first the schoolmarm had been hailed as a martyr. However, the morning of the interment, officials announced that the source of the inferno was her very own classroom, and asked pointed questions about kerosene and a peculiar mountain of ash. As well, reports suggested that on the night of the blaze, a bevy of young ladies had wakened to the smell of smoke and someone cackling opera. They ran to the cricket pitch from which they saw Miss Budgie dancing from window to window like a latter-day Mrs. Rochester, setting fire to the curtains with flaming sheets of foolscap. Gossip spread faster than influenza. Memories stirred of her infatuation with the unspeakable Mr. Fontaine. Overnight, it was common knowledge that the Academy's teaching staff was a collection of arsonists, perverts, and sexual hysterics.

Miss Bentwhistle was aware of the rumours. Not that anyone said anything to her face. Rather, she knew from the increasingly smug tone of her sympathizers. Mrs. Mandible was particularly solicitous. "It must be so difficult to check references," she commiserated. More telling was the sudden and precipitous drop in the school's enrollment. Within days, the only girls left were those whose parents preferred they risk immolation than darken the family door.

It didn't help that these delinquents were now loose in the community. Churches providing space to the Academy reported trashed Sunday schools, defaced hymnals, and cigarette butts in the choir loft. At St. James, the Reverend Mandible's vestments went missing, only to be discovered in shreds, plugging the toilets. Worse, someone absconded with the cathedral's silver candlesticks and chalice, and its nineteenth-century European oil paintings: *The Annunciation, The Beheading of John the Baptist,* and *The Martyrdom of St. Sebastian.*

The Academy's credibility, like its woodwork, was up in smoke. It had no securities with which to rebuild. There were no revenues to pay for the rented classrooms. The room and board money had already been spent. Gossip foreclosed fundraising. And insurance monies would be stripped by past creditors.

As for Miss Bentwhistle, she was living on the charity of church mice. How long before they turned to rats? The wolf might not be at the door, but one could smell him from the verandah. She began to plan for the inevitable day of judgment.

The headmistress knew it was time to put her plans into effect when Mrs. Mandible brought her this morning's breakfast tray. Coddled eggs, cured ham, sausage, crumpets, and plum jam had replaced the customary boiled egg and toast. What unexpected kindness. She'd better watch her back.

"The mayor was wondering if you'd be up for a delegation of well-wishers," Mrs. Mandible enquired. "Say around ten?"

"I'd be delighted. Say around eleven."

They meant to humiliate her, of that she was certain. Let them dare. She polished off her breakfast, reviewed her strategy, and placed a call to her secretary. "Gird your loins, Dolly. The enemy is at the gates." Then, dressed in style and fashionably late, she floated down the rectory staircase, into the parlour, past her visitors, and onto the Mandible's finest floral wingback at the head of the room.

She gazed around the circle of starched collars, reserving a special nod for Mrs. Mandible, simpering by the tea trolley in the back corner. "And what can I do for you, gentlemen?"

The men shifted their weight, fiddled with their trousers, and cast sideways glances at the mayor. His Worship rose. "Sorry to trouble you, Miss Bentwhistle, but, uh, over the past couple of weeks there've been problems around town."

"In that case, you had best deal with them."

Pause. "Yes. Well, uh, that's why we're here. You see, these problems, well, they seem to involve your young ladies."

Miss Bentwhistle stared at the centre of the mayor's forehead. He shuffled. He dabbed his brow with a handkerchief. He sat down.

"What Herb means to say," said the town clerk, "is that ever since the Academy moved into our Sunday schools, there's been theft and vandalism at the churches."

"What makes you suspect my young ladies?" Miss Bentwhistle bristled. "Why not an insurrection of local Bolsheviks?"

"London doesn't have any Bolsheviks."

"Oh, doesn't it, though. I know a Ukrainian grocer when I see one," she said with a withering glance at Alderman Cole, formerly Kulesha. "Nor let us forget the bog Irish in our midst."

The room leaped to its feet. "And who do you suppose is raiding our liquor cabinets?"

"I wouldn't know," sniffed Miss Bentwhistle. "Perhaps your wives?" A sea of bobbing Adam's apples. "Come, gentlemen, half of you are married to known tosspots. I'm sure they're only too happy to use my girls as window dressing for their debaucheries."

The town clerk shook his fist. "It was your little vixens, and none other, whom I found in my living room playing strip poker with the neighbour boys!"

Miss Bentwhistle gasped. "How dare you have left them unsupervised!" She swept the crowd with an eyebrow. "I have entrusted to you the flower of this nation's youth. And what have you done? By your own admission, surrendered them to booze, boys, and bedlam! You ought to be sued for breech of trust, reckless endangerment, and contributing to the delinquency of minors!"

"No one's looking for trouble," the Reverend Mandible soothed. "It's just that we're going through hell providing for your Academy, without a penny of compensation."

"So that's it!" Miss Bentwhistle sneered. "Money! It always comes down to money with your sort. For generations, this town has been sustained by my family's generosity. More recently, my girls have spent their trust funds in your shops. Now, in our darkest hour, as we mourn our dead, you seek to beggar us! You seek to extort recompense for your self-confessed derelictions of duty!"

"We seek nothing of the kind."

"Do you take me for deaf? Your effrontery is beyond preposterous! It is an outrage! I will not have it! No! I will not allow the good name of Bentwhistle to be spat upon by ingrates! Better that the Academy should fold than suffer mob attack! Indeed, I shall shut its gates forever and forthwith!"

The righteous burghers, whose stores indeed had benefited from the Academy's clientele, scrambled to make amends.

Miss Bentwhistle would have none of it. "You call yourselves town fathers. Town eunuchs is more like it. Gelded pigs. Well you've killed the goose that laid the golden egg. I'm already packed. Yes! I'm leaving this little piss-hole you're pleased to call home. I'm off to greener pastures. To a world that appreciates my gifts." There was a knock at the door. Miss Bentwhistle checked her watch. "That will be my secretary and her brothers.

They have arrived to fetch my bags and convey me to the station. Good day."

Before the delegation could pick their dentures off the floor, Miss Bentwhistle had sailed from the rectory. Her grand plan was in motion. She was about to take on the greatest role of her life, a role commanded by destiny.

VII

The BARONESS and the SHOWGIRL

OPENING NIGHT

The new revival tour got off to a rocky start. All the way to Flint, Brother Percy shook with fury at the advertisements for the Miracle Maid decorating the Olds. On the bright side, he didn't say much; his outpouring at the Twins had been so impassioned that he'd popped a few sutures. As a result, the only time he ventured a word was at the Sarnia/Port Huron border. The customs agent asked, "Do you have anything to declare?"

"YEZ!" Percy announced. "JEZUZ CHRIZE IZ MA PERZONEL LORE AN ZAVER!"

Floyd had made reservations at the Walden Hotel. The moment they drove up, a gaggle of curiosity-seekers mobbed the car. "It's her! It's her! Like in the movies!" Two police officers cleared a path, the doorman hustled them inside, a bellboy packed them into an elevator, and — bingo — they were on the third floor in front of their rooms. Mary Mabel was put in the middle. "The rose between two thorns," Floyd joked.

After they'd had time to freshen up, Floyd knocked on their doors and asked if they'd care to join him for supper. Brother Percy preferred to fast. Until his jaw was healed, he'd be out of commission preaching-wise; he hoped this might inspire God to get a move on with his recovery. Mary Mabel wasn't hungry, either.

"Butterflies," Floyd said with a wink. "Get a good night's sleep. Tomorrow's a big day."

"Thanks for reminding me." Mary Mabel closed the door and flopped on her bed. Her premiere was in less than twenty-four hours. What if there were critics? What if they hated her?

Should Mr. Cruickshank do like "Auntie" Irene? Before opening nights at the Milwaukee Little Theater Guild, she'd send the local reviewer a box of chocolates.

All week, Floyd had reassured her. Their hosts were filling the first half with local children's choirs. This guaranteed a crowd of appreciative parents. After intermission, she'd talk about Timmy's resurrection, a tale she knew backwards. Then there'd be preselected questions from the audience, a freewill offering, the choirs would return, she'd give the kids a hug, the crowd would sing "Amazing Grace" and everybody'd go home happy: "It's as simple as cows."

Mary Mabel took ten deep breaths. What right did she have to worry? She had food, shelter, and a future. And not just any future. The chance to perform — to fulfill her childhood dream! She counted her blessings over and over, even managing a thought for her hotel room. It was so different from the ones she and her papa had stayed in during their vagabond days. For one thing, she could look under the bed without blushing. For another, the mattress didn't bite.

Soon Mary Mabel was off to the land of Nod … and a most peculiar dream. She imagined that she'd woken to a commotion outside her room. "She's in here!" the crowd shouted, hacking through her door with fire axes. "Don't let her get away!" She hid in the closet. To her surprise, it was filled with nurse outfits. She swam through rows of uniforms, the mob in pursuit. *What'll I do when I reach the back wall?* she panicked. But there wasn't a back wall. The closet kept growing. Soon there was no light. No air. She was tangled in clothes. Choked by coat hangers. Suffocating in fabric.

That's when she woke up for real, twisted in bed sheets, to an argument coming from Floyd's room. Whatever her partners were yelling about, she had a sneaking suspicion it had to do with her. She retrieved the water glass by the bathroom sink, pressed it against the wall, and cupped her ear. The reception came in dandy. Floyd's end of it, anyway.

"If the car bothers you so much, we'll get a new paint job. All black with flaming orange letters. 'The Doomsday Special: Repent or Burn.' Okay? Or how about 'Brother Percy: The Hell and Back Tour'? Think that'll draw crowds? Face it. Folks don't give a rat's ass about you. It's her they want. God answers her prayers."

"Whadeja mean he answers your prayers, too? Your prayers killed a kid. Hers brought him back to life."

Howls of outrage.

"Who cares if it's bullshit? It's what they think."

More outrage.

"Don't threaten me, you sonovabitch!"

Door slam. Stomping back and forth in the hall. The stomping came to rest outside her room. She held her breath. More stomping.

"Keep it down," someone called from the end of the corridor.

A rant, followed by the sound of Brother Percy's door banging shut. He was still raving. Mary Mabel tiptoed over and pressed her glass to the wall. It was like he could see her. "SHE-DEVUH!" he roared through the plaster. "SHE-DEVUH!" His wastepaper basket hit the wall by her ear. She leapt back. He pummelled the wall with his fists.

Then his phone rang. They froze. It kept ringing.

Percy answered. "WHOZIT?" Incomprehensible grunts and explosions. His caller appeared to be talkative. On a hunch, Mary Mabel scampered over to listen at Floyd's wall. Success.

"How many times do I have to say it? I'm-sorry-I'm-sorry-I'm-sorry!" Floyd exclaimed. "It's just, right now we need her … Whadeja mean 'why'? Cash flow, you idiot. She's a hot ticket … Look, will you keep it down? You want the front desk to call the

cops? You want to wreck your opening night?... Of course it's
your opening night. Who cares if you're not preaching? You'll
be introduced and applauded. And once you're back to normal,
you'll headline ... No, I'm not lying. Heck, you're God's anointed.
Heir to Billy Sunday ... I am not making fun. I swear on the grave
of my grandmother ... Yes, Perce, of course we're friends. Best of
friends ... I care about you, too. Now say your prayers, get some
sleep, and don't do anything you'll regret ... Amen, pal." Click.

Silence. Mary Mabel put her glass to Brother Percy's wall and
heard a strange sound. Brother Percy was crying.

Mary Mabel tossed and turned all night. She'd known that
Floyd played with truth. But did he really think her miracle
was a fraud? What were his actual plans for Brother Percy and
her? Speaking of Percy — should she be moved to pity, terror,
or both? By morning Mary Mabel wasn't fit for company. She
stayed in her housecoat, huddled in a blanket with the drapes
drawn. Floyd honoured her DO NOT DISTURB sign till ten. Then
he knocked with a cheery, "Rise and shine."

She opened the door a crack. "Mr. Cruickshank, I hate to be
rude, but like the sign says, I don't want to be disturbed."

"We have an invitation for lunch. The Chamber of Commerce."

"Send my regrets."

"Can't. They're the sponsor. No sponsors, no cash flow."

"Rumour has it *I'm* the cash flow."

A careful pause. "I'm not sure what you overheard last night,
but when Perce and I get to arguing, sometimes I say things I
don't mean to keep him in line."

"Oh. And do you ever say things you don't mean to keep *me*
in line?"

His eyes flickered. "You owe me an apology."

"And you owe me an answer."

He leaned in. She could smell his breakfast. "I won't be called to account in a public hallway. Lunch is at noon. I'll pick you up at eleven-thirty."

The Chamber of Commerce was a crowd of very loud men in very loud suits. They stank of cigars. They thought they were funny. Floyd was in his element. Brother Percy, on the other hand, feared for his life. He got stuck between two bankers who slapped his back with the enthusiasm of Swedish masseurs. Mary Mabel was spared the more robust shenanigans, including the bun toss. In fact, the only thing that threatened her was the conversation: "So you're from Canada. Any igloos in your neck of the woods?"

"Can't wait for the show. Will you be tap dancing?"

"As a healer, what do you recommend for a cold?"

At first she tried to make herself disappear by staring at her mashed potatoes, but Americans are relentlessly friendly. "If you don't mind my asking, how long have you had that mole?" She closed her eyes and pretended to pray. Even that didn't work. "Look, she's fallen asleep! Isn't that the sweetest thing? Wakey-wakey!" When a geezer in plaid came up, pinched her cheek and remarked that she was the spitting image of his daughter, she'd had enough. "Pinch me again and I'll bop you one."

Back in the car, Floyd lit into her. "Threatening a sponsor! Making sculptures with your damn potatoes! What on earth were you doing?"

"Getting a preview of Hell."

"The Chamber of Commerce has busted its butt to make tonight's event a success. The least you could have done was pretend to enjoy yourself."

"I'd need a can of laughing gas."

"That's snooty, selfish, and just plain spoiled. Brother Perce is a walking bruise. Do you hear him complain? No sir. If somebody pinched his cheek, he'd turn the other one." (Righteous whimpers from the back seat.) "You may not care for those boys, but they're doing their best, clinging to families and businesses by their fingernails. Despite that, they volunteer for their town. They think you can help. You oughta feel privileged."

She lowered her head. "You're right. I was mean. I'm sorry."

"I don't want you to be sorry," he replied, tossing her his handkerchief. "I want you to shape up. You're an actress. Act."

"I'll do my best," Mary Mabel promised. She blew her nose. In future, she resolved to be kind. She resolved to be generous. Above all, she resolved to act.

All Mary Mabel's stage training, she owed to her "Auntie" Irene, a woman who, like herself, had had a childhood fantasy of becoming an actress. When Auntie Irene had told her parents her dream, they were so horrified they ran out and found her a husband. He was a third-generation undertaker by the name of Bigelow. Auntie Irene spent the rest of her days wearing black. "'I am in mourning for my life,'" she'd say. And indeed she was. The closest she got to a life on the boards was bossing the Milwaukee Little Theater Guild.

Rehearsals were held on Tuesday and Thursday evenings and Saturday afternoons, except if there was a death in town, in which case they'd be cancelled. Auntie Irene was expected to attend the visitations. A visitation on a performance night meant the curtain was held till nine. In order not to delay things further, she'd wear her costume under her funeral duds and greet the mourners in full makeup. "The show must go on."

Auntie Irene began each practice with exercises in elocution and gesticulation. Guild members would stride about in grand circles, while she'd bellow instructions from the sidelines. "Breeeeeathe from your diaphragms! Expaaaaand those resonating cavities! Chins up! Chests out! Keep your mouths wide! Your foreheads high! Emote!"

Her actors looked pretty simple, but Auntie Irene reminded them that they'd be performing on a stage, not in somebody's kitchen. "Dramatic art is larger than life. King Lear raged on a heath, he didn't pick fights at the donut shop. Thanks to the magic of theatre, the audience shall willingly suspend its disbelief." Guild members agreed, noting Auntie Irene's recent triumph as Juliet.

Mary Mabel was cast in every production. When the play didn't have parts for children, her auntie put her on stage as a kitten or a footstool. This was because there wasn't anyone back at the funeral home to keep an eye on her. In addition to yard work, Brewster was up to his ears stacking coffins, clearing mice out of their upholstery, and cracking the joints of unruly cadavers.

As for Mr. Bigelow, he didn't keep an eye on anything but his corpses. Even when Auntie Irene took Brewster to her bedroom for private acting lessons, he'd stay below ground in the Land of the Dead — that's what Mary Mabel called the basement room where he did the preparations. When the upstairs vocalizing got out of hand, she'd wander down to keep him company. He rarely noticed her. When he did, he'd give her a nod as if she were a spirit passing through. Then his gaze would return to the middle distance, and he'd slowly inhale fumes from the jar of embalming fluids by his side.

His addiction didn't bother the bereaved. They appreciated his calm demeanor and took the glassiness of his eyes as shared grief. Like Auntie Irene, he was an actor who could play his role pickled, knowing exactly when to make a comforting gesture, or to pass a tissue, or to say: "Good evening, it's a great tragedy, so glad you could come."

Mary Mabel liked Mr. Bigelow. He cared about the dead more than most people care about the living. All of his clients' rough edges were smoothed away, their hair combed, ties knotted, and jewellery adjusted with absolute devotion. They were also treated to sympathetic patter. He'd wax enthusiastic about their obituaries, or tell jokes. When he worked on a child, he'd sing lullabies. For those who died friendless, he'd make up stories about stacks of condolence cards, and tell them not to be disappointed by a low turnout, there was a bad storm brewing. If they looked afraid, he'd hold their hands. "Don't worry," he'd whisper, "you'll be fine." And they were. By the time they went on display, his clients appeared more lifelike than the actors at the Guild.

Mary Mabel liked to sneak into the visitation room to look at the baskets of flowers around the caskets. Mr. Bigelow made sure there were lots, even for those who couldn't pay. After admiring the flowers, she'd wander up and stare at the deceased. She was fascinated by their hands; they all seemed to be wearing pale silk gloves. Mostly, though, she concentrated on their eyelids. If she stared long enough, she began to imagine that the bodies were breathing. They weren't lost in a terrible void. They were sleeping soundly, at rest in a land where dreams are good and every dream comes true.

She wished her mama had had a Mr. Bigelow. Her mama wasn't at peace when they closed the lid. During the waiting-in, Mary Mabel had tried to climb into her coffin. They'd pulled her away, but not before she'd seen her mama's face. It was hard and disfigured. The mouth crooked. The chin black. The tips of the nose and ears missing. Mary Mabel was too young to understand about death, much less about frostbite. All she knew was that something terrible had happened to her mama and it was all her fault.

After lunch, Mary Mabel went over her speech in front of the bathroom mirror till it was time to go to the auditorium. The children's choirs were already there when she arrived, as bubbly as soda pop except for one little boy who sat in the back row crying. He'd gotten so excited he'd peed himself. Mary Mabel knew how he felt.

Soon the audience was gathering in the hall and the choirmasters were bundling their charges into nearby classrooms to await their entrance. The house opened. The crowd spilled in. Mary Mabel ran to her dressing room at the side of the stage, a closet filled with brooms, dustpans, and old boxes of decorations for school assemblies. Her heart did back flips. What if she froze? What if she fell into the orchestra pit?

Floyd gave her the half-hour call. The ten. The five. A thumbs-up. She peeked through the closet door to watch the first half. The house lights dimmed. The chatter subsided. The school band struck up "The Star and Stripes." The audience clambered to its feet and the show was off and running.

Floyd began by thanking the Chamber for its hospitality, stressing how the evening's proceeds would help to pay for downtown renovations. "Your attendance tonight is a tribute to your community spirit. Give yourselves a big hand." They did. "However, you haven't come to hear me speechify," he continued, preparing to introduce Brother Percy. "So with no further ado, please welcome a very special someone. The one — the only —"

The audience cheered before he could finish. At the sound of the roar, Brother Percy bounded on stage in his secondhand tails.

He strutted about, flapped his arms, and crowed like a rooster. This continued for some time until he realized that the crowd was staring at him in stunned silence. A confused voice pierced the hush. "Who's he? Where's Sister Mary Mabel?" A murmur of shared puzzlement.

Brother Percy clawed his head, bent over, and squinted into the auditorium. Bright red circles ballooned on his cheeks. There was a titter. Apparently people thought he was a clown doing a warm-up act. Brother Percy reeled upright. He put his hands on his hips, elbows out, and glowered. The titters grew. He popped his eyes. Squeals of delight. He wagged a bony finger. The house was in stitches. He foamed at the mouth. He shook his fists. He brayed. Yet the angrier he got, the more they laughed. Soon everyone was holding their sides, rolling in the aisles, pointing. Brother Percy stomped from the stage to a rousing ovation.

The children's choirs were also a hit. And then, in what seemed a blink, it was intermission. Proud parents slipped out for a smoke. Floyd gave Mary Mabel a fistful of recipe cards containing the audience questions that would conclude the show. He'd prepared a snappy answer for each. She was so afraid of blurting something stupid that she memorized them whole. A rumble of high spirits rolled back into the auditorium. The audience had returned for the star attraction.

Again the house lights dimmed. Again the chatter subsided. A spotlight on Brother Floyd. A fulsome introduction, thunderous applause, and suddenly Mary Mabel found herself outside her body, watching as she entered, curtsied, and blew kisses to the crowd.

She'd read that there are tribes in Africa that refuse to let anyone take their picture. They think it robs them of their soul. *They may be right,* she thought, *for that's how it is with stories. Each time we tell a memory, it becomes a little less our own. Soon our most sacred moments have been turned into public spectacle.* This truth overwhelmed her as she heard herself recite her miracle with the empty conviction of a parrot.

The first times she'd told it, she'd been an apostle aflame with a holy gospel. Yet weeks of rehearsing it to anyone who'd listen had doused her fire. She gesticulated like a puppet, while Auntie Irene strode inside her head bellowing, "Chin up! Chest out! Emote!" Mary Mabel's text was letter-perfect, but it rattled from her lips as false as Miss Bentwhistle's teeth.

The crowd didn't care. They'd paid to see a star, and fix up Main Street. Mary Mabel struggled to breathe, as she mimed an elaborate laying on of hands. "It was at this moment that Timmy Beeford came back to life," she declaimed.

Applause. Her interview followed. Instead of answering the audience's questions, she spouted the quips she'd learned in her dressing room.

"What's your favourite hobby?" asked a pleasant woman in the front row.

"My favourite hobby is liking people."

"Can you tell us about your parents?"

"Papa is a man of many talents. He's not afraid to get his hands dirty. Oh, and he loves to travel. Mama, alas, passed away when I was two."

Oohs and *ahs*. The easy commiseration filled her with guilt.

A dozen more inquiries, then the children's choirs regrouped for the grand finale and Floyd announced a special free-will offering. The plates got passed as the crowd rose for a heartfelt sing-a-long of "Amazing Grace." Tears and hankies all around. At song's end, Mary Mabel clasped her hands to her breast. "May sunshine fill your hearts, and happiness warm your tomorrows."

An eruption of cheers and whistles. She wanted a bath. *At least it's over*, she thought. She was wrong. At that moment, the auditorium doors crashed open. Standing in the entrance was a tramp clutching a white cane in one hand and a tin cup in the other.

"Where am I?" the blind man cried.

"The auditorium," someone volunteered.

"I'm looking for Sister Mary Mabel McTavish!"

"I'm here," Mary Mabel called out uncertainly.

The man lurched forward, swinging his cane with abandon. The audience froze, except for the ones by the aisle who ducked. Brother Floyd led him to centre stage, where he fell on his knees and raised his arms in supplication. "Sister, you see before you a miserable wretch! A beggar man blinded by moonshine! I repent of my sins! Help me to see the light, I beseech you, for I would be whole!"

Mary Mabel's head reeled, stomach heaved. *Mama*, she prayed, *please do something*. But her mama was as far away as the moon.

A voice rose from the middle of the auditorium. "Heal the man, Sister!" Others joined in. "Heal the man! Show us your stuff!"

She glanced helplessly over the crowd. "I can't!"

"Why not?" the blind man pleaded.

"Do like the Lord," yelled the pleasant woman in the front row. "Spit on your fingers! Touch his eyes!"

The air swarmed with buzzing tongues. "Do it, Sister! Do it! Do it!"

"Give 'em what they want," Floyd whispered. He took her hands and forced them to her lips. Her fingers were cold as icicles. She placed them on the blind man's lids. He let out a series of high-pitched yelps and convulsed, flopping about the floor on his back. Spittle spewed from his mouth. Then he bounced to his feet. Threw away his cane. Rubbed his eyes. Danced.

"I can see!" He spun her around. "Praise Jesus, I can see."

The audience was on its feet, stomping and cheering.

"The plates!" Floyd screamed at the ushers. "Pass the plates, goddammit!" He grabbed the tramp's arm and hustled him out the back door, as collection plates materialized throughout the house under a glare of flashbulbs. The audience surged forward. Souvenir programs were thrust in Mary Mabel's face.

"Stay back!" It was her friends from the Chamber of Commerce. They formed a human shield and shuffled her out back to the Olds. Her beggar had vanished.

"Best show we've had in Flint, ever!" cheered the Chamber president, thrusting bags of cash at Brother Floyd. "Come back anytime!"

They peeled rubber, tearing into the night with a police escort.

The escort departed at the edge of town, and they headed off to their next stop: Kalamazoo. Brother Percy's forehead bubbled with dark thoughts.

Floyd tried to cheer him up. "They loved you, Perce."

"Dey affed!"

"Yeah, but they weren't laughing *at* you. They were laughing *with* you!"

Mary Mabel agreed. At the sound of her voice, the reverend screeched like an eaglet.

"So be a Grumpy Gus," Floyd said, and turned to Mary Mabel. "You were the cat's meow." He cataloged the virtues of her performance: the confidence, theatrical flair, and elocution "clear as a bell at the back of the house." (Thank you, Auntie Irene.) Last but not least, he spoke in awe of her healing. "Yes sir, you have the gift. I knew it from the moment I laid eyes on you."

"I don't understand," she said. "There was no fire running down my arms. My hands were blocks of ice."

"Could've fooled me. You were damn electric. Did you see that bugger twitch?" They neared a railway crossing. Floyd pulled the car to the side of the road. "Just a sec." He got out and opened the trunk. From its depths, the tramp unfolded like an accordion, clutching a knapsack and a bottle of booze.

"Much obliged for the ride."

Floyd gave him a wad of cash. "Adios, amigo." Two seconds later, he was back in the car and they were off, leaving their friend by the side of the tracks.

Mary Mabel was dumbfounded. "Why was our blind man hiding in the car?"

"He wasn't hiding. He was hitching a ride to his favourite terminal."

"In the trunk?"

"He's a little ripe for the back seat, don't you think? Besides, these years of darkness have made him sensitive to the light."

"That doesn't explain why you gave him money."

"A little gift to get him started on his new life. Surely you don't begrudge charity?"

Mary Mabel glanced in the rear view mirror at Brother Percy. He was staring out the window, fevered lips moving soundlessly in dark communion with the heavens.

DÉJÀ VU *in* KALAMAZOO

By the time they hit Kalamazoo, it was the middle of the night. Mary Mabel checked into her room and crawled under the covers, but sleep was out of the question. Each time she closed her eyes, she imagined she was behind the wheel of the Olds, careening down a mountain with Floyd's foot on the accelerator. She dove for the brakes, but there weren't any. She tried to steer, but the wheel came off in her hands.

She turned on the bed lamp. Truth is simple; facing it is hard. With help from Floyd, the papers had invented her past. As of tonight, folks also thought she'd healed the blind. But that was a lie, wasn't it? In her mind's eye, she saw the Olds fly off the road and plummet into a bottomless canyon.

The phone rang. It was 4:00 a.m. She gritted her teeth, determined to give her partner a piece of her mind. Only it wasn't him.

"What's up, Buttercup?"

"Mr. Doyle! Do you know what time it is?"

"Best time to catch you unescorted. By the way, nice show tonight. Especially that bit with the blind guy."

A hole opened up in the pit of her stomach. "You were in Flint?"

"The Chief's put me on your tail with a byline."

"Where are you calling from?" she whispered.

"Down the hall. I drove in as soon as I wired my story. Mind if I drop by?"

"I don't entertain gentlemen in my room. In any case, I'm sleeping."

"Too bad. We've got lots to talk about."

"No we don't."

"Bets? I just got back from Cedar Bend."

She dropped the receiver.

"Hey, you still there?"

"Yes," she recovered.

"I'm doing a feature on your childhood for the national rotogravure. If you're worried about your reputation, I'll meet you in the lobby."

Mary Mabel's biographer was sprawled on an easy chair in the conversation nook to the left of the registration desk. A worn briefcase was on the coffee table in front of him. They were alone, except for the night clerk dozing by the switchboard. Figuring the best defence is a good offense, she strode over, head high. "How dare you trouble my former neighbours? You have no right to spy on me."

Doyle looked up casually. "Says who?"

"How long do you intend to hound me?"

"How long do you intend to stay in business?"

"I'm not in business."

"Spare me. I hear your ministry claims you found a missing toddler through the power of prayer."

Mary Mabel took a deep breath. "Mr. Doyle, I know you plan to ruin me. At least let me ruin myself. For the record, I never found anyone."

"Oh?" He gave her a wry look. "That's not what they say in Cedar Bend." She stared in disbelief as he pulled a deck of photographs from an envelope in his briefcase and handed her the one on top. "See anyone you recognize?"

It was a picture of a group of men outside the barber shop. "That's Mr. Whitby, the barber," she said cautiously. "When I was three or four, he'd spin me around on his chair." She pointed at a man in suspenders. "I think he ran a junk shop. And this man raised chickens. He always wore bandages on account of they pecked his hands raw. The rest I don't remember. Why?"

"They're the town council. Each of them swears you saved not one child, but a couple of dozen. They also say you rescued an old woman from a bear and resurrected a dog."

"I didn't."

"Are you calling the town council a pack of liars?"

"Yes ... no ... I ..."

"You were young," he prompted. "You've forgotten."

"I'd have remembered things like that."

He shrugged. "Commemorative plaques are popping up everywhere."

"Mr. Doyle, those stories aren't true and you know it."

He held up his hands. "I only know what folks tell me. So zip your lip. False modesty will spoil your reputation and insult your friends."

Mary Mabel paused. "Why are you protecting me?"

"You don't know?"

Her stomach did somersaults. "You care about me?"

The mention of affection made Doyle itchy. He cleared his throat. "I have a few more pictures. Let me know if they spark memories. Any details'll help my story."

The first photo was easy. "That's Mr. Woo. He hasn't changed a bit. He bribed me with almond cookies to stop playing hop-scotch in front of his restaurant." The next few were of Slick's Lodge. She played dumb. After these were pictures of the house where she was born. The place looked smaller than she remembered, and it was odd and a little sad to see that tree growing through it; when she was little, its branches barely tapped her window pane.

Then came pictures of the park. "That's the war memorial. Teenagers went there to smooch. In winter, these picnic tables were moved into a big circle around an outdoor skating rink." He passed a picture of the playground equipment. Mary Mabel paused. "That's where they found Mama," she said quietly. "It always felt strange to see kids having fun where she died." She didn't mention that when the wind whistled through the swings, she thought it was her mama's voice, crying her name. She'd run around in circles screaming, "Mama, I'm here. Mama, I'm here."

"One to go," he said, and handed her the final snapshot. It was of two women and a baby. At first, Mary Mabel didn't recognize them, but when she saw how Doyle studied her reaction she took a closer look.

"Oh, my God. Mama! She looks different than I remembered."

Mary Mabel gazed at the photo in wonder. Time had betrayed her memory as surely as the visitations had blinded her eyes. But the longer she stared, the more her childhood resurrected before her. *Yes*, she thought, *this is Mama, who washed me in a tin tub, brushed the curls off my forehead, and told me stories to keep away the night.*

Doyle passed her another surprise. It was a small package wrapped in newspapers and elastic bands. She opened it and nearly fainted. There before her was a green saucer with gilt around the rim, the mate to the teacup her papa had smashed when he stormed off from the Academy.

"What's the big deal?" Doyle asked. "It's only a chipped piece of china."

"It's not!" she exclaimed. "It's a sign. Oh Mr. Doyle, you've been sent by an angel. You're the answer to a prayer." She gripped his arm and kissed him on the cheek.

He jolted backwards. "You're pretty frisky when you're off your leash."

The night clerk roused. He gave them a look and coughed. Mary Mabel removed her hand from Doyle's arm. The clerk pretended to read the sports pages.

She lowered her voice. "I have a confession. Timmy Beeford's resurrection wasn't as advertised. It wasn't God inside me. It was Mama. Sometimes she's come to me as a voice in my head, other times as a vision of light. Mr. Cruickshank said not to tell anyone: 'Talk to God, they call you holy: talk to ghosts, they call you nuts.' Anyway, lately she hasn't come at all. Tonight, when I touched that blind man's eyes, I felt absolutely cold. Then, on the road to Kalamazoo he got out of the car trunk and Mr. Cruickshank gave him money. I had a terrible feeling the whole thing had been faked. I was afraid Mama had abandoned me."

Doyle blinked like he'd inhaled smelling salts. "You do understand that I'm a reporter, don't you?"

"Yes," she replied smartly. "But you won't betray my secrets."

"Why not?"

"Because Mama sent you. There's always a reason for what she does, even when I don't understand it."

"Slow down. I wasn't sent by your mother. I was sent by Mr. Hearst."

"That's what you think. I prayed for her to give me a sign if tonight's healing was real. Well, she answered right away, didn't she? You brought me her picture and her saucer, things I thought had been lost forever."

"That's not a sign," Doyle said. "It's coincidence. I met the man who took that picture by accident: Jimmy McRay, father of your mama's best friend, Iris, the other one in the picture. As for the saucer, finding it was luck, taking it was chance."

"The world's too full of 'coincidence' for coincidence to be only coincidence. What looks like chance is part of a grand design. It's destiny."

"You read too many books."

"History has stranger twists than fiction," Mary Mabel shot back. "Everyday life, too. We say 'What a coincidence' and 'What a small world' all the time because in *real* life so-called flukes happen regularly. Oh, Mr. Doyle, if you want to know the truth about life, you mustn't limit yourself to the ordinary."

He gave her a curious look. "How much do you know?"

"Everything and nothing," she said, beaming.

"Well, you're right about one thing. I'm keeping your secrets. My reasons, however, have nothing to do with the supernatural."

Mary Mabel laughed. "You men can never admit you're wrong."

It was almost dawn. Mary Mabel happened to glance out the window. A tramp with big ears was squatting on the curb across the street. He rolled over, avoiding her eyes. *Poor man*, she thought, *I wonder how long he's been watching us, envying our comfort.*

She turned back to Doyle, about to say something, when her skin went alive with goosebumps. That tramp across the road, there was something familiar about him. She knew him from somewhere, from a moment tucked in her memory she couldn't quite find. Impossible. She'd never been to Kalamazoo before in her life.

She looked back across the road. The tramp was gone. Was she losing her mind? No, just tired. Déjà vu from too little sleep. She shook it off. *Folks on the skids have the same look everywhere,* she thought.

"I should get to bed," she said. "I look forward to talking to you again, though. Tomorrow, maybe? Mama never steers me wrong."

"Sure," he winked. "Keep that saucer, if you'd like. The pictures, too. They've already been shot by *King Features*."

"Thanks." She shook his hand.

He held it. "Be careful who you talk to about this 'mama' stuff."

"Oh, I'm very careful, Mr. Doyle."

"Another thing. 'Mr. Doyle' makes me feel like an old man. Call me K.O."

"K.O. All right ... K.O." Mary Mabel collected her new treasures. "Good night ... K.O."

The feel of his name on her tongue gave her tingles. "K.O., K.O., K.O.," she whispered to herself as she skipped upstairs. The name tickled her lips. In fact, it was the most exciting name she could imagine. "K.O., K.O., K.O."

She couldn't wait to whisper it again.

The BARONESS

There were cheers and tooting horns as word spread that the train carrying the baroness had pulled into the station. The chief of the Los Angeles Police Department, supported by thirty of his finest, ordered the crowd to stay behind the barricades.

Meanwhile, on Track 3, the baroness and her handmaid descended from their private car. They were met by a short, chubby gentleman sporting flashy cufflinks, dyed hair, and astonishingly white teeth. He offered the baroness his arm and led the pair along the red carpet that had been rolled along the platform, through the station, and outside to a white stretch limousine. Two security men followed, flanked by sharpshooters. They carted an imposing strongbox filled with jewels to a waiting Brinks truck. Everyone knew these jewels were worth ten million dollars.

A convoy of police motorcycles, sirens blazing, spearheaded the drive to the Beverly Hills Hotel, where the baroness had taken the Presidential Suite. She rode with her limousine window down, waving at clusters of well-wishers, and noting with pride the many billboards along Sunset Boulevard that welcomed her arrival.

Los Angeles area papers featured front-page photographs of the baroness being greeted by the hotel staff, who were spiffed up in gold braid, crisp collars, and wingtips. Press and radio reported the ceremony that followed in the Polo Lounge, during which the manager presented her with the keys to the hotel, and the mayor offered her the keys to the city.

For her part, the baroness read a gracious statement thanking Los Angeles for its hospitality. "We look forward to the opportunity to thaw and revivify in this City of Angels, having laboured to teach the social graces to the colonial rustics of Canada." She concluded with the announcement that the following day she would be receiving delegations from city and state banks. The day after that, she would be giving an audience to those intimates to whom her secretary had sent official invitations. The list was select and confidential. She trusted that the press would respect her privacy.

The idea that she was a baroness, or rather that she *ought* to be a baroness, had first occurred to Miss Bentwhistle in a dream she'd had shortly after moving in with the Mandibles.

Maybe it was because of sleeping at the rectory, or maybe it was the extra laudanum, but Miss Bentwhistle dreamt that the entire town had turned up at her reception for Mary Mabel dressed in Bible clothes. She wasn't entirely sure that it was appropriate for the Reverend Mandible to be wearing dress socks with a toga, but this was the least of her worries. She had just discovered that she was stark naked. Not only that, but she was pinned to a cross, and everyone had crowded around to stare at her privates.

"Let him who is without sin cast the first stone," intoned the Reverend Mandible. The entire St. James Board of Session began throwing rocks at her head. She was further plagued by an insufferable whining from the cross to her left. It was Clara Brimley. "If you don't get me down from here, I'm telling my father!"

"Go to hell," snapped Miss Bentwhistle. Lo and behold, the ground opened up and a screaming Miss Brimley was spirited off by a cauldron of devils chewing at her entrails. That didn't stop the wailing. Now it was coming from the cross to her right. There dangled head secretary, Miss Dolly Pigeon. "What's to become of us, Lizzy?"

"Fear not, oh good and faithful servant," replied Miss Bentwhistle, "for you shall be with me in paradise."

No sooner said than done. The clouds parted, it was a beautiful sunny day, and Miss Bentwhistle wasn't on a cross, she was dripping ermine and pearls on a chaise lounge beside a swimming pool. Dolly was there, too, sitting on a beach towel in a maid's uniform, giving her a pedicure. A waiter set down a tray of highballs. It must be a party. Miss Bentwhistle recognized a number of the guests. Wasn't that Douglas Fairbanks and Mary Pickford playing footsie in the shallow end? And W.C. Fields passed out on an inner tube? Why, there was Harpo Marx chasing a dazzle of chorus girls down a water slide, and Charlie Chaplin doing the dog paddle.

"So you're the Baroness." The voice was familiar. She looked up to see Clark Gable, eyebrows at a rakish tilt. Was he referring to her? Absolutely. She couldn't quite remember how it had come to pass, but beyond question she was a baroness. The Baroness Bentwhistle of Bentwhistle in fact. No wonder everyone had started to bow and curtsy.

Next thing she knew, she was in the back seat of Mr. Gable's roadster with her legs in the air. She licked her lips. He smelled of marmalade.

"Want me to put some butter on it?" Mr. Gable asked.

"Mmmm," she moaned. "I'll take it any way you give it to me."

"As you wish."

How strange. Mr. Gable sounded like the rector's wife.

Miss Bentwhistle had opened her eyes. Mrs. Mandible was standing over her with the breakfast tray.

"Doesn't anyone knock around here?" the headmistress grumped as she propped herself up against a pillow.

"I *did* knock," Mrs. Mandible countered. "Three times. I asked if you'd care for your breakfast. You hollered, 'Yes, yes! I want it now!'"

Miss Bentwhistle eyed her with suspicion. "What else do you imagine I 'hollered'?"

"I'm sure I don't remember." Mrs. Mandible smiled discreetly. She placed the tray on Miss Bentwhistle's lap and departed.

The headmistress wasted no time. She put her breakfast aside, snuggled back under the sheets, pulled the covers up to her ears, closed her eyes, and tried to picture herself back in that roadster. Mr. Gable! Oh, Mr. Gable! Oh! Oh!

Oh, it was no use! She cast a critical eye at the light fixture on the ceiling. The closest she'd ever get to Clark Gable would be at the movies. As for the rest of it, being a baroness ...

Her eye fell on her family crest and genealogical parchments from the Heralds' College of Westminster sitting on twin easels at the foot of the bed. At the Academy, those squiggles tracing her lineage back to an eleventh-century English barony had seemed important. They made her an aristocrat. A minor aristocrat, perhaps, but an aristocrat nonetheless. That mattered in a colonial hinterland like London, Ontario, where dynasties were counted on three fingers and indoor plumbing was a source of pride.

It mattered not a whit, however, in the world of her dreams. In that world, the world of international affairs, soirées, and pool parties, she was but a social asterisk, a squiggled worm at the end of a hook descended from Horatio Algernon Bentwhistle V, himself a worm on a hook on a line on a document teaming with hundreds of other worms and hooks on lines, all leading back to that scurvy pair of worms at the top of the parchment — Henry the Bent and his child bride Mathilde. And who were they, this army of Bentwhistles? They were nobodies, that's who. Savages and imbeciles whose sole function in life was to have reduced the space available for her inscription on the family tree.

Miss Bentwhistle knew this for a fact, thanks to a certain Dr. Archibald Moorehead, an itinerant professor from Liverpool who years ago had given a lecture tour throughout the Dominion to various chapters of the Imperial Order of the Daughters of the Empire. According to Dr. Moorehead, Canada was teeming with blue blood whose birthrights had been forgotten in the dustbins of history. It was a tragedy that he would rectify for a modest fee.

Intrigued, the headmistress had invited him back to the Academy. She was thrilled to discover the name Bentwhistle listed in his well-thumbed copy of *Debrett's Peerage*, and immediately hired him to research her genealogy. She also agreed to underwrite the publication of his research, and to pay for his efforts in securing official documents from the Heralds' College of Westminster. The Bentwhistle Family Tree and Coat of Arms subsequently graced the Academy's dining hall. However, the monograph, all copies bought up at her expense, graced its fireplace.

It seems that *paterfamilias* Henry the Bent had arrived in England with the Norman invasion. He was reputed to have been a fierce warrior who took particular delight in dismembering the battlefield dead. William the Conqueror made him a baron for clearing the Whiftle Bog of Saxons. The original manor house was essentially a cave in one of the few outcroppings of rock on the barony. From here, the Baron of Bentwhiftle presided over a few thousand acres of inhospitable moors noted for swamp gas so vile it was rumoured to drive men insane. The family needed no such excuse. Lacking other diversion, it rutted itself into a frenzy of inbred half-wits, their spawn the tangle of worms and hooks and lines that cluttered Miss Bentwhistle's prized parchment. These were her relatives, dammit, addled cousins, legitimate and illegitimate, a hundred times removed. Worse, many were still alive, breeding like maggots in north England bog country, spreading like germs throughout the Empire.

Now, lying in bed staring at her family tree, Miss Bentwhistle was overcome with despair. It was all so squalid. She dabbed her eyes and reached for the laudanum. A capful turned into a tumbler, and soon Miss Bentwhistle was possessed of the most wondrous visions. History came alive as she imagined innumerable lines of Bentwhistles poisoned, garroted, and beheaded, their skulls cleft by broadswords, their gullets stuffed with coals, and their bodies drawn and quartered, dipped in lye, and roasted on spits. Those living when Dr. Moorehead wrote his drivel fared no better. Worm by miserable worm, she saw them sucked into the quagmire whole, or succumbed to scurvy and pox, consumption and clap, their puling infants ground beneath carriage wheels, poor things, or savaged by birds of prey.

Last but not least, she conjured the death of the current baron. According to the monograph, the barony had become so reduced that he and his family lived without servants in a small cottage, subsisting on the goodwill of squatters. The headmistress pictured them gobbling a tin of tainted veal. As they fell to the earthen floor, befouling themselves in agony, vermin feasted on their living flesh.

In the midst of such happy thoughts, Miss Bentwhistle became aware of distant knocking and a voice remarkably like Mrs. Mandible's asking if the breakfast dishes might be cleared.

"Go away," Miss Bentwhistle replied, or imagined she replied. Her voice was low and gravelly, like a gramophone winding down. Nonetheless, it roused her sufficiently that she realized she was no longer in bed. She was standing in front of that genealogical chart from Westminster. Something odd caught her eye, something she had never noticed before. A tiny *d.* and date of death were attached to every name but her own.

Why, it was a miracle, the document transformed in accordance with her visions!

A light dawned through the fog, a truth self-evident. As the sole surviving descendent of Henry the Bent, she wasn't simply the beleaguered headmistress of some bankrupt girl's academy (correctional institute) in the colonies. She was the rightful heir to the family barony. Indeed, she was none other than the Baroness Horatia Alice Bentwhistle of Bentwhistle!

Stunned by the revelation, the baroness staggered to the chest of drawers for support. En route, she realized that her left hand held the pot of India ink from the writing table. A recently dipped quill was in her right. Even in her fragile state, the nature of her miracle was apparent. Her father had been a master calligrapher, a skill which he had put to good use revising the wills and financial statements of his clients. She had clearly inherited his gift. Her alterations of the little *d*'s for death appeared genuine, the script exact, the chronologies plausible. A veneer of dust from the rectory's window sills and who would be the wiser?

All the same, Miss Bentwhistle was horrified at the knowledge that she'd altered a royal document. It was one thing to play tricks on the neighbours, quite another to forge one's way into a barony. She imagined an army of Beefeaters descending on the rectory to cart her off in leg irons. She slipped the evidence under the bed and ran to the closet, where she hid for the next half hour.

Things became clearer in the dark. There was no need to worry about the law. No one knew about her inventions but herself. Besides, she owned the document and could do with it as she pleased. The worst that could be said about her was that she had wished her relatives dead. Well, who hadn't?

Miss Bentwhistle crept out of the closet, navigated to the bed, and retrieved her folly. The sight of her handiwork no longer terrified her. It made her heartsick. Oh, the fruits of delirium! The addenda could never be erased. Her precious parchment, her pride and joy, was ruined. In happier days, she might have ordered another, but the Heralds' College demanded cash in advance, and royally certified gilt calligraphy was now beyond her means.

This was but another entry in her catalogue of woe. She fretted through the index: her Academy's implosion, her financial straits, her inevitable confrontation with the town, and the humiliation sure to follow. It was too much to bear.

Miss Bentwhistle rarely thought about God. Since she was a regular at St. James, she figured she didn't have to. At the moment, however, there was no one else to turn to. So with nothing to lose, she fell on her knees and did what she always did during her bouts of piety. She made God a bargain. If He would fix her problems, she'd believe in Him and never sin again. To prove she was serious, she began to mortify her flesh, whipping herself silly with the sash of her housecoat.

The stratagem paid off. Whether from boredom, amusement, or a sense of professional obligation, God threw her a lifeline. His assistance came by way of a powerful memory of the "Introduction to Philosophy" course Miss Bentwhistle had taken at Trinity College, University of Toronto. Professor Slater had peered around the lecture hall and declaimed: "If a tree falls in a forest, and no one is around, does it make a sound?" He'd proceeded to yammer away about some eighteenth-century Irishman by the name of George Berkeley who believed that nothing exists unless it is perceived — "to be is to be perceived" — and, consequently, that material objects are no more than ideas. What nonsense. Trust the Irish!

Still, Miss Bentwhistle had appreciated the practical applications of this philosophy. Dust behind the tea cabinet didn't exist unless one rearranged the furniture. Neither did young men in women's dormitories, provided they were spirited in after dark. Poverty and injustice likewise disappeared the instant one turned one's back on them.

A convert to Mr. Berkeley's thesis, she'd stopped attending her classes in the hope that they, too, would cease to exist. Come the mid-term report, however, her professors concluded that it was *she* who didn't exist. Happily, they altered their deduction at year's end thanks to the perceived evidence of essays, which she'd bought, and exams, which she'd arranged for friends to write on her behalf.

Such were the memories that the good Lord sent the headmistress now in her hour of need. He also tossed in an epiphany. Miss Bentwhistle grabbed it. "'To be is to be perceived,'" she exclaimed in full eureka. "*Ergo, ipso facto, a priori*, to be perceived is to *be!*"

In a blaze of tautological insight, she grasped that it wasn't important for her to actually *be* a baroness; it was only important for people to *perceive* that she was. She cackled with the enthusiasm of a madwoman. Empirically speaking, hadn't the use of appearances been her principal *modus operandi* since her father's demise? If she'd managed to wring privileges as a mere Middlesex County Bentwhistle, think what she might accomplish as an English noble!

Euphoric, Miss Bentwhistle saw her problems resurrected as opportunities. The annotations on her family tree, for instance. According to Mr. Berkeley, material objects are simply ideas. The document from the Heralds' College was a material object. *Ergo*, the irrefutable syllogism: "My document is simply an idea! An idea I've improved upon!" Best of all, those improvements provided her with *prima facie* evidence of her aristocratic *bona fides*.

The joys of philosophy.

She paused to remember dear Professor Slater and his lonely tree in the forest, the one that fell unobserved. Did it make a sound? The answer was clear. Of course not. A corollary to the riddle: "If somebody commits forgery, and no one notices, has a crime occurred?" Likewise, no. More to the point, who cared? If her peccadillo ever came to light, she'd blame it on one of her girls. She'd choose a delinquent whose family hadn't contributed to an endowment fund. It would serve them right, the cheap bastards.

However, there was no need to fear discovery. The current Baron of Bentwhistle was an illiterate pauper who stuck to his bog. If he wouldn't know what she'd done, who would? The title "Baron" might impress folks on this side of the pond, but when it came to British nobles, barons were the lowest of the low. Even lower in the case of her family, according to Dr. Moorehead, whose monograph had kindly noted that it was "over a century since the last Baron of Bentwhistle took his seat in the House of Lords, owing to the law excluding the bankrupt and insane." In short, the name Bentwhistle was a nothing beneath notice, its barony a pustule on the rump of history. She could forge a new life undetected.

Too much happiness is hard on the nerves. In mid-cavort, Miss Bentwhistle collapsed in despair. A new life? Here? In London, Ontario? Her credit was exhausted. A peerage would buy less than a month's reprieve. If she was to fulfill her destiny, she'd have to relocate. But where? She thought of the other London, the *real* London across the sea — but *that* London wouldn't give two hoots for her title. She imagined the city's hostesses turning to their butlers: "What, a baroness to tea? Put her in the kitchen with the squires." If not London, England, the continent? That would mean dealing with Frenchmen. As for those *other* continents? Be serious.

Down for an instant, Miss Bentwhistle bounced back like a punching doll. For God had tapped her on the shoulder and reminded her of this morning's dream. Mr. Gable. Hollywood.

Of course! There was nothing that fascinated Americans more than British nobility: it was the one thing they didn't have. And although being a baroness wasn't as good as being a queen, it was close enough for a cigar. She imagined herself as a sought-after house guest, rotating her way throughout the mansions of Beverly Hills and Hancock Park, with getaways to exclusive oceanfront retreats and Palm Springs spas. She'd have the nouveau rich and famous eating out of her hand. Most certainly, she'd be eating out of theirs.

Miss Bentwhistle paused. People see what they expect to see. All the same, if one's hawking a fake painting, it helps to have a nice frame. And if one's passing oneself off as a peer of the realm, it pays to look the part. She took a little medication and considered her needs. No self-respecting baroness would be caught dead without a fabulous wardrobe, a fortune in gems, and a maidservant. Miss Bentwhistle had none of the above. Not to fret. Thanks to Mr. Berkeley, she knew that material objects were simply ideas. *Ergo*, what she really needed were props.

Miss Pigeon flew over the moment she was called. She almost fell on her backside when Miss Bentwhistle pointed out the fine print on her family tree.

"I am the last of the Bentwhistles, Dolly," the noblewoman sighed. "The recent fire has awakened me to my ancestral duty. Much as I treasure my young ladies, I must close the Academy and take my proper place in society. Know that we have chosen you, dear friend, to serve as our cherished handmaid."

Miss Pigeon wasn't sure about the proper etiquette. To play it safe, she dropped to her knees and kissed Miss Bentwhistle's school ring. "Does this mean we're going to England?" She didn't like to complain, but damp weather got to her bones, and she had a fear of fog. What a relief to discover that they'd be taking an extended vacation to Los Angeles instead.

The headmistress tapped her nose. "Naturally, this must remain confidential until we leave town."

"When will that be?"

"Perhaps weeks, perhaps days. In the interim, you are to scurry here before and after school. To refine your social graces, you shall be quizzed on the finer points of Emily Post. To acquire a proper accent, you shall mimic the recordings of Beatrice Lillie. Further, you shall memorize lists of aristocratic titles and shall invent personal anecdotes relating to each. These tales will be dropped at L.A. cocktail parties."

"You want me to lie?"

"In America, it's not lying. It's expected. In any event, better a liar than a bore. Putting one's hosts to sleep is an unforgivable sin."

Miss Pigeon had another concern. Would she be expected to drink alcohol at these parties?

"Not at all. You can stand at the front door and hang coats."

Finally, Miss Pigeon was troubled by her new title: Mistress Dolly, Keeper of the Wardrobe.

"What's the problem?"

"'Mistress.' It's unclean."

The headmistress sighed: Baptists could be so literal.

Miss Bentwhistle still needed baronial gear and seed money. To acquire both, she placed two suitcases, her lacquered jewellery chest, and the decorative packing box from the Heralds' College in the truck of her Packard and drove to Toronto.

Her first port of call was Ends and Means, a discount store in the garment district that sold end-of-line quality fabrics to the formerly well-to-do. Shy of being seen in a thrift shop, its customers entered through a side door, collars up. Inside, they made their way down a set of stairs and along a dim corridor to a dingy showroom where they could buy the finest of satins, velvets, linens, and wools, providing they weren't fussy about colour or style.

Miss Bentwhistle grabbed the last quarter bolt of an alarming green brocade, a dozen yards of mauve taffeta, enough lace to curtain a house, ten pounds of Edwardian upholstery material, some ribbons and bows, and a box of assorted ivory buttons carved in the shapes of flowers, birds, and nuts. These textiles would be transformed into frocks and ballgowns overnight, courtesy of Mistress Dolly, a Rumpelstiltskin at the Singer sewing machine. Fortunately, English aristocrats weren't expected to be fashionable.

Next the headmistress headed to an appointment at Sleeman's and Sons, a firm at Bay and Bloor that dealt in antique jewellery. Mr. Sleeman was waiting for her at the well-lit table in his oak-panelled cocoon at the back of the store. The decision to sell her family heirlooms had been difficult, as the role of baroness required decoration. Miss Bentwhistle needed cash, however, and had scads of quality costume jewelry donated over the years for use in school plays.

She dickered with Mr. Sleeman for an hour, finally agreeing to trade her past for her future and a thousand dollars and change. It might have been more, but her granny's rubies turned out to be glass, and her opals were paste. "If they had been real, you would have lost them," Mr. Sleeman consoled. "Now you keep something more precious than money: a memory of your grandma."

"Spare me your folk wisdom," Miss Bentwhistle sniffed. She stuffed her jewellery box with lower-denomination bills, locked it in the trunk of her car, and headed off to the Rosedale address of Mr. Cornelius Blunt, a well-connected art dealer who'd done business with her father.

Suspiciously tidy for a bachelor, Mr. Blunt lived alone in an airy mansion full of well-dusted antiques. He escorted Miss Bentwhistle to the drawing room, where he drew the curtains and invited her to display her wares. She opened the lid of the decorative box from the Heralds' College, withdrawing the spoils that were hidden under her family tree: the stolen silver and artwork from St. James. (It was a relief to have the booty out from under her floorboards. Since the robbery, she'd been terrified the police would scour the rectory. Thank God they'd set their sights on her girls. She'd resolved never again to take laudanum before going to vespers.)

Mr. Blunt twiddled the left point of his waxed mustache. "An auction is out of the question," he observed dryly. "Fortunately, I have a ready customer for your *Annunciation*. Another gentleman of my acquaintance will be amused by your *Beheading of St. John*. As for the *St. Sebastian*, well, my dear, that's a little number few could resist." He picked up the St. James chalice and sighed. "We can't do much about the hardware, I'm afraid. It would be noticed hereabouts, and Europe's awash. Best to melt it down. I'll make the arrangements."

Discussions were brief. There was no one else she could trust to fence the goods, and although Mr. Blunt feathered his nest, he was eminently fair, understanding that unhappy clients could exact revenge with a well-placed phone call. He opened the secret vault behind his dart board and withdrew thick wads of cash; cheques could be traced. As he did so, Miss Bentwhistle made a mental check of her travel budget.

First, her assets: $4,000 from Mr. Blunt, $1,000 from Sleeman's, and $3,000 from Academy endowments. That made a grand total of $8,000.

Second, her expenditures. Bus trip to Chicago for herself and Miss Pigeon, $40. Three days at the Fairmont, $260. Private rail car to Los Angeles, $700. (This extravagance made her ill, but a baroness simply *cannot* ride in coach.) The Presidential Suite at the Beverly Hills Hotel, $175 a night x 7 nights = $1,225 a week. (Highway robbery, but a baroness needs the right address.)

Obscene tips, a driver and a stretch limo to taxi them to the best restaurants, $1,000 a week, including food and beverage. In short, it would take a grand to get to L.A., and over two a week until she got connected.

For a moment, Miss Bentwhistle considered banking her nest egg and staying put. With the average wage hovering at eighteen dollars a week, her current take was enough to allow her to tease out her days as a pitied boarder at the Twins Bed and Breakfast. The thought of it made her tremble. Yet she trembled even more at the hard truth that she stood to lose it all, for a successful launch required more than money. This fact had hit home the day before when Miss Pigeon had brought over a box of movie magazines, insisting that *Galaxy* and *Starlight Confidential* contained important information about their neighbours-to-be. "Things to talk about at cocktail parties."

The magazines were chock-a-block with publicity shots of the stars, articles about their impossibly happy lives, and invitations to join their fan clubs. Miss Bentwhistle had enjoyed a grim chuckle at the thought of thousands of plain Janes sitting at endless cafeteria tables in studio dungeons stuffing envelopes while waiting to be discovered. Then she'd realized the joke was on her. The stars had battalions of such envelope-stuffers, whereas she had a single secretary. One who had trouble with the word "mistress."

Miss Bentwhistle had been struck by a terrible corollary to Professor Slater's riddle: "If a baroness comes to town and nobody notices, did she ever arrive?" Before her title could take her anywhere, she'd have to attract public attention. But how? At first she'd taken comfort in Mary Mabel's success: "If the penniless seed of some drunken hobo can reap fame and fortune, so can I." Still, Mary Mabel had raised the dead. She, on the other hand, ran a burned-out school for delinquents.

Another prayer to God — "Save me and I *really* promise to sin no more" — had brought an inspiration. Its success, however, was contingent on Mr. Blunt.

After putting the art dealer's cash in her decorative box, Miss Bentwhistle pulled out a hankie and drew his attention to the tragic circumstances documented on her family tree. "I'm afraid there's been a death in the family. In fact, there've been a lot of deaths in the family."

Mr. Blunt arched an eyebrow. "Someone's been naughty."

Miss Bentwhistle ignored him, explaining that she was about to take a trip to California. "Might you have a client in Los Angeles who could introduce me around town? Particularly at the banks? I'll be bringing the fabled Bentwhistle Jewels."

Mr. Blunt smiled. He knew exactly the person she needed. Dr. Howard "Howie" Silver, Dentist to the Stars. Dr. Silver had a thriving Bel Air practice, thanks to a winning combination of nitrous oxide and gossip which he dispensed with such indiscretion that his patients begged to book root canals. Keen to be seen, and to be *seen* to be seen, he was a fixture at all the right parties, the sort of man who'd be delighted to be known as the consort to a baroness. Especially a baroness trailing a treasure trove in fabled jewels.

Miss Bentwhistle paid Mr. Blunt a hundred dollars for his contact, put her loot in the trunk, and tootled over to Diana Sweets to celebrate her good fortune over a Honeydew and a double Toasted Ritz. Her ducks were in a row. She couldn't wait to confront the town fathers. What fun she'd have, telling them off and sailing out the door. If she succeeded, the rewards would beggar imagination. If she failed, she'd make a grand *jeté* from the Hollywoodland sign. It was as simple as that.

• • • •

Dr. Howard "Howie" Silver, Dentist to the Stars, was on cloud nine. Whether downing a highball or drilling a molar, he alerted everybody he knew that his good friend the Baroness of Bentwhistle was coming to town with the barony's fabled jewels. Not only that, he let them know that he was to be her Lord High Secretary and Steward of the Calendar, *pro tem*, responsible for lining up her social engagements in the city.

"The Baroness of Bentwhistle?"

"Yes," he gushed, "*the* Baroness of Bentwhistle."

After a little repetition the name invariably rang a bell. "The Baroness of Bentwhistle ... , oh yes. Isn't she the one who, uh...? Didn't she, um, uh...? Don't tell me. It's on the tip of my tongue."

Word spread.

A number of Dr. Silver's well-heeled patients and associates claimed to have spotted the baroness on trips to England, at Wimbledon and/or Trafalgar Square. One recalled sitting next to her in a box at the West End. Others remembered her winning horse at Ascot, while still others understood that the king had praised her charity work with the families of unemployed chimney sweeps. There was confusion as to her height, weight, age, and complexion, but on one point they were unanimous: they'd love to see her again. Could Dr. Silver arrange a luncheon? The dentist's social stock, always good, went through the roof. So did his rates.

Expatriate Brits in the Hollywood film community were caught by surprise. At parties and on the set, people asked them questions about the baroness. Pleading ignorance was inconceivable for those who'd padded their pedigrees or played royalty in period costume dramas. Besides, it's always useful to appear in the know. So they smiled, confirmed every rumour, and conveyed the impression that they had inside information to which they were sworn to secrecy. Things got dicey when studio honchos started to leave messages asking them to bring the baroness to upcoming galas. They agreed, and made a mental note to be hospitalized on the days appointed.

Meanwhile, as requested by the baroness, Dr. Silver made a point to speak to his contacts in the financial community. The bankers were excited at the prospect of representing a baroness. Customers had been shy since the Crash. Securing the confidence of British nobility would be terrific publicity. They thanked Dr. Silver for his referral, and put their staffs on high alert; any communication from the baroness was to be given top priority.

Miss Bentwhistle waited to telephone personally until she was safely holed up in Chicago's Fairmont. A call from the Windy City had more clout and raised fewer questions than one from the Canadian boondocks. Her conversations with the bankers were brief. "The Baroness of Bentwhistle here. We are en route to L.A. with the family jewels. May we pencil in a tour of your facilities?" Booking bank presidents turned out to be easier than booking parent-teacher interviews.

While Miss Bentwhistle lined up banks, Miss Pigeon scavenged old bricks and concrete chunks from derelict buildings. These were used to fill her ladyship's strongbox, giving weight to the legend of the Bentwhistle Jewels. The errands took thirty-five trips and ruined the inside of Miss Pigeon's purse.

Then it was off to the train station. It was the first time they'd worn their Ends and Means finery in public, and Miss Pigeon was embarrassed. "We look like the Easter Parade."

"Chin up, Dolly. We aristocrats are famous for our eccentricity."

Heads turned, children pointed, and undercover cops kept an eye out as the pair waltzed to the head of the ticket line trailing a dozen porters toting bags, wardrobes, and a most imposing strongbox. The station manager was there in a jiffy. One peek at the money in her suitcases and she was whisked to the V.I.P. lounge. Over a gin fizz, she booked a private sleeper car and a masseur. She also insured the bricks in her strongbox for ten million dollars.

As the train rattled across the country, L.A. was in a frenzy of anticipation. The banks openly warred to secure the Bentwhistle Jewels. Wells Fargo was the first to erect a sign welcoming the baroness. The others hopped on board. Overnight, billboards praising Her Ladyship sprouted like dandelions along Sunset Boulevard and Rodeo Drive. The Beverly Hills Hotel decorated its Polo Lounge for a special reception. The mayor insisted on making a speech. The press demanded front-row seats — especially Louella and Hedda, who breathlessly reported every rumour confirmed by the Hollywood Brits. At the station, vendors stocked up on Union Jacks. The L.A.P.D. prepared a motorcycle escort. And all over town, citizens made plans to attend the arrival of the city's latest curiosity.

The Baroness Horatia Alice Bentwhistle of Bentwhistle left the ceremony in the Polo Lounge of the Beverly Hills Hotel for a relaxing bubble bath in the marble tub of the powder room off the Spanish Colonial boudoir of the Presidential Suite. Everywhere she looked, she saw sprays of orchids, statuary, gold faucets, porcelain mosaics, and towels as thick as Devon cream.

"Heavens," she enthused, "I should have killed off my family years ago."

VIII

The RADIO CITY REVIVAL

HER SWEETIE

"**H**ow come you can put three tablespoons of sugar in your coffee and still stay skinny?" Mary Mabel asked.

Doyle batted his eyes. "It's my destiny."

She gave him a swat with her serviette. The two of them were having a pre-show snack in the backstage dressing room at the civic light opera house in Peoria, Illinois. Floyd and the stage manager were setting light levels, while a couple of ushers sat in the foyer folding programs. Aside from that, the theatre was empty.

She and Doyle had been seeing a lot of each other since Kalamazoo. It was hard not to. They were staying in the same hotels and her partners were no company whatsoever. Aside from work, Floyd's whereabouts were a mystery. Brother Percy, for his part, had gotten odder by the day. After being laughed offstage in Flint, he'd vowed to rest his jaw till he could "scorch those hyenas with a lick of hellfire." Now he was a hermit with no interest in hygiene, much less conversation.

That left Doyle.

Their socializing had begun quite innocently; Floyd had invited him on their visits with local sponsors. There were advantages all around. Doyle got material for his column, a heartwarming series on how Mary Mabel fulfilled heartland dreams, while their hosts got national exposure for their pet projects. This exposure, in turn, led to endorsements from county and state bigwigs. All of which enabled Floyd to double their guarantees.

Doyle was Mary Mabel's godsend at these events. Whenever she was about to die of boredom, she'd look his way and he'd toss her a grin that tickled her inside out. In fact, he was so much fun that she suggested he ride in the Olds. "Brother Percy can sit up front with you," she begged Floyd, "while K.O. keeps me company in the back."

Initially, Floyd welcomed her newfound warmth for the press, but he soon grew suspicious of her happiness. When Doyle raced her to the car, Floyd grumped, "Here comes Little Mary Mabel Sunshine." When Doyle gave her the giggles, he griped, "When was the last time Jesus bust a gut?" And when Doyle stretched his arm across the back seat behind her shoulders, he growled, "Don't touch the merchandise."

"I'm not merchandise," Mary Mabel shot back, "and K.O. is a perfect gentleman."

"Think of your image."

"My coverage does more for her image than any two-bit lecture from you," Doyle said.

It was true. His articles spared no detail of the tour or of Mary Mabel's growing list of miracles. Each night, folks swore that a touch of her hands had improved their lumbago, sinus, toothache, or palsy. Sometimes Doyle's descriptions went overboard. In Gary, Indiana, an old woman rose from her wheelchair; he reported that she danced the Charleston. In Muncie, a man born deaf and dumb made sounds; he had him reciting the Pledge of Allegiance.

Mary Mabel asked Doyle to stick to the facts. He said that's exactly what he'd done. When she protested, he said he guessed they had an honest difference of opinion about what happened. Then he accused her of wanting to censor the news and lectured her about the virtues of a free press.

As tales of the miracles multiplied, so did the crowds and the size of the tour's venues. Hearst gave Doyle more column inches, and had him snap photos for the rotogravure. Doyle was overjoyed. According to him, people were much more likely to read news that came with pictures, and to believe it, too.

If Doyle was hard-headed, he was also softhearted. That's what Mary Mabel loved most about him. Once a day, he snuck off to talk on the telephone. She'd thought he was placing bets at the track. It turned out he was phoning his mother. "Ma's an invalid," he said. "I feel guilty being away like this. She devoted her life to me, and now I'm gallivanting about the country when she needs me most."

He saw his ma as often as possible. Whenever the tour had a few days off, he'd take the all-night bus to Buffalo. Mary Mabel offered to go along to say a special prayer for her or to lay on hands. It's the only time she saw him really mad.

"Save it for the customers," he said. "Ma's sick. She's not going to get better."

"I don't offer guarantees. But what would be the harm?"

"The hope! The hope would be the harm. If you laid on hands and nothing happened, she'd blame herself."

"Why?"

"Wake up! If God answers prayers for some, why not others? Do they sin? Lack faith? Don't you feel responsible when prayers fail? Or when people throw away their pill bottles and suffer a relapse?"

"I'm not the one making claims in your newspaper," Mary Mabel said quietly.

He looked away. "It's not your fault. You're just doing your job. People can believe what they want to. As for Ma, I shouldn't worry. She's not one for malarkey."

Neither am I, Mary Mabel thought. But he was hurting so bad, she let it pass.

At first, the other press syndicates had economized by using stringers, but as Doyle's tales boosted Hearst's circulation, they assigned full-time reporters of their own. This meant Doyle had to rent his own car again, since Floyd couldn't afford to play favourites. He also informed Mary Mabel she'd best stop giving him special attention at host functions.

Nonetheless, the pair still managed to find private time. Mary Mabel insisted on having Floyd take her to their venues in the late afternoon. Doyle would arrive separately, parking his car some blocks from the hall. They'd hole up in the makeshift dressing rooms, munching treats and swapping tales, the door left open in the interests of public decency. If other reporters had discovered the arrangement, they had an alibi; they were doing an interview and would be happy to have the others join them. Fortunately, they were left to themselves. Doyle's rivals considered the tour a dog-and-pony show; luncheons aside, they drank till dawn and slept till curtain time.

On the day of their Peoria engagement, Mary Mabel had more on her mind than Doyle's addiction to sweets. Ever since they'd gone on the road, she'd felt uneasy. She'd put it down to nerves, bad dreams, and doubts about her partners. Still, her fear hadn't gone away, and now she'd placed it. She waited till Doyle had gobbled the last of his donut and slurped his coffee.

"K.O.," she said slowly, "I think I'm being watched."

"No kidding." He licked icing sugar from the down on his upper lip. "You've got a full house each night."

"I'm serious. Someone's following me."

Doyle paused. "Following you?"

"Yes. I feel like an animal being tracked."

He closed the dressing room door, pulled his chair beside her and leaned in. "Okay," he said. "Shoot."

"I've had the creeps since Kalamazoo. There are these eyes. They're everywhere. When I leave the hotel. Before and after the show. Sometimes I even feel them when I'm alone backstage or at night in my room."

"Do these eyes have a face?"

"No. To tell you the truth, I've never actually seen them. But they're there. Around the corner. Outside my window. Everywhere. It's a sixth sense."

He held her hand. "Tell Cruickshank to give you some time off."

"This isn't nerves," she said, pulling away. "Don't tell me you've never had a hunch."

"Okay," he allowed. "Sometimes I've spooked myself."

"And sometimes you've been right."

"So call the cops."

"With no proof?"

"Get Cruickshank to hire security."

"He'd say it would bring bad publicity."

At the mention of his name, Floyd waltzed in. "I suppose a breeze must have blown the door shut." He stared coldly at Doyle. "It's time for Sister to get ready."

"Sure thing." As he rose to leave, Doyle whispered in her ear, "I'll keep an eye out."

SCANDAL

William Randolph Hearst was immersed in clarity: the lake of spring water that filled the Neptune Pool at his castle at San Simeon. Soon guests would be arriving from Hollywood for a weekend of horseback riding. Early birds Erroll Flynn, Dick Powell, and Charlie Chaplin had already unpacked and hit the tennis courts. Marion was playing hostess. He'd join them, but for the moment preferred his solitude, swimming brisk lengths over the green mosaics that lined the basin floor, past the marble statues of Venus, mermaids and cherubs that graced the deck, and between the Roman colonnades that bracketed this piece of heaven.

It was a great day to be alive. At his age, every day was. Not that he wasn't at the top of his game. He'd been the first to puff Mary Mabel McTavish. He'd had the smarts to scout K.O. Doyle, too. Between the girl's story and the kid's rat-a-tat-tatty prose, the public couldn't get enough. Neither could he. As the miracles multiplied like the loaves and fishes, his brain had been on fire. Mary Mabel's life was the stuff of biopics. A natural for his Cosmopolitan Pictures. A vehicle for his sweetie. Marion was a bit old for the part, but so what? Better too old than too young. The idea of Shirley Temple raising the dead gave him gas.

"W.R.?" His secretary, Joe Willicombe, stood at the water's edge.

Hearst swam over. "Wipe that frown off your face, Willicombe. It's a glorious day to be alive."

"Oh yeah?" Willicombe handed him a teletype.

• • • •

Bobby Green, Bertie Green, and their friend Sammy Potter were kids with a dream. They wanted to be famous bank robbers. Stars of movie serials and comic books. They called themselves the Green Gang. Sammy'd wanted it to be the Potter Gang, but he got outvoted.

At ten, Bobby was the oldest and strongest, which is how he got to be leader. His first order of business was assigning the gang's handles. He called himself "Pretty Boy" on account of three girls had tried to kiss him. He called his brother "Scarface" on account of the cat scratch on his chin. And he called Sammy "Baby Face." Sammy complained that he wasn't a baby face, he was eight. Bobby said tough luck, he was the boss and if Sammy didn't like it he'd beat him up.

The Green Gang spent Saturday mornings in the alley behind the pool hall smoking their fathers' old cigarette butts. Between hacking fits, they argued about how to start their life of crime. The quarrel was usually about whether to rob the bank on the corner or one across town. If they robbed the bank on the corner, Miss Wilson the teller might recognize them and call their mothers. On the other hand, a bank across town meant making their getaway on bicycles.

One day Bobby arrived with sandpaper he'd swiped from his dad's toolbox. He said no matter which bank they robbed they should rub off their fingerprints. By lunchtime, they still had fingerprints, but they hurt like hell. Bobby said it didn't matter, this was their gangland initiation, and if they touched fingertips they'd be blood brothers. Bertie said that was stupid, they were already brothers except for Sammy. Sammy said who cared, he didn't want to be brothers with a couple of goofballs, anyway. The gang broke up for three days.

When they got back together again, Bobby said that rather than knocking off banks, maybe they should start small and work up. Sammy volunteered how he'd heard the cashier at the local Piggly Wiggly was epileptic. Maybe they could wait out front till he had a fit, and rob the place while he was flopping around. Bertie said they could be waiting forever; instead, maybe one of them could pretend to have a seizure and the other two could rob the place while the cashier was checking out the disturbance. It seemed like a pretty good plan. They took turns seeing who could do the best fit. Sammy won on account of he could spit, flail, and go cross-eyed at the same time.

Full of beans, they headed off to the Piggly Wiggly, but by the time they arrived Sammy had cold feet. Bobby was exasperated. All you have to do is fall down and start twitching, he said. Sammy wanted to know what if the cashier thought he was making fun of him and went wacko? Or what if the cashier thought he was for real and took him to the hospital? Or what if while he was jerking around he accidentally knocked over a wall of cans and they fell on his head and turned him simple?

Bobby said if the cashier went wacko he'd be so distracted they could steal the money for sure; that if Sammy tried to weasel out, *he'd* send him to the hospital; and that as for cans falling on his head, Sammy was already simple.

Sammy looked to Bertie for support. Bertie kicked a few stones; maybe Sammy was right, maybe this wasn't such a good idea.

Bobby blew up. How were they ever supposed to become famous bank robbers if they couldn't even steal a few bucks from a stupid Piggly Wiggly?

At that moment fate intervened. A blind hobo with a white cane and a knapsack tapped his way down the street. He set up shop near the store's entrance, arranging himself in a pitiful heap. The boys watched as occasional customers and passersby dropped spare change in the tin cup in front of him. Gosh, there was probably more money in that cup than in the Piggly Wiggly cash register.

A new plan was born. Sammy would go up to the blind man and pretend to be a good Samaritan. While they were talking, Bobby would steal the tramp's knapsack and Bertie would steal his cup. The boys tiptoed over. Bobby and Bertie got in position while Sammy cleared his throat. "Excuse me, sir. My Sunday school class is having a 'Good Deeds Week.' Can I do anything to help you?"

"Yeah," said the blind man. "You can bugger off."

"Nice talk," said Bobby. He dove for the knapsack. Bertie went for the tin cup.

"Jesus Christ!" the blind man swore. He swung his cane. The hook caught Bobby round the neck. The blind man yanked. Bobby sailed backwards and cracked his head on the pavement. On the backswing, Bertie got whacked on the forehead. The brothers were out cold.

Sammy ran screaming into the Piggly Wiggly, the hobo in hot pursuit. "Goddamn little fuckers!" the hobo hollered as he chased Sammy around the aisles pitching cans at his head.

The cashier got in the way. "This store is for customers only."

"Screw your granny!" the beggar roared, and shoved a jar of pickles through his teeth.

The cashier staggered backwards. He grabbed the gun from under the till. "Hands up!" The stress was too much. Bright lights flashed before his eyes. A white pain seared his brain. He lurched forward in full epileptic seizure, his finger jerking spastically on the trigger. *Bang! Bang! Bang!* Bullets ricocheted everywhere as he thrashed about the store. *Bang! Bang! Bang!* Racks toppled like dominoes. Produce sailed through the air. Bottles exploded like grenades.

Within minutes, three cop cars, an ambulance, and a cab of reporters were on the scene. It didn't look good. The windows of the Piggly Wiggly were blasted out. Two boys lay splayed and bloodied on the curb. The cashier, clutching a smoking gun, sprawled in the doorway drooling teeth. The brigade prepared for the worst. Then, through a haze of flour and cornstarch, came a little boy's voice: "Over here!"

In the far corner, Sammy Potter stood in triumph on the Coca-Cola cooler. When the bullets started to fly, the beggar had hopped inside for cover. The latch snapped shut. He was trapped.

The picture in the newspaper showed Sammy held aloft by the Green brothers in front of the grocery store. The caption read: "Potter Patriots to the Rescue." The accompanying article told how the young heroes had thwarted Wallace "Wally" Jones, a.k.a. "Whacker" Jones, a.k.a. "Wally the Cane," a desperado who'd tried to knock over the local Piggly Wiggly disguised as a blind man. The mayor announced that the boys would get medals for bravery. Meanwhile, "Whacker" Jones was in the clink, charged with robbery, aggravated assault, attempted murder, and loitering.

That should have been the end of it. But when the cops told Whacker he could make one phone call, he didn't ask to speak to a lawyer. He asked to speak to Brother Floyd Cruickshank of Holy Redemption Ministries.

Hearst closed his eyes. According to Doyle's teletype, Cruickshank was reached at the Biggs Hotel and Grill in Tulsa. Whacker Jones demanded money to pay for a big-time lawyer. Cruickshank denied knowing him and hung up.

"I've just spoken to Doyle," said Willicombe. "There's more."

Hearst held up his hand. "Let me guess. Whacker Jones feels betrayed. He's accused the ministry of interstate fraud, conspiracy, and racketeering. Claims he was hired as a plant. He wants to cut a deal with prosecutors. If the Piggly Wiggly charges are dropped, he'll sing."

Willicombe nodded. "Doyle says reporters from the competition cornered Cruickshank in a booth at the hotel grill. He repeated the line about Whacker being a stranger."

"At which point," said Hearst, "I presume they pulled out a picture of the two of them together."

"On stage. In Flint. With Sister Mary Mabel."

"Life is so predictable."

Willicombe smiled grimly. "Suddenly Cruickshank's memory improves. He remembers Whacker; he could have sworn he was legit. To hear him tell it, he's been duped by a two-bit extortionist. He and Miss McTavish are victims."

"The boys don't buy it."

"Natch. So he plays double or nothing. 'It's his word against ours,' he says. 'Print a word and I'll sue.' Then he makes a run for it."

Hearst slapped the water in fury. "We've invested a lot in this story!" He soothed his hands on the cool mosaics. "How does Doyle think it'll play?"

"On the one hand, he says Cruickshank's right. There's no proof of ministry wrongdoing. If folks read that the girl's been conned by a murderous tramp, she might even get sympathy."

Hearst watched a sparrow wash its feathers in the lap of a marble cherub. "On the other hand?"

"He thinks the threat to sue was a mistake. The boys are buzzing like flies on a dog turd. By tomorrow, they'll be running other claims of fraud, real or bought. Then watch out. When shit hits the fan, everyone stinks."

"Exactly." Hearst knew the game better than anyone. News is something that somebody doesn't want printed; everything else is advertising.

He kicked off and swam a savage backstroke. Plants are a dime a dozen, but why had Cruickshank sunk to the likes of Whacker Jones? Surely he could have found a law-abiding widow who'd toss her cane for a bottle of pain killers and a month's rent. Besides, Miss McTavish didn't need plants. Adrenaline propels the lame two steps. Hysteria provides shadows to the blind. And a holy rap to the head can make the deaf hear bells.

Damn Cruickshank. His link to Whacker had popped the soufflé. If the public loves a saint, it loves a scandal even more. Each day, there'd be fresh dirt. Rumours. Allegations. Innuendo. The girl would be buried alive.

Worst of all, Hearst had lost control of the story. So far he'd had the inside track, negotiating its curves and straightaways like a demon. Now he was trapped in a demolition derby: Mary Mabel was roadkill; Marion's vehicle was a write-off; and he was in a pileup, rammed on all sides, while the competition streaked by, threatening to hijack advertisers en route.

Hearst was so angry, he lost track of his backstroke and conked his head on the end of the pool. When he came to, he was flat on the deck, a doctor checking him for concussion. Hearst shoved the doctor aside. "Willicombe," he announced, "I've had a vision."

Willicombe observed the mad dilations of his pupils. "W.R., are you okay?"

"Okay?" Hearst laughed. "I'm back in the driver's seat. Rent me Radio City Music Hall. On the double. And don't forget to book the Rockettes."

• • • •

Next morning, the following editorial appeared on the front page of Hearst newspapers across the country.

SISTER MARY MABLE: SAINT OR SINNER???
THE HEARST PRESS DEMANDS THE TRUTH
An editorial by publisher
Mr. W.R. Hearst

We Americans are a God-fearing people. It is therefore natural that we pay heed when we hear reports of Divine providence.

As publisher of the Hearst chain of family newspapers, I take it as my highest obligation to keep the public informed. Consequently, I have spared no expense to bring you, my readers, the most up-to-the-minute news on the alleged healings of Sister Mary Mabel McTavish.

Miss McTavish has convinced many that she is a conduit for miracles. Others allege that she is party to chicanery, greed, and corruption.

If she is a healer, she well deserves the accolades she has received. However, if she is a charlatan, she is the most despicable of wretches; for she will have betrayed the faith on which our great nation was built, in the process abetting the insidious forces of godlessness and Communism.

In light of the current controversy, this newspaper has rented Radio City Music Hall for Saturday evening, two weeks from today, at 8:00 p.m. At that time, we demand that Sister Mary Mabel McTavish submit to an onstage lie detector test. Saint or Sinner,

Miss McTavish: which are you? America
deserves the truth.

Signed,
Publisher Mr. W.R. Hearst.

*Editor's note: The previously sched-
uled performance by Mr. Edgar Bergen
and Charlie McCarthy has been cancelled. Tickets will be refunded or
may be exchanged at the Radio City
Music Hall box office, courtesy of the
Hearst Press. Mr. W.R. Hearst wishes
to apologize for any inconvenience,
and to extend his thanks to Mr. Bergen
for his co-operation in this matter
of national interest.*

ON *the* RAILS

General Secretary Comrade Seamus Duddy, founder and guiding light of the Independent Collective Proletarian Brotherhood of the International Industrial Bolshevik Workers Alliance of the United States of America (I.C.P.B.I.I.B.W.A.U.S.A.), had concluded a rousing call to arms to his troops and retired to the roof of their boxcar to cry. In five years, despite a nonstop recruitment campaign, the I.C.P.B.I.I.B.W.A.U.S.A. had never had more than six members. No sooner were new comrades educated in the finer points of dialectical materialism, than they'd get arrested, miss the train, or form a splinter group.

Comrade Duddy had persevered, convinced that he was destined for revolutionary greatness; it was a matter of historical inevitability. Lately, however, the inevitable was beginning to appear doubtful. Duddy wanted to change the world, but he feared that all he'd ever change were his socks.

A fifth-generation miner, Duddy had been a bright, handsome lad. Before the Great War, his intelligence caught the attention of a union organizer for the Industrial Workers of the World (I.W.W.), who taught him reading, writing, and Marxist revolutionary theory, while his looks attracted the attention of the mine owner's daughter, Lydia, who taught him more immediate ways to screw the bourgeoisie.

One night, Pinkerton's men caught the pair *in flagrante*. Duddy was wrapped in a blanket, beaten with a baseball bat, and brought before the girl's father. Randall Blackstone was at his wits' end. He'd soon be reduced to filling abandoned mine shafts with the bodies of his daughter's lovers. That would clean him of workers by spring. Cutting his losses, he had the couple married by dawn and shipped north to well-heeled cousins in Connecticut. They ran Pinecrest, an exclusive elementary school outside New Haven. Duddy was given a bath, a suit, and a class of forty first-grade students.

He was a favourite with the children, although his attempts at political re-education left them confused. In the words of Master Winston Van Buren IV: "If I was a worker, I'd quit and ride ponies."

Duddy started to drink, especially at formal dinner parties arranged by his in-laws. He'd knock back the brandy until the guests were comfortably into their entrées, then launch into vivid descriptions of black lung disease. His wife was not amused: an affair with a worker was romantic; marriage to one was sordid.

Duddy's career and marriage came to an abrupt end at the annual Pinecrest Thanksgiving Weekend. He'd organized the first-grade pageant. Wealthy parents filled the auditorium, expecting to see their little Pilgrims and Indians roll out a papier-maché turkey, shake hands, and recite the Pledge of Allegiance. Instead, the Pilgrims grabbed the turkey and threw the Indians to the ground, shouting: "We steal your land, and make you our slaves."

At this point, Master Van Buren ran on in coveralls, waving a hammer and sickle. "Workers of the world unite!" he squealed. "Throw off your chains! Death to the capitalist bosses!" With bloodcurdling screams, the little Indians leapt to their feet and attacked the pilgrims with rubber tomahawks. The moppets staggered around squirting ketchup. Mothers fainted.

There was so much commotion that no one paid any attention to the explosion in the main office. Duddy's mining experience had come in handy. One stick of dynamite had blasted away the door to the school vault. The sound was muffled by sandbags stuffed with the fur coats of visiting parents. Duddy hopped the 7:45 with two suitcases loaded with tuition fees and tuck money. He never looked back.

He spent the Great War organizing strikes for the I.W.W. in New Jersey, Minnesota, and Washington State. When the I.W.W. collapsed, he joined the Communist Labor Party, which begat the Communist Party of America, which begat the Workers Party of America, which begat the Communist Party of the United States of America.

Comrade Duddy was happy to follow the party line until the Communist International decreed that labour leaders were greater enemies to workers than fascists. Duddy was outraged. He made a rude joke about Lenin and sheep, and was promptly expelled from the Party. He didn't care. Within the week, he'd founded the Independent Bolshevik Alliance, a syndicalist group dedicated to industrial slowdowns and sabotage. The Great Depression had taken care of slowdowns, but it was still fun to blow stuff up.

The Independent Bolshevik Alliance peaked at three members. To expand his power, Duddy merged with the two-member Proletarian Alliance to form the Independent Proletarian Bolshevik Alliance. This entente was known as "The Great Leap Forward." There followed "the Second, Third, Fourth, Fifth, and Sixth Great Leaps Forward" as Duddy swallowed up the Proletarian Brotherhood and the Independent Proletarian Brotherhood, not to mention the Industrial Workers Alliance, the Collective Workers Alliance, and the Bolshevik Workers of America.

Since these cells included visionaries much like Duddy, doctrinal disputes were as common as manifestos. Marked by charges of revisionism and factionalism, they generally lasted till dawn and ended in black eyes and schisms. As a result, after years of leaping forward, Duddy's I.C.P.B.I.I.B.W.A.U.S.A. had grown in name only.

At least the cell could feed itself. Once every couple of months, Duddy would blow up a bank and the gang would hightail it to

Mexico to drink tequila till the dust settled. Knocking off banks wasn't stealing, according to Comrade Duddy. It was an act of revolutionary heroism in solidarity with the workers of the world.

Unfortunately, the revolutionary heroes had hit a snag in Laredo when their getaway car ran out of gas. Only comrades Duddy and Lapinsky had managed to scramble across the border ahead of a posse and tracking dogs, hauling ass for three days through a swamp filled with every biting insect in creation. They showed up delirious at Casa Mama Rosa, their heads the size of beach balls.

Duddy wished his fellow survivor was someone other than Lapinsky. The man was loyal, but he was also psychotic. Years ago a train had severed his left hand. Ever since, he'd worn it on a rope under his shirt. He used it as a back-scratcher. True, he doused it in aftershave to keep down the smell. All the same.

During the course of recuperation, Comrade Duddy spent much of his time retching in the outhouse. It was here that he met his latest recruit, Comrade Johnny Canuck; he got the nickname Johnny Canuck since he was from Canada.

Canuck claimed he'd been betrayed by his child and fired by his employer. Drunk as a skunk, he'd hit the rails and landed in Texas, where he vaguely recalled playing poker. The next thing he knew, he was in his underwear on a mule cart under a pile of rotting potato skins. The driver threw him on the roadside by Casa Mama Rosa. He'd been here ever since, cleaning the brothels' bedpans and sheets in exchange for room, board, and a weekly tumble with one of the girls.

Canuck's Spanish was limited to *"sí,"* *"mañana,"* and *"muy bonita* tits." Consequently, he had no idea about anything, except that he was stuck in a foreign whorehouse. When he'd heard Duddy grunting English in the crapper, he'd thrown open the door, fallen to his knees, and kissed the comrade's crusty boots.

Duddy was so desperate to replenish the troops that he recruited the lost soul on the spot. It was a move he regretted. Comrade Canuck wasn't interested in Communist theory regarding the means of production; all he cared about was the sharing part. As the gang trekked back to America, he'd helped himself to most of their supplies.

Now Stateside, Comrade Duddy was filled with despair. He'd just delivered an oration on the I.C.P.B.I.I.B.W.A.U.S.A.'s glorious return from exile, and of its triumphant storming of the border, hidden in a boxcar, disguised as sacks of chicken feed. Nobody listened. As he preached revolution, Comrade Canuck had made a bed out of a pile of crumpled newspapers, while Comrade Lapinsky had picked dried sinew from a knuckle on the Hand. "Dammit!" Duddy cursed as he climbed to the boxcar roof, "The revolution is wasted on morons!"

"Comrade Duddy?" Johnny Canuck scrambled up beside him. He had an earnest look and a fistful of newspaper. He pointed to an article with a big picture. "Can you read this for me?"

Duddy glanced at it. "It's bullshit. Bread and circuses. Sister Mary Mabel McTavish is playing Radio City Music Hall. She's going to be strapped to a lie detector."

"I have to see her."

"That whore? That stooge of the capitalist bosses?"

"Watch your mouth," said Comrade Canuck. "You're talking about my daughter."

NEW YORK, NEW YORK

Hearst's editorial made Mary Mabel feel like a criminal. Doyle, on the other hand, said it had saved their bacon. The prospect of a polygraph test would distract the public from the daily dirt. He called it her "trial by fire."

"Right," she snapped. "Like what they had for witches."

Still, Mary Mabel could see that Hearst appeared to want her to succeed. Aside from the challenge, he'd sent them under-the-table instructions. They were to cancel all performances till after Radio City. Officially, so the Miracle Maid could rest. Practically, to keep her clear of mischief.

Mary Mabel thought they should carry on as normal to show a clear conscience, but Doyle explained that if the tour didn't cancel first, nervous sponsors would likely cancel on their behalf. Bad press. Besides, rival syndicates might try to create news, organizing pickets at the theatres, planting hostile questions, or arranging riots. No, until Radio City the tour was to stay in seclusion, except for photo shoots with former sponsors. These would appear with Doyle's articles, which he promised to pack with testimonials from fans and hatchet jobs on accusers.

"You're focused on public relations," Mary Mabel said. "What about truth?"

"Public relations *makes* truth," Doyle growled. "Facts never saved a soul from Old Sparky."

As expected, Doyle found that former sponsors were too busy to be seen with him. That meant the Miracle gang was left to cool its heels in Tulsa, the reverends and Mary Mabel sticking to their rooms until two days before show time, when Hearst would fly them to New York.

Effectively they were prisoners. Floyd checked in on Mary Mabel occasionally, but decency required that he stay in the hall. As for Brother Percy, his room next to hers was so quiet she asked Floyd to see if he was dead. Floyd assured her that his friend was happily praying in a corner.

One thing broke Mary Mabel's solitude: her evening phone calls from Doyle. He'd tell her everything was going well and she'd say, good, she was feeling terrific. In fact, she was crawling the walls. To escape the claustrophobia, she'd lie in bed and study the picture of her mama. If she stared hard enough, her mama appeared to be breathing. Other times, she'd curl up by the window, hold the saucer, and imagine her mama was sending messages in cloud formations, or in the whistle of the wind, or in the birds that landed on the ledge. Then she'd get a chill and wonder if maybe she was crazy.

If she was crazy, maybe her miracles *were* in her head. But that would mean the people she'd healed only *imagined* they were well, in which case they'd be crazy, too. Who makes the rules about who's crazy, anyway? If it's a matter of opinion, then K.O. was right: reality is just successful advertising.

Too much thinking is hard on the brain, but at least it passes the time. Before it seemed possible, Mary Mabel was packing her bags for the flight to New York.

Hearst's plane was a marvel. The passenger cabin looked like a sitting room. It was panelled in rosewood and mahogany with leather sofas, armchairs, and coffee tables bolted discreetly to the floor. The panelling was covered in art, including a pair of Rembrandts and a da Vinci.

None of the trio had flown before and they were all a little anxious. Brother Percy had to be carried on by the plane's butler; Floyd had given him a sleeping potion and he'd passed out. *Thank heaven for small mercies*, Mary Mabel thought. She'd been worried that mid-flight he might throw open the door to stroll the clouds in search of Paradise.

The pilot came on last and invited her to sit in the cockpit. As the plane took off, Mary Mabel's nails nearly ripped the armrests, but she soon relaxed. The hum of the engine was soothing as a cat's purr, and the clouds as whimsical as cotton candy. The earth spread out below like a giant quilt, patches of farms and towns stitched together by threads of road and fence.

We're flying over millions of people with hopes and despairs, she thought. *Yet from up here, nothing matters but the weather.* She marvelled at cloud shadows sliding across rivers and fields: how strange that things can be worth nothing and everything at the same time.

There are three things Mary Mabel remarked about her suite at The Belvedere. One: it was so big it took her forever to find the bedroom. Two: there were so many pillows on her bed it took her forever to find the mattress. Three: the bathroom had two toilets, one of which they called "a bidet."

Doyle met them in the lobby. They had an hour to unpack before he was to escort them to a luncheon interview with Hearst opinion-makers from the *New York Journal-American* and the *Mirror*. "Don't worry," he said, "the Chief's wishes are known. You just have to show up and pay homage to the court." Playing chauffeur was a big deal for Doyle. He was the new kid on the Hearst block, and showing Mary Mabel off was a great way for him to meet the big boys.

Happily, Brother Percy wouldn't be around to embarrass him. The reverend had arrived at the hotel reeling from the after-effects of his sedative, and insisted on riding the luggage cart like a train conductor. "Doot! Doot! All abore vor da Burly Gades!" Floyd had popped him another pill and the bellhops tucked him into bed.

Lunch was at the Stork Club, the New Yorkiest joint in New York. The maitre d' whisked them to Table 50 in the Cub Room. Five men and a woman were having a spirited conversation. Their host rose. "Please welcome K.O. Doyle," he said to the others. "A member of the younger degeneration."

"K.O. Doyle!" said the woman. "You're quite the scribbler."

Doyle blushed. "May I introduce Sister Mary Mabel McTavish and her producer, Mr. Floyd Cruickshank."

"Winchell," said our host, extending his hand. "Walter Winchell. Welcome to my home away from home. From your left, Mr. Damon Runyon, Mr. Westbrook Pegler, editor Mr. Arthur Brisbane, city editor Mr. Eddie Mahar, and table ornament Miss Dorothy Kilgallen."

"Pinch a loaf, Walter."

Hoots all around. They shook hands and sat down. Mary Mabel tried not to stare at Runyon. He was one of her favourite short story writers.

Winchell ordered a round of drinks, two bottles of champagne, and menus. Since Mary Mabel was on a tight budget, she asked for a glass of milk and a salad.

"Salad-schmalad. Make it a steak and a Waldorf. It's on the Old Man."

"Yes, and he's very generous," said Kilgallen. "Damon, tell Miss McTavish about your bill for that trip to Canada."

Runyon rubbed his hands. "There's this guy and this doll on the lam, see? The Old Man sics me on their tail and I get stuck in some burg the far side of Bumhole. Nothing to do but get stinkeroo, in the course of which enterprise I punch a yokel in the snoot and wind up in the town sneezer. Fine, I shmooze my way out with a couple of Cs and send the chit to the Chief. He was madder than somewhat. 'What's this for?' he barks. I say, 'Funeral expenses for my dead sled dog and flowers for the bereaved bitch.'"

"Along with his expenses, Damon sent a story that goosed the weekly run." Kilgallen laughed. "The Old Man says he can't afford us. The truth is, he can't afford not to afford us."

"Mr. Runyon," Mary Mabel asked, "was that story 'A Dead Cold Setup'?"

His jaw dropped. "You read it?"

"I read all your stories. At least all the ones I can find. 'The Idylls of Sarah Brown' is my favourite."

Runyon loosened his tie. "I like this kid."

A stumpy man in a white linen suit advanced on the table with a soft-cheeked companion. A phalanx of handsome young men in dark suits followed at a discreet distance. The lead pair were always in the news. Winchell shook their hands like they were old friends. "You know the usual suspects; let me introduce our guests, Sister Mary Mabel McTavish and Floyd Cruickshank." To his guests: "May I present F.B.I. Director Mr. J. Edgar Hoover and Assistant Director Mr. Clyde Tolson."

How-de-ja-dos all around.

"You gents care for a seat?"

"We're on our way out. Just came by to say hello."

Runyon cocked his head. "What brings you to town?"

"The Radio City show." Hoover's eyes slid in Mary Mabel's direction. "I've been following your progress, Sister."

"Gosh," she replied, "I've been following yours, too. All those gangsters and Communists to catch. You're everywhere."

"Crime never sleeps. Neither does the Bureau." He sounded so much like he did in the newsreels that Mary Mabel wanted to laugh. Hoover tipped his hat. "Till tomorrow." A nod and he was out the door: a hard-boiled egg leading a side of beef.

"Edna Hoover and Mother Tolson. Interesting fans," Runyon observed.

"Keep your trap shut," Pegler hissed. "You want to get us in trouble?"

"Boys, boys, settle down," said Winchell. "Have a drink."

Kilgallen raised her glass. "Here's to the game."

There was a walnut Marconi in Mary Mabel's sitting room. At suppertime, Doyle told her to tune in the *Lucky Strike Magic Carpet Show*; they'd be the lead on Winchell's report. The familiar voice came in loud and clear: "Ohhhkaaay Aaamerica! Good evening Mr. and Mrs. America and all the ships at sea. Let's go to press. Tomorrow Radio City plays host to Sister Mary Mabel McTavish. Are those magic fingers the old phonus-balonus, or are they the real McCoy? Call me a chump, but I bet the holes in my socks, her curls are screwed on straight."

Next morning, the advance press was mixed. One tabloid said, "She plays the role of L'il Orphan Annie, assuming God to be her personal Daddy Warbucks," but the Hearst press glowed. Arthur Brisbane wrote, "In these dark times, we need a little pixie dust. Don't let us down, Miss McTavish. Fly right and lift our hearts to the heavens."

After breakfast, Hearst's limousine took her to Radio City to get familiar with the auditorium and the polygraph equipment. Doyle and Floyd came along for the ride. Not Brother Percy. According to Floyd, he was boycotting the entire event on account of the Showplace of the Nation was a flesh-pot sucking souls to Hell.

They went in by the stage door. The doorman gave them a peek of the lobby, with its sixty-foot ceiling and thirty-foot chandeliers. Light bristled off towering gunmetal mirrors, steel, chrome and aluminum foil. "It's visual jazz!" Doyle exclaimed as they entered the theatre, a six-thousand seat lollapalooza capped by a symphony orchestra pit and a vast deco sunset. By the footlights, Mary Mabel saw a bank of radio mikes that would broadcast the show live, coast to coast, and on a small platform in the pit, the newsreel cameras of Metrotone Presents.

Mr. Leonarde Keeler was on stage making adjustments to the lie detector. He'd invented the most up-to-date improvements on the instrument and had been hired to conduct the interrogation. His authority would put the results beyond doubt. After introductions, he had Mary Mabel sit in his chair to try out the straps and sensors that would feed him information on her blood pressure, pulse, and respiration.

The basic equipment was simple, but for theatrical purposes Hearst's people had added some decorative elements. The chair was oversized and covered in diamond mirrors and gold foil, the straps were painted silver, and she was to wear an enormous futuristic headdress with circular neon rings designed to make her look like a creature from Fritz Lang's *Metropolis*.

The chair would be positioned under the trap door at centre stage. The show would start with a symphony overture, a dance by the corps de ballet, a vocal chorus, and then the Rockettes. Their tap dance would climax with fountains of water jetting from the stage floor. As the applause peaked, the lights would dim and an amplified voice would announce the Inquisition. The orchestra would play "Thus Spake Zarathustra" and Mary Mabel's chair would rise twenty feet in the air on a hydraulic dais of glitter and light. She made a mental note to keep her knees together.

The rest of Mary Mabel's day was so packed with activities she didn't have time to be scared. But at 6:30, when Hearst's limo arrived to take her to Radio City, she had a palpitation.

She and Floyd were at the elevator. When it arrived, she stepped in. Not Mr. Cruickshank. As the door closed, he called out, "Meet you in the lobby," and darted down the corridor to Brother Percy's.

Downstairs, Mary Mabel grew increasingly alarmed. Was there a problem with the reverend? News that Percy was boycotting the show had been a relief. She hoped there wasn't a hitch. After a ten-minute fret, she determined to go upstairs to see what was up, but at that moment, the elevator door opened and Floyd stepped into the lobby whiter than his starched shirt.

"What's the matter?" Mary Mabel demanded.

"Nothing. Everything's taken care of."

"What do you mean?"

"What I said," he replied. "Now hurry up, we're late." He grabbed her by the elbow, and whisked her into the back of Hearst's limo.

Unsettled by the twitch in his eyes, Mary Mabel was too frightened to investigate further. Nor was she in any shape for the tumult at the Radio City stage door. Hustled along the red carpet, heart beating a mile a minute, she thought she heard a familiar voice call to her from the crowd: "Yoo-hoo, baby doll! Over here, it's me!"

She turned to the voice and nearly fainted. There in the sea of faces — was it her papa?

Autograph books were waved in front of her face. Flashbulbs exploded everywhere. When her vision cleared, whomever she'd seen had disappeared.

Her knees wobbled. Police helped her the rest of the way, to a dressing room filled with so many baskets of flowers she half-expected to find one of Mr. Bigelow's caskets. She closed the door and sat in front of the makeup mirror staring at the stranger staring back. Over the speaker, she heard the audience piling into its seats. It was too much. She had to run.

It was then that she noticed a battered shoebox by a vase of roses. The box was tied with a string and had her name on it. Inside, wrapped in tissue paper, was a first edition of *Guys and Dolls* inscribed by Mr. Runyon.

"Dear Miss McTavish," he wrote, "If they ever make *Sarah Brown* into a picture, you're my gal. You got a noodle, kiddo. Break a leg. Don't let 'em break your heart. Your pally, D.R."

From the depths of despair she filled with joy. Her mama'd arranged to send her luck.

Doyle burst in. "You better sit down. Bad news."

The REVELATIONS of BROTHER PERCY

After his opening night humiliation in Flint, Brother Percy had collapsed by his bedside. "Dear Lord," he'd wept, the crowd's laughter ringing in his ears. "It's not that I doubt You. It's just I'm at the end of my rope. Talk to me. Say something. Please."

Miraculously, God had obliged. He spoke to Percy that night and every night thereafter. The preacher had to listen very hard, for the Almighty spoke in a strange language, low and rumbling, punctuated by hisses, clanks, and knocking. Fortunately, Percy had been blessed not only with tongues but with the gifts of prophecy and divination. *The Lord moves in mysterious ways*, he thought, as he sat before various hotel radiators, taking dictation in his little black books.

Percy was determined to keep these communications private. The godless would say he was crazy. Small wonder. The first time the radiator spoke, he'd covered his head with a pillow and tried to get back to sleep. But God was insistent, reminding him that He'd appeared to Moses as a burning bush, so what was the big deal?

"You might be Satan come to my room to trick me," Percy said.

God replied that Satan already came to his room to trick him.

"How does the Fiend get in?"

"Seek and ye shall find," God rumbled.

Percy went on a tear. He searched for a secret passageway to Hell under the bed, in the closet, and behind the chest of drawers and medicine cabinet. Nothing. He was about to give up when he became aware of a slow drip coming from the bathtub faucet. Percy crawled into the tub and put his ear to the drain. A hollow sound as delicate as breath rose from the pipes. It seemed to be coming from deep in the bowels of the earth. As Percy listened, the sound filled with distant wails of loss and regret. This was no mortal sound. It was the sound of lost souls in Hell.

God was right! Percy panicked. *Satan's using the drains to sneak into my hotel rooms and drive me mad.* These drains were surely connected. All over North America. Perhaps all over the world. No wonder the devil moved slick as a gopher. He simply popped down one hole and out another. The money boys who built these drains — the bankers with the funny names — they were in on it. Satan's minions. He'd always guessed it. Now he had proof.

Percy plugged the tub and turned on the taps. When it was full, he blessed the water, that it provide a holy seal between himself and Hell. He likewise secured the sink, then turned to the W.C. It didn't seem right to consecrate water in the toilet, but what if the Serpent slithered up through the bowl? Percy had an inspiration. He covered the lid with a towel and put his Gideon Bible on top.

God's revelation changed Percy's life. His first order of business on checking into a new room was to secure the drains. The wiring in his mouth had made brushing his teeth impossible. Now he stopped bathing as well; he didn't want his nether parts to defile the holy water. As for bodily functions, he squatted above the lip of the john and launched his load with a hearty, "Get thee behind me, Satan!"

To further protect the holy water, Percy dry shaved, but he nicked himself so often that his cheeks became dotted with bits of toilet paper applied to staunch the blood. Consequently, on God's advice, he let his beard grow. His hair, too. This prevented heathen barbers and chambermaids from collecting the clippings for voodoo dolls. In order not to look peculiar, he stuffed his matted locks in a rubber bathing cap covered by a fedora.

After a week or two, Floyd began to leave his car window open: "For Christ's sake, Perce, you're high as a cat's litter box."

Better the stink of the saved than the stench of the damned, Percy thought. It thrilled him to know that his whoremonger partner was hell-bound. The Lord had passed word by means of the radiator: It turned out He had intended to fry *Floyd* in London. Unfortunately, He'd been so full of wrath that His lightning bolt had hit the Beeford boy by mistake; when He'd resurrected the kid, You-Know-Who had stolen the glory.

Percy said it wasn't fair that a stray bolt had left him with a broken jaw, playing second banana to a witch. God told him to buck up, the righteous were destined for affliction, it was part of His grand design. In any event, "Soon the she-devil shall be cast down, and ye shall be raised to glory, a star shining brighter in Mine firmament than all the saints and the apostles." Since a thousand years is a day unto the Lord, Percy wanted to know how soon was "soon." "I will come like a thief in the night when ye least expect it," the Almighty clanked. Then He rattled a bit and shut down.

Every night for two months God made the same promise. Percy got so impatient he almost gave the radiator a kick. Then Whacker Jones hit the headlines, Hearst made his challenge, and the preacher did cartwheels. Yea, the harlot would be exposed and he would be exalted; God's prophecy would be fulfilled.

Percy rapped on Floyd's door and demanded to open the show at Radio City.

"Mr. Hearst only invited Mary Mabel," Floyd scrambled.

"Doo bat," Percy replied. "Ma invitashun es fwum Gah!"

"Congratulations. Did He mention how you're supposed to preach with a mouth full of wires?"

"Ee zez dey muz be re-mooft."

"Fine, we'll remove them." The wires had been due for removal weeks ago, but given Percy's tenuous grip, Floyd had hoped to let sleeping dogs lie. Or rust. Now he had to act.

Percy selected a doctor from the phone book; Floyd arranged for the house call. When the doctor arrived, Floyd slipped him a twenty-dollar bill and a note that read: "Beware. This patient likes to bite people. These wires were installed as a muzzle."

The doctor found the note questionable, the appearance of a bribe moreso. All the same, the rubber bands dangling from the reverend's bathing cap were certainly peculiar, and when he tried to wash his hands in the sink, Percy went berserk. Playing it safe, the doctor advised Percy to consult his regular physician in Canada. The radiator hissed and clanked. Percy ranted incoherently and burst into tears. The doctor prescribed sedatives.

Floyd administered the pills in triple doses. For the rest of their stay in Tulsa, Percy slept peacefully. (Floyd was tempted to ease him into the bathtub. Drowning in holy water. What a tragic accident.) He remained drugged on the airplane ride to New York, rousing only to throw up on Floyd's lap, and to cause a scene when they entered the Belvedere. Not to worry. A few more sedatives from Floyd and the bellhops had been able to tuck him into bed without incident.

But Percy didn't stay put. When Floyd arrived to spoon-feed him soup, he found the evangelist on the floor. In case the upchuck on the plane had eliminated some medication, Floyd slipped an extra pill in the broth. But when he came by next, Perce was slumped by the radiator. After that, in the bathroom, Floyd took no chances. He emptied half a bottle of pills down Percy's throat.

The next morning, Hearst's limousine picked up Mary Mabel for last-minute activities. Floyd tagged along, returning every few hours to check his friend. Relief. Whenever he opened the door, Percy was exactly where he'd left him, out cold under the shower curtain sucking his thumb.

For supper, Floyd gave him an over-the-top-up, then dressed for the show. At 6:30, the phone rang; Hearst's limo had arrived for the trip to Radio City. Floyd collected Mary Mabel and escorted her to the elevator. But as he was about to step inside, he had a terrible premonition. "See you downstairs," he said, as the door closed, and raced down the corridor into Percy's room.

His worst fears were realized. Percy sat at his desk, dressed in his secondhand tux, a top hat on top of his shower cap. Greasy hair billowed from under the cap and flowed into his beard, matted by various soups and stews. "I knew you wouldn't leave without checking in on me," Percy said. "Care for a mint?" He offered a bowl of bile-coated sedatives.

Floyd stared blankly. "Your jaw is free. You're talking."

"Yes, just out of surgery," Percy replied. It was then that Floyd noticed the pieces of wire on the desk, the pliers and cutters, and the blood and saliva dribbling from Percy's mouth, down his beard and onto his clothes.

"We need to get you to a hospital."

"Nonsense," Percy said. "We need to get me to Radio City." He rose gingerly, pliers in one hand, wire cutters in the other. "Tonight God's prophecy is fulfilled! Tonight I preach glorious hellfire!"

"You're not stepping out of this room."

"Stop me!" Percy tottered forward. He swung his bony arm. The pliers grazed Floyd's temple. Floyd staggered backward. Percy swung again and again. "Stop me, Profligate Beast! Defiler of Virgins! Licker of Toads!"

Floyd scrambled over the bed. He grabbed a pillow for protection. The preacher attacked. "Woe unto thee, Fountain of Iniquity!" Floyd tumbled off the bed as the pillow shredded apart. He retreated on hands and knees over the shower curtain.

"Prepare to meet thy God!" Percy raised his weapons high and bounced from the mattress onto the shower curtain. It slid beneath his feet. He pitched forward. Floyd rolled to the side. Percy's head cracked against the radiator.

There was a terrible silence.

BEST LAID PLANS

Brewster hadn't wanted to kidnap his daughter, but Comrade Duddy had insisted. "Religion is the opiate of the masses," he railed the night Brewster showed him Mary Mabel's picture in the paper. "It's pie in the sky when you die. We need salvation here and now. Control of the means of production."

Whenever Duddy went on about "control of the means of production," the comrades had a snooze. They could picture owning hammers and saws, maybe even a toolbox, but Duddy always talked about factories. Who the hell wanted a factory? They couldn't agree on the time of day, much less how to organize shift work. Why not stick to blowing up banks?

Fortunately, on this occasion Comrade Duddy kept the yackety-yack short. He had a plan. If they made tracks they could hit Manhattan in time for Mary Mabel's big show. Brewster would greet her at the Radio City stage door. After a tearful reunion, he'd lead her to an alley five blocks away where Comrade Duddy would knock her out with a hankie doused in chloroform. Comrade Lapinsky would stuff her in a burlap bag and the three of them would haul her to a hideout on the Lower East Side. Here she'd be indoctrinated into the wonders of Communism, re-emerging to preach the Gospel According to Marx. Her fame would draw converts and contributions. General Secretary Comrade Seamus Duddy would become a leader in the glorious revolutionary struggle and they'd all live happily ever after.

Brewster's plan was much simpler. He'd show up on Mary Mabel's doorstep, stake his claim as her father, and his comrades could bugger off. "After all," he told them, "she's *my* daughter. Why should I give you a cut of the action?"

Lapinsky picked his nose with the Hand. "Because if you don't, we'll kill you."

Comrade Duddy was more diplomatic. "Right now your kid's pot of gold goes to the God racket. You won't get a cent. Help us rescue her and you'll be rich."

In that light, kidnapping his daughter was smart thinking: Whoops — kidnapping — wrong word, that could get a guy strung up. He was simply protecting his child's nest egg from preachers. At least that's what he told himself as he left the gang's hideout on Avenue D and headed to Radio City.

When he arrived, he found police barricades from the street to the stage door. Brewster was astonished at the size of the crowd. It would be hard to get close enough for Mary Mabel to see him. Nonetheless, by the time her limo pulled up, he'd groped enough bottoms to get within earshot.

Mary Mabel got out of the back seat, flanked by police. A sea of fans reached over the barricades. Some wanted autographs. Some wanted to be healed.

"Mary Mabel!" Brewster shouted, waving his arms among the sea of other arms. "Yoo-hoo, baby doll! Over here! It's me!"

For a second he almost caught her eye. Then he felt a golf bag pressed against his back. "If it isn't the proud pappy," came a voice from the past. "Marge sends her regards."

As the mob cheered and waved, Slick Skinner wrapped his free arm under Brewster's ribs and drew him backwards. "Help me!" Brewster cried to the people around him. "Help me!" Nobody heard. Like quicksand, they filled his space as Slick pulled him backwards. In seconds, Brewster was swallowed by the crowd.

Slick Skinner had been stalking the tour since Kalamazoo, confident that sooner or later McTavish would show up. After all, pigs know where the truffles are.

Tracking had been a snap. He'd travelled in the expansive trunk of the Olds. Picking the lock was easy; the trick was to squish himself under the back blanket until the bags were unpacked and the car parked. Hunting food was a breeze, too. Towns were well-stocked with raccoon, squirrel and neighbour-hood cat. As for the stakeout, it held a bonus attraction: nights when the fire escape passed by Mary Mabel's window. She was a sweet thing asleep in her nightie. Once he'd killed her pa, he'd jimmy the sash and pay his respects.

Still, time was wasting. After months of rubbing the bul-let-etched B.McT., his prey hadn't shown a whisker. Skinner didn't know if Brewster was dead or in jail. Either way, he'd decided Radio City would be his last stand. If McTavish didn't show there, he wouldn't show anywhere.

Stowing aboard the Hearst plane was impossible. Instead, Slick got to New York courtesy of newlyweds Elmer and Mona Mackenzie. Minutes away from their wedding reception, he used his hunting knife to carve his way from their trunk into their back seat. Mona thought this was another prank of her goddamn alco-holic Uncle Fred till Slick stuck his shotgun in her ear and suggested Manhattan was a better honeymoon destination than Topeka.

The trapper camped out in Central Park to await Mary Mabel. By day, he slept under a bridge near the boat house. By night, he offered not to shoot people in exchange for their wal-lets, stashing the loot inside the lining of his jacket — his "money coat" he called it. The afternoon of the big show, he stuffed him-self on roast pigeon. Then he wrapped his shotgun in a blanket, slipped it into a golf bag he'd scavenged from a Fifth Avenue gar-bage can and headed to Radio City.

Ah, the thrill of the hunt. Slick loved it. Mostly he loved to hunt humans; unlike cows, they understood death. Why, you could walk right up to a cow, shoot it between the eyes and it wouldn't even notice. But humans had fear. That's what he loved most. Watching their fear before he blew them away. It was why he liked to kill them up close. And to let them know death was coming.

That's why tonight, pulling McTavish from Radio City Music Hall, Slick had the biggest boner of his life. He was about to avenge his manhood — yahoo! — with the victim being the greatest coward he'd ever hunted down. Exactly five blocks from Radio City, Brewster fell to his knees beside an alley and blubbered, "Don't shoot me in the street."

"Don't worry." Slick laughed. "I aim to shoot you down an alley."

"Not down *this* alley," McTavish quivered. "*Please*, Mr. Skinner, *please* don't shoot me down *this particular* alley."

Slick hadn't given the matter much thought, but McTavish's desperation made this particular alley seem mighty attractive. "Yeah, this particular alley. This here'll do us just fine," he grinned. McTavish snivelled to his feet. Slick prodded him forward. "Get moving."

The alley was too dark for Slick to get a picture for his album. Who cared? The tabloids were sure to have plenty. Headless bodies were a rarity. Especially skinned. Once out of sight, Slick stuck his shotgun at the base of Brewster's skull. "Say cheese." That was the last thing Slick remembered before he woke up in the drunk tank at 54th and 8th.

Comrade Duddy dropped the chloroform hankie beside the snoring hunter.

"What took you so long?" Brewster demanded.

"I should have taken longer," Duddy said.

Comrade Lapinsky stared at Slick. He scratched his head with the Hand. "Gee McTavish, your daughter sure don't look like her pictures."

BROTHER PERCY RESURRECTS

GR-GR-PHEEEKT! GR-GR-ZEIKKKT! KRYPA KRYPA KRYP! The radiator was working overtime. Percy blinked. His head hurt. The room was pitch black. Where was he? What time was it?

"*GRECKT!*" God bellowed. "You're in New York! It's show-time!"

In a panic, Percy struggled to get up, but all he could do was roll around. Floyd had hog-tied him with the curtain cord. "Sweet Jesus, what can I do?"

"*GZOOT! GZEIT!*"

"Pardon?"

"FIND THE WIRE CUTTERS, YOU IDIOT!"

The ROCKETTES GET RELIGION

"**W**hat do you mean, bad news?" Mary Mabel said. She rose from her dressing table and looked Doyle straight in the eye. With the show about to start, bad news was the last thing she needed.

"J. Edgar Hoover has muscled his way into the show," Doyle replied. "He and a couple of G-men will stand guard while you take the test. If you pass, he'll be in on the pictures. If you fail, he'll arrest you for racketeering and slap you in jail."

"Can he do that?"

"He's J. Edgar Hoover."

"Well Mr. Hearst is Mr. Hearst. Have him keep Mr. Hoover off stage."

"And have Hoover open his secret files?" Doyle looked at his shoes. "Besides, from the Chief's point of view, having the F.B.I. on stage will sell papers."

Mary Mabel began to shake. He gave her a hug. "Look, the test can't be used against you in court. At worst, you'll be booked and released."

"Oh? If Hoover names me a public enemy, I'm finished."

"On the bright side, if you get his blessing, you'll be free of suspicion forever."

"*If.*"

"The polygraph only cares that you believe what you say. You do, don't you?"

"Yes."

She bit her lip. The truth was, from Miss Bentwhistle's study to Radio City was as far as the earth to the moon. The more she'd seen of life, the more she'd begun to wonder how anyone could believe in anything.

Upstairs, the Rockettes were tapping up a storm while Kate Smith sang "God Bless America." It was time to be led to the Chair.

"Just stay calm and you'll be fine," Doyle said.

Calm? As they strapped her in, Mary Mabel's head swam, her heart skipped, her breath raced, and she sweated so much she was sure she'd be electrocuted on a loose wire.

Applause for the Rockettes. Hoover was introduced. More applause. The orchestra struck up "Thus Spake Zarathustra." *Oohs* and *ahhs*. The hydraulic gears turned. The dais lit up. Mary Mabel rose amid jetting fountains. Screams and whistles. It was Coney Island and the Salem witch trials all in one.

Keeler asked her questions about her life and miracles. She didn't know what she was saying. She was only aware of the lights, keeping her knees together, and wondering why she hadn't killed herself at Riverside Bridge when she'd had the chance. The next thing she knew, Hoover and Keeler were in a spotlight. Cameras whirred, drums rolled, and colour wheels danced stars across her chair.

"Mr. Keeler, you are the world authority on the lie detector."

"That's what they tell me," her interrogator said stiffly.

"Based on the results of tonight's polygraph test, is there any reason to believe that Sister Mary Mabel McTavish has lied about her life or her miracles?"

"No. There is not."

"Is there a shred of proof that she has said anything but the truth?"

"None whatsoever."

"Thank you, Mr. Keeler." Hoover turned to the audience and beamed. "Ladies and gentlemen, as director of the F.B.I., it is my pleasure to report that America's sweetheart is vindicated."

The audience was on its feet. Canes and crutches went flying.

Keeler wanted to say something, but stage hands directed him offstage. Mary Mabel's dais descended. Two G-men unstrapped her from the chair. Hoover took her by the arm and placed a pudgy hand against her back. A solemn hush fell over the crowd.

"Sister Mary Mabel McTavish," he said, "on behalf of all patriotic Americans, we at the F.B.I. applaud your courage in standing up to the forces of godlessness and Communism. Our enemies are everywhere, poised to attack. But you have shown them the moral armour of this great republic: the power of a pure heart. Your truth has made believers of us all. The nation salutes you."

Cheers and tears. The orchestra struck up "America the Beautiful." Hands went to hearts.

Then chaos. Rockettes erupted from the wings: "Help! Help! A madman!"

Brother Percy was on their tail, swinging a pair of wire cutters and a Bible. He flew downstage toward the audience. "Behold, it is I, Brother Percival Homer Brubacher, sent by God to lay waste to these Satanic abominations! Death in the fiery pit awaits, you potbellied buzzards of Beelzebub!"

Before Brother Percy could get out another word, a special agent tackled him from behind. He came down hard on his jaw.

Hoover dropped his knee on the small of Brother Percy's back. He slipped on cuffs, as a phalanx of G-men filled out the pose for the press. The last Mary Mabel saw of Brother Percy, he was being carried offstage by the F.B.I. while a swarm of Rockettes savaged him with tap shoes.

IX

HOLLYWOOD

An INVITATION

The FBI handed Brother Percy over to the New York Police, who took him to the local lockup and booked him on charges of disorderly conduct, public nuisance, and threatening with a weapon. A hearing and psychiatric assessment at Bellevue would follow, with bail denied until doctors had given the all clear.

"Percy's a loon," Mary Mabel said, "but he's not dangerous."

"You saw those wire cutters," Floyd replied. "Who knows what he might get up to."

Once things broke up at Radio City, Mary Mabel and her entourage — Floyd and Doyle — were chauffeured to Hearst's digs at the Clarendon. He'd flown in for the show and slipped away with Keeler following Brother Percy's arrest.

A private elevator brought the trio up to the first of Hearst's three floors. They were met by Mrs. Hearst, who was showing Keeler out. "You must be Miss McTavish," she said, nodding. "I understand you had quite the show. My husband is down the hall in the library. Have a good evening." She and Keeler sailed onto the elevator and disappeared.

Hearst stuck his head into the corridor. "What's keeping you?" He waved them into the library, wasting no time on introductions. "What can I get you?"

Doyle had warned them that Hearst was a teetotaller. Mary Mabel chose milk, the others coffee. Hearst beamed, pulled the velvet cord by the pipe organ, and led them to a semicircle of chairs and sofas arranged before a cozy fire. No sooner were they seated than a servant appeared and took the order.

"What a shame Mr. Keeler couldn't stay," Mary Mabel said.

Hearst winked, a little boy trapped in an old man's body. "Hoover's speech left him in a pickle."

"Why?"

"His polygraph *didn't* vindicate you. There wasn't any proof you lied, but there wasn't any proof you told the truth, either. Your pulse and respiration were off the chart throughout the entire interrogation. The test was meaningless."

"Does that mean I'll have to take another?"

"Don't be absurd. You've been cleared by the director of the F.B.I. on live radio. Tomorrow there'll be headlines coast to coast. And don't forget the newsreels."

Floyd stuck a finger under his collar. "What if Keeler goes public?"

Hearst smiled. "Leonarde's smart enough not to embarrass Hoover. I've also reminded him of our confidentiality agreement, and of my ownership of tonight's test, the record of which has kindled our little fire." A pause as they considered the blaze. "In any case, I've sent him on a long and well-deserved holiday trip to Europe." Hearst turned to Mary Mabel, hands folded behind his head. "On the subject of travel, have you ever been to Hollywood?"

"No."

"That's a crime I'd like to remedy. I want the movie rights to your story. Cosmopolitan will co-produce with Warner Brothers. Miss Marion Davies will star. Mr. Busby Berkeley will direct. I'd like you to meet the gang. You'll like the air out west. It has space. Manhattan's fine, but no sky, and a helluva lot of pipsqueaks nipping your ankles. Whaddya say?"

"We'd be delighted," said Floyd.

Hearst turned to Doyle. "As for you, young man, you're coming, too. I want to expand that syndicated column of yours.

L.A. has the sort of scoundrels a fellow like you could sink his teeth into."

Doyle hesitated. "Could I have a few days back home?"

"Don't worry about your mother. Bring her along. I'll see to the bills. Buffalo's no place for arthritis. Heck, it's no place for anything."

Doyle's eyeballs nearly bounced off the floor. "How, uh, how do you know about my mother?"

Hearst chuckled. "I take an interest in my employees. Especially the ones the competition might like to steal."

"Th-thank you," Doyle stammered.

"Yes," Mary Mabel seconded. "Thanks for everything."

"No, no. It is I who thank *you*," Hearst said. "You've let an old man dream."

The TEMPTATION *of* BROTHER PERCY

The night of the big show, Staff Sergeant Francis Malloy had been on desk duty at the Midtown North Precinct, 54th and 8th. Malloy was an honest cop. He didn't care about free home renovations. He didn't care about fur coats for the wife. He didn't even care about free Dodgers tickets. All he cared about was ridding New York of gangsters. Cops with that kind of attitude got themselves killed or stuck on the night desk, which is exactly where Malloy had been stuck for the past thirty years.

His job was to sort the incoming riffraff. Pickpockets, stickup artists, and three-card-monte operators were booked and locked in a nearby holding cell to await arraignment hearings in the morning. Winos were dumped in the drunk tank, a retch-hole far enough away that their rants wouldn't get on the nerves.

Malloy had the company of a handful of rookies. They played poker and drank gin out of paper cups while he did all the work. This gave him migraines. Tonight's migraine was worse than usual thanks to the arrival of Brother Percival Homer Brubacher. The reverend believed that if he prayed loud enough the Angel of the Lord would descend in a blaze of light, put a spell on the guards, cast open the cell doors, and deliver him unto freedom. Apparently this had worked for Peter the Apostle.

Since Brubacher was up on charges, he'd been put in the holding cell, but after hours of animated prayer it was even money who'd kill him first: his fellow crooks or the rookie cops. Dead prisoners meant paperwork. When the preacher collapsed in tongues, Malloy did them both a favour and threw him in the drunk tank.

Brother Percy was confused. He'd expected to emerge from his religious ecstasy a free man. Instead, he found himself in a dark room face down on a tile floor that smelled of urine and vomit. From all corners came sobs, snores, screams of delirium, and the sight of shapeless forms rutting the air in agony. It was Hell with the thermostat turned down.

The reverend gasped. In front of his nose was a drain hole the size of a pie plate. A monstrous black fly with a ripe, hairy body crawled up through the grate. It was slow and lazy, with thick-veined wings and eyes like darkened glitter balls. The fly stared at him. "Good evening, Brother Brubacher," it said.

Percy wet himself: God had rendered him unto Satan.

"Fear not," said the fly. "I've come to save you."

"Tempt me not, Satan!" Percy cried. "The Lord God Jehovah is my saviour! I am His prophet"

"Oh yeah?" The fly rubbed its front legs together in mock prayer. "What kind of saviour treats his prophet like shit? Blows up his family? Steals his ministry? Locks him in a drunk tank?"

Percy's eyes welled. "Enough. Please."

But Satan went on and on. He told him secrets that Percy had always known in his heart but had been afraid to face. The Almighty had lied to him. He'd never intended for Percy to be famous. For all He cared, Percy could rot in a madhouse, alone and anonymous; the butt of some sick cosmic joke.

Percy began to cry.

"It was ever thus," the fly consoled. "God abuses everyone who loves Him. He ordered Abraham to kill his son. He abandoned His chosen people in the desert. He tortured His own boy on a cross. And did He ever once say, 'I'm sorry'? Not on your life. He doesn't give a damn about the faithful."

Percy smote his head on the tiles. He stuffed his fingers in his ears. "Stop. Stop. You'll lead me to Hell."

"So what? It's a nice place. Interesting people." The fly flicked its sucker on a speck of dung. "Face it, Perce, you've been had. Sunday school is a pack of lies."

"Why should I believe you?"

"What have you got to lose?"

"My immortal soul."

"Oh that."

"Yes," Brother Percy wept. "That! That and eternal paradise."

"Paradise is a bore. Nothing but flying around with a harp singing 'Hallelujah.' You wanna spend eternity bowing and scraping to some jerk who's played you for a sucker? Follow me, Perce. I'll give you fame, fortune, and glory everlasting. They won't laugh at you with me around. No one will ever laugh at you again."

Brother Percy thought about his life. His sacrifice and ruination. Tears streamed down his face. Satan was right. God had betrayed him. Laughed at him. Over and over and over. It wasn't fair. It had to stop. It would. Here. Now. He, Percival Homer Brubacher, was going to get even.

"Time for Communion," the fly said.

Brother Percy nodded grimly. In one swift move, he gripped the fly by its wings, popped it in his mouth, and swallowed.

"That's my boy," Satan buzzed inside him. "Now here's a plan to get us out of this joint. See that guy passed out over there? The one with the big red ears?"

The rookies were well-hootched when the riot exploded in the drunk tank. Malloy went to investigate. He peered into the cage. Despite the dim light, it was easy to spot the chief rabble-rouser. Although Malloy hadn't remembered the reverend being so broad-chested or having such big red ears, the mangy beard, rubber cap, top hat, and tails gave him away.

"Go to sleep, Reverend."

"I ain't a reverend. Turn on the lights. Some bastard's stoled my stuff. I aim to see who done it."

Malloy laughed. "What stuff?" On arrival, prisoners were frisked. Belts, shoelaces, pocket knives, and other potential weapons were put in a basket. The reverend had come up clean, except for a handful of bent wires.

"None of your damn business, what stuff." The prisoner rattled the cage. "Now turn on the goddamn lights. You're pissing me off."

The rookies were delighted to learn that Brubacher was the source of the trouble. They needed some exercise. "Come on boys," hollered flatfoot Tony Dolittle, whapping his nightstick on the palm of his hand, "Let's play us some baseball." Beating the shit out of loonies and drunks was like shooting fish in a barrel. They were too afraid to fight back, they never complained, and who'd believe them if they did? Malloy warned the boys about the perils of paperwork, but they pushed him aside. "Who's up for a home run?"

Unfortunately for the rookies, "the reverend" wasn't the pushover they'd imagined. The minute Dolittle swaggered into the cage, the reverend yanked his arms from their sockets, flipped him ass-over-teakettle, and stomped on his head. Then he grabbed Dolittle's night stick and made lunch meat of his pals. Malloy called in reinforcements. By the time the battle was over, the reverend was in a straitjacket at Bellevue, and the rookie cops were at St. Vincent's in body casts.

The drunk tank was released in the morning. Brother Percy grinned. Satan had delivered him as promised; it had been His idea to switch clothes with that comatose stranger. The man was tall like himself, while the oversized tails allowed for his fuller frame. Still, it was a close call. Snapping the shower cap above those big red ears had roused the beast. Luckily Percy had managed to hide under a pile of hoboes.

There were newsies hawking papers on every corner. Each had a banner headline heralding the triumph of the Miracle Maid and a large photo of Mary Mabel shaking hands with J. Edgar Hoover. They had a smaller picture of him too, face-down, being mugged by Rockettes, along with a sidebar about a "disgruntled former employee" now locked up in Bellevue after starting a riot in the midtown cop shop. He was variously identified as Pierce Homer Brewbeaker, Pierce Homer Broobunker, or homely Perce Brubinker.

Another injustice to be avenged. However, first things first; he needed to eat and he had no money. He held out his hand. "Spare change?" The crowd hurried by as if he didn't exist. Percy was outraged until it dawned on him that Satan had given him the cloak of invisibility. Delighted, he made faces at the passersby. Then he skipped across the street to a sidewalk vendor, grabbed a hot dog off the grill, and waved it in front of the vendor's nose. He expected the ghostly effect would make the man scream. Instead, the man asked what the hell Percy was doing and demanded two bits or he'd call the cops.

Percy dropped the hot dog and fled. He hid in a stairwell. The smells from the grill had made him even more ravenous. "What must I do, Lord of Darkness?" Satan told him to check the lining of the jacket he'd stolen from the stranger. There was a small hole at the bottom of the inside breast pocket. Percy reached through into the lining. To his astonishment, it was full of bills.

• • • •

Things were moving too fast for Slick. One minute he'd been about to plug McTavish. The next he'd woken up in a stinking hole, minus his money coat. Then he'd knocked heads with an army of cops calling him a reverend, and gotten jabbed with a hypodermic. Now, from what he could see, he was in a strait-jacket facing a table of shrinks.

Mind you, what he could see wasn't much. In the paddy wagon to Bellevue, the cops had renovated his face. His nose wandered from ear to ear, his cheekbones were somewhere in his forehead, and his eyes dripped like rotten cantaloupes.

The chief psychiatrist cleared his throat. "Good morning, Brother Brubacher."

"I ain't Brother Brubacher. The name's Slick Skinner. I'm a trapper from Canada."

The table smiled indulgently. "Perhaps you could tell us what a Canadian trapper is doing in New York?"

"I heard you had a bunch of the-aters. Thought I'd catch me some girlie shows."

The psychiatrists doodled. "How long have you been in New York?"

"Long enough."

"Where are you staying?"

"Around."

"What are you living on?"

"I got me a money coat."

Pause. "A 'money coat'? What exactly is a 'money coat'?"

"Whaddya think? It's a coat with money in it."

"I see. And how did you happen to get this magical 'money' coat?"

Slick thought of all the tourists he'd robbed in Central Park. "I dunno," he said. "Guess it was a birthday present. Or maybe I found it."

"Could you show it to us?"

"Nope. Some bastard stoled it."

The chief psychiatrist wiped his glasses with the end of his tie. "It's no use pretending. We know the truth about you, Brother Brubacher."

A question floated into Slick's head. He'd have frowned, only it hurt too much. "Why do you keep calling me Brother Brubacher? Why would that fella be in jail?"

"Perhaps you can tell us."

"Dunno. He's strange, maybe?"

"What do you mean by 'strange'?"

"You know, he talks to hisself."

The table exchanged glances. "How do you know he talks to himself?"

Slick's entrails congealed; he couldn't very well say he'd stalked the miracle tour. "I s'pose I don't."

"Sure you do," the chief psychiatrist said gently. He ambled over to Slick's chair, knelt slowly and whispered in his ear. "When Brother Brubacher talks to himself ... Slick ... is he talking to you?"

Slick's eyes bugged. "I'm not an imaginary friend if that's what you're asking."

"It's not what I'm asking," the psychiatrist said calmly. "What I'm asking is ... when Brother Brubacher talks to himself, are you the one who talks back?"

"Hold on. I'm Slick Skinner. I'm real."

"Do you talk to him, Slick? Do you tell him what to do?"

"I ain't some crazy voice, dammit! I'm real!" Slick struggled in his chains and straitjacket as if his life depended on it.

The chief psychiatrist conferred with the table. The judgment was unanimous: Only a true psychotic could lie with such conviction. The chief psychiatrist turned to the guards. "Return

Brother Brubacher to solitary. Keep him restrained. And tell the ward nurse we'll be ordering a full range of injections."

MAKING PICTURES

Doyle was given a few days with his mother to discuss the move to California. If she agreed, he'd pack up the apartment and fly out with her by week's end.

Meanwhile, Floyd and Mary Mabel traveled with Hearst to Los Angeles. Hearst's friend, Marion Davies, greeted them at the airport.

"So I'm going to be you," she said, giving Mary Mabel a big hug. She insisted that the young woman stay in her place at Warner Brothers. "It's sitting empty while I'm at San Simeon, and there's a four-room trailer next door for your manager."

Hearst had arranged a small luncheon to introduce Floyd and Mary Mabel to the Misters Warner and Berkeley. It was held at his beach house in Santa Monica. He'd wanted a relaxed get-together with Marion and her dachshunds, but Warner hijacked the agenda. As soon they'd settled into their deck chairs and the waiters had served the appetizers — shrimps, avocado and mango slices — he flashed a serious set of teeth. "Great project, W.R. Only one problem. Who's gonna play the girl?"

"That would be Marion," Hearst said tightly, tossing a shrimp to one of the dogs.

Warner gave Mary Mabel a look. "You a school kid, angel cakes?"

"Till recently."

"A virgin?"

"Of course!"

"So, no offense, Marion, but like I said, we got a problem."

Hearst's face went blotchy.

"Come on, Pops," Marion said. "Jack's pulling your leg."

"Is that right, Jack? Are you pulling my leg?"

"Depends which one."

Marion laughed. Hearst didn't. He banged the table so hard the silverware clattered. "Marion's cast!"

"Okay, okay." Warner rolled his eyes. "And who do you want for the dead kid?"

Hearst collected himself. "I want Mayer to loan us Mickey Rooney. Or do you think *he's* geriatric, too?"

"Not if he's playing opposite Marion. Just kidding. Rooney's a swell kid, swell. Providing you don't mind having your chorus girls knocked up. By the time that friggin' midget's through puberty there won't be a virgin north of La Jolla. Except, of course, for Marion."

Hearst yanked the tablecloth off the table sending salads, glasses and cutlery flying. "This party is over!"

Mary Mabel and Floyd froze in horror. To the rest it was business as usual.

"Don't be such a Droopy Drawers," Marion teased.

"I think you've had too much ginger ale, my dear," Hearst said, his eyes drilling holes through Warner.

Marion winked at the waiters cowering in the doorway. "We need a tidy-up out here." She rose and whispered something in Hearst's ear. It did the trick.

"Forgive my rudeness," he apologized. "We'll have our sandwiches indoors."

They relocated to the dining room, except for the dogs who stayed to help clean up the food. The conversation switched from casting to content.

Warner got to the point. "They tell me your mom's dead."

"Yes," Mary Mabel said.

"This I like. No, this I love. We can make her into an angel."

Mary Mabel was speechless. Hearst was appalled. But talk of an angel got Busby very excited. He made a big frame with his hands. "I got it! The Miracle Maid sees visions, right? Well guess what! Her visions are production numbers! Picture it. She prays to the sound of a heavenly choir. Dissolve to a rotating staircase of clouds filled with tap-dancing angels! Chorus girls with harps and wings! Lots of mirrors. Dry ice. Strings. The camera pans up and up and up. Bingo, we're at the Pearly Gates! Fifty, sixty choir boys flying around in silk pajamas and —"

"Busby, what the fuck are you on?" demanded Warner.

"Cloud nine!"

"Cloud moolah-moolah. Those angels of yours better have big tits."

Busby spun around to Hearst. "It'll make Marion the talk of the town! At the climax of her vision, she sails up to Heaven on a star. The Pearly Gates swing open, she waltzes in, and there's God!"

"Who's God?"

"Paul Muni. His head, anyway. It's enormous. It beams light." Busby gave a sly shrug. "Who am I kidding? Jack's right. It's too expensive."

"How much?" Hearst's eyes had an odd light.

"A hundred big ones."

"No problem," Hearst announced grandly. "For Marion, the works."

"Great," said Warner. "You pay for heaven, I'll spring for the avalanche."

"What avalanche?" Mary Mabel asked.

"The one where the kid gets killed."

"But he died in an electrical storm at a tent revival."

"Yeah. An electrical storm at a tent revival in the Rockies. The storm sets off an avalanche. The kid gets electrocuted and carried off in the slide. Your prayers lead to where he's buried. Voila! His little fried frozen body gets dug up by a bunch of Indians, French fur traders, and some schmuck Mountie on a horse. You lay on hands, the kid resurrects, happy ending, roll credits."

"That's not how it happened."

"It is now. This is the pictures, baby doll. You want reality, hang out at the morgue."

"Excuse me, Mr. Warner, but if you want my co-operation I'd appreciate some respect."

"Respect? Who the hell do you think you are? You're not even the writer."

"Jack, Miss McTavish, why don't we work out the details later?" Hearst intervened.

"Sure thing," Warner said. "Like the little detail about who's payin' the friggin' bills." He whirled around and stuck a finger in Mary Mabel's face. "You better learn to play nice or you'll be doing miracles up in heaven with your mama." He glanced at his watch. "Two o'clock. Gotta scram. I have a private meeting with Miss Crawford, if you know what I mean." As he left, he called over his shoulder, "Gimmee a shout, W.R. Marion's cast, but have a think about de Havilland. Or maybe Deanna Durbin." He was gone before Hearst's plate hit the door.

There was an awkward silence. Busby took his leave.

"I'm sorry," Hearst fumed to Mary Mabel. "Jack is Jack. I'll deal with him. In the meantime, please know I want you to be happy. There'll be no more talk about an avalanche."

"Or trappers, or Mounties or tap-dancing angels. I don't mean to be difficult. I just don't want to be humiliated."

"None of us do," Marion said softly. She turned to Hearst. "You know, Pops, Jack may be right about me being wrong for the part. No, really. I'm not a spring chicken anymore."

"Hush, hush." Hearst took her hand and stroked it tenderly. "You will never grow old, Marion. Never. I forbid it."

• • • •

The next morning, the storm had blown over. Hearst called the ministry to say he'd had an inspiration. He thought there should be a part in the film for a heroic young reporter, a certain "K.O. Doyle," to be played by Clark Gable. He hoped Mary Mabel would approve.

"Approve? You've made my day!"

"I have a second present for you," he enthused. "I've arranged for a private bus to take you and Mr. Cruickshank on a tour of the city."

It was a wonderful tour, although Mary Mabel felt odd travelling in a big bus alone with a tour guide and driver, while a waiter served her beverages and hot snacks and a masseur rubbed her neck and feet. Floyd had begged off. He said he was tired, but he smelled of hangover.

Mary Mabel returned to her dressing-room-cum-mansion in the late afternoon. To her surprise, a stretch limousine was parked in front of Floyd's trailer. A chauffeur was standing on the curb in full livery.

Floyd sauntered out of his trailer. He had a big smile on his face. "Hey kid," he whispered, "come see what the cat dragged home."

Mary Mabel peeked inside. There at the table sat Miss Bentwhistle.

A MODEST PROPOSAL

The Baroness Bentwhistle of Bentwhistle had been leading the life of Riley. In a few short months she had become a fixture in the society columns of the Los Angeles dailies. Dr. Silver, Lord High Secretary and Steward of the Calendar, *pro tem*, took his responsibilities seriously, reserving her Ladyship's time for the most exclusive of exclusive functions. Securing the Baroness, and consequent media coverage of one's event, required considerable wooing.

The success of the Baroness had been immediate. Everyone had heard about her meetings with the banks. Preliminary auditions had been held in the sitting room of her presidential suite at the Beverly Hills Hotel, where the Baroness sat on a throne flanked by her Coat of Arms and Family Tree from the Heralds' College of Westminster. Institutions sending less than their presidents were refused a hearing. Those whose presidents lacked personal pedigrees were summarily dismissed, for Miss Bentwhistle knew that the very rich were too polite to ask each other personal questions, and, in her situation, the fewer questions the better.

Local media gave full play to her selection: Wells Fargo. There were front-page photographs of the Baroness and her strongbox of jewels surrounded by the bank's board of directors.

Wells Fargo had nearly lost out. C.E.O. Mr. John C. Wilcox III had asked that it be allowed to appraise the jewels. "What are you suggesting, young man?" the Baroness demanded of the sixty-year-old Mr. Wilcox. "If the Baron were with us, God rest his soul, I should not be forced to suffer such impertinence."

Mr. Wilcox assured her that his request was standard practice.

The Baroness was shocked. "To think that your world is so steeped in chicanery and vice that even nobility cannot be trusted. What a sad comment on democracy. Be that as it may, while the humiliation of its clients may be standard practice at Wells Fargo, such treatment is as foreign to me as baked beans. Trust, Mr. Wilcox, is central to my relationships. It has been prized by my ancestors for over nine hundred years. Good day."

Mr. Wilcox apologized profusely. In her case the bank would make an exception.

She refused to hear of it. "Do you honestly believe contrition can repair this breech?"

The Baroness forgave him when Mr. Wilcox amended his apology to include the complimentary use of a limousine and driver.

Following publication of the Bentwhistle/Wells Fargo entente, rumours of the jewels' value spiralled upwards, from ten million, to fifteen, to twenty. When asked to confirm the speculation, both parties smiled discreetly. "No comment." The stock of the jewels shot up again.

All the while, Dr. Silver was an angel. The Baroness had only intended to stay at his home for a week. However, he insisted on a second and a third. Eventually, she and Mistress Dolly took up permanent residence, venturing forth as valued weekend guests at the tony getaways of the city's elite.

Dr. Silver came along for the ride. Now that he was consort to a baroness, he was much more than a flamboyant social butterfly; he was a player. In order to keep his prize catch, he catered to her every need. He made her a new set of dentures with her name inscribed in gold on the inside of her right molars. He even arranged a milk bath. "There is nothing for the complexion like soaking in fresh milk," the Baroness had enthused. She'd been drunk at the time. Confronted by a room-temperature tub of the stuff, she was nearly sick. She soaked for ten minutes, then insisted that the milk be rebottled and sent to a downtown soup kitchen as an act of charity. That afternoon she had to stay indoors; the flies wouldn't keep off her.

Despite a few such misfires, life *chez* Silver was Shangri-La; a parade of occasions that offered special delight to Miss Pigeon. As a Baptist, she loved being scandalized. In fact she made a point of it. "God disapproves of dancing," she told Miss Bentwhistle at one particular dinner dance, standing in Dr. Silver's foyer hanging coats.

"It's not dancing, Dolly," the Baroness replied. "It's choreography."

The Mistress of the Wardrobe sniffed. "I also suspect that our host is 'artistic.' Dancing will do that to a man."

"Heavenly days, my dear," said Miss Bentwhistle, "Dr. Silver's not artistic. Just sophisticated."

The day Mary Mabel arrived in Los Angeles, the Baroness was in her housecoat enjoying a blueberry muffin. Dolly read her the announcement in the papers. The Baroness thought she was having a heart attack. It turned out to be gas.

The glory of her disguise had been that a baroness was simultaneously important and inconsequential. A star in local society, a mere extra in national life. In other words, someone who could make a splash without fear of getting wet, providing she didn't swallow a truckload of pills or run off with a busboy.

Mary Mabel, however, had the connections and motive to blow her cover. Miss Bentwhistle considered hiding. Where? For how long? No matter the town, big fish swim in the same bowl.

And it wasn't as if the name "Bentwhistle" wouldn't ring bells. Oh, if only she'd been born the Baroness Jones.

The Baroness called Dr. Meredith Whitehead for a house call. Dr. Whitehead was a distinguished heart specialist. To be more specific, he was an unemployed actor who'd once played the role of a distinguished heart specialist. Socialites didn't care; he was better than the real thing. He had a winning bedside manner, a keen desire to get to the bottom of things, and a stethoscope that wouldn't quit. The moment he walked in a room, female patients opened their mouths and said "Ah."

Dr. Wilson's consultation put the Baroness in a jolly mood. His acting career was proof that disaster is simply another word for opportunity. In that light, Mary Mabel's arrival might actually be a cause for celebration. Her "eureka" moment happened as Dr. Wilson poked about in search of her prostate. She hadn't the heart to tell him she didn't have one: Actors are so fragile, a criticism can ruin their performance; so instead she screamed encouragement. "Oh, God! You're almost there! Yes! Yes! A little more! Oh! Ah! Eureka! EUREKA!!!"

Years of small-town intrigue had taught Miss Bentwhistle that the surest route to security is to turn one's enemies into dependents. Her "eureka" was a plan to dominate Mary Mabel and enrich her own finances in the bargain.

Millions in presumed collateral had enabled the Baroness to enjoy the generosity of the city's elite. Her cash flow, however, was non-existent. Holy Redemption Ministries had the opposite problem: cash flow, but no collateral. In different ways, the Baroness and the ministry were each dependent on the goodwill of the gullible. Why not marry their strengths and eliminate their weaknesses?

Miss Bentwhistle recalled that Floyd had been an ally with respect to her Academy gala. Dr. Silver placed a call. Happily, Mary Mabel was sightseeing; Floyd was home and eager to talk.

• • • •

Floyd recognized the former headmistress the moment she stepped from her limousine. He was more amused than surprised; merchants in imagination have a talent for turning up in the unlikeliest places. He offered the Baroness a drink and congratulated her on the tragedies leading to her inheritance. "So," he said as they clinked glasses, "what's on your mind?"

"I want to make you rich beyond your wildest dreams."

"I'm all ears."

The Baroness inclined her head. "There's a little radio station just outside the Hollywood Hills. WKRN. It broadcasts country music, weather reports, stockyard prices, and local obituaries. Understandably, the owners have been trying to unload it for years. It could be yours for a million."

"What would I want with a money pit?"

"A money pit? You mean a gold mine! Sister Mary Mabel knows how to fill a collection plate. Imagine if that collection plate was passed throughout the greater Los Angeles area. Sister will star in a range of new programs. Breakfast sermonettes, lunchtime prayers for the sick, and on-air supper calls from the healed. The station will also feature hourly pitches for Sister's Charity of the Week."

Floyd's mouth watered. "One problem. I don't have a million in seed money."

"But I do." The Baroness beamed. "Wells Fargo will loan the money. A small portion of my jewels will serve as collateral. The repayment of principal and interest will be your responsibility, said costs and other expenditures to be deducted from your donations. You'll have fun doing the books." They shared a smile. "Incidentally," she added, "as silent partner, I shall receive 50 percent of the gross."

"The net."

"If you insist. Providing we use my accountant."

Floyd licked his chops. A 50/50 split. Not bad. In theory, he had the added cost of Doyle's 15 percent, the payoff for the Metrotone newsreel. In practice, he hadn't paid the kid a cent, and wasn't about to start. The reporter had asked for payments every six months, but events had outpaced expectations; Hearst had handed him a syndicated column and cash for his mother. If Doyle tried to play hardball now, Floyd would rat him out as a two-bit extortionist.

So ... Holy Redemption Ministries would enjoy its full 50 percent of the pie. And what a pie it promised to be. As the Good Book said: "To them that have shall be given." Say what one might, the Lord was no Communist.

Floyd raised his glass. "Here's to the deal."

"You men are always in a hurry," the Baroness purred. "WKRN is only the beginning. The promotional tool to launch the deal of the century!"

"I beg your pardon?"

"Dear friend," — she placed her hand on her bosom — "I refer to the greatest sensation to hit Los Angeles since the quake. The Heavenly Dwellings!" Miss Bentwhistle proceeded to sketch her vision on the back of a napkin. "The Heavenly Dwellings will be a complex of apartment buildings extending from a central Prayer Tower, a.k.a., the WKRN transmitter. Purchasers may buy permanent residence, or a week of recreational access per year."

As with the radio station, Wells Fargo would loan the money, the Bentwhistle jewels serving as collateral, and the ministry would repay principal and interest. The wrinkle? The ministry and the Baroness would hold joint title on the complex in trust for their purchasers, the Heavenly Dwellers.

"The faithful will be attracted by their access to Sister Mary Mabel," the Baroness enthused. "Our little star will take her radio microphone outside at noon each day for a live laying-on of hands at the Prayer Tower. Now there's a show worth a listen!"

The Dwellings would also be marketed to spiritually minded organizations. Churches could buy apartments as retreats for their ministers, deacons, and parishioners. National service groups could underwrite whole blocks in exchange for promotional considerations broadcast on Sister's Charity of the Week.

Best of all, units would be sold for less than market value, even though 60 percent of all payments would be skimmed by the ministry and Baroness "in consideration of professional services rendered." This financing would be possible thanks to the miracle of ever-expanding markets. As the Baroness explained it, down payments on apartment two would help to build apartment one; down payments on apartments three and four would help to build apartment two; and so forth.

"Sounds like a Ponzi scheme," said Floyd.

The Baroness brushed the air with her hand. "Capitalism is a Ponzi scheme. Boom and bust, boom and bust. Has the Depression taught you nothing?"

"Yeah. The bust part. What happens when we go belly up?"

"Don't be absurd. We're not selling a South Seas Bubble. We're selling L.A. real estate. Location, location, location. And our location will be next to God's heart. Not to mention a hop, skip, and a jump to the ocean. Besides, Sister will attract the hopelessly infirm. God willing, they'll drop dead before they hit the beach, leaving us their deposits and a mention in their wills."

"What if they all survive?"

"In that unfortunate event, we make the Dwellings our permanent Charity of the Week. I can see the billboards. 'Suffer the little children,' saith the Lord. Support a Heavenly Dwelling for the sad little ragamuffins of skid row.' Or, if you prefer, 'Pity the sick and dying. Give them a Heavenly Dwelling till Jesus calls them home.' As a bonus incentive, we'll promise a lobby display of donors' names engraved on marble scrolls headed *The Heavenly Angels*. Depending on the size of their contributions, we'll list them as Archangels, Cherubs, or Members of the Choir.'"

Floyd grinned. "Who'd have thought a Baroness could be so crafty."

"Nothing to it," Miss Bentwhistle demurred. "After all, I've run a girls' school."

Outside, Hearst's private bus drove up. Mary Mabel had returned from sightseeing. Cruickshank went out to greet her.

Miss Bentwhistle gritted her teeth. She'd won over the producer, but Mary Mabel would be a harder sell. As the girl approached the trailer, she prepared to swallow her pride. Miss Bentwhistle hated eating crow. However, eating crow was better than eating dirt.

PARTNERS

Mary Mabel was flabbergasted at the sight of Miss Bentwhistle. Moreso when she discovered her old headmistress was posing as a monied baroness. "You don't have millions in jewels!"

"I certainly do, my dear. Ask anyone."

"'Anyone' can be deceived."

"People who live in glass houses," Miss Bentwhistle replied.

Floyd interrupted to say that the Baroness had come with an interesting proposal.

"She can leave with it, too," Mary Mabel said. "Use me once, shame on you; use me twice, shame on me."

To Mary Mabel's astonishment, Miss Bentwhistle fell on her knees. "You are right, my dear. I have sinned against you. Grievously. Pray, forgive my temper. Forgive my abuses. They are but several of my many transgressions. It is difficult at my age to try and set right a lifetime of wrongdoing, but with your help I should like to try."

The sight of Miss Bentwhistle on the floor was embarrassing. She was much easier to deal with when she was ornery. Mary Mabel helped her back into her chair with misgiving.

"Thank you, my lamb," the Baroness said and pulled her hankie from her sleeve. "Admitting the truth is a frightening but necessary step on the road to salvation. As I have described to Mr. Cruickshank, the destruction of the Academy was my wakeup call. I had given it my soul, trampling on anyone and everyone to ensure its success. God took it from me that I might see the wretched hollowness of my life. I did. And was ashamed. Fortunately, as the Reverend Mandible likes to say, 'The good Lord never closes one door without opening another.' In the

midst of my desolation, I discovered that I had inherited the family barony and the jewels that go with it. Like Saul at Damascus,
I resolved to be reborn, resurrected into a life of good works.
I have so admired how you have overcome adversity, my dear;
adversity in which I, alas, have played no small part. I decided to
come to you with my good fortune, not only to seek forgiveness
and to make amends, but in the hope that I might contribute to
the happiness you bring to others."

At this point, Miss Bentwhistle was overcome. She blew her
nose and motioned for Floyd to outline her proposal.

He explained that the Baroness had offered to provide the collateral for the ministry to buy a radio station. It would broadcast
Mary Mabel's message of hope across the state. Across the country, if it blossomed into a network. Moreover, the Bentwhistle
jewels would secure a loan to enable the construction of "a city of
God on earth — the Heavenly Dwellings," a set of charitable and
low-income apartment blocks designed for the sick, the destitute,
and the dying.

Reaching into homes to offer comfort to shut-ins, putting
her name to the service of homes and retreats for the poor — the
possibilities made Mary Mabel's head swim. But no sooner was
she prepared to accept Miss Bentwhistle's charity, than her pride
rose up, telling her to stay clear of the dragon at all costs.

How cruel, Mary Mabel reproached herself. *Miss Bentwhistle
has humbled herself to me and begged to change her life. Why
should I do anything but rejoice?*

Pride said that a snake could change its skin, but it was
still a snake. Didn't Mary Mabel think her confession was a
mite rich?

It's her manner, she answered back. *Besides, what about forgiveness? What about turning the other cheek? It's what Mama
would do.*

Pride answered that if her mama hadn't been so forgiving she might have left her papa and had a decent life. There's turning the other cheek, and then there's being plain stupid. What proof did she have that Miss Bentwhistle was even a baroness?

Well, Mary Mabel thought, *I've seen her Coat of Arms and Family Tree often enough. They hung in the Academy's dining hall for years. If Miss Bentwhistle's descended from a baron, she might well have inherited the title. The banks and everyone else in town believe so. Am I smarter than the world? Down, Pride, down! I only have to look in the mirror to know that anything's possible.*

Pride kept Mary Mabel's stomach in knots, but it wasn't going to make her deny the needy out of spite.

"I'm sorry for being so harsh," she said to Miss Bentwhistle. "Life takes us on such curious journeys. I'm glad we have the opportunity to put away a difficult past. Working on a radio station and building projects for the poor would be an honour. I thank you for the opportunity. I know my mama thanks you, too."

"God bless you," Miss Bentwhistle wept. "And God bless your mama."

And so it came to pass that within days the Miracle Maid was sitting behind the microphone of Holy Redemption's WKRN: "This is Sister Mary Mabel McTavish, Helping Heaven Help You." The response was so positive that Floyd was soon making down payments on stations in the Midwest. It seemed proof to Mary Mabel that the collaboration with her enemy had been ordained. Her mama must be smiling.

Over the next months, Mary Mabel's schedule was gruelling. As well as the radio shows, she appeared at the Hollywood Bowl and the Los Angeles Coliseum. Floyd said it was important for her to stay in touch with her public, and that the publicity from these services would benefit the start-up of their emerging network.

There was no question that they got publicity. Owing to the size of the venues, Floyd invested considerable time and money on production values. Once he had Mary Mabel roar up the aisle dressed as a cop on a motorcycle, siren roaring. She was joined by what seemed like the entire L.A.P.D. The gimmick was that she'd arrived to arrest sin. It made for great front-page photographs.

Mostly though, Floyd filled the stage with animals. He got them from the McConaghie Family Circus and Petting Zoo. The McConaghies had spent their lives touring county fairs throughout California. Most of their animals had been caught in the hills and desert around Los Angeles: mountain lions, coyotes, bobcats, elk, turkey vultures, prairie dogs, and assorted lizards, snakes, and barnyard animals. They also had alligators, crocodiles, an old blind camel, a white horse painted with black stripes to look like a zebra, and a dead elephant stuffed with hay which they propped in a cage, its trunk in a tub of water.

The McConaghie Family Circus had featured human acts, as well. The McConaghie boys had dressed like Tarzan and wrestled the crocodiles: The crocodiles were drugged; so were the boys. Little Belinda McConaghie, the youngest, wanted to be a ballet dancer, so her dad had put her in a tutu and stuck her on the high wire; she fell off so often that the routine turned into a trampoline act. For their part, Mr. and Mrs. McConaghie had performed on the trapeze. People flocked to see their midair collisions. Also to see Mr. McConaghie end the show by being shot out of a cannon.

By the time Floyd found them, The McConaghie Family Circus was a more-or-less stationary attraction, set up by the roadside in what might best be described as a one-family trailer park. The boys, tubby fifty-year-olds, still wrestled the crocodiles. The crocs were now embalmed, but visitors didn't care; it was scary enough seeing the brothers in their loincloths. Meanwhile, baby Belinda had given up the trampoline for fortune-telling, Mrs. McConachie sold lemonade and stale Crackerjack off a beat-up card table, and Mr. McConachie sat on his rocker swatting away flies.

Mr. McConachie was surprised that Floyd wanted to rent his sheep. "They're cute, but stupid as shit." That was fine as far as Floyd were concerned. They just had to stand still, while Mary Mabel entered the stage carrying the littlest. "Hello," she'd say to the kids in the audience. "I'm Sister Mary Mabel and this is Sally. She's the little lamb that lost her way; the little lost lamb that went astray." The kids would giggle. "Would any of you like to come up and pet little Sally?" Squeals of delight.

The mountain lions were even more of a sensation. They appeared in a sermon called, "Dare to Be a Daniel," based on the story of Daniel in the lions' den. "Would you like to come up and pet the lions?" A surprising number of parents were eager to have their children cuddle predators. Fortunately, the McConachie lions were senile, toothless, and doped to the gills. In fact, Mary Mabel had seen livelier rugs.

Despite all the work, she had some wonderful getaways. Hearst invited her and her partners to various parties at San Simeon. It was tricky getting away, but Hearst was sensitive to refusals, so when possible, Sister's appearance schedule would be rearranged and she'd make an audio recording for WKRN to play in her absence.

Doyle was a little jealous of Hearst's invitations. He told Mary Mabel it was because he missed her company, but she suspected it was really because he was dying to go himself. An invitation to a Hearst party meant you were a star. She dropped a few hints in Hearst's ear about what great company Doyle was, and hoped for the best.

But even if Doyle missed Mary Mabel when she was in San Simeon, he was at all her public appearances. She said that for a non-believer like him her shows must be torture. He joked that the real reason he came was in hopes of seeing a lion eat one of the kids. She smiled. Despite his tough guy routine, he loved the little moppets.

Usually he brought his mother. He said the fresh air was good for her. Mary Mabel liked Ma Rinker a lot. After the show, Ma would invite her back to her new home for cookies and cocoa. Scrapbooks of Sister's adventures were prominently displayed on the coffee table. Or perhaps it would be more accurate to say she displayed scrapbooks of her son's accounts of Sister's adventures. Her eyes beamed with pride whenever he was in the room.

"K.O. tells me you're very kind," Ma confided one day when he'd stepped out on an errand. "He likes you."

"I like him, too," Mary Mabel said.

"Good." Ma smiled knowingly.

"I like him as a friend, Mrs. Rinker. That's all."

"Mmm-hmm."

Doyle and his mother had chosen a tiny bungalow in Pasadena. Neither of them could stand Los Angeles. They thought it was a contradiction in terms: a city of angels without souls. Pasadena on the other hand was small and neighbourly, with orange groves and mountains and fresh air. "Not too big to get lost in, and not so small that you feel alone," is how Ma Rinker put it. There was a hospital nearby that could handle emergencies, and Doyle's drive to work was a country breeze.

"Pasadena won't stay like this forever," Mary Mabel said.

Doyle shrugged. "Nothing ever does. But it's here for now and that's what counts."

Mary Mabel never offered Ma a laying-on of hands, nor did Ma ever ask for one. Still, when it was time to leave, Ma would hold her hands longer than necessary. Doyle would get annoyed. "Ma, she has to get back for the supper show."

One evening as he drove Mary Mabel to work he said, "She listens to your programs."

"That's nice."

Doyle didn't smile. "Yesterday I caught her touching the radio during your healing hour."

"She says she's feeling better."

"She's gotten out of Buffalo."

Mary Mabel paused. "K.O., lots of other people are touching their radios and claiming miracles. You write about them."

"My mother's not 'other people.' She's sick, not senile. Tell her to knock it off."

"You tell her."

"Why me? I'm not the one who claims to have magic fingers."

The following day they were friends again. Doyle skipped into the station waving an embossed card. "Guess what? I'll be seeing you at San Simeon this weekend. Mr. Hearst's invited me and Ma to his costume ball! She'll be so proud." He picked Mary Mabel up and twirled her around. She had an itch to tousle his cowlick.

WESTWARD HO!

While Mary Mabel was preaching on WKRN, Brother Percy Brubacher was engaged in a national tour of sacrilege. Satan had told him to get out of New York fast; it was only a matter of time before the loony bin realized it had the wrong guy. Percy wondered if he could pick up his stuff at the Belvedere. Satan said, "What, are you nuts?" The money coat enabled him to buy a cheap suitcase, toiletries, nondescript travelling clothes, a new little black book, and a book of bus schedules. A shave and a haircut made him unrecognizable.

Satan had warned him that when the cops wised up they'd be looking for a pattern to his movements, so Percy avoided one. He'd go to the bus station, close his eyes, and randomly point to a destination on the schedule board. The buses were rarely full. Percy would sit alone at the back making graven images of the Fly with toothpicks and chewing gum.

On arrival at each new town, he'd eat a plate of mash, then set off to desecrate the church closest to the terminal. His abominations were non-denominational: he peed in Catholic confessionals, put toads in Episcopal holy water, stole from Presbyterian offering plates, and wrote dirty jokes in Baptist hymnals. Mormons he left alone; they were already a desecration, so what was the point?

In addition to run-of-the-mill sacrilege, Percy determined to violate each of the Ten Commandments. Graven images aside, he'd already worshipped Satan, blasphemed God, stolen church collections, dishonoured his father's memory, coveted Mary Mabel's success, borne false witness against her in various rants, and forgotten the Sabbath — indeed, he no longer remembered the days of the week. He was on a roll: eight commandments down, two to go: adultery and murder.

Adultery was hard. The idea of sex was terrifying, much less sex with someone other than himself. Percy decided to start small and work up. He fantasized Floyd with a hooker. It was a revelation. Percy took to self-abuse like a duck to water. Soon his pockets were stuffed with wads of toilet paper and a hip flask of bleach to burn away the germs.

After a month of practice and a severe skin rash, Percy was ready to go for the Scarlet Letter. He asked Satan to take him to a house of ill repute. Satan, who'd appeared as a cab driver, dropped him off at Lucille Stout's. She was a part-timer who turned tricks whenever her husband Rudy was in the slammer, which was mostly. The minute she unhooked her brassiere, Percy ran screaming into the night.

The next night he returned with a plan. He closed his eyes and pretended he was Floyd. After ten minutes of awkward grop-ing, Percy's member remained as limp as an overcooked bean. Then Lucille took him in her mouth and Percy had a flash. He wasn't Floyd; *Lucille* was. Out of the blue he saw stars. Fireworks. His little legume erupted into a prize-winning cucumber.

Percy was confused, troubled by the memories that surfaced of his early days rooming with Floyd. Sleeping in a twin bed in the same room as his partner had been heaven. If Floyd had asked him for a neck rub his world would've been complete. Instead, his pal had slipped out to be with landladies and harlots. The waves of hurt, anger, and jealousy had been unbearable — though not as unbearable as Floyd's suggestion to fold the tent and part com-pany forever, or, more recently, of being jilted for Miss McTavish.

Percy wobbled off Lucille's verandah consumed with the remaining item on his agenda. Murder. The thought of killing Floyd overwhelmed him with despair. No matter how cruel,

Floyd was the closest thing to a friend that Percy'd ever had. Mary Mabel, however, was another kettle of fish. The idea of driving a stake through her heart gave Percy goosebumps.

It wasn't the first time he'd imagined her dead. Page after page in his little black books had been filled with prayers that she be trampled to death by well-wishers.

Fat chance. Those prayers had gone to God, who'd played him for a sucker. Now he sent his prayers to Satan. Satan encouraged him to take a more active role in the death of his enemy. Her murder would conclude his initiation into the world of darkness. And it would make him famous beyond his wildest dreams.

Percy was delighted by the suggestion. He hopped off Lucille's verandah and tap-danced down the street.

Next stop, Los Angeles.

Fitz Feeney was the lawyer engaged by Floyd to represent Brother Percy in the wake of the Radio City disturbance. Floyd had hired him because he was cheap and incompetent. With any luck, his former partner would spend the rest of his days confined to a penitentiary or asylum.

Feeney was a good Catholic who spent an hour a day in confession. As a lawyer, he more or less had to. His priest, Father O'Hara, thought Feeney's biggest sin was continuing to practise law; his stupidity had sent innocent men to Death Row and widows to the poorhouse. O'Hara gave him a plaster statue of St. Jude and insisted he pray to it daily. (The priest made statues of the saints as a hobby. St. Jude, patron saint of lost causes, was his favourite. He gave it to shut-ins and the sick. He also presented it at baptisms, since babies invariably turn into sinners.)

Fitz Feeney had prayed diligently to St. Jude re: the Brubacher file. If ever there was a lost cause, the preacher was it. He'd committed his crimes in front of six thousand witnesses, been arrested by the director of the F.B.I., and shipped to Bellevue after disabling five of New York's finest. According to the shrinks, despite a month of drug and deprivation therapy, his schizophrenia had deepened. Brubacher's alter ego, "Slick Skinner," now claimed to own a hunting lodge in Cedar Bend — significantly, the home town of his estranged colleague Miss McTavish. "Skinner" also believed that he shared his cell with a horse. Refusing to answer questions, he bounced off the padded walls hollering, "Ask the mare, ask the mare."

"I can't imagine he's appealing to Mayor LaGuardia," confided the chief psychiatrist. "It's no doubt a reference to his mother. 'Mare', as in a mama horse, or '*mere*' as in the French." He tapped his nose. "The mother. It's always the mother."

Something troubled Feeney. If his client weren't crazy, he'd swear he was sane. "What about the mayor of Cedar Bend?" he asked. "Has he been contacted?"

The doctors were horrified. "Never encourage a patient's delusions. Given half a chance, psychotics will have you believing black is white."

Much like lawyers and psychiatrists, thought Feeney. That night, egged on by St. Jude, he placed a Hail Mary phone call to Cedar Bend.

The mayor hesitated when asked about Skinner; since he'd gone hunting, the town's disappearances had stopped. Nonetheless, he described Slick perfectly and confirmed each of his claims. "Is Slick in trouble?" he asked hopefully.

"No," Feeney replied. "As a matter of fact, he's about to come into a fortune."

• • • •

The next day, Fitz Feeney's letter on behalf of his client sent shockwaves through the Bellevue Psychiatric Institute, the N.Y.P.D., and city and state bureaucracies. Especially after a new set of fingerprints established that the "Percy Brubacher" incarcerated at Bellevue was not the same Percy Brubacher who'd originally been fingerprinted at the Midtown North Precinct house. Feeney's letter read as follows:

Dear Sirs:
Respecting the Case of Mr. Slick Skinner:

Whereas Mr. Slick Skinner, a respected Canadian businessman and tourist, was mugged and left for dead in a New York alleyway;

And whereas officers of the New York Police Department did find his body, and did deny him assistance, and did unlawfully confine him, during which confinement he duly was robbed a second time, and beaten beyond recognition by officers of said New York Police Department;

And whereas Mr. Skinner was thereafter illegally committed to the Bellevue Psychiatric Institute, during which detention he was subjected to deprivation, drug, and other psychiatric treatments and therapies against his wishes and in violation of his rights under the constitution of these United States of America and of international jurisprudence;

And inasmuch as I have been retained by said Mr. Skinner to seek punitive damages on his behalf against the aforementioned New York City

Police Department and the Bellevue Psychiatric Institute, as well as the City and State governments of New York;

I ask that you or your representatives contact me at your earliest possible convenience, but no later than the close of tomorrow's business day, failing which I shall be compelled to initiate civil and criminal proceedings against you, and to so advise the press.

Sincerely yours,
Mr. Fitzroy Feeney,
Attorney-at-law

In an out-of-court settlement, Feeney negotiated Slick's immediate release. Subject to Slick's silence on all matters relating to the case, charges of assaulting police officers were dropped, and he was awarded $10,000 in cash, less Feeney's contingency fee. Doctors suggested he might like to spend a day or two under observation till the drugs wore off; he looked a bit jumpy.

Slick wouldn't hear of it. "Gotta get a move-on. Time's wastin' an' I got things to do."

Later that afternoon, police made a terse announcement that due to a clerical error Brother Percival Homer Brubacher had been accidentally released from custody. Brubacher was described as armed and dangerous. A nationwide manhunt was underway. Citizens were urged to be vigilant. Citing security concerns, authorities refused to provide further details.

• • • •

The Baroness Bentwhistle always remembered a face. Especially a face that had aimed a shotgun at her head. One week after Slick's release, her limousine was pulling away from the WKRN radio station when she noticed the hunter peeking out from behind some bushes. She ordered her driver to stop. "Yoo-hoo. Mr. Woodsman," she called from the window. "Over here."

Slick stepped awkwardly from his hiding place. He was somewhat confused. Did he know this woman?

"Still looking for Mr. McTavish?" the Baroness inquired sweetly.

Slick had a flash of the laundry basket. "What're you doing here?"

"Oh, this and that. About your friend, McTavish, he hasn't shown up yet, but I suspect he will. I'm guessing we have similar dreams for his future. Give me a number where you can be reached. The moment I see him, I'll let you know."

Slick obliged. Since his payday he'd been staying in hotels. Nothing fancy, but they came with a front desk, and packs of matches with the phone number on them.

"Ta ta." The Baroness drove off. She'd worried about what to do when McTavish arrived to see his daughter. Her connection to Mary Mabel ensured he'd show up on her doorstep with blackmail on his mind. Now, thanks to her woodsman, she could rest easy.

X

ARMAGEDDON

The COSTUME BALL

O f all Hearst's parties, his costume balls were the best. He wanted his company to look spectacular, so he let them borrow outfits from Cosmopolitan Pictures' wardrobe department. On this particular weekend, Doyle and his mother were going as d'Artagnan and the Queen of France. Mary Mabel was to be the Match Girl, and Floyd, Rumpelstiltskin. The Baroness had selected Little Bo Peep, and ordered Dr. Silver and Miss Pigeon to play her sheep. She planned to lead them around on jewelled leashes.

As usual, Hearst had arranged for a private train from Los Angeles to San Luis Obispo County; his fleet of cars would taxi his guests the final leg to his castle. The train was a terrific ice-breaker, particularly for first-timers like Doyle and his mother. By the time it pulled into the station, everyone was in a festive mood and on a first-name basis.

Still, Mary Mabel wanted to drive. Her life was so full of people she wanted a few hours of privacy. So did Brother Floyd and the Baroness. They kept company in the back seat of her limo behind a panel of tinted glass; Mary Mabel sat up front with the chauffeur, reading a book, peering through her binoculars, or waving out the window to Dr. Silver and Miss Pigeon; they followed in the Olds in case the Baroness had car trouble. "Heavens," she'd said, fanning herself, "what if we got stuck in the middle of nowhere, fending off turkey vultures with a road map?"

For Mary Mabel, the best part of the trip was the ride by the Santa Lucia Mountains. The Pacific crashing against the cliffs created mists and wisps of cloud. It was like travelling through dreamscapes. And then to see the Hearst castle in the distance, glistening atop La Cuesta Encantada. It seemed every name came from fairy tale and myth.

She had a second reason for wanting to travel by car. Something had been bothering her, but every time she'd broached the subject, her partners had been too busy to listen. A two-hundred-mile car ride denied them any excuse. She waited till they were an hour out of town before knocking on the glass panel.

"Just a minute." There were sounds of a scramble, then Floyd slid open the glass. "Yes?"

"I'm sorry to bother you," Mary Mabel said, "but there's something I have to get off my chest. I love performing on the radio, but I wish you weren't forever handing me scripts about the Heavenly Dwellings. I'm either praising their spiritual benefits, chatting up buyers, or praying for donations. I feel like a real-estate agent."

Miss Bentwhistle and her partner stared blankly and rolled down their side windows. They pretended they couldn't hear her over the breeze.

"We have to talk," Mary Mabel shouted.

Floyd ordered the driver to pull over and take a walk. He did. The Olds stopped ahead of them. Dr. Silver came running to see what was wrong.

"We're fine," said Miss Bentwhistle. "Go entertain Dolly. Nibble her ears. Tell her tales of your youth." The dentist brightened and hurried off to shock his Baptist.

"Okay," Floyd said coldly to the troublemaker. "Economics 101. We want to spread hope, right? So we bought more radio stations, remember? They don't come cheap. Pushing Dwellings is the fastest way to raise the boodle."

"But how does money raised to build apartments end up buying radio stations?"

Miss Bentwhistle sighed. "You clearly have no head for business."

"Perhaps not," Mary Mabel said. "But I know how to spell fraud."

Floyd bristled. "It's not fraud. It's borrowing. Each new station enlarges our pool of donors and buyers. Their contributions repay the Dwellings accounts."

"Mr. Cruickshank, we're soliciting money under false pretenses."

Miss Bentwhistle tapped Floyd's knee. "She was always a difficult child."

"I'm not a child. I'm not a grifter, either. From now on, I won't solicit for the Dwellings, I demand to see the books, and I insist they be above board."

"Mind your place," Miss Bentwhistle snapped. "You may be a star, but to us you're the help."

"I'm a partner," Mary Mabel snapped back. "I'm also the one with the story. Back off or I'll take it elsewhere."

Floyd smiled. "Actually you won't. According to our agreement, I hold the rights to your career. You perform when and where I say."

"Is that so?" Mary Mabel coughed. "I seem to be coming down with permanent laryngitis."

"Don't play cute. If you don't push apartments, sales will dry up. Without those sales we'll lose the new stations, their income, and all we've invested. Shazam, the Dwellings will fold before they're built, with no cash to repay buyers. Enter the F.B.I."

"If the operation is crooked, I ought to turn it in myself."

"But, as you say, you're a partner," Miss Bentwhistle observed. "Moreover, the partner soliciting the cash. If there's a problem, you'll be the first to be nicked."

"You and your poor Mr. Doyle," said Floyd. "Rat us out and I'll destroy him."

How? Mary Mabel wondered, but was afraid to ask. "There's a smell in this car." Mary Mabel jumped out and drove the rest of the way with Dr. Silver and Miss Pigeon.

By the time they arrived at San Simeon, the other guests had eaten at the refectory and dressed for the party. Hearst's secretary, Willicombe, got them settled and asked the kitchen to send up dinner trays. He said the night would be grand. There'd be jugglers, fire-eaters, magicians — oh, and the McConaghie Family Circus was going to shoot a clown out of a cannon. Tomorrow, Hearst would like to talk to them about their movie.

"Terrific," Mary Mabel said, but she had more important things on her mind than her biopic. As soon as Willicombe left, she whipped into her Match Girl outfit and tore off in search of d'Artagnan.

He was sitting by the Neptune Pool with his mother, talking to Henry the Eighth: Charles Laughton munching a turkey leg. Acrobats and fire-eaters circled around them, juggling torches, and breathing flames. Across the pool, a trio of clowns were setting up the McConaghie Family's human cannonball act.

"May I steal your musketeer?" Mary Mabel asked.

The company laughed. Doyle said he'd happily be of service to a match girl. She marched him off towards Hearst's private zoo. "Keep a smile on and pretend to be talking about the animals."

"What's the matter?"

"You tell me." Mary Mabel recounted the conversation with her partners. "What I want to know is, what have you done? How can Mr. Cruickshank bring you down?"

Doyle gripped the bars of the antelope cage and took a deep breath. "I'm sorry," he said. And then he told her how he'd extorted 15 percent of ministry earnings in exchange for puffing her miracles. His eyes begged her to say something, but she couldn't, she just stood there.

"I didn't take a penny," he pleaded. "Cruickshank never deposited to the account."

"Then I guess you're scot-free."

"In court. But if the story leaks, I'm finished. Who wants a writer who uses his column to front frauds and solicit bribes?"

"I wouldn't know. All I know is, I trusted you. You used me."

"I didn't mean to. I was thinking of Ma."

"Don't hide behind your mother."

"I wanted the cash to save her from the county home. I'm sorry."

"It's easy to be sorry when your chickens come home to roost."

"What makes you so self-righteous?" Doyle demanded.

"Pardon?"

"Don't play dumb. You knew Cruickshank was a flim-flam artist."

Mary Mabel shifted uncomfortably. "I didn't. I've just thought about doing good."

"Nice excuse."

He was right, and Mary Mabel knew it. True, she could pretend she didn't know the ministry was corrupt. But there's knowing and *knowing*. She'd ignored so much, claiming her mama as her guide; yet her mama would never have led her into temptation. Her wishful thinking had betrayed her mama's memory.

Doyle turned away and slumped against the cage. Mary Mabel paused, then put her arm around his shoulder. He squeezed her hand. "I'm afraid. I don't know how to tell Ma what I've done. She'll be ashamed of me."

"No she won't. She loves you."

"That makes it worse."

They stared through the bars at the antelope.

Mary Mabel remembered how her papa had mocked her for reading so much. "Why waste your time with lies?" he'd said. *But the thing is,* she thought, *lies can make truth.* Whether real or imagined, her miracle had led her into a life of deceit with no escape. To remain in the ministry was unthinkable: every second she continued was a crime against her mama. But bringing the ministry down would bring ruin to the two people she cared about most: Doyle and Ma Rinker. *Mama,* she prayed, *forgive me. Please. Help me to get out of here.*

Suddenly there was a terrible explosion at the Neptune Pool. Guests were screaming, scattering in all directions: "They're everywhere! Run for your lives! We're surrounded!"

What?

Doyle leapt to attention. "Don't move!" he said. "I've got to get Ma!" He took off in a flash. Mary Mabel went to run after.

"Not so fast." A man grabbed her by the shoulder.

She whirled around. "Papa?" she gasped.

"Shush up. I've come to get you out of here."

REVOLUTION

When Comrade Duddy felled Slick Skinner with a hand-kerchief of ether, there had been fevered discussion about what to do next. Comrade Canuck was all for a summary execution. "He's a bourgeois counter-revolutionary. A stooge of the capitalist bosses."

It was the first time Duddy had heard McTavish talk remotely like a Bolshevik, so he was a little suspicious. "Why did this guy want to kill you?"

"I screwed his wife."

Duddy explained that screwing somebody's wife didn't make the husband a counter-revolutionary, and that Slick didn't exactly look bourgeois. McTavish replied that if Skinner lived he'd track them down, thus imperilling the grand revolutionary struggle to come. Lapinsky agreed. He thought it would be fun to choke Skinner with the Hand.

The commissars broke off their dialectic with the arrival of the cops, who were sweeping the alley for drunks. Comrade Duddy grabbed Slick's rifle and golf bag, and the trio escaped to the street beyond.

With Skinner alive and no doubt on the warpath, the comrades decided to stage a strategic retreat to Casa Mama Rosa, by way of small-town banks in Ohio and Arkansas. Once settled into the girls and tequila, McTavish and Lapinsky wanted to stay put. Comrade Duddy said that any more whoring and they'd turn into capitalists. The comrades didn't care. But Duddy was still determined to kidnap Mary Mabel for the revolution. When he heard that she was in Los Angeles, he found a way to motivate them. "L.A. is the hooker capital of the world. Only there, they call them starlets."

The comrades hopped a train to an area of bush near Hollywood. There was a road nearby that went to town. While the other two set up camp, Duddy scouted Mary Mabel's radio station. He reported back that Skinner was there in sniper position, sitting under a nearby tree pretending to read the *Saturday Evening Post*. A long thin object wrapped in black tissue paper lay at his side.

Lapinsky volunteered to surprise him with a knife in the ribs. Duddy pointed out that a murder would raise security and make their job more difficult. Instead, he'd comb the papers for word on Sister's upcoming appearances. With luck they'd find a venue that the hunter would ignore.

A spread in the *Herald-Examiner* provided inspiration. There was to be a costume ball at San Simeon; the guest list included Sister Mary Mabel. Duddy was certain that Skinner would steer clear; the hunter would never imagine that McTavish would be stupid enough to try and crash Hearst security.

"And he'd be right," said McTavish. "How do you propose we get in? How do you propose we get out?"

Comrade Duddy smiled.

Mr. McConaghie was in a fine mood. He'd been doing a brisk trade in circus rentals. It had started with his animals. Now it had progressed to his hardware. The newest clients were a trio of clowns in full makeup, red noses, and yellow fright wigs.

"The truck and the cannon haven't been used in years," said McConaghie. "Gimme a couple of days to scrape out the rust and touch up the paint job."

The biggest clown, Leo the Large, tried the cannon on for size. It was a tight fit.

"You boys know about explosives?" asked McConaghie.

The littlest clown, Duddles, honked a horn. "I've worked in coal mines."

McConaghie gave him a sheet of instructions about the amount and placement of the fuse and gunpowder, and where to set the safety net. Oh, and he'd need some identification and a signed release before letting his stuff off the lot.

Friday morning the clowns returned with a driver's license. McConachie checked it over. "You sure you're fifty-two, Mr. Jenson?"

"Fifty-two, whoo-pitty-do!" sang Duddles and rang a little bell.

Belinda McConaghie came running out of her trailer, eyes popping. She wore a purple cape over her brassiere, and a jewelled fortune-teller's hat. There were runs in her leotards. "I see an explosion!" she exclaimed, and stabbed her forefinger at Leo. "You will come out of a cannon. There will be much surprise." She cackled and ran off to her mother's card table for some lemonade and Crackerjack.

Under the circumstances, McConaghie didn't figure he had the right to be asking the clowns any more questions.

Duddles took the driver's seat. He blew a kazoo.

"Knock 'em dead," McConaghie hollered as the truck pulled onto the highway.

Comrade Duddy ordered the commissars to shut-the-fuck-up as he drove up to the Hearst castle security post. At least the truck looked official. The touch-ups to the side walls reading THE MCCONAGHIE FAMILY CIRCUS were in crisp reds and golds, and the sparkles and stars on the cannon were a nice touch. Duddy

knew the circus's name would ring a bell, too; it had been cred-
ited in the press for providing Sister with lambs and lions.

The guard gave the truck a once over and peered into the cab.

"McConaghie Family Circus," said Duddy brightly. "I'm
Duddles, and these are my pallys: Leo the Large and Mr. Spiffy.
We're doing the Human Cannonball act."

The guard frowned. They sure looked like clowns. Still, they
weren't on the list of entertainers. "I'll have to check with the
Chief," he said.

"Okey-dokey," chirped Duddles. The guard entered his
booth and got on the phone. Mr. Spiffy whimpered; Leo the
Large drummed the fingers of the Hand on the dash.

"McConaghie's Family Circus?" Hearst said on the other
end of the line. "Of course, let them in." (Another surprise from
Marion, he smiled, or maybe a treat from Sister.) "Have them set
up by the Neptune Pool. Instead of a net, ask them to splash down
in the deep end. We'll have a cannonball to end all cannonballs!"

The guard passed them through.

From now on it'll be easy, Duddy thought. After the act,
Comrade Canuck would get his daughter to the truck — she'd
go quietly or be ethered — then, bingo, they'd slip her down the
cannon barrel and escape.

The comrades set up while the guests ate. As the cannon was
manoeuvred into final position, Brewster spotted Mary Mabel
across the pool. She looked well. It pissed him off. How dare she
have fun with the mucky-mucks, while he slaved with the proles?
He watched the little slut wander up a garden path with some
highfalutin' sugar boy. He'd soon wipe that smile off her face.

Out of nowhere, Little Bo Peep sashayed by accompanied by
two balls of wool crawling on all fours. It couldn't be. "Who's Bo
Peep when she's home?" Brewster asked a fire-eater.

"You don't recognize the Baroness Bentwhistle?"

"The *Baroness* Bentwhistle?"

"Her jewels are worth twenty-five million," the fire-eater confided. "Excuse me, I have to go suck some kerosene."

Twenty-five million! What an unexpected honey pot. Brewster would have to drop by and pay his respects. Alone.

Suddenly, klieg lights lit up the cannon. The castle's drummers and coronet players assembled at the side of the pool and played a fanfare. From all corners, guests surged around, filling the deck and marble stairways. W.R. Hearst appeared at a microphone, Willicombe at his side. A hush fell over the crowd.

"Glad to see you, my friends," Hearst said. The microphone squealed. Willicombe adjusted the volume and all was well. "I hope you were as tickled as me to see the McConaghie circus truck pull in. It brought back memories. Tonight, I understand they're favouring us with their Human Cannonball act. So, with no further ado, may I present Duddles the Clown."

Duddles did a handspring into the light. He honked his horn. "Hi there, boys and girls, ladies and gents," he squeaked.

"Hi there, Duddles," the crowd called back affectionately.

"Before we get started, let me introduce my pallys. This is Mr. Spiffy." Caught in the glare of the klieg, Mr. Spiffy covered his head and fell to the ground, bum up. Much laughter.

"And this here's Leo the Large." Lapinsky marched forward waving the Hand. Duddles rang his little bell. "Give Leo a hand. A left hand." The crowd hooted. They expected a real paw to pop out of the empty sleeve. It didn't.

Yet there was no time for shock. Leo was already being squeezed down the cannon barrel. It was a tight fit. So tight he had to stick the Hand in his mouth. Duddles and Mr. Spiffy pushed with all their might. Leo's shoulders plugged the end of the barrel; his head was stuck outside. Duddles made a great show of trying to force it down with a toilet plunger.

The veins on Leo's neck bulged. "Get me outta here!"

"You asked for it!" Duddles yukked. He ran back and lit a fuse as long and thick as a skipping rope. Drum roll. As the flame snaked and sparkled its way along the deck and up the butt of the cannon, Duddles stuffed his fingers in his ears.

Three. Two. One. There was a tremendous explosion.

The cannon elevated two feet off the ground and crashed down. Duddles and Mr. Spiffy were somersaulted backwards. There was only one problem. Leo the Large hadn't budged. He was the immovable object meeting the irresistible force.

Leo raised his eyebrows. He looked surprised, as his head dropped off the end of the barrel, bounced twice, and plopped into the swimming pool.

The cannon wobbled. It tilted downward. Guests held their breath in the hope that this was a magic trick — that a whole Leo the Large was going to slide out the end. Instead, what slid out was two hundred and twenty pounds of lasagna.

Even Jack Warner was sick.

Comrade Duddy knew the jig was up. He'd be put on trial for murder. But if he was going to face the electric chair, he wouldn't go down as a clown. Instead, he'd go down as a hero in the grand revolutionary struggle. "Workers of the world unite!" he roared into the microphone. "Throw off your chains!"

The crowd gasped. An emulsified clown was one thing, a Communist insurrection another. How many armed fanatics were in their midst masquerading as waiters? Elves? With visions of fire-eaters setting them alight, and an army of Okies storming the castle walls, the high and mighty fled screaming in all directions.

In the confusion, Brewster tossed off his red nose and wig. Soot coated his clothes and makeup. He was one of the mob. He ran up the path where his daughter had disappeared. He saw her. Grabbed her.

"Papa?"

"Shush up. I've come to get you out of here."

To his surprise, she didn't need ether.

The HIDEOUT

There are so many things to say to a long-lost father. Things such as, "Oh, my God," or "What are you doing here?" Yet when Mary Mabel saw her papa, all she could think to say was: "Can you hot-wire a car?"

They stole Miss Bentwhistle's limousine. Brewster bonked the chauffeur on the head and they were away. Nobody noticed or cared: those with cars were too busy scrambling for their own; those who'd come by train were running for the safety of their rooms. They tore out of the parking lot, past Bo Peep; she was on the ground, hoop skirt over her head, tangled in leashes and sheep.

Brewster's recent adventures had taught him about getaways. He gunned the limo full bore, taking potholes head-on and riding the air currents as they bounced skyward. In what seemed like no time, they passed a railway crossing. There was no one ahead of them or behind. Brewster killed the headlights and turned off the road. For once he took care; he didn't want to leave tracks.

They drove by moonlight for several miles, keeping parallel to the rail line as they manoeuvred around cactus, brush, and shadow. At last they came to a deep gully. "End of the road," Brewster said. They got out and he pushed the car over the edge. It careened down, crashing on the dry riverbed beneath.

"This way," he said. He led Mary Mabel to where the trestle track crossed the ravine. They sat together and waited for a train.

"I've missed you," she said. It was a lie, but the truth would have been cruel. "How did you find me? Here? Tonight? Why did you come?"

"To rescue you from the opiate of the masses. Something like that."

Mary Mabel squeezed his arm. He was Mama's answer to her prayer, a sign of forgiveness and deliverance. She told him every-thing — all about the Heavenly Dwellings and Miss Bentwhistle being a baroness. She also told him how good it was to finally be free, to know she'd never be going back. It would be morning before they knew she was missing. There'd be search parties, but she'd have vanished off the face of the earth.

Brewster grunted and put his ear to the track. "She's com-ing." Five minutes later, the freight train passed. As he predicted, it slowed to a crawl crossing the bridge. They hopped a flatcar, no trouble. There were a couple of hoboes already on board, sleep-ing soundly at the far end. "Five hours to the crack of dawn," he said. "Time for some shut-eye."

She couldn't sleep. She felt badly about leaving Doyle and his mother without a goodbye. Still, they weren't in any danger. Neither were the Heavenly Dwellings nor Doyle's reputation. She knew Brother Floyd and Miss Bentwhistle would turn her disap-pearance into a bonanza. They'd hawk her photograph, complete with forged signature, maybe even set up a miracle shrine at the entrance to the Dwellings where the faithful could light candles and drop cash.

"Get ready. This here's our stop."

Mary Mabel barely had time to blink herself awake before Brewster had her by the hand, counted to three, and jumped. They landed in gravel and grass, no worse for wear save for scraped hands and a small tear in her dress. He led her over a hill and through a patch of forest to a clearing. There were four lean-tos around a burned-out campfire. Three of the lean-tos had a satchel under their thatched roofs and a few clothes airing on their supports. The fourth covered some pots, tin plates, assorted cutlery, canned vegetables, beer bottles, whiskey jugs, cans of lighter fluid, and a pile of old newspapers held down by a chunk of cement. A few yards from the site was a pit of food scraps and an old car seat.

"Where are we?"

"Two miles outta Hollywood."

She froze. "I thought we were getting as far away from L.A. as we could."

"You thought wrong." He undid his belt, a double length of binder twine, and used it to tie her hands behind her back.

"What's going on?"

"You've been kidnapped."

"You said you came to rescue me."

"How else was I to get you to go peaceable?"

He tied her legs with strips of green bark and told her how originally she was supposed to be turned into a Bolshevik mouthpiece. Now, with his partners gone, life would be simpler. There'd be a ransom note demanding a million bucks. He'd collect the cash and hand her over. She'd make up a story — say her kidnapper was a Swede or a Ukrainian — and he'd retire to Mexico where he'd buy up the Casa Mama Rosa and have a different girl every night of the week.

"I'll be home-free," he said. "Even if you tell the truth, they won't come after me. Bad publicity."

"There's only one problem," Mary Mabel replied. "How do you propose to send a ransom note? You're illiterate."

"That's easy. You're going to write it for me."

"Not on your life."

Brewster laughed and poured himself a whiskey laced with a dash of lighter fluid. "A hothead, just like your mother. She cooled off, and so will you."

"How dare you talk like that?"

"She's not around to care."

"She was a saint. She died to save me. And look at you. A lecher. A kidnapper."

"Spare me the violins. Your mama died because she was a nag, plain and simple. Always at me about my drinking. If I had it to do over, I'd toss her out again."

"What?"

Brewster helped himself to another shot. "I was in my cups. She wouldn't let up. So I threw her outside and locked the door. Then I passed out. I woke up freezin' my butt, the door wide open. You were away on your errand of mercy, but she was long gone."

Her mind reeled. "You let everyone think she ran off to save me. I grew up believing I killed her."

Brewster shrugged. "What was I supposed to do? They wouldn't hang a two-year-old for murder. It was her fault anyway for wandering off. She'd shoulda stayed put by the door. But hey, what's past is past. You're a rich bitch now and the truth don't matter."

"God forgive me," Mary Mabel said, "but I wish she were alive and you were dead."

He laughed. "Take a number, get in line."

BAD NEWS

The Hearst press scooped the opposition. Police confirmed the front-page report that San Simeon had been overrun by a cutthroat army of Bolshevik anarchists. Though hopelessly outnumbered, a brace of Hollywood's leading men had apparently beaten back the nefarious insurgents, one of whom was dead, another in custody. The rest of the Red Battalion, including a mysterious "third clown," had fled to secret camps in the tunnels and caves of the Santa Lucia Mountains. The F.B.I. were combing the territory with tracking dogs.

It was also noted that the fanatics had snatched the limousine of the Baroness of Bentwhistle. Late editions reported that it had been found in a gully near some rail tracks. Authorities believed the cowardly ringleaders might have hopped a train to San Francisco.

The other front-page story concerned the disappearance of beloved healer Sister Mary Mabel McTavish. It was unknown whether she was in hiding or had been kidnapped during the melee. There were prayers for her safe return from Mr. W.R. Hearst, Mr. Jack Warner, Miss Marion Davies, and others connected with her upcoming biopic. Mr. Floyd Cruickshank of Holy Redemption Ministries urged her followers to send offerings to pay the expenses of volunteers mounting a round-the-clock prayer vigil.

Doyle was worried sick. A week had passed with no sign of Mary Mabel. If she'd run off in panic, she could be lying at the bottom of a ravine with broken legs, either dehydrating and starving or prey for coyotes and mountain lions. Police said these scenarios were unlikely; if she were in the area, the tracking dogs would have picked up her scent. All the same, if she'd been kidnapped where was the ransom note?

So far there wasn't even a lead.

Comrade Duddy refused to talk as he was laid up with a coma in the Alcatraz infirmary. *The Daily Worker* claimed brutality by prison interrogators, but the warden maintained that Duddy had deliberately beaten himself senseless in order to avoid questioning. The public was enraged: those damn Commie bastards would stoop to anything!

(Duddy's subsequent trial for the murder of Leo Lapinsky created the biggest international furor since Sacco/Vanzetti. He was found guilty and sentenced to be electrocuted. However, by the time his case wound its way through the appeal courts, America was at war and Mother Russia was an ally. Duddy was pardoned and sent to Connecticut where he became head foreman in a munitions factory.)

Aside from Comrade Duddy, investigators had questioned the McConaghies. Belinda McConaghie had shown up in a cape, leotards, and turban, bearing her crystal ball. She claimed to have had a psychic vision: Mary Mabel had been kidnapped by her father and was tied up in a clearing outside Hollywood. Police said thanks and told McConaghie he ought to put Belinda in a home.

The other McConaghies were equally useless. "We can describe them perfectly, Officer. They had yellow fright wigs, red noses, and flowers that squirted water." The McConaghies were released after being charged with keeping a rotting elephant on their premises and renting lions without a permit.

Three days later, the case broke wide open. Police made an arrest.

Doyle wept as he wrote the front-page story. Sister Mary Mabel McTavish wasn't lost. She wasn't kidnapped. She was dead.

• • • •

Brother Percy had been arrested at two in the morning trying to set a fire in the garbage bin behind WKRN. Satan had told him that his hour was at hand, and it very nearly was. The vigil volunteers who tackled him were in a surly mood. For over a week, they'd been praying in eight-hour shifts, taking turns in sleeping bags lined up on the radio station parking lot. There was no place to shower and only one sink and toilet to brush their teeth, shave, and et cetera. The last thing they needed was some firebug disturbing them with a rant about the joys of eternal damnation.

Percy hadn't been sure that he was actually setting a fire. As far as he was concerned, it was a very live possibility that he was only dreaming that he was setting a fire. The last time he'd been able to distinguish between his waking and sleeping life was … well … a while ago. In fact, around the time he had his last decent meal. It wasn't that he couldn't afford to eat. Rather, Satan preferred that he lift rocks and search for grubs.

The police took Percy to the station. He was happy to confess to whatever they wanted, providing they promised to spell his name correctly and get his story on the front page of the newspapers. He told them that he was world famous except that there was a conspiracy to hide this fact from the public.

The interrogators left him alone. Percy struck up a conversation with the fly buzzing around the bare light bulb and made faces at himself in the two-way mirror.

Police on the other side of the mirror were slack-jawed. Somehow they'd lucked onto Brother Percival Homer Brubacher, the escaped lunatic wanted for questioning in the case of missing evangelist Sister Mary Mabel McTavish. Brubacher's little black books had been sent with the rest of his belongings from the

Belvedere Hotel to the Bellevue Institute. Psychiatrists had been shocked to read his lurid fantasies of her death.

When the interrogators returned and confronted him about Mary Mabel's disappearance, Percy didn't blink. He knew about the incident at San Simeon from reading the papers. Indeed, the more he thought about it, the more he *thought* he knew about it, because, well, he was starting to be pretty certain that he'd been there. He might even have been the so-called mysterious "Third Clown." Come to think of it, he *was*. He remembered a big crowd and everyone laughing at him. He also remembered driving in a car with Mary Mabel and wishing she was dead.

Satan stopped flying around the light bulb and landed on his shoulder. "Well done," he buzzed. "Tell them the idea we laughed about on the bus. You know, the idea about the wood chipper."

Percy giggled. The interrogators all had notebooks. They were taking pictures. He leapt onto the interrogation table and beat his chest. "I confess," he exulted. "I killed Sister Mary Mabel McTavish."

And then he told them how he did it.

Miss Bentwhistle was astonished at the outpouring of public grief. Love offerings were pouring into the Sister Mary Mabel Memorial Fund. Superimposed photographs of the dead girl ascending into heaven were selling at a brisk clip, and manufacturers were competing for the rights to make plaster statues of the fallen evangelist in sizes ranging from paperweights to lawn ornaments. Best of all, sales of the Heavenly Dwellings were booming. Buyers had been assured of a complimentary lock of Sister's hair; Miss Pigeon was next to bald.

Looking into the future, there appeared to be no end to Mary Mabel mania. Her death hadn't even put a dent in new miracles.

Patients were crawling out of hospitals convinced that the healer had cured them in a dream.

The Baroness wiggled her toes. Mary Mabel dead was more valuable than Mary Mabel alive. And a good deal less bother. Over crumpets and tea, she made a "to do" list for future projects.

> *Item: Market replica stationery from the desk of*
> *Sister on which the sick can write prayer requests.*
> *Item: Consider collectibles. Commemorative plates*
> *and coin sets a must.*
> *Item: Ask Miss Davies to donate dressing-room*
> *in which M.M. spent her final days. Ideal for*
> *bus tours.*

Her labours were interrupted by an unexpected phone call.

"You've come up in the world," said the voice at the end of the line.

"Excuse me, but have we made your acquaintance?"

"Damn right, Cuddles. Remember those feather dusters?"

"Mr. McTavish!?"

"I have your kitten. It's alive. It'll cost you a million bucks."

"I'm afraid we no longer need it," the Baroness demurred.

"It hasn't eaten in ten days."

"Quel dommage."

"It's starving."

"Then be a dear and put it out of its misery."

A pause. "Naw. I'll just look for another buyer. The press, maybe. I'm sure they'd love to hear it purr. By the way, I'll let them know you wanted it put down."

The Baroness pictured the headlines. "You shall have your million."

"That's more like it. Ten o'clock tonight. Unmarked bills. I'll be on Barclay Side Road, two miles north of Mulholland Drive, where the rail line takes the bend. Come alone. And don't play games or I'll blab your past to the world. Speaking of which, my silence will cost you extra. A hundred grand for starters."

Brewster hung up the telephone outside the booze store and left with a cart of whiskey. He'd meant to send a ransom note made up of glued letters cut out of newspapers. It would have looked more professional. But after ten days without food, Mary Mabel still refused to spell, so he'd had to launch the operation himself. *On the bright side*, he'd figured, *my voice'll put a fright into Horatia.*

The fear of God was more like it. The fact that Mary Mabel should be alive was bad luck; that her father should be alive, too, was Divine malice. What with demands for ransom and black-mail, Miss Bentwhistle was between a rock and a hard place. She had to admit that it was an appropriate location for one whose collateral was in bricks.

She took a glug of laudanum and fished Slick's matchbook from her smalls drawer.

That night, Miss Bentwhistle backed her new limo into an alley two blocks from Slick's hotel. In case McTavish checked the back seat, she stowed Skinner in the trunk. She planned to follow McTavish into the brush, out of view. Her woodsman would follow.

As instructed, she turned off Mulholland Drive and drove two miles north along Barclay Side Road. McTavish appeared out of the darkness.

"Where's the money?"

"In the trunk."

"Let's see it."

"Not till I see my precious."

"I thought I was your precious," McTavish snickered. "This way."

Miss Bentwhistle followed him through the woods that ran between the side road and the rail line. She walked slowly. Mr. Skinner had sworn he could follow a trail at night, but she couldn't be too careful. Besides, her fortifications for the evening's adventure had left her somewhat wobbly. "How much further?" she asked when they hit the tracks.

"Just over that hill."

"Let me catch my breath." Miss Bentwhistle sat on the rails and pretended to nurse an ankle. This was quite far enough, thank you very much. She couldn't understand what was keeping her hit man. Honestly, whatever happened to the Protestant work ethic?

(As it turned out, Slick was back at the limo having an interesting conversation with police. A passing patrol car had pulled over when it came across the apparently empty vehicle. Officers had become even more curious when they saw the woodsman emerge from the trunk.)

Back at the tracks, McTavish got a glint in his eye as he watched his former sweetie stroke her ankle. He had a notion why she was lingering. Well, why not? They had the time. He sat down beside her. "You smell as pretty as a bag of potpourri," he leered.

The Baroness wished she could say the same of him. Still, it's amazing what a couple of drinks will do for a man's looks, especially observed by moonlight. A wink and a tickle and she found herself reconnected to the handyman's secret appeal. It was delightfully freakish. The biggest distraction she'd ever encountered. "Oh, Mr. McTavish," she gasped as they thrashed about on the tracks, "All is forgiven. I appoint you the Head of my Privy Chamber!"

Her body tingled with vibrations. The earth moved. But it wasn't because of McTavish. It was because of the rumble of an approaching train.

"Mr. McTavish, I believe a train is coming."

"That's not all that's cummin', dearie."

"Mr. McTavish! A train! A train!"

Sadly, McTavish's member had drained the blood from his brain. All he could think was: "YES, YES, YES, YES!"

Then, out of nowhere — BANG!

Miss Bentwhistle saw stars. Not stars from the explosion, but stars from the sky. They were shining through the hole in McTavish's head where his face used to be.

Slick Skinner was ten feet away, his shotgun smoking.

Miss Bentwhistle wrestled with her lover's body. How would she ever explain this to the cleaners? "Get this thing off me," she exclaimed.

"Sorry." Skinner stuck a toothpick between his teeth. "I'm in a hurry." He bounded up the hill beyond the tracks.

Miss Bentwhistle heard a train whistle. She looked ahead. This time she didn't see stars. She saw the moon. It was large and round and luminous. A lovers' moon. A moon to inspire poets.

It was the headlight of the Santa Fe Express.

MR. SKINNER!

W hen Brewster left the camp, Mary Mabel expected to see him return with Miss Bentwhistle. Instead, a stranger loped out of the woods with a shotgun.

"Hi there, Sister," the man said, slicing her bindings with a hunting knife.

"Where's Papa?"

"Here and there." He yanked her to her feet and hauled her over the hill to the railroad tracks. Moments earlier, she'd heard the blasts of a train whistle and a screeching of brakes that went on forever. Now she saw the end of a caboose, slid to a stop a half-mile away. Some men were running back, yelling.

"Keep moving," said her rescuer. They ran through a patch of woods and came out on a side road. "Coast's clear," he said and raced her toward the limo. It was parked on the shoulder beside an empty police cruiser.

"Where are the officers?" she asked, bewildered.

"People should mind their own business," he muttered. He shoved her into the passenger side and told her to keep her head down. Then he jump-started the car and they drove off.

Mary Mabel took it as a good sign that he hadn't stuck her in the trunk. On the other hand, she was concerned that he might be connected to the ministry. "Thank you for rescuing me from Papa," she said. "But if you're planning to take me back to WKRN, forget it."

"Don't worry," he smiled. "You won't be going there ever again."

She breathed easier.

They turned off the side road on to Mulholland Drive and headed into the Hollywood Hills. "By the way," she asked, "who are you? Where are we going? And why are you helping me?"

"You're quite the one for questions."

"Yes, and I'd like some answers."

He grinned. "You don't recognize me?"

She struggled to place the face, lit in starts by the street lamps. She knew she'd seen him, somewhere, but it was more like he came from a dream. "Did we meet on tour?"

"Not exactly. Though I s'pose you could say I've followed your career."

She froze. These were the eyes she'd felt staring at her from behind corners and on the other side of windows. The stranger who'd stalked her nightmares. The words fell from dry lips: "Kalamazoo. I was talking to my friend in the lobby. You were the tramp across the street."

"I seen you other places, too," he said. "In bed. Yeah. I liked watchin' you in bed."

"Let me out of this car. Now."

He kept driving. "I got into your room, you know. Lots of times. Sat on your mattress. Smelled your nightie. Felt your sheets. I coulda had you any time I wanted. But I waited till I had your pa."

Light fell on his big red ears. The penny dropped. "Mr. Skinner."

He tipped his head. "You were prettier when you were little. Just as scared though. I like that in my girlies."

They drove higher into the hills. The houses had disappeared. The lights, too. "Why didn't you kill me at the camp?" she whispered.

"Accidents are cop magnets. I'd have had to be quick." He sucked his teeth. "And I mean to skin you slow. Skinning's an art. You'll be alive for most of it." The wind whistled past the car. "There's a cabin off the road a piece. Won't be nobody come by. We can have some fun before we get started. Eh, Sister?"

She tried to scream, but her throat locked.

"Cat got your tongue? I was hopin' to cut it out. Screamin' don't sound human without a tongue. Sounds more like cows. Hey, there's a thought. Body parts. I can pickle your organs and sell 'em to the ministry. I hear there's a market for relics."

"You're the Devil incarnate."

"Yup."

There was only one way to escape.

Mary Mabel raised her knees and jammed her feet hard on the accelerator. The car revved forward. Skinner kicked at her legs. She kept them rigid.

Struggling for control, he held the wheel with his left hand, grabbed her hair with his right, and snapped her out of her seat. She twisted her head and bit into his wrist. He slammed her cheek on the dash. She sunk her teeth deeper.

Then she grabbed for the clutch. The gears shredded. The limo spun like a top. The rear swung into a guard rail. The trunk buckled. The lid popped open. The bodies of two police officers bounced onto the road as the limo careened forward.

She jammed the accelerator again. The limo veered onto gravel, swerved across the pavement, hit a second rail, missed a bend, and smashed headlong into a pile of rocks.

Skinner flew through the windshield. She didn't see where he landed. She was too busy running in the opposite direction.

The CAT'S MEOW

Slick shook himself out and limped back to the car. Mary Mabel had vanished. He'd better do the same before anyone saw the wreck, not to mention the dead cops. He retrieved his shotgun and jerked his way to the guard rail.

The city spread out below, a pan of twinkling lights. Slick experienced a moment of vertigo and pain, then adrenaline took over. Descending the steep incline on a zig-zag, he skittered past brush and boulders, periodically hopping across the gaps in eroded ledges. Things were going well until he hit a patch of dry clay. It crumbled under his feet.

Suddenly, Slick found himself on his ass, tumbling straight down. A scrub tree on a narrow footpath stopped his fall. The trunk snapped. So did his back. His rifle flew out of his hands and clattered away. Silence.

Slick was relieved to be alive, until he realized he couldn't feel anything below the waist. Still, no time for self pity. He had a hunter's instinct. And that instinct told him he was being watched. By whom? Mary Mabel? McTavish's friends? The cops? Passersby? All he knew for sure was that he was exposed.

A few yards away, the foot path widened into a small plateau covered in brush. Perfect camouflage. He dragged himself over and paused. He was still being watched.

Slick determined not to panic. He pulled himself another three yards. He tried to pull himself further, but encountered a peculiar resistance. It fact, it was more than resistance. He was being pulled backwards. Perplexed, Slick looked over his shoulder. He froze. A mountain lion had his knee in its mouth.

Slick would have screamed, but the cat leapt on his ribcage, driving the air from his lungs. It stretched itself luxuriously along his back, its front paws crimping his shoulders, its hind legs braced in the dirt on either side of his thighs. It nuzzled his neck. Licked its hot, wet tongue over his cheek and ears. Slick had the unsettling sensation the beast was aroused. *Dammit*, he thought, *I'm about to get buggered!*

He wriggled onto his back. "Get yer goddamn paws off me!" he wheezed and landed an uppercut to the lion's chops.

The lion was delighted to find its toy so playful. It reared up and gave Slick a love tap across the stomach. *That*, Slick could feel. He scrabbled backwards fifteen feet on his elbows. The cat didn't move. Slick was flushed with pride. He'd shown the critter who was boss. He confidently retreated another five feet. And another five feet.

It was then that he noticed a peculiar grey rope glistening in the moonlight. The rope ran in a straight line between himself and the lion. In horror, Slick understood why the cat wasn't moving. Its front paws were firmly planted on the end of his large intestine. As he'd retreated, his insides had been unravelling. The lion sucked them back like a string of spaghetti.

As the beast eyed his liver, Slick sighed. It was all over but the dung beetles.

TRUTH *and* CONSEQUENCES

The discovery of a second trashed limo belonging to the Baroness of Bentwhistle set off a sensation. The fingerprints in the trunk matched the bodies of the dead cops on Mulholland Drive; the same cops who were missing from the cruiser by the site where the Santa Fe express had collided with that pair of rutting hoboes. There was little physical evidence to identify the tramps, aside from some skid marks and miscellaneous flesh. However, when investigators found a set of dentures inscribed with the Baroness Bentwhistle's name, the tabloids had a field day.

The limo yielded two other sets of unexpected prints:

One was traced to a skeleton found a hundred yards downhill from the car; forensics made the identification based on a partial thumb print. This print matched that of a Mr. Slick Skinner, a Canadian businessman lately released from Bellevue. When his wife was contacted, the phone line crackled with whoops of glee.

The second set of prints, tragically, belonged to Sister Mary Mabel McTavish. Police also found a bow from her Match Girl costume, which had snagged on the limo's clutch.

The discovery of Mary Mabel's prints established conclusively that Brother Percy Brubacher hadn't murdered the evangelist. Not only were his prints nowhere to be found, but he'd been incarcerated before the replacement limo had even been bought. In any event, police had been growing suspicious of his confession. Brubacher had given them a dozen false leads regarding the whereabouts of the murder weapon, and he barely had the mechanical smarts to flip a light switch much less operate a wood chipper.

Brother Percy was furious to have his guilt challenged. This was another example of the conspiracy to deny him his place in history. Fortunately for Percy, the public didn't care about the truth. With his wild eyes and mangled jaw, he made a perfect villain. His face became a popular Halloween mask, and at Fourth of July fireworks "The Little Red Schoolhouse" became "Percy's Little Red Chapel." A lawyer for the state also licensed his name for use in Hollywood shorts, the most famous of which was *Hell's Bells* starring the Three Stooges. In this flick, a look-alike Brother Percy chases the Stooges through a haunted house while hammers and cement blocks are bounced off his head.

Alas, fame didn't bring happiness. Brother Percy was plagued by nightmares about the wood chipper and hellfire. Claiming that Satan was a fly who'd betrayed him, he begged God's forgiveness and swallowed a bottle of insect repellent.

He was much happier after the lobotomy. He'd sit quietly in a corner of the ward, blessing the white-robed angels who brought him meals and pills, and nodding his head in time to the beautiful piped music. Percy had secretly feared that Heaven would be filled with cherubs singing hymns with little soprano voices and harps. What a pleasant surprise that God preferred recordings of Cole Porter.

Meanwhile at the Heavenly Dwellings, Floyd had assumed that Miss Pigeon's hysteria was connected to the death of her old friend. However, when Wells Fargo announced that it would search for the baroness's will in the strongbox containing her jewels, she came to him and confessed. The collateral for his Ponzi empire was two hundred pounds of bricks and a handful of pennies and pins.

"What should I do?" Miss Pigeon wept.

"You should pray, Dolly," Floyd said, as he stuffed an overnight bag. "You should pray very, very hard."

Miss Pigeon's prayers were soon answered. She escaped the cage by singing like a canary. She knew nothing about Doyle, but her full-throated warbling on the subject of Hollywood parties made an instant bestseller of her subsequent autobiography, *Baptist in Babylon.*

The F.B.I., in concert with the R.C.M.P., followed up on Miss Pigeon's remark that Floyd liked to stay at the Twins Bed & Breakfast in London, Ontario.

The Twins entertained the detectives over homemade rhubarb pie and tea.

"Yes, indeed, Mr. Cruickshank stayed with us frequently over the years," sniffed Miss Millie, "but he was a no-account scoundrel who never paid his bills."

"He took advantage of poor spinster girls," Miss Tillie confided.

"That he did," Miss Millie agreed. "So, when he showed up on our doorstep a few nights back, we sent him on his way for good."

The detectives nodded sympathetically. "Any idea where he is now?"

"Hell," said Miss Millie.

"At least we hope so," her sister added.

The detectives accepted a second piece of pie and a tour of the garden. "Good luck with that new rose patch."

"Thank you," said Miss Millie. "We were up all night digging."

"Oh yes." Miss Tillie beamed. "And laying in the fertilizer."

Several years later, the Twins' rose patch spawned a prize-winning cultivar. They dubbed it "The Floyd."

"It's a rambler," Miss Tillie told the press. "If it tries to take over your garden, just take a good stiff shovel to it."

• • • •

While much was unknown, this much was clear: Sister Mary Mabel McTavish had undoubtedly met a terrible end. Police believed her body was probably buried in a shallow grave somewhere in the vicinity of Barclay Side Road or the Hollywood Hills. Whether it would ever be found would depend on luck: a sickening discovery by bird watchers, hikers, or area wildlife.

There was national mourning. Sensing the mood of its readers, the press syndicates devoted special sections to the Miracle Maid, so tragically taken in the prime of her youth. Sins of the Holy Redemption Ministry were laid at the feet of "financial advisors who abused an innocent's trust." None were foolish enough to question the public myth-making.

What with the general bloodfest, Hearst's plans for a musical biopic seemed somewhat tasteless. The project was shelved. This was a killer as Gable was signed to play the reporter. With typical Hollywood "can-do," however, screenwriters rewrote the vehicle as a comedy about a showgirl and a boxer called *Cain and Mabel*. It was the second-last film of Miss Davies's career.

Doyle didn't care about the hoopla. He was off the beat, numb with grief. In this, nothing upset him more than his mother's good intentions. She was a believer in things turning out for the best, even though experience proved the opposite.

"They haven't found the body," she'd say.

"They haven't found God, either," he'd reply.

One day she went too far. He'd stepped out to get them groceries. When he got back, she was at the door without her walker.

"K.O.," she exclaimed, "I've just received a message from Mary Mabel. She wants me to tell you she's fine."

"Please, Ma." There were lots of these kind of reports circulating in the papers and on the radio. Supernatural visitations and dreams in which Sister would comfort the bereaved. Surely his mother had better sense than to give in to mass hypnosis.

"I've seen her, too," she said, trembling. "Wearing her Match Girl outfit. Oh, and smiling. Radiant as an angel."

This is it, he thought. *It's time for the home.*

"I can tell you don't believe me," she scolded. "Here. See for yourself."

She handed him the photograph and letter that had come with the morning mail.

> *Dear Mrs. Rinker,*
> *Please give this to K.O. so he won't worry.*
> *Yours,*
> *Mary Mabel*

> *Dear K.O.,*
> *Sorry it's taken so long to get in touch. I've had my reasons. Don't ask. Just know I'm fine.*
> *I send this in care of your mother in case anyone screens your mail. I plan to stay dead. Please don't betray my trust. I know you won't. If you think hard, you'll know where to find me.*
> *All my love,*
> *M.M.*

HOME

After the car wreck, Mary Mabel had headed back to the camp. She knew Skinner wouldn't be near the place. Too many cops.

It took her three hours on foot. By the time she got to Barclay Side Road, there were barricades. There was also a crowd of gawkers, watching the ambulances, police cars, and fire trucks come and go. She made a wide detour above the tracks, figuring the authorities would still be dealing with the crime scenes.

She was right. The camp was untouched. She bobbed her hair with a rusty scissors and changed into the smallest set of clothes hanging on the lean-tos; Brewster'd said they belonged to a Comrade Duddy. If she was going to hit the rails on her own, she figured she'd better do it dressed as a man.

After she'd changed, she packed some cans of food and a can opener in Duddy's satchel. She also packed her Match Girl outfit which she'd been wearing since San Simeon; it was pretty high, but she thought that someday she'd like a souvenir. Finally, she took the money stash hidden inside the junked car seat by the compost; she'd seen Brewster dip into it before heading out for groceries and whiskey; better to take it than leave it to rot, she figured.

Mary Mabel hoisted her new belongings and walked along the track away from the accident. At length, she reached a trestle bridge, where she waited till the trains were back in operation, and hopped the first one east. She had no clear idea of where she wanted to go, so she let the rails decide for her, swapping flatcars as the mood struck. Some nights she'd camp out in the middle of nowhere, and bathe in a stream if there was one handy. Other times, she'd curl up and fall asleep to the rhythmic clickety-clack of the track.

After about a week, she started to overhear tramps discussing reports of her death. They mourned openly. It was humbling and liberating. A good time to stare at the stars and to think.

Why did Mama set me on this journey? she wondered. At first the answer seemed obvious. If she'd refused the call, Timmy Beeford would be dead. Or would he? Perhaps someone else would have laid on hands. Who can tell about anything? She remembered how Miss Bentwhistle had demanded that she deny her mama's miracle or be put on the street. She'd refused and ended up a star.

Gosh, she thought, *am I just a bubble of happenstance?*

No sooner had the idea occurred than she had a vision. Not of paradise and angels, but of a place she had to go for her journey to be complete.

It took her a week to ride into Canada, and another few weeks to get east. In Winnipeg, she stopped to buy a dress. From there, she went by bus to Cedar Bend. The buildings stood where they'd always stood, but something was different. When she'd been little, the town's focus had been the mill. Now it was the tourist sites commemorating the early life of Sister Mary Mabel McTavish.

She walked up and down Main Street, sticking her head into stores to see if she'd be recognized. If so, better to know now than to be surprised later.

The stores were empty. She found the owners at the barber shop. When she walked in, the men froze. At first she thought it was because they knew her, but it was because she was a woman. She breathed a sigh of relief. Of course no one recognized her. The camera plays tricks. More important, Mary Mabel was dead.

"What can I do you for?" asked the barber.

"My name's Ruth Kincaid," she said, pressing her luck. "I'm looking for a Mr. Jimmy McRay."

The room paused. "We used to have a Ruth Kincaid McTavish in town," the barber squinted. "She was the mother of our Mary Mabel. Might you by any chance be a relative? You bear a slight resemblance."

"As a matter of fact, Mary Mabel was a distant cousin," she said. "We didn't have much in common, but I knew her a little."

"Dying so young, it's such a tragedy. But she'll be remembered, oh yes, long after we're gone."

The room nodded solemnly.

"You wouldn't happen to have the touch, would you?" asked a man with an overbite. "You know, being a relative and all?"

"I thought I did, once upon a time. But I'm no Mary Mabel McTavish."

The man nodded. "She was one of a kind, poor thing."

There was a moment of silence. Then the barber said, "Now about Jimmy ..."

Mr. McRay was on the porch, as if expecting her arrival. He knew her at once. "I figured you'd be by sooner or later; I never do trust the papers." He smiled. "That reporter fella passed on the photo of you and your mama, eh? I was hoping he might. How long you planning to stay?"

"I haven't decided."

Mr. McRay said he'd love to give her his spare room, but it wouldn't be proper. However, his daughter, Iris, lived just a few blocks over. She'd never married. "Iris was the bosom friend of your mama. She'll make you welcome."

"Thank you. But please, Mr. McRay, no one can know it's me."

"I understand."

They walked to the cemetery, and he showed her where her mama was laid to rest. There was a white marble stone that read:

HERE LIES RUTH KINCAID MCTAVISH
1903–1922
LOVING MOTHER OF MARY MABEL MCTAVISH
"IN OUR HEARTS AND MINDS FOREVER"

"Your papa didn't have much time for markers. But thanks to you being so famous, town council put up this memorial. It's in the visitors' guide." McRay pointed to his wife's grave. "If you need me, I'll be just over there with Gracie."

Mary Mabel nodded thanks. She sat on the ground and closed her eyes. There was a light breeze. She smiled.

She stayed with Iris and got a job looking after the library. Town council voted her a stipend and looked after room and board. It was a mess; the last librarian had had glaucoma so bad he couldn't see to sort the books. But in short order, she put things to rights, and more and more people began to drop in. She set up a children's book club for Saturday mornings, and taught adults to read in her spare time.

Naturally, word got around that she was a shirt-tail cousin of Mary Mabel. Every so often, townsfolk and tourists would come by to tell her a tale about her famous relative, one that she mightn't have heard. She got to love hearing these stories. In the end, legends about Mary Mabel McTavish were no different than legends about Robin Hood or Pocahontas. They had their own truth, even if it was a truth that never happened.

In her heart, she grew to know and accept that she wasn't Mary Mabel McTavish anymore, and never would be again. Mary Mabel was a saint whose memory gave hope to believers. She was a town librarian who offered comfort through books. The Miracle Maid had died and she had been reborn in her passing.

. . . .

One night she wrote a letter to Doyle to let him know that she was well. Mr. McRay dropped by a few weeks later to say: "A friend of yours is in town. He's staying at the Lodge."

Doyle waited till closing time to put in an appearance. They didn't say a word. Just beamed at one another. Then they laughed till the tears came. "Give me a hug" — the words came from their lips at the same time.

He took her to Mr. Woo's for supper: wonton soup and a hamburger. They had banana splits for dessert and he proposed.

She got very serious. "K.O., you're a true friend," she said, "but you're talking fairy tales."

"I'm talking destiny."

"Here's destiny: your life is a continent away."

He looked down. She held his hand. He shook her off and paid the bill.

They took a long walk beside the river. Doyle stopped to skip stones across the current. "You're right," he said at last. "This is a whole other world. But what if I came up for summer getaways? I'd like to get to know you. Here."

She smiled. "I'd like to get to know you, too."

Doyle shuffled. "I know you can't make promises, but …"

She held up her hand. "With a little luck and imagination, anything's possible."

"I hope," he said, and gave her a peck on the cheek.

They sat on the riverbank and talked till dawn. What would happen would happen, if it happened. Now was enough for now. It was a wonderful night. She felt no need to call on her mama for guidance. Nor did she ever feel the need again. In Cedar

Bend, her mama was simply in the air she breathed. Her mama was at home, at peace.

And so was she.

ABOUT *the* AUTHOR

Allan Stratton is the internationally acclaimed author of *Chanda's Secrets*, which was made into the Cannes Film Festival hit *Life, Above All*. His books are published in over twenty countries. Before turning to fiction, Allan wrote *Nurse Jane Goes to Hawaii*, one of the most produced plays in Canadian theatre history. His citations include the Canadian Authors Association Award, the ALA Michael L. Printz Honor Book, the CLA Best Book for Young Adults Award, the Children's Africana Award, the Dora Mavor Moore Award, two Junior Library Guild selections (USA), three ALA Best Book nods, a *Times of London* Book of the Week; and nominations for the Governor General's Award (for both children's literature and drama), the Forest of Reading Award, and the Stephen Leacock Medal for Humour. He lives in Toronto with his partner and four cats. You can visit him online at *www.allanstratton.com*.